"I HAVE TO SEE YOU."

Mila forced herself into total consciousness, taking in small breaths, keeping her eyes open. What day was it? Or what night? Was it the weekend? "Who is this?"

"It's Garrick. Garrick McClellan."

Mila rolled onto her back. "You have to see me? Didn't—didn't you just jump out of a car to get away from me?"

There was a pause, and Mila wondered if she'd fallen back to sleep, but then he said, "I'm—I'm sorry. I want to explain. And I want to ask you something about . . ."

"What? About what?" Mila asked.

"Us," Garrick said. "Us."

Sitting up, Mila leaned against her pillow, her mouth open slightly. *Us?* What was he doing calling her like this after a night like that? After he almost made himself roadkill rather than sit next to her? She wanted to laugh at him. To tell him to take a hike. But then, through the phone, she felt so much that she wanted to lie down flat on the bed and weep. Images were coming to her, feelings, thoughts. Garrick's. So much hurt and loss and pain. He had been so alone. So afraid.

What time was there? she wondered. What time was there but this moment? She knew from wasting time how valuable it was.

"Now," she said. "Come over now."

Other titles by Jessica Inclán

Believe in Me
When You Believe
Reason to Believe
Intimate Beings
The Beautiful Being

Published by Kensington Publishing Corporation

BEING WITH HIM

JESSICA INCLÁN

ZEBRA BOOKS
KENSINGTON PUBLISHING CORP.
http://www.kensingtonbooks.com

ZEBRA BOOKS are published by

Kensington Publishing Corp.
119 West 40th Street
New York, NY 10018

All Kensington titles, imprints, and distributed lines are available at special quantity discounts for bulk purchases for sales promotion, premiums, fund-raising, educational, or institutional use.

Special book excerpts or customized printings can also be created to fit specific needs. For details, write or phone the office of the Kensington Special Sales Manager: Attn.: Special Sales Department. Kensington Publishing Corp., 119 West 40th Street, New York, NY 10018. Phone: 1-800-221-2647.

Zebra and the Z logo Reg. U.S. Pat. & TM Off.

ISBN-13: 978-1-4201-0113-3
ISBN-10: 1-4201-0113-7

First Zebra Books Trade Paperback Printing: February 2008
First Zebra Books Mass-Market Paperback Printing: September 2010

10 9 8 7 6 5 4 3 2 1

Printed in the United States of America

Prologue

In her dream, she isn't alone. Not ever. Not in all the times she's conjured it up from her subconscious. Always in the darkness, there are the other children, so many of them, their voices echoing in the small strange place that holds them.

Two of the children are somehow related to her, belong to her, are connected to her by blood or heart or time. She looks at them—turning to her left and then right—but even in the dream, she blinks, unable to see them clearly, as if her eyes are filled with glue, cloudy and sticky. Are the children blond like her? Do they have dark eyes? Do they have long thin limbs? Do they always wonder who they really are?

She thinks she can see one of them—a boy—looking at her, saying something, his voice and face so serious and kind. She knows that she trusts him completely, but she can never hear his words, his voice a young, soft warble in the darkness. And she isn't really sure that she's hearing his voice as much as feeling it inside her head, her body. She knows he is talking with her, but is his mouth moving? Is hers when she tries to reply?

This dream confuses her. She doesn't know where they are or who they are or where they are going. She knows they are moving because she feels the vibrations from some large engine, but it is as if she is almost anesthetized, amnesiatic, drugged. She can't figure out anything. How old is he? How old is she? Of course in the waking world, she isn't a child, but in her dream, she forever is, trapped in time and place. Maybe she is about two or three. Maybe one. Maybe four. She's not sure exactly, but as she sits with the other children, she looks down at her body and sees little girl legs, little girl arms, and strange little girl clothes, skirt and top a light shade of orange. But no matter the clothes or her size, she knows this is her body, her life, her experience, even though she is now twenty-eight, grown, a single woman with no siblings, an only child. Always the only child.

But in the dream, she doesn't know where she is because it is dark and closed in and crowded. She is sitting, her back against something hard. This dark is a place she only sees in the dream. But it is not scary. It is a place where she is surrounded by the children and by adults, who talk in soft whispers. Everyone in the dark place is like her, can do the strange things she does. Can do the things she has to hide in her real life. And even though there might be something outside the dark place that is bad and wrong—and she thinks there is—they are all protected. And as they sit and wait and watch, they are traveling, going somewhere she thinks will be better.

For an instant in the dream, she can almost see the bad people and the bad things they do. She lifts her small hands to her eyes, knowing she doesn't want to see what she can remember, but the thin, wispy, bad bodies of the people slip into her thoughts. There are horrible, red, wet things that happen because of the bad people. This is why she and the other children and the adults are in the dark place, run-

*ning away. The shape and sound of the thing the bad peo-
ple do is lonely and black and hollow and empty, and the
adults are trying to keep this from the children. But all the
children know. All the children understand. All the children try to forget.*

*The boy next to her talks. The body of the other child
presses close. The three of them are holding hands, shoulders
together, small legs touching. The adults that are their
adults aren't there, but for now, in this dream, that's okay
because at least the three of them are together. They are still
together.*

*The other children around them hold hands, too, talk in
soft sad tones. Some cry, and others comfort them. Now and
then, there is laughter. Sometimes, someone giggles. They
love each other. They all love each other.*

*And somehow in the dream she knows this: there is an-
other child in the dark place who is hers. Not in the same
way of the two next to her, but in a way that is different,
matched. She looks into the dark place, but she can't see
him, can't see anything really. She knows he's here, though.
She can almost hear him think, can almost feel his mind in
hers. And she feels his energy, the opposite of hers. Her
magic in the mirror, backward.*

*As the place seems to shift, dip, move, adults come and
lean over them, smile, wipe the children's eyes and their
own, hug them over and over again. The dark place rumbles, and the dream goes on and on in a gummy, sad same-
ness until it begins to break apart, turn gray and grainy,
slowly slide out of view.*

No, *she cries out.* Don't leave me here. Don't leave
me again! Please come back. Please tell me how to
find you! I'm lost now. I don't know where to go.

*But the dream pulls away like a rolled-up carpet, and she
turns on her side, falling into a dreamless sleep.*

Chapter One

Garrick McClellan stood at the end of the enormous museum gallery, holding a double scotch and wishing that he were at home. Or at work. Or at a bar. Or anywhere but this party. The room smelled like boiled shrimp, bad champagne, and acrylic paint, and he had been stuck listening to the perpetually giddy Meredith Stone talk about Aruba for going on fifteen minutes. Aruba this, Aruba that. Now and then as she spoke, she put one slim, tanned hand on his arm, and the very act made Garrick want to growl.

Get the hell off me, he thought, but, of course, Meredith didn't hear his thoughts. No one did, even though he heard theirs loud and clear, twenty-four-seven, turning them off just to save his sanity. And he knew, from experience, how important sanity was, how useful it was when trying to deal with others.

"The Mirabelle is simply the best resort there," Meredith said, smiling at Garrick as she did, her teeth so bleached he wondered if she'd mind if he put on his sunglasses to block the almost blue glare.

"We must go, then," said a woman to Meredith's right, a San Francisco socialite Garrick had been introduced to many times but whose name he always forgot. "The sun would do wonders for me this time of year."

"There's nowhere else this season," Meredith said, but her thoughts were not on Mirabelle, the warm aqua-colored water, the scuba diving, or the frothy pina coladas served up at the beachfront bar. No, not a thought there. Garrick could hear Meredith's sex channel loud and clear. Keeping her eyes averted, she was thinking about what she perceived as Garrick's enormous bulge in his tuxedo trousers.

God, she thought, talking about in-room Jacuzzis at the same time. *Get me a room alone with him. At Mirabelle or the Holiday Inn Express on Harrison. I don't care.*

Garrick pushed back his coat, smiling, wanting her to get an extra glimpse of his solid, strong, six-foot-two frame, but then, with a sigh, he let the jacket fall forward. It wasn't fair to take advantage. He'd made a pact with himself, but he smiled, knowing that it wasn't just Meredith who had admired him in that way. But he shouldn't be around her or any woman. Nothing good ever came of it. Nor would it ever.

"Maybe you should go back to Aruba soon," Garrick said, moving away from Meredith and her greedy hands. He winked, giving everyone, including Meredith, the notion that he was kidding. "If you took another trip next week, I know it would do me wonders. Ladies. Gentlemen."

He bowed slightly, pulled away from the group, and strode off. If it wasn't for the donation his company made to the museum's fund, he wouldn't be here at all. But he was the one person the museum requested. Garrick McClellan, top producer for the largest finance firm in the city, Calder Wilken Brodden, to present the five-million-dollar check to purchase additional future collections. He could see the headline in the Datebook section of the *San Francisco Chronicle* now. And as if to corroborate, he heard a sharp "Mr. McClellan."

Turning, he faced a man with a camera and then there was a click and a flash.

"Great. Thanks. Love the show," the photographer said, striding away to find another society victim.

Garrick put his drink down on a small table and pushed his blond hair back from his forehead. He leaned against a wall and shook his head. Some show. Modern art. This stuff looked like crap. Stripes and boxes and what looked like spills. Blobs of color. One painting was just blue. A blue box. Another piece was a shovel hung from the ceiling and a bucket. Both painted white. Garrick almost laughed when he listened to some woman say, "It's the negative space that makes this piece so arresting."

Arresting, Garrick thought. *Someone should arrest the artist. Get the forty thousand dollars back they paid out, too.*

He picked up his glass and downed the last of his scotch. He had to make nice, as he always did. He'd learned long ago that no one wanted someone different around to make a scene, to say something weird, to act "inappropriately." Who said what was true, who acted crazy, unless, of course, it meant that someone was an artist hanging shovels and painting buckets. But there wasn't space, negative or otherwise, for a person who didn't fit in.

"Garrick, love, come see the new collection with me," Meredith said, back at his side, her hand like a snake's head on his arm. She smiled up at him, and Garrick realized there wasn't anything really wrong with Meredith except for her preoccupation with money and travel and upward mobility. That and marrying a man she perceived could help her maintain all of the above. She was pretty in a rich skinny tanning booth way, her hair long and dark, her eyes, while slightly flat in affect, wide and blue and pretty. "It was just unveiled last week."

Garrick sighed, started to walk with Meredith, when his phone vibrated in his coat pocket.

"I'll catch up with you," he said, and she winked at him this time, walking away slowly enough so that he could notice the flip of her skirt, the roundness of her ass, the intensely worked out curve of her calves.

Maybe, he thought as he took out his phone and clicked it on, she wouldn't be so bad for a night or two. And with his power, he could make the night last a long time. He and Meredith could have sex over and over for what would seem like days. Now, that would be better than a vacation in Aruba. Much, much better.

He looked down at the number flashing on his phone and almost put it back in his pocket. It was his aunt Linda calling for about the eighth time that day, the first seven calls he'd let slide into voice mail, never listening to any of them. What was worse was that he'd blown her off two weeks ago, calling at the last minute to avoid a Sunday brunch at her house, where he knew there would be at least one single woman.

But maybe talking to his aunt would keep him away from Meredith Stone, her round ass, and the emptiness that would follow any night with Meredith or any woman.

"Linda," Garrick said, turning to look at a painting composed of swirls and bell shapes and what looked like little fat angels. "How are you?"

"Don't Linda me. And where's the 'Aunt' part anyway?"

"Hi, *Aunt* Linda," Garrick said, feeling slightly silly at twenty-eight using the appellation.

"Oh, stop it and listen to me. I have been calling you all day!" she said, annoyed, her voice high pitched and slightly nervous sounding. "You never answer when I call. You watch it go into voice mail, don't you? And then you don't listen. I never knew you were such a bad nephew."

Garrick put a finger in his glass and swirled the ice. "I've been busy. And now I'm at S.F. Museum of Modern Art at a charity event."

"Then this is perfect," she said. "What a coincidence. How amazing!"

He rolled his eyes, looking around him for a waiter who could get him a refill. Or a bottle. Something to ease the pain of having to talk with his aunt, Linda. He could see a mile off where this conversation was headed. "What's perfect? What's amazing?"

"Her paintings are there. Right now!"

A waiter passed by, and Garrick waved him down with his free hand, taking a glass of red wine. Maybe he'd have a headache tomorrow morning from mixing drinks, but it would be better than the pain in the head he'd have now without it.

"Who is *she*, Linda? I have no idea what you are talking about."

"Mila Adams. The girl I fixed you up with. She's an artist, and her work is showing right now in a special collection of local artists."

From across the large room, Meredith waved to him, turning slowly so he could get a perfect look at her form, which was indeed pretty dammed perfect. Garrick took a sip of wine, listening to Linda go on.

"And it's just so amazing that you are in the same building with her paintings as we speak."

"Linda, it's not that amazing. I'm here once a week for something."

"You are so cynical. I don't know why you are that way, Garrick."

Garrick breathed in, turning around to look at another painting hanging behind him, this one orange and pink with a black-lined border, the horizon on it flat and almost tasting of sorbet.

He sighed. His parents had kept his childhood problems between them and the doctors, and Linda had never heard the stories about hospitals and tests and procedures. She hadn't a clue what made him the way he was, so Garrick couldn't be mad at her. He couldn't hang up on her for not understanding, for kidding him when she really didn't know that his very life had made him this way. The way he was made him this way. What he could do made him this way. And he couldn't tell anyone ever again. He would never trust another person with his story. He'd learned that, at least.

"So, who are we talking about again?" Garrick took another sip.

"I told you. Mila Adams."

Garrick almost spit up his drink, wiping his chin and putting his glass down. "You mean of the Paul Adams family? Judge Adams? I told you, Linda. No more society girls. No more trust fund babies. No more debutantes."

"But I promise! She's not a debutante. Pretty, of course. But no debutante. Well, okay, she was a debutante. But she's not the white glove kind of girl. Certainly not now. In fact, Mila Adams has really sort of taken a turn, you know. An artistic turn. She was in the stock market for a while, but now she takes classes and paints. She's not like those girls you've complained about to me before. She's unique. She's an in-div-id-u-al. Just go look at her artwork. I did. It's really quite, well, unique."

Garrick tried to conjure forth Judge Adams' daughter, but all that came to him was a swath of blond hair and a shy smile, a downward look, quick steps away from the group. Not tall but not short, a nice form, long legs. Maybe a better body than Meredith over there, who was still flitting and turning so he could watch her show.

When had he met Mila Adams? Or had he? It was likely he was remembering a photo taken by the same jerk who'd just accosted him.

"I told you the last time, I don't want to do another setup. I can meet plenty of girls on my own," Garrick said. And it was true. He had no problem meeting women. He just didn't want to stay with them. He didn't want to let them see anything that would mark him as different. As weird. As not right.

All of his relationships ended before he even thought of them as relationships, just before who he was became noticeable.

"None of them can stop smiling," Garrick went on. "And they wear dresses that aren't really dresses but carefully placed scarves. Not that I don't like a good flesh exposure now and again. But did they forget about imagination?"

"I know, I know. It's the style, dear. But I've known Mila since she was in grammar school, and she's like you somehow. Really, you two look remarkably alike. Blond hair and all. Those dark, mysterious eyes with all their secrets."

"I thought you said she was an in-div-id-u-al," Garrick said, a laugh in his voice.

"Oh, stop it. Say you will come. Say you will have dinner at the Adamses' with me. Tell me you'll come to dinner next Saturday night. It will be nice. I promise! And if you don't like her, well, no one will say it's my fault. Everyone will say you are too hard to please."

Meredith did another turn, sashaying across the marble floor, her dress floating around her knees in a black cloud. She smiled, and Garrick grew impatient with his aunt. But Linda was all he had left now that his parents had moved to London, and he had to have something besides work to connect him to life. Linda was family. She really was there for him— on holidays that without her prodding and insistence that he come over for a prime rib roast, he would either spend staring out his condo window all night long with a few drinks or go out partying with his friend Jim, and find himself at four in the morning hungover in some woman's bed.

And if he was here at this ridiculous art show for a

company who owed him more than he owed it, why
wasn't he willing to do something to please his only
relative? The only person who truly seemed to want
his happiness.

"Fine," he said, nodding at Meredith and smiling.
He could bail out on the party at the De Young Museum he'd already RSVP'd to, claiming an emergency family situation. And in a way, he wouldn't be
lying. "Next Saturday."

"Oh, this will be so wonderful. I'll call Adair and
Paul right now. And go look at Mila's work. Right
now! It will be lovely to talk about at dinner."

"Good-bye, Linda," Garrick said, irritable suddenly and hot under his tux collar. He'd helped out
his aunt but now he was going to be saddled with
Mila Adams and her princess ways.

He yanked at his tie and took one last sip of his
wine, looking around for a waiter for another and
then giving up. Garrick took the lack of wine as a
sign. He'd go look at the art so he could woo for one
night the shy daughter of Judge Paul Adams, the
debutante turned stockbroker turned artist. But
after looking at all the horrid ugliness of Mila
Adams' work, he would ignore Meredith's annoying
voice and conversation and take her home and sleep
with her, for one or two or three nights, as many as
he wanted, knowing that she would only remember
one. Even if it wouldn't be perfect. Even if he'd probably never sleep with her again.

"Never mind this section," Meredith said, pulling
hard on Garrick's arm. "It's just the local artists, my
love. Nothing of consequence."

Figures, he thought, looking down the long broad wall of canvases, a couple of sculptures on daises on the floor space. From just a glance, he could tell there were squiggles and blobs and fat angels everywhere. He was ready to take Meredith to her place, but he'd promised Linda.

"Do you think you could find me some wine?" he asked. "No, make it a scotch. Could you do that for me, Meredith?"

Garrick smiled, watched her face change expression, going from fake confidence to hope.

"Of course. I'll be right back," she said. Then finding her flirty bearings, she added, "Don't disappear in an artistic frenzy."

"That will never happen," he said. "But the company wants me to look at the entire exhibit."

Turning so that her hair swirled around her, Meredith disappeared into the crowd. Garrick took in a breath and began to make his way down the first wall. And the art was just as he expected. Not art. Wires forming large spindly balls, swirls and twirls of strange color combinations, white canvases probably teeming with negative space, and then—he stopped walking, his exhale stuck on his tongue.

What is that? What does it mean? he thought, his body a map of shivers.

There on the canvas in front of him was the usual mélange of color and shape he'd seen all night in some fashion, but this one was different. He understood it. He knew it. What was that in the middle? Purple, round, dark, the shape of something Garrick had always known. He turned back to see if Meredith was coming, but she'd never made it past the first group on her way to the bar. Sweaty and hot, Garrick

moved closer to the painting, which wasn't a paint-
ing as much as it was a creation of paints and fabric.
Purples and blues and a swirl of black in the middle.
He didn't know how to say it but he'd been there.
He'd been inside this painting, felt all of this color
and sensation.

Home, he thought. *Home.*

Shaking his head, he closed his eyes, unwilling to
feel this need, this desire. To feel anything so
strongly again. He knew he should turn now and
walk away. Go back to his usual routine. Go to Meredith and take her by the arm and hop into the limo.
Uncork a bottle of Dom. But he couldn't. He knew
that, too.

Taking in a large breath, Garrick opened his eyes.
Moving closer to the wall, he looked at the tag, know-
ing somehow what he would read: THE RIDE. MILA
ADAMS. 2008. ACRYLIC, LINEN, PENCIL, AND COTTON.

He looked up at the painting again, hit again by
the vivid colors, the circular motion of the paint that
told him about movement. He thought he could almost hear voices, the sounds of children. He felt the
darkness creep over him, the black paint telling him
a story he could almost remember.

Run, the story told him. *Hide.*

Staggering back, Garrick put his hand on his
mouth, trying not to call out to something, someone.
For a moment, he couldn't blink, couldn't swallow,
couldn't move a muscle. All he heard was his heart
beating against his ribs, blood banging in his ears.

It was too much. He couldn't look anymore. He
wouldn't feel like this again. He wouldn't go back to
the agony of his teenaged years, knowing that there
was something so different about himself and want-

ing to share it with his parents. With a doctor. With anyone. No one listened. No one cared, and he wouldn't do it again. Not ever, and without saying good-bye to Meredith, he rushed out of the gallery, the museum, and into the San Francisco night.

"The least you could have done was say good-bye," Meredith's voice was saying into the answering machine. "I didn't think you were such an ass."

And then there was a click, her voice only a thin echo in the room, and then there was silence.

Garrick sat at his desk, the computer on, the screen bright. He didn't have to be with Meredith to read her thoughts this time. He heard her hurt through the telephone wires, felt her upset, and he wanted to care, but his mind was fixated on Mila Adams and her painting, so purple, so familiar.

Meredith was right. He was an ass.

He clicked on the search engine and typed in Mila's name. When three hundred entries popped up, he thought he should shut the computer down and go to bed, dealing with the hangover he would have in the morning. He looked at the bottle of scotch he'd opened when he came home, the glass he'd splashed full still unsipped.

Mila Adams. Garrick clicked on the first entry, an old site, something from Smith Barney. And there was a black-and-white photo of Mila.

Our newest junior partner, the blurb said. *Head of corporate stock option sales. Stanford M.B.A. graduate with three years of corporate experience . . .*

But Garrick barely read the blurb, focusing on the photo. He was glad it wasn't in color because she seemed far away, slightly grainy, stiff, formal. She was pretty. Linda had been right about that. Long hair, dark eyes, shy, natural smile. If he stared at the photo long enough, he felt, he would understand everything about her. Or he would understand that he already did. That was it! He knew her. And he knew her in a way he didn't want to. From the dark time. From the dreams and visions. A face from the days and nights in hospital beds drugged up so he would forget what he'd remembered. A face . . .

Garrick sat back, picked up his glass. The phone rang again, and he threw the full glass at the phone, the scotch a flume of amber, the glass hitting the phone, knocking it off the stand but unable to stop Meredith's now tearful voice.

"Garrick, I can't believe you haven't called back. I've called your house. I've called your cell. I—I—" and then she hung up.

Garrick stood up quickly, looking out at the city lights below him, a fan of yellow and gold, the bay a dark blanket hugging Angel Island. No matter how successful he became, no matter the women he had, the houses he bought, the trips he took, Garrick would never be able to forget the first time it happened. The first time he moved time backward. He relaxed and then suddenly he was back ten minutes, an hour, a day, time he had to live through to get to a new, fresh moment.

How old had he been? Five? Six? He'd run into his parents' room, probably for the third time that night. But they only remembered the time that was happening now.

"It's just a bad dream," his mother had said. "That's all. A very bad dream. You thought you went back in time, but it was just a little nap. You can't move time. No one can. Hush, now."

"No," Garrick had cried. "I've already seen this. I've already been here tonight. I'm scared, Mama. I don't know what to do. I thought about not liking to sleep in my room alone and then I was here. Just like now. It keeps coming back."

His parents turned on the light, watching him sob, looking at each other over his tiny, heaving body. Finally, he'd fallen asleep, too tired to move time back, unable to think himself into the path because he was unconscious.

But then in dreams, there was the purple, the twirl, the movement, the cries of children. The dream that Mila Adams had somehow managed to paint.

Garrick turned from the window, sitting down again at the computer, his hands on his thighs, his long legs stretched out.

Mila Adams. Who was she? How could she do this to him? How dare she? How was she able to knock him out of his world, this ordinary world he'd worked so hard to craft? Who was she to make him think about those years? To make him feel it all over again?

He turned to the computer, looking at her face for a moment before clicking to another site. This one about art, the photo of the very painting that had been in the gallery tonight. *No!* he thought. *No more.*

So he clicked and clicked until the computer was off, gone, her image and the painting swallowed up into air.

Goddammit, he thought. He'd worked too hard to get here, alone and happy in his high-rise. He'd gone through his parents' disbelief, their growing horror at what Garrick insisted he could do, the outrage that he seemed to know their thoughts. He had known everything they were thinking, from before he could remember. He just couldn't tell them. And all the fighting. One night his father threw a coffee cup against the kitchen wall, after one more "blasted rerun" of the same backward time story. Even his mother seemed to pull away, regarding her boy, her son, with fear. Maybe with loathing.

But they had been good, caring parents, wanting to take care of their boy. As a teenager, Garrick started living backward in the past, coming up to where he'd started, and flipping back into time. When he was twelve, maybe thirteen, he faced doctors in hospital rooms who took extensive notes when he said, "I can move time backward. All I have to do is close my eyes, let myself relax and be still, and then it's some time before. Sometimes five minutes, sometimes a month. I can't figure out how to control it. I can't make it stop. I don't know if people jump back with me or it's just me by myself. I'm scared."

The doctors shook their heads, wrote down more notes, sighed, and gave sympathetic nods to Garrick's parents, who sat against the wall on a stiff bench, their arms crossed.

Finally, when he couldn't sleep at night, his teeth chattering out of fear that he'd let himself slip back in time again, he found himself in a cold, harshly lit hospital room, nothing but a bed and a chair pushed against a flat white wall, his body laced tight in a straitjacket. Then there was the last time, the time that made him commit to saying nothing, to being like everyone else, to not saying another word to his parents. That night, he found himself on a stretcher, being wheeled into a room with machines, electrical machines.

Even now, he could still feel the electricity on his tongue and heat in his mouth, the whiz of energy in his chest, the sad emptiness of his mind.

A month later, he was in a new school, sitting at the head of the class, listening to a lecture about westward expansion. After all this time not caring about anything but his dreams and thoughts, he realized that girls liked the way he looked, thought he was "cute," but he kept his eyes on the teacher. He didn't want to notice anyone else's gaze, needing to talk about history. He was the one raising his hand, answering his teacher's questions. He was the one making the funny comments, his every sentence followed by laughter.

Sometimes during a lull in the conversation, after a test, just before the bell would ring, he would grip his desk, wanting to blurt out the truth, how he wished to move back time every so often, wanting to do over what he'd already lived, to fix the mistakes he'd made.

But Garrick ignored these feelings and impulses, went off to college, partied with his fraternity brothers, made his parents proud of his perfect grades. Never again did his father raise his voice to Garrick. There were no more thrown mugs or plates or dishes. No more hospital stays. No more machines. And eventually, when it seemed that Garrick was truly all right, his parents left the city, settling in first Paris and then London, a good place for Garrick to visit but not necessarily stay. Everyone in their corners, safe until the bell rang for another round. But

Garrick had vowed there would never be another round.

It was late, the sky beginning to turn a soft luminous indigo, the sun a thought forming behind Mt. Diablo in the east. This morning, he would go to work just like any other day. He would forget about the purple swirl of memory that Mila Adams gave him through her painting. He would forget about her dark eyes and her shy smile. He would forget about the past and his power to move time backward. He would do his job. He would go out after work with his friend Jim, and maybe after a drink or two, he would call Meredith and apologize for his very rude, evil behavior.

As for the Saturday date with the Adamses, well, he wouldn't let his aunt down, not again, but he wouldn't let some dilettante deb rock his entire world, knock him on the path he so carefully, painstakingly had put himself on. So when he went to the Adamses' house, he would be cool, cold, clear, and barely there at all. Locked down tight, his thoughts tamped. He wouldn't listen for anything but for the sound of dinner ending, the pushing back of chairs, the clearing of silverware. He would be polite. He would be cordial. But he wouldn't look to Mila for any answers about himself. He wouldn't look to her for anything.

Chapter Two

"**M**om," Mila Adams said into the phone. "Mother. Mother! Listen, I am not coming over for another dinner. It's completely pointless. I'm not good at dates, and you certainly aren't good at setting them up. You know this. We've already tried it too many times. I'm doomed to be eternally single. Do I need to spell out that word? D-O-O—"

"Nonsense, Mila, darling," her mother, Adair, said, a sniff of irritation in her voice. "You have simply *not* met the right man. Frankly, it's rather hard when you are sitting alone in that horrifying cavern you call an apartment eating macaroni and cheese from a box. Surrounded with all those messy vats of paint and whatever it is you stick all over the canvases."

"Fabric, Mom," Mila said, as she always did whenever her mother questioned her art. "I work with mixed media. Fabric and paint. And I am not sure at all how a *loft* can be a cav—"

"And, darling," Adair went on. "It's been ages since you had a reasonable date. Linda Tilden is especially bringing her nephew just to meet you! Garrick McClellan works for Calder Wilken Brodden! And you know what a reputation that firm has. He's quite the catch. Quite the young man-about-town. And even so, you have just got to get over the idea that there is the one perfect man. How ridiculous! There are hundreds of perfect men, Mila. Just let me try to introduce you to one!"

Mila sighed. By accident and because of two glasses of wine on a lonely winter night, she'd let slip to her mother during a phone conversation her hope. No, not hope. Her knowledge that there was one man for her. Just one. The one who completed her. The one who was perfect. She'd said, "Mom, I know he's out there. I'm just waiting for him to come through the door."

"Nonsense, dear. You just won't look at anyone who walks through any door," Adair had said, and now, each time Mila refused an invitation, Adair brought up the conversation, holding it out like a stinky sock.

"Mom," Mila said. "I—"

"He's quite the most eligible bachelor of the year. Maybe of the last *two* years. And so good looking, too. Linda brought over a photo from the Black and White Ball . . ."

Mila looked out her bedroom window onto the swath of San Francisco Bay, barely paying attention as her mother talked on. For a few minutes, she went "Hmmm" and "Yes" and "Of course," hoping that her mother would slow down, forget the direction of this familiar and particular conversation. But Adair was a wall, a wave of forceful water coming at Mila for twenty-eight years now. For the nth time this month alone, Mila found herself in the terrible position of trying to think of a plausible excuse to get out of a dinner at her parents' Pacific Heights house. Sure, it was nice to go home, eat a wonderful meal filled with organic vegetables and the freshest ingredients prepared by the Adamses' personal chef, Nidia, sit on the covered porch with an espresso and watch the boats float like bath toys in the bay. But lately, ever since she'd quit her job for Smith Barney and decided to paint full-time in her live/work space in the Mission District, her mother had been hell-bent on making her normal.

"Mom—Mom," Mila interrupted. "Do you really think that a man is going to make me better in some way? That suddenly because of a man I won't be living here or doing my art? Suddenly I'll want to go back to the office and work twelve-hour days? That somehow I'll be the daughter you want me to be?"

"Nonsense! How can you say that? You are the daughter I want you to be. But truly—" Adair began, and even on the phone line, Mila could hear her thoughts, the *Of course a man will make you better. He would never put up with that mess. He would want you to live in a respectable house!*

These were the thoughts—same tone, different content—Mila had faced her whole life. Making Mila normal had been Adair's life quest. But being a stubborn, wildly adult daughter who didn't follow any of the social rules was the worst situation of all, her mother's worst nightmare. San Francisco was really a very small town socially, some of the families' connections going back to the gold rush. The Adamses were such a family, and Adair couldn't handle having a bohemian daughter. From the beginning, Mila had

faced Adair's "Let's make our daughter normal" poli-
cies, which always made Mila feel more of what she
usually felt: abnormal.

But instead of delving into Mila's feelings, Adair
had gone about her plans. Mila attended only the
best schools—Drew for high school, Stanford for her
B.A. and M.B.A.—and had the best advantages—
summers in Rome, Paris, London, Barcelona, where
she studied art and language and literature and
music. She was forced into dance lessons when she
was thirteen, paired up with sweaty boys as they all
learned the box step, the waltz, square dancing, the
tango. Then there were sports classes: tennis, golf,
swimming. When Mila hit puberty, there were the
weekly beauty treatments at Beau's spa. Shopping
trips to Neiman's. Pedicures and manicures a must,
and she still shivered about the time she let Adair
talk her into getting a bikini wax. What a painful mistake!

She of course was a deb, introduced into San Francisco society in a tight white dress, elbow-length
white gloves, and a date with pimples on his chin.
She spent much of her time after the first few dances
in the bathroom, listening to the Steve Kearney Band
while sitting on a toilet.

After Mila graduated from high school and then
college came the parade of parties, galas, openings,
the interminable social engagements, the glossy photos in *Focus* magazine. The teas at the Fairmont
Hotel. The fetes at S.F. MOMA, the Palace of Fine
Arts, the Legion of Honor, the remodeled De Young
Museum.

Once Mila tried to complain to her father, Paul,

but he just laughed, said, "Your mother knows best," and kept writing checks to camps and academies and tutors.

What Mila knew that Adair and Paul could not was that she would never be normal. Or even close to it. Not in a million years. No matter the number of strappy Italian leather shoes or low-cut ball gowns or Laura Mercier makeup products Adair brought over to Mila's loft in enormous shopping bags. There was no policy or solution to the "normal" problem at all.

And it really was more than just fitting into Adair's perceived social rules. It was the longing that Mila had felt her entire life, her longing for a connection she had no right to ask for. No one did. Sometimes, she could feel it, touch the energy coming at her, given to her by a man.

Who was she kidding? She was just lucky if her dates knew what acrylic paint was. Or could recite a poem from memory. Or knew that Euclid invented geometry. Or had a car for that matter. Or knew how to use fabric softener.

But this longing wasn't anything she could articulate to her mother, who, now launched into her tirade about being realistic and finding love in marriage, would go on all afternoon.

Mila dove back in. "I'm not going to change for a man, Mom. I'm not going to be someone else miraculously, suddenly Cinderella if I fall into a swoon over a man. No one has that power," she said. "I don't want to give that power to anyone."

"But if you won't even try meeting men, how could you ever know what a man would do in your life?" Adair said. "How do you know you won't change? How do you know what your life would be like? You have to give it a chance. Linda says that her nephew—"

Mila said, "Mom? Mom? Can I—" and then waited for Adair to pause, but no dice, so she pulled the phone away from her ear and closed her eyes. She could take care of this annoying conversation with her mother in an instant. She knew this. If she let herself fall into a state of complete stillness, if she thought nothing and felt her body turn into the air around her, she could push time ahead.

Like magic, this call would be over. In fact, she could make it the hour after this so-called dinner engagement with Garrick McClellan had ended. She could arrange it so that she was standing on the porch with her parents, waving good-bye to Linda and her annoying nephew, Garrick McClellan. Then she could sit down and have a shot of espresso and talk about art with Nidia, who came from Madrid and was a fan of El Greco.

But after getting out of tight spots too often (bad dates, hard exams, boring workdays), she'd promised herself she wouldn't move time anymore, even though it was something she had done since it first happened in first grade. Mila would never forget the feeling, how irritable and bored she had been with her classmates, as they sat in a small circle during reading time. Mrs. Verona droned on about Tim and Tom, the little mice who ran away from home with only one tiny piece of cheese between them. Mila knew the book by heart, had read it all by herself at the beginning of the school year, the same way she had read everything on the first grade reading list. Reading and math and everything else came easily to her. But Mrs. Verona refused to let her read from the second grade list, and here Mila was again, listening to the stupid story, knowing that on page six, the mice would argue about the cheese and on page eight would lose it, both so very, very hungry.

All she wanted to do was go outside and play on the climbing structure. She wanted to run on the bridge and slide down the rope. She wanted to spin on the tire swing, let her best friend, Kimberley Wheeler, push her around and around. Mrs. Verona kept reading, and Mila closed her eyes just for a tiny second, letting her body relax. The story went on, slowly fading from her ears, Tim and Tom drifting away. *The structure*, she thought. *Now! Now, now, now!*

And then she was jolted into air that was not the still, quiet air of the classroom. Instead, she was in the midst of noise and a light breeze and the sounds of laughter. She opened her eyes and had to grab on to the bridge rail as Kimberley ran by laughing, calling out, "Let's get on the swing! Come on, Mila! It's our turn!"

Mila gasped and tried to find her breath. She was outside on the playground! On the structure. She closed her eyes for a second and then opened them slowly, the world filtered through her eyelashes for a second, seeming almost, maybe . . . no. Not normal. Not even close.

She glanced back toward the classroom and saw Mrs. Verona putting the chairs from the reading circle back under the tables where they belonged. For a minute, Mila stared, her eyes wide, thinking that she had to go right this second to the office and call her mother to come get her. She was sick. Really, really sick. Adair would send Mr. Henry, their driver, and when they arrived home, Adair would tuck Mila into her bed and feed her soup, telling her, "It's all a dream. That's all. You are fine. You fell asleep. You were very groggy and stumbled out onto the playground. That's all."

Mila was just about to jump off the structure and run to the office, when something inside herself stopped her. It was like a hand held her back, pressing on her shoulder. It was like a voice saying, "No."

She didn't know why, but she obeyed the hand, the voice, and breathed in, turning to see Kimberley twirling on the tire swing. Kimberley waved at her and laughed.

"Come on!" she cried, and Mila found a way to walk to her friend, to forget that somehow, she managed to move time ahead so she didn't have to hear about Tim and Tom and their tiny piece of cheese one more time.

And since then, all her life, she'd never mentioned the shifts of time to anyone. Even when she felt crazy. Even when all she wanted to do was whisper, "I move time," into a friend's, a lover's, a parent's ear. Every time she felt the words in her mouth, she felt that same restraint, that same warm pressure above her heart that said, "No."

"So you see," Adair was saying, the conversation never varying from the one-two punch of Adair's desire for Mila to come absolutely to dinner. "You just must. After that latest dating debacle with—what's his name?"

"Tomas," Mila said, looking at her nails, paint rimming each like colored slivers of moons. "Tomas Javier Oliveto."

"The artist," Adair said, but for a second her voice softened, held the pain that Mila had felt when Tomas packed up his paintbrushes and moved to Miami with Andrea, the nude model from his water-color class. Andrea, the gorgeous brunette, with her liquid eyes and lovely body. For weeks, Mila would find her image in her apartment, Tomas's sketches everywhere.

Mila nodded, her cheek pressed against the phone. "The artist."

"I never liked him. Not one bit," Adair said. "So this time, Mila, I won't take no for an answer. I simply won't. You will come to dinner and meet Garrick. You won't be disappointed."

Mila nodded at her mother's recitation of de-mands, knowing that the problem with moving time is that there is so little of it. So limited. So precious. All those occasions she pushed herself forward into another chronological space wasted her life. It didn't matter what the boring, horrible experience was: PAP smear, the dentist's waiting room, traffic jams, long, dull lectures, the prelude to a breakup, sorrow and pain of any kind of stripe. All that boredom, pain, and suffering were parts of her life.

And it wasn't just her life she had to think about; she might also have wasted the lives of the people around her, though she wasn't sure about that. How could she know? She couldn't just sidle up to her friends and family and loved ones and say, "Hey, you know that twenty minutes of the speech the bride's father gave the crowd? Do you remember it? Did you find yourself thankfully eating cake instead of listen-ing to him go on for one more second?"

Mila had tried to research her "affliction," and on

another long, lonely night, she searched the Internet for hours, Googling the paradoxes of "time travel" and "chronological disruption" and "astral projection," and while she didn't run into anyone who said he or she could project themselves anywhere, she at least knew that it was possible. There was even a site that promised that the witchy experts therein could instruct you on how to leave your body, fly around your neighborhood, and meet your deceased loved ones.

And no matter how hard Mila tried, she had never found a way to reverse the order, to go back to a time in the past and reclaim the moments she had squandered. When she tried, she found herself floating in a swirl of nothing, in neither the present nor the future, and this interim feeling scared her, so she never attempted it again. And thus her policy of not pushing forward anymore. Mila knew she needed to live her crazy, weird life the way it unfolded, one boring, happy, long, dull, joyful event at a time.

And for better or worse, moving time wasn't her only affliction. She also had the ability to hear other people's thoughts, ideas, and feelings that were unspoken, unsaid. And often just unnecessary. Adair used to be surprised when Mila knew it was time to leave for a shopping trip before being told or answered questions before they were asked. But she learned very early on to ignore people's thoughts because people often thought things they didn't want to say aloud. The mind was like a beautiful, horrid quilt, bits and pieces patched together, some spots ripped and torn, some smooth and lovely. Mila didn't want to hear secrets, hatreds, loves, desires. So she cloaked her mind, holding herself back, pushing others away.

"Mother! Mother!" Mila interrupted now, catching Adair midstream in yet another reason why Mila should attend the dinner.

"Yes, dear?" Adair sounded satisfied, obviously hearing the acquiescence in her daughter's voice.

"Okay. I'll come. I'll be there." Mila sighed, wondering what she would wear, knowing there wasn't much in her closet that met with her mother's approval anymore.

"Wonderful. I'll have Henry come get you next Saturday at seven thirty."

"Fine."

"And, dear?"

Mila shook her head, hearing what was coming. "Yes?"

"Try to look presentable, will you? None of that faux animal print silliness of yours. Or all that tight black material. That *jersey*."

Mila smiled, remembering the leopard-print miniskirt she'd worn the last time, a skirt she'd had to borrow from Farrah, the girl in the space downstairs. Mila wanted something completely bizarre so that that setup with the retired banker would fall flat and die.

"I promise," Mila said. "Bye, Mom."

She hung up and looked out the window again. This was her life. She was a weird person in a normal world. She was alone but what else could she do? Almost her entire life, she'd known that there was no one else in the world like her and there was no one on this world who would understand. She had a skill she had never been able to talk about with anyone, and so what? In recent months, she was finally doing what she wanted: painting and taking art classes and going to art shows. She spent hours engrossed, surprised by unexpected combinations of color and texture. She wasn't wasting her time. Not at all. She lived through every single real second, and though her parents often drove her insane, they were her parents. Even though she'd never really understood them and their lives, she wanted them to be happy. They loved her, despite the series of sad bachelors they presented to her over gazpacho and pasta, despite the strange lonely distance between them sometimes. Mila knew she had a good life, a privileged life, a life that was just about on the verge of happiness. She had to stop dwelling on what she didn't have. That's what all the books told her. She just needed to live.

So she would go to dinner. Mila would spend her time with her parents in the best way she could. And most importantly, she would have a nice meal, good-looking, fantastic, wonderful, wealthy Garrick McClellan or no perfect, talented, *so so* sexy Garrick McClellan. Period.

Even though the dinner was set for Saturday at eight, Mr. Henry came in his car to fetch Mila an hour early. In the moments just before he arrived, Mila found herself standing in front of the mirror, looking at herself, trying not to see her image in Adair's eyes. Or trying to see herself in Adair's eyes. Or both. What would her mother think tonight? And why, Mila wondered, did she still care? Would she be a sixty-year-old woman still worried about what her mother would think of a skirt?

But she couldn't help it. She did care. And

tonight, her long blond hair was pulled neatly back in a ponytail, Mila making sure to use at least some of the products Adair had given her earlier in the week— especially a glop called "Smooth and Shine," which seemed to do just that, her hair a smooth shiny rope of gold. She'd dug in her closet for a simple black silk skirt and a red long-sleeved sweater that clung in the right places.

"If I had a figure like yours, dear," Adair always said, "I would show it off. Thin is in and so are breasts. Yes, don't look at me like that. They are. So show it off! Not too much, but just enough to advertise."

The red sweater did just that. Garrick McClellan would have at least one nice thing to say to his friends when he got home, ready to tell the tale of another blind date gone bad. And to finish off the entire date costume, Mila had slipped on her black pumps and glossed her lips with an almost translucent shade of red just when Mr. Henry knocked on her large loft door.

Pulling the door open, she smiled, wanting to step into his space but knowing that she could not. All her life, Mr. Henry had been a permanent fixture, the one who picked her up from school every afternoon, who stood in the kitchen talking with Nidia as Mila ate her snack, who listened to Mila and her friends laugh and talk in the back of the Lincoln Town Car.

"My," he would say. "My, oh, my."

But he never let her touch him, throw an arm over his shoulder, hold his hand as they walked from the school office to the car. Mr. Henry wasn't like her father, Paul, who would hold out his arms and say,

"Come to me, my beamish gal!" Mila would run to her father, try to roll him over with her slight weight, giggling as he lifted her into the air.

No matter how much time passed, Mr. Henry seemed to stay the same: short dark hair trimmed carefully, a smooth, placid face, a slim, compact body dressed in a driver's dark suit. She was completely unclear about how old he was, and there were no physical clues. No gray hair, no facial wrinkles, no age spots. He could be thirty-five or sixty-five. It was a mystery. Maybe if he varied his appearance now and again, she might be able to discern some changes, but she had never seen him dressed in anything but the suit, not once. No Hawaiian shirt on weekends, no Dockers and loafers, no polo shirt or button-down blue oxford.

Once Mila asked her mother where Mr. Henry came from, and Adair looked slightly pinched, somehow slightly pale, and then shrugged her shoulders.

"Oh," she said. "He was recommended. By the best people."

"Who?" Mila asked, but Adair shrugged again and clacked away in her perfectly shined pumps, leaving Mila thinking that Mr. Henry had power over Adair, apparently the only person on the planet who did.

Another time, she snuck very briefly into his upstairs room, pulling open a dresser drawer about an inch before she got scared and slipped back out of the room and closed the door, her heart beating so hard her ears thumped. She loved him, and she didn't want him to know she needed to spy, wanted clues. She didn't want him to know she had no idea who he was at all.

And really, she didn't want him to know that by

trying to figure his life out, she was trying to figure out hers.

"So, are you ready for the onslaught?" Mr. Henry asked, his lips in their usual light smile. "Are you ready to meet the next new man of your dreams?"

Mila laughed. "Is that what my mother is saying now?"

"Oh, he's a 'keeper,' " Mr. Henry said. "He's the man who could take care of you for the rest of your life. He's your equal. He's probably Mr. Perfect, but she's not willing to go out on that limb quite yet. But it's very possible that he's the man you've been waiting for since before you can remember."

Shaking her head, Mila picked up her purse and a sweater, just in case the night turned chilly, the fog blowing in from the Pacific. For the first time, Adair was sounding as if she believed in Mila's sad theory about her soul mate.

"She's lost her mind this time. Gone over the total deep end," Mila said, grabbing the door handle as she walked out. Then she stopped. "But wait. Do I look 'acceptable'?"

Mr. Henry took careful stock of her, his eyes knowing Adair Adams' preferences almost as well as he knew the ins and outs of San Francisco streets, avenues, and alleys.

"You'll do," he said. "You'll do just fine."

Mila closed the door to her studio and followed behind Mr. Henry, knowing that those words were the highest praise indeed.

"Mr. Henry, could you take me to the Slanted Door instead? I need a margarita. Maybe a plate of spring rolls? We could sit by the window and watch the ferries load and unload. We can laugh at the tourists in their shorts," she said, as they made their way down the flight of stairs. "The weather is wonderful! And I am the best company."

"Yes, you are, but if I don't get you to the house soon, your mother will give me that look. Her terrible evil eye," he said. "But I promise if you make it through dinner, I'll drive you home fast, running every red light I can."

Mila snorted. Mr. Henry had never broken a driving law in his life. "It's a deal. And I will take you up on it."

Mr. Henry smiled and they walked to the car. He opened the door and as she sat down, Mila looked up into his face. For a second, she thought she saw something other than his affection for her. Something different. Something like irritation. Or maybe even anger.

"Mr. Henry," she began, but as she began to talk, his face changed, and he was the man she had always known, all these years.

"Don't worry," he said just as he was closing the door. "It will be over before you know it."

"That's what you always say. And didn't I have to endure three dinners with Vic Shiffrin, the mortgage broker? Or what about that long Sunday lunch with Doug Epstein, the guy who said, 'You know what I mean?' after every sentence? I am still feeling those meals. Right here!" Mila pointed to her head. "And here," she said, pointing to her stomach.

Mr. Henry stopped, blinked, his face calm. "But you know it's true. In an instant, it's all over."

Mila shrugged and sighed, knowing that he was exactly right. It was always over before she knew it, and sometimes over sooner. But not tonight. Tonight, time would go unchanged and on and on and on.

* * *

Mila was sitting on a plush leather chair in her mother's perfectly appointed living room, when the doorbell rang. Adair answered it herself, letting in her old friend Linda Tilden and a man Mila knew must be the famous Garrick McClellan, the man of her flipping dreams.

Taking a deep, calming breath that she learned in yoga class, Mila stood up, put her drink down on the carefully placed coaster, and wiped her hand on her skirt. She knew what she would do. She would smile, shake his hand, sit back down, and ask Linda a bunch of questions about her fund-raising for the youth art museum downtown. She would smile, make nice, and then Nidia would let them know that dinner was ready. Garrick—sensing that she was enthralled with Linda—would talk with Paul and Adair and then somehow, he would end up at the wrong end of the table from Mila. Halfway through dinner, Mila would go to the bathroom and stay there for seven minutes, and when she returned, there would only be about fifteen minutes left. Coffee would be served out on the porch, and she could stay in the kitchen with Nidia, ostensibly helping with the dishes instead of what she was really doing: hiding out. The whole evening would be painless, and, most importantly, her mother would be happy that Mila showed up in nylons and black pumps.

"Mila, love," Linda Tilden said, walking into the living room. "So good to see you. You look absolutely wonderful."

Not glancing at the man behind Linda, Mila shook her mother's friend's hand. "Good to see you, too, Linda. You look amazing yourself."

Amazing was the right word. In recent years, Linda had gone through a number of cosmetic treatments. The first were pretty innocuous: BOTOX and Restalyne and laser sessions that left her slightly red around the nostrils even days later. But lately she had started to develop the pinched and tight and lifted look of the intensely, perhaps arctically windblown.

"Thank you, dear. But here. Mila," Linda said, turning to pull Garrick forward. "This is my nephew Garrick McClellan."

Before she looked up at Garrick McClellan, Mila thought that it must be sad to be a man who could be led around town by his bossy aunt. Here was a man with no balls, no gumption, no drive, no energy, no mojo. Nothing. Or maybe here was a man who was hungry. Who couldn't cook. Who couldn't take care of himself and needed Linda in order to survive. He probably didn't know how to do one thing for himself. He lived with roommates, sent his laundry out, and ordered takeout every night. He was inept, stupid, watched football, and drove something expensive, small, and shiny with two doors.

She knew that his parents had moved out of the country a few years before, so he clearly couldn't live on his own, attached by the hip to his annoying aunt.

What a loser, she thought, lifting her eyes up his body slowly, noting his long, lean legs, his flat stomach, his broad chest under a crisp button-down shirt, the stripes of which matched perfectly with thousands of dollars of dark blue silk in his suit. For a second, she imagined asking if she could have the suit for the piece she was currently working on, but then she looked at his hands, tanned and strong, the fingers long and graceful. Her gaze reached his face and with a bigger breath, she let herself look into his eyes, feeling some kind of woozy heat fill her as she did. His eyes were dark and lovely, but somehow closed to her. Shut off. Slightly mean looking even with his handsome face, a face that had known a lot of smiles from the slight crinkles at the corners of his eyes. He wasn't available to her at all.

Here we go again. Another loser. A loser in a gorgeous suit, she thought. *And an amazing, gorgeous body under all that gorgeous fabric.*

Suppressing the idea that she'd like to use part of his suit fabric in a painting, Mila stood up, smiled a thin smile, and reached out her hand. But Garrick McClellan didn't lean forward to meet her halfway. He didn't move forward; he wouldn't take her hand, and didn't reach out or toward her. He didn't even do more than nod and quickly turn to Linda and Adair. Mila was right. Here he was—another loser.

"Wonderful room," he said. "An amazing house. Thank you so much for the invitation."

"Thank you," Adair said a bit stiffly, pulling her arm back and holding it next to her side. Even she seemed a bit taken aback by Garrick's entry and lack of greeting. "It has always done well for us. We've been very, very happy here."

As they spoke, Mila tried to reach into Garrick's thoughts, usually something so easy for her to do with anyone, but there was nothing coming from him. No pictures, no image, no words. Not even a whiff of feeling. It was as if he'd locked everything down tight and thrown away the key. Clamped down tight like Fort Knox. After his shrug, he wouldn't glance at Mila, and she stood there blinking, unsure of what to do.

Linda looked surprised, her face frozen not from cosmetic surgery but from embarrassment. She looked at Adair and Mila, trying to find words to cover the empty space in the room.

"Garrick," she said. "Tell Mila about seeing her painting."

Linda turned to Mila, her face reverting to her earlier happy expression. "He was just at MOMA and saw your work! Isn't that a coincidence?"

Mila watched Garrick, saw him take a deep breath before he replied. "Yes, I was there for a fund-raiser. I saw your painting."

His face was totally expressionless, not containing any of the interest or even the pretend interest people usually had when talking to Mila about her work.

"I have three there," Mila said. "Which one did you see?"

After that question, Garrick looked up at her. For just a moment, his eyes contained an ache she could almost feel inside her head. It wasn't a thought. He was not letting anything out somehow, but she knew he'd been hurt. Wounded. And that somehow, she was responsible for some of it.

"The one with the purple swirl," Garrick began, his voice flat, but as he seemed to want to say something else, Mila's father walked into the room.

Everyone turned away from the painting conversation to greet Paul, but before Garrick turned to introduce himself to Paul, he gave Mila a look that would have hurt had it been made of metal.

What did I do? she wanted to say. *What have I done to hurt you?*

But why bother saying anything? After all, who was he to her? He was a blind date, a date already gone bad. A jerk who couldn't muster the social niceties both of them had grown up with. This situation wasn't horrible enough to move time, but it was bad enough to ignore the niceties of conversation and pretense. All she needed to do was eat dinner and then she could go home. She would wash off her makeup, take off her acceptable outfit, stand before her easel, and stare into color and form.

Adair gave Mila a wide-eyed look, and Mila could hear her mother think, *This isn't working out at all.*

"Mila, why don't you come help me and Nidia in the kitchen," she said, and Mila breathed out, thankful that her mother was saving her from the living room conversation. Garrick McClellan could talk big boy stuff with her father and Linda could listen on, conjuring up other single women for her prize jerk nephew.

"Okay," Mila said, smiling, following her mother out of the living room, through the dining room, and into the kitchen.

"How rude he is," Adair hissed. "Good looking but rude."

"Don't you mean well off and rude, too?" Mila whispered.

Adair pursed her lips and shook her head. "And the way he talked about your painting."

"*Didn't* talk is the operative word," Mila said as they pushed through the double doors into the large kitchen. Nidia stood at the steel counter, organizing soup bowls.

"How is it going on the date?" she asked.

"Don't ask," Mila said.

"I think I just did," Nidia said, and they all laughed, even Adair.

"Suffice it to say," Adair said, stirring the soup with a shiny steel spoon, "that we will want all the courses at once, Nidia dear. Maybe we should just start with dessert."

They all laughed, but Mila looked toward the dining room, wondering why this man couldn't even look at her, touch her. Why did he pull away before he had the need to? He didn't even know her and he rejected her. She stopped laughing, picked up a soup bowl, and moved toward her mother, who was ready to ladle out the soup.

Garrick McClellan seemed to see into her, see her flaw, the one she'd been trying to hide all her life.

"Well, then, I think you will fill the bowls only half. Soup over early," Nidia said.

"An excellent idea! This is why we love you so much," Adair said, and she ladled a tiny dollop of soup into the bowl Mila held out. "There. Give this to *him*."

Mila smiled, breathed out, relaxed. Adair chuckled to herself and then filled the bowl full.

Mila knew she could handle this dinner. She could get through this five-course dinner despite Garrick McClellan's dark haunted stare and rude behavior. And she would be gracious and kind and even give him a full bowl of Marta's delicious gazpacho.

Linda must have started it, and Adair—probably in a last-minute effort to reclaim the date—must have condoned it. So without Mila or Garrick having much of a say, Mr. Henry was driving both Garrick and Mila home.

The limo was new, airtight, and thoroughly upholstered and carpeted, so the only noise was the occasional loud traffic blare and the rich whoosh of tire on asphalt.

Mila smoothed her skirt and tried to keep her eyes trained to the night cityscape: the lights, the cars, the buildings. She worried that she was breathing too loud, the rapid speed of her breath a monitor of her almost welling panic from being trapped in the car with Garrick. And Mr. Henry was of no use, keeping his head resolutely forward, his hands on the steering wheel, never turning back to say a word.

This situation, she thought, *is completely untenable. Horrible. The worst.*

Garrick guffawed and she looked up, but his head was turned toward the window. His long legs were stretched out, the muscles under his suit pants taut. She paused, looking at him, but finally blurted out, "What is so funny?"

He didn't look at her but said, "Nothing. Nothing is funny at all."

"Why did you laugh, then?"

"No reason."

"So you just laugh for no reason. Do you have some kind of disorder?"

Garrick turned to look at her, his face no longer containing a ripple of his laugh. His dark eyes were filled with feeling that seemed old and deep and angry. "I don't think I'd call it a disorder. Do you have a disorder? Or are you just rude enough to ask people if they have one?"

Mila swallowed, looking down at her hands. He was right. She had been rude. Why had she said that? All her life she'd worried that people would think she was off or touched or crazy, and then to say something like that? "I'm sorry. I just wanted to know what was so funny."

He shrugged. "It's not hard to find what's funny about this ride. Here we are, two grown people being treated like children. Stuffed in a car with each other, even though both of us would rather be elsewhere."

"We wanted to be elsewhere about three hours ago," she said. "I know I wanted to be somewhere else the minute you walked in the door."

He smirked. "Exactly. We let ourselves be dragged into a blind date. I knew better, of course, but here I am all the same. It's, well, untenable."

Mila jerked her head up, staring at him. Did he pull that word out of a vocabulary hat? Or was it one of his favorites, as it was hers? Or had he heard her thought?

"Anyway," he went on, "that's why I laughed. I'm tired of evenings like this. I'm tired of trying to make my aunt happy. That's what I do all day at work. I just want to go home. And forget about—everything."

Mila stared at him, biting her lip for a second. "Do you know," she said, "that this is the most you've said to me all night?"

Garrick looked at her. She could see the rise and fall of his breath, his shirt and tie moving up and down slowly. He shook his head. "We don't have much to say to each other."

Mr. Henry made a turn, Mila sliding slightly on the leather seat. Her foot hit Garrick's leather shoe, and he pulled back from her, crossing his long legs.

"You chose to not say anything. There is plenty we could have said. We are about the same age, grew up in the city, worked in the same profession. Small talk was made for us."

He pushed his blond hair away from his forehead, his hands the kind of hands that made her feel safe. Hands that could do things that were necessary: open jar lids, change tires, fix small appliances. But also beautiful hands, tanned and smooth, the kinds of hands that she'd thought about—maybe even dreamed about. The kind she wanted to see with a paintbrush, the kind that could encircle a lush wet pile of clay. The kind she wanted to see on her arm, her shoulder, her thigh.

Stop it, she told herself. *You are acting loony over a guy who would rather be watching* Conan *right now.*

"Your painting," he asked, his words coming from him slowly, as if he had to pull each word out of his mouth by a string, "the one with the purple swirl?"

"The Ride," she said, changing her gaze, moving it from his hands to his face. She was startled by his pointed expression. "What about it?"

"What does it mean?" he asked. And when Mila looked at him, she could see such an intense curiosity burning from behind his indifference, she wished she could open the car door and fling herself out. No one had ever looked at her like that before, not her parents, not a lover. No one ever paid that much attention to her, all at once. "What is it saying? Where does it come from?"

"It's just something from my imagination. Something I think about. All the time."

"Why? Why do you think about that shape? That color? What do you think?" He was leaning forward now, his face alight, his eyes filled with something like heat. "It's like there's movement there. Like the shape is going some place. Like it's carrying people, important people."

Mila blinked, startled. She'd only ever talked about *The Ride* with her art instructors, the museum gallery director, her classmates. "I don't know why you care. You certainly didn't show any interest earlier."

"I—I . . ." Garrick stopped talking, shaking his head. He jerked his head up and noticed where the car was. "Never mind. I shouldn't have done this. I never should have come, Linda or not. Driver."

"His name is Mr. Henry."

Garrick leaned forward. "Mr. Henry, you can let me out here."

Mr. Henry didn't turn but said, "It's a mile yet."

"That's fine. Right here. Let me out here." And when Mr. Henry didn't seem to slow down, Garrick almost yelled, "Stop."

Mila sat flat against her seat watching this beautiful angry man do everything in his power to get away from her. If it wasn't so upsetting, she thought, she'd be able to craft some kind of story about it to tell her friends at the beginning of open studio, recounting the evening with verve and style, a jaunty yarn about the blind date from hell. The man who endured asphalt raspberry burns rather than ride a final mile in a one-hundred-thousand-dollar limo with her.

"Here we go, sir," Mr. Henry said, and Garrick opened the door, and he started to push through to the outside. He stopped for a second, and she could see him take in a big breath.

"Look," he said, turning back to her, one foot already out on the pavement. "It's not about . . ."

It's not you, it's me. Yadda, yadda, yadda, Mila thought. *Get out of the car, jerk.*

Garrick stopped talking, and she thought she heard him laugh. But his eyes weren't happy.

"Good luck with your painting," he said, leaving for real this time, the door closing heavy and hard.

As the car pulled away, Mila watched him as long as she could, until Mr. Henry turned left down the hill, heading toward the Mission District.

"Well," Mila said finally as they sailed through traffic. "That was so much fun, I hope I can do it again next Saturday!"

"He seemed a little strained," Mr. Henry said. "A little tense."

"He needed—well, he didn't need me, that's all I know."

Mila sat back, letting the ride home take her over. If she wasn't laughing, she would cry. And vice versa. It was too ironic. Here was a man who if he hadn't acted like such an ass, she actually would have loved to see again. And for no good reason, except for a strange feeling she'd had ever since he walked into her parents' living room. Some kind of zing, a flurry of energy in her body.

But his good looks and some kind of chemistry weren't enough to overcome his clear lack of manners or caring. So now it was over. She'd survived the dinner, her mother would likely not try another setup for months, and Mila could scratch another San Francisco bachelor off the long list her mother seemed to keep on file. Maybe now after this debacle, Mila thought, it was a good time to kiss that list good-bye.

* * *

She didn't even have a chance to look at the clock before picking up her cell phone, fumbling in the dark bedroom to find the button to answer it.

"What?" she asked, blinking into the early morning light, her blankets piled around her.

"I have to see you," he said.

Mila forced herself into total consciousness, taking in small breaths, keeping her eyes open. What day was it? Or what night? Was it the weekend? "Who is this?"

"It's Garrick. Garrick McClellan."

Mila rolled onto her back. "You have to see me? Didn't—didn't you just jump out of a car to get away from me?"

There was a pause, and Mila wondered if she'd fallen back to sleep, but then he said, "I'm—I'm sorry. I want to explain. And I want to ask you something about . . ."

"What? About what?" Mila asked.

"Us," Garrick said. "Us."

Sitting up, Mila leaned against her pillow, her mouth open slightly. *Us?* What was he doing calling her like this after a night like that? After he almost made himself roadkill rather than sit next to her? She wanted to laugh at him. To tell him to take a hike. But then, through the phone, she felt so much that she wanted to lie down flat on the bed and weep. Images were coming to her, feelings, thoughts. Garrick's. So much hurt and loss and pain. He had been so alone. So afraid.

"Oh," she said, trying to find words. "Oh."

"Can we meet?" he asked, unaware of what she was pulling in from his mind.

"Yes. Yes," she said. "We can meet."

"When?" he asked.

What time was there? she wondered. What time was there but this moment? She knew from wasting time how valuable it was.

"Now," she said. "Come over now."

Chapter Three

Garrick stood in front of Mila Adams' loft door, a finger poised to ring the bell. It was late—or early—about 3:00 A.M., and his eyes felt grainy from lack of sleep and wired from meeting Mila.

Before the date, he'd tried to make sure nothing could connect them, nothing could interest him. He tamped down his thoughts, closed off his ability to read into anyone's mind, and decided to be cordial but quiet, nice but cool. He wouldn't bring up the painting or her inspiration for it. He would eat and get the hell out, probably dampening his aunt's need to fix him up again. Life could go on as it had since he'd come back from the hospital all those years ago when he was a boy.

But from the moment he walked into the Adamses' house and set his eyes on Mila, he'd wanted to run away and toward her. She sat there on the couch and looked up, and it was as if his dream—every dream, all dreams—was in front of him.

How stupid could he get? How ridiculous to believe that dreams come true, like a stupid song from a stupid movie. Nothing in his life had ever suggested a happily ever after.

So instead of focusing on her eyes, the soft dark way they held him, or her smile, the way she tried to befriend him, he'd been a total ass. A jerk. He didn't even lean over to shake her hand. And he didn't touch her probably because her hand wouldn't have been enough. Even though he didn't know her, he wanted to step over the coffee table, stand her up, and press her next to him. Holding her, taking her in. It wasn't like with Meredith or any of the other women he'd been with. It was different. He wanted to love her and protect her and care for her.

And he knew this from one look? And from that one look, how did he know he couldn't touch her? As if one tiny slide against her soft skin would make something wonderful, horrible, amazing happen. He knew that the same way he knew he could move backward through time, the idea ridiculous but true. So he ignored her outstretched hand, shoving his hands in his pockets and admiring the scenery.

Then in some nightmare date coup de grace, Linda and Adair arranged for Mila and him to go home together, packed like kids into the back of the limo, that slightly strange driver whisking them off. It was all he could do to keep himself from jumping next to her and grabbing her by the shoulders, asking her the questions he knew she'd have the answers to.

So he'd thrown out the question about her painting and then bolted from the car like an embarrassed teenager. What must she think of him? Why would she think of him at all?

Garrick dropped his hand. He couldn't go through with this. Maybe it was time for a visit to his parents. Maybe it was time for a sabbatical from work. Italy. Italy sounded perfect.

The door flew open, and Mila stood in front of him wearing a bathrobe, her hair slightly mussed, her eyes intense. "Maybe it's time you told me what's going on?"

Garrick stepped back. "What?"

"Maybe instead of running away, you could let me know why from the moment we met, you've been acting like an idiot." She pulled open the door, giving him space to walk through.

Garrick looked at her. Was she reading his thoughts? Could it be possible? When he was in college, he'd gone to three psychics hoping that one of them would be able to hear him. He'd gone to the Haight District, sitting in cramped rooms that were filled with the dense smoke of incense and lies. He'd sat down and looked at the women, shooting out quick hard thoughts to all, and none had answered back. So was this for real?

Are you reading my thoughts? he thought.

She looked at him, her eyes wide, and nodded. *Yes.*

Garrick stopped walking, his body suddenly perfectly still, perfectly calm. *You can do that, too?*

Mila blinked, took in a small inhale, brought a hand to her chest. "Yes," she whispered. "Forever."

Garrick stared at her, this woman who somehow knew his dream, who somehow was his dream, who could hear him when he didn't even speak. "Me, too."

Mila sighed. *I don't know what to think. I mean, no one—*

No one, Garrick thought. *No one ever. Not once. Not in all these years.*

They looked at each other just inside her doorway, and he wanted to reach out and take her hand this time, squeeze it tight. But he still didn't know exactly what would happen if he did.

He didn't know what to say, how to mark this bizarre coincidence, how to let her know how relieved he was to find one person on the planet who knew what he could do, at least partly. What should he say? Something like "Wow, isn't it weird?" Or "What are your tips on how to deal with it?"

But as he thought all this, he knew that she knew what he was thinking. She'd already seen the seedy Haight Ashbury neighborhood, the red-handkerchief-headed women, the beads and feathers and crystal balls, his eager, hopeful questions. She'd already felt his frustration and sadness that he truly was alone.

"Let's . . . well . . . come in," Mila said, and he walked past, hearing her close the door behind him. He waited for her, and she came up to him, smiled, and led him down a short hallway into a space that opened up wide. She'd turned on some lights, and Garrick felt his body rock as he took in her work that hung in the room.

He scanned the ceiling, the walls, taking in all the color and light.

"This place," he began as he walked around the wide open space of Mila's loft, "is . . ." He didn't have a word that did justice, so he said what word worked best. "Amazing."

And the space was amazing, large and light and highlighting her work, large framed canvases that were full of swirls of darkness and color, black, yellow, purple, burgundy.

"How do you do this? It's what? Paint and—"

"I guess you could call it assemblage art." She stood with her arms crossed.

"Like a collage? But that's not what it looks like."

"No, it's not collage. Paint. Etched textured compound. Acrylics. Fabric."

"So," Garrick said, breathing in the color and almost sound of the images in front of him. "It's paint first?"

Mila shrugged. "My art teachers always talk about fat over lean. I choose the layers pretty carefully and then they have to dry. Usually paints and then the texture."

Garrick turned, faced another wall, and there it was—*The Ride.* Or no—it was like the painting at the museum, but this was another version. Another take. It didn't matter; he still stood there, almost gasping at the memory. The feeling that had grasped him two weeks ago as he stood in the gallery looking at his own memory in ink and paint and canvas. And as he stared, he imagined that he could hear the roar of an engine, the pulse of heat and travel.

He looked back at Mila, his mind, for once, almost blank.

"What?" she asked.

"I know this somehow. It's a place," he said. "I think I've seen it, and I don't mean your other painting. It's so familiar to me. That's what I wanted to talk about with you in the car."

Mila shrugged. "I don't know how you could have seen it or know it. It's from a dream. Not a place, really."

But Garrick stared at the canvas, knowing that he had seen it somewhere before. Or thought of it. Maybe it was from a movie. Or a television show or a book. But it seemed to him that he'd been there. Because they could share thoughts, he wanted to ask Mila if he could look at her dream, slip into her memory of it and look around, but before he could, she was talking about her work, probably too quickly, her words coming out fast due to nerves. She was nervous just like he was.

"I did this during my first year of art school. You know, exorcise the inner demons. Try to purge myself of feeling like a nut bar all the time. But then I changed to lighter subjects." She led him to a wall where a series of canvases covered in textured yellows and oranges hung. "I try to call this my 'bright' period, but it doesn't really seem to fit. Maybe it's just more of an 'I ran out of black and indigo' period."

"The mind reading. That's why you feel like a 'nut bar'?"

Fear and shame from her thoughts came to him, and he almost closed his eyes, recognizing her feelings, the same ones he'd had growing up in a world of normal people.

No, she thought. *Not just that.*

"What else? What do you mean?"

"Can we sit down?" She pointed to a couch and a chair in the corner of the large space, but even that space was crowded with art.

Garrick followed her over to the couch, sitting down, crossing his legs and then uncrossing them.

He'd never felt this uncomfortable in his whole life.
But how could that be? For the first time in his life,
someone was actually like him.

"It's weird. I know. I don't know what to do with it
yet. But I thought you must—well, after the way you
acted at my parents' house, I thought there had to be
something you were hiding."

"So, what did you mean?" he asked, ignoring what
she said, no matter how true it was.

She nodded, looked down at her lap. "There's
something else I can do besides read minds."

"What?" he asked, feeling the air escape him.
"What?"

"It's going to sound crazy," she said, and as he
tried to reach into her mind, he realized that she had
closed it off.

"Look," he said, leaning forward, his elbows on his
knees, his chin in his hands. "It can't be much
stranger than what we've already talked about."

He stared at her, waiting. And she looked up at
him, her face in such repose, so calm, so beautiful.
And she lifted her head, slowly, taking in a slight
breath and nodding.

"All right," she said. "But I've never told anyone
before. Never."

Garrick wondered where she had gotten such
strength. He'd been so little, but he'd run immediately to his parents with his fears. He'd blabbed to
everyone: the nurses, the doctors, the shrinks. If she
had anything in her arsenal like he did, she must be
stronger than he could even imagine.

"I'm ready," he said, his heart a gymnast in his
chest.

"I can move forward in time," she said, her words

clear and perfectly formed. "I could move us through an hour if I wanted to right now. I could have gotten us through that miserable dinner tonight in, well, no time. We could have been here, skipping over everything else."

Garrick listened to her words, staring at her, unable to really pull in the words that were in the air right in front of him. Can. Move. Time. Forward. He sat back, feeling a full welling of feeling in his solar plexus. He turned to look out of the window, trying to find breath. He found himself smiling, happiness a feeling he actually understood for the first time. He could feel it on his face and in his body.

"I should never have told you," she said, starting to stand. "Please don't tell anyone. Please just forget about this."

He turned back, leaned forward, almost touching her knee to keep her still, pulling back before touching her knee. "No. No. Please sit. I needed to think for a second. Or feel."

Mila sat back down, crossing her arms. "What do you think? Or feel about this?"

She pushed her long hair behind her shoulders, and Garrick wanted to move to the couch, sit next to her, kiss her on the shoulder, the collarbone, the neck. He wanted to take her in his arms and say, "Me, too. Yes."

But he couldn't. He closed down his mind again, not wanting her to see the place they couldn't connect. Garrick knew that something dangerous was crackling between them like lit pine needles, and he couldn't walk into it. He wasn't sure what the danger was. He just knew that if he touched her, nothing would be able to stop what happened next. So her lovely neck and shoulders were out of bounds. For now. Maybe forever.

"I won't be able to forget about what you've said," he said. "Because I can move time, too."

Staring at him, she blinked once, twice. Her lips opened slightly, and she stared at him. "You can?"

"Yes. Since I was a boy. I guess about five." As he told her, he imagined himself running to his parents' room, so afraid of time repeating. He was trapped in a maze of hours, and he didn't know how to escape.

"Oh my God," she said, now standing up, clutching her ribs. "There are two of us. I can't believe it. I always thought—no one . . ."

Mila paced under her paintings. "I just never thought to ask anyone about this. Mind reading was one thing. You know, it's all around us, clairvoyants on the corner and that irritating man on TV. The one who supposedly can talk to the dead. But time?"

"It's a power I don't like to use," Garrick said. "In the past, more often. But now I try—I try not to do it. I have to relive the time I push back, so I try not to move one more minute, except . . . well, I try not to do anything more than once."

"I don't go forward anymore, either," she said. "I can't bear to lose more time."

Mila looked at him and started to laugh, covering her mouth with her hands. The sound was happy at first, and then she crossed the line from laughter into tears. She slumped against the wall, her shoulders shaking.

"Mila," Garrick said, standing up, feeling something he never had before. He wanted to attack what was making her upset, but he was what was hurting her. What he had told her was making her cry. "It's okay."

She held up a hand. "I know, I know. It's just that I never imagined I'd have this conversation with anyone. I . . ."

Her sobs came again, a soft, sad tug of sound.

He stood up, walking closer to her. "I can't stand that I am making you cry. Please stop. It's okay."

She nodded, her hair hanging in front of her face. He wanted to reach forward and tuck it behind her ears. He wanted to kiss her cheek and hold her close. And why didn't he? What could possibly happen to him that hadn't happened before? Time might move, but he'd be with someone who would understand.

Garrick put out a hand, but he heard the flames crackle, the kindling explode with heat. So instead, he leaned against the wall next to her. "Look, I never thought I'd meet someone else who could do it, either. I always thought it was crazy. It's what you said in the car. A disorder. My parents tried to rid me of it for years. But they couldn't get rid of what they didn't believe in."

Wiping her eyes, she looked up at him. "You told your parents?"

"That was my first mistake. I kept trying to tell them my entire childhood. After no one would listen, I finally gave up. My life got a lot better. But I always hoped I'd find someone I could talk to about it. I always . . ." He stopped talking, feeling as though he might start crying, too. "I always imagined this. Maybe we weren't so upset in my imagination. But I

always hoped I'd find a person who would understand."

Mila nodded, found a smile, pulled it forth, her
face relaxing. "I imagined it, too. But I never figured
out the context. I thought maybe it would be a shaman
from another country or a circus performer or a
woman in a black cape. I didn't think you'd be—"

"Like you?"

She nodded again. "Yeah. As if we were perfectly
normal."

"Normal isn't the right word, but I know what you
mean."

"No one had ever asked, 'What's really bothering
you? Why do you look so confused? Why are you so
unhappy?' " Mila said. "And if they had, what would I
have said? Something like 'Listen, here's the scoop. I
can hear your thoughts and I can move time. Really.
Pretty amazing, huh? I know you are thinking about
how much you hate your mother-in-law and how you
wish you could get into the pants of the bag boy at
Safeway. I heard you wish you could take a nap right
now during the CEO's presentation. Yes, really. And I
can whip right through this entire discussion if it
starts to annoy me. Isn't that something? Do you
promise not to take me to the nuthouse now?' "

"I wasn't as smart—"

"No, no, I didn't mean that." Mila's eyes were
wide. "I just didn't know how to ask questions."

Garrick shrugged. "I asked too many. And they
did throw me in the nuthouse."

She watched him, breathing lightly. "I am so
sorry."

There was a pause in the conversation, and Garrick pushed away from the wall. "Let's sit down again. Start over."

Letting out a long sigh and wiping her eyes, Mila moved from the wall and back to the couch. As she sat, Garrick saw a long lovely slip of leg under her robe, his eyes and body reacting as he did. He made sure his thoughts were tucked in, not wanting to let her know how drawn he was to her, how much he wanted to touch her; how much he did not.

He sat down a good two feet from her and crossed his legs.

"I—" he began, but Mila took over.

"What do you think?" she said. "Tell me. What are we? Why do we have these powers?"

Garrick wanted to shrug but didn't. What were they? As a boy, he'd read science fiction novels almost as if they were religious tracts. In the pages of every novel were people like him who could move through time and read minds. They could do other amazing things, too, even weirder things like fly and shoot fire through their fingers and disappear and reappear elsewhere. They lived on different planets and led unearthly lives, but somehow they were humans, somehow they were like him despite the worlds upon worlds of difference. Only in fiction had there been anyone to relate to. When he looked up from the words, all he saw was an ordinary planet full of normal people who were confined to the laws of nature he learned about in class.

"I don't know," he said. "No one ever had an answer for me. One doctor even suggested to my parents that I might be possessed by a spirit. A demon. Sort of the whole *Exorcist* thing. Spinning heads and all that. He even recommended a guy who could ex-

orcise me. Someone with proven results, a renegade
Catholic priest."

Mila shook her head, her voice a slap in the dim
light. "How is thinking someone is possessed any different or any weirder than what we can do? How is
that normal? Why didn't they give that doctor electric shock treatments? How could your parents even
listen to that?"

"I know the whole story sounds terrible. But they
were all desperate. My parents would have done anything to make it, me, stop. It was about then that I realized I had to shut up. I had to stop trying to find an
answer. I had to stop thinking that there was anyone
who could help me."

"What do we do?" she asked, staring into his eyes,
and Garrick felt what he often called déjà vu, but this
sensation was more of a memory, a memory of someplace dark and warm and safe.

He shrugged, slipping down a little on the couch,
trying to find a comfortable spot, though nothing
made him feel good now. "I have no idea. I never
have. It's like I've been treading water all my life
until now, waiting for the rescue boat or total fatigue."

She looked down at her hands, clasping them.
"Do you know why we can do this? Why aren't my
parents like me? How come they don't have this ability?"

He stared at her. She didn't know. Garrick could
already hear the apology he'd have to say; his stomach churning, his whole body uneasy. How could he
tell her this, too? He was glad that he had decided to
cover his thoughts, because he needed time to say
this. But was there enough time? Maybe he could slip

them both back, let them do this whole conversation over again in a better way, slower, more comprehensive. He would already know that she could move time, so there wouldn't be any surprises for him, and he could guide her through this truth.

He cleared his throat. "Did they ever talk about you when you were a baby?"

Mila seemed taken aback. "Of course they did. Like all parents."

"I mean, is there anything weird in that story? Any plot points missing? Never any, well, discussion of—" He couldn't say anything else, unable to find the words that would lead her to this next truth.

"I don't understand what you are saying," she started. "I know the story of my entire birth. How my father rushed to take my mother to the hospital because I decided to come three weeks earlier. How he drove the Mercedes they had at the time as if it were a Porsche, barely missing a ticket and three accidents. How I had to stay in the hospital for two days to be observed. How I had colic. All the early stuff. They wouldn't lie to me. They would have—I mean, my parents are far too into every single aspect of my life to tell me a story."

"I'm adopted," he said, his voice calm and quiet, trying to layer the room with calm. "They decided to take me in when I was about three. Their story is a little strange, but I figured it out over the years. Looking through records. Reading my birth certificate, which is very odd. But I've always known. In a way, I think that's why I imagine they've been able to leave the country now. Things are going well, they've done their job, and they're out of here."

"But I'm not adopted," she said. "I told you. I

know the whole story. They've told it to me over and over again. So that's not me. Your adoption doesn't explain anything."

"It's the only explanation I have. I knew I wasn't like my parents, like anyone else in my entire family. I came from people who were like me, and I was given away for some reason. I couldn't find the people on my birth certificate. A couple of years ago, I hired a private detective to find them, and they just don't exist."

Garrick paused, breathed, wished he could get over his fear, and put his hand on hers. "I have to think because you have the same abilities I do that you aren't your parents' child."

She blinked, almost snorted, shook her head. "Don't try to bring me into your scenario. I am not adopted. And this is hardly the place for some kind of weird discussion straight out of *Oprah* or something. I just want to know where this, well, skill came from. Why I'm like this. Why you are."

Garrick didn't know what to say. She hadn't been down this road at all, not even once, not even in all her figuring of how she was able to move time and read minds. He had to go very slowly. "So your parents are like you? They can do this? They understand the time shifts? The mind reading?"

"Of course not. I've told you already. No one but you can." She crossed her arms, her face and her mind completely shut down.

"Listen, let me ask you this. Have you ever told them about what you can do? Have you ever tried to explain?"

"No," Mila said, no longer angry, her sadness at keeping the core of herself secret from her parents rising in her chest, the thrum of despair like heavy water. "I've never told anyone anything. I didn't have the words. I never knew where to start."

She paused, and it was as if Garrick could feel what she was thinking, his old friend aloneness tugging at her, at him, insistent as always, its voice telling them both, "No one will ever understand. You are mine. You will never have anyone but me."

"So do you have a better explanation?" Garrick went on, and as soon as he let the question out into the room, he wished he hadn't. He'd gone too far. Between them connecting over their impossible skills and the adoption, he'd overwhelmed her.

Mila stood up, and he could see that she was trembling, her legs shaking slightly, her lips quivering. "I think you should go."

"Mila," he said. "I'm sorry. We don't have to talk about the adoption anymore."

"Stop it!" she said. "You don't know anything about me. How can you come in here and tell me I'm adopted when my own parents haven't told me a thing about it?"

He stood, wishing that his feelings could bolster her, hold her up. "I know all of this is a lot to take in, but it sort of pales in comparison to our abilities. We can figure all of that out together. We can work together."

Shaking her head, she moved around the coffee table and walked toward the front door, talking to him as she did. "I can't think about this anymore. Not tonight. You need to go."

Everything that was in his body told Garrick to stay. His body, his mind, his heart. He wanted to run to her, pull her close, and tell her that it would be all right. That they would figure out everything, not just their powers but their families. That they were stronger together than apart.

But even as he thought that, he felt the fear, the electricity, the burning crackle of warning.

"All right," he said. "But can we talk about this later? Any of it. I—I need to talk with you about it."

Mila reached the door, and Garrick slowly followed her. She looked up, her eyes wet, her nose red.

"Maybe," she said. "I need time to think about this."

"Time is what I have. What I can have over and over again," Garrick said. "All the backward time you want. Part of me wants to push us back and do this all over again. I wouldn't have to mention your parents, but I want to be true with you. And I know you could have gotten rid of me by now, pushed me out the door, and already gone back to bed. But you didn't. You must want this in some way, too."

She wiped her eyes, looked away, opened the door. "Good-bye," she said.

He bit the inside of his mouth, knowing that a half hour ago was only a second away. So easy to fix this, just as he had fixed things before with people. Say something stupid, do it again. Give it another go. Like someone? Have more time with her. Want to kick someone's ass? Here's your chance. It was like life with Tivo.

Garrick pushed the hair off his forehead, staring at Mila. He didn't ever want to be anything but real with her. In real time, together.

"Okay," he said. "But can we talk about this another time?"

Mila was still for a moment, and then she shrugged. "Maybe."

"I'll call you," he said as he walked out the door. "Soon."

He turned to look at her one more time, but all he saw was the door, closing hard behind him.

Outside, the sky had turned to a flat pewter, commuters already heading for the freeway on-ramps. He heard the sparkle hiss of Muni as it rumbled by on the street below. He was going to figure out why he was scared to touch her. He was going to get to the bottom of the adoption issue. Maybe he'd call the detective he'd hired before.

Walking down the steps, Garrick sighed. For a moment, he thought that he should be frustrated, but what he was really filled with was relief. He'd finally found someone who was the same as he was. Mila was like him and lovely, his nerves jangling him as he thought about her eyes, her smile, her rare, low laugh.

And even if she wouldn't talk to him now, she would eventually. She had to.

"Man, what form of gone are you?" Jim Ryan, Garrick's best friend since their freshman year at UC Berkeley, said after Garrick mumbled something about having a great time on Aunt Linda's setup. "I know your crazy aunt was going to drag you around town on Saturday, but don't tell me it worked! Don't tell me you fell for a blond, flouncy deb! Don't tell me that she wears tiny dresses, big sunglasses, and carries a Chihuahua around in her Prada. Then don't tell me you fell for her and her little dog, too."

Garrick looked out his twentieth-floor office window toward the Bay Bridge, holding the phone to his ear, barely hearing what Jim had to say.

"I mean, I understood the deal with Susan what's-her-face. She was hot. Really hot. Yeah, yeah. Don't say it. She was kind of slow. But in a cute way, all those pouty *uhs* and *ohs*. And then, wow, there was that Roxanne. She had that enormous rack. And weren't you just with Meredith Stone? What gives on that front?"

Garrick bit the inside of his cheek, wondering how fast he could get off the phone. It was Jim's habit since college to call Garrick every Monday to check the score—the three things that made a guy a dude. Women. Money. Partying. But for at least five years now, Garrick had only tolerated these calls because Jim worked for another big firm in San Francisco. And sometimes still, he made Garrick laugh, especially after Garrick had a second martini, which most often made his mind switch to "normal" for at least an hour.

"This is different," Garrick said, unable to even begin to tell Jim what his meeting with Mila was like. "Nothing happened."

"Nothing? So why, like, the total gaga?"

"We—we connected. That's all." Garrick swung his legs off his desk and sat up straight in his Aeron chair. "Look—"

"When are you going to see her again? For lunch? In an hour? For the rest of your life?"

"Soon. I've got to call her," Garrick said. "Very soon."

Now, he thought. *Now. I want to talk to Mila a half hour ago. All day long. All night long.*

"Wedding bells are going to chime," Jim taunted.

"I knew it had to happen. When giants fall, they fall big. Or basically you've finally lost it. And that doesn't bode well for the rest of us. What's that quote? 'Madness in great ones must not unwatched go.' "

"Listen," Garrick said, shaking his head, unwilling to believe that not only did Jim know about Shakespeare but he could also quote from *Hamlet*. Rather than comment on it, he began to wish that for once that his assistant, Brody, would buzz him from the outer office, needing Garrick to sign a form, a letter, anything. "I've got to go."

"Just call me for the bachelor party." Jim clicked off the line, and Garrick sat back and sighed. Wedding bells? Bachelor party? He never thought he could get married, scared to tell anyone ever again about what he could do, much less tell a wife. How would she be able to stand it, knowing that he could read her mind? Wouldn't she think he was a freak because he could think his way back to something that had already happened? And wouldn't she, like Garrick, want to know who or what he was? Where he came from? Who his parents were? Wouldn't the mystery drive her as crazy as it had him?

And Jim was right about one thing: madness. Wouldn't any normal loving wife begin to think her husband was crazy? Wouldn't she do exactly what his parents had? Try to fix him by any means?

Putting down his phone, he thought of Mila, her face beautiful even as he had asked her about being adopted. The way it felt when she read their minds, as if their thoughts met midstream somewhere, mingling, touching.

Garrick looked at the clock. He'd waited almost thirty hours, not calling, not e-mailing, not text-

messaging until now. He told her he was going to call
her, soon. Maybe she'd had enough time to think about
what he'd said. Maybe now she was ready to talk. He
picked up his phone again and dialed her number. He
had it memorized after only one call.

Mila hadn't wanted to meet at his place or hers,
and Garrick half expected to see her arrive at the
Italian restaurant Amarata with Mr. Henry, the stoic
driver as ready and necessary protection.

But she arrived just after he did, all alone. She was
dressed in a simple black dress, a soft red jacket in
her arms. Her face was blank as the hostess led her
over to the table, almost as if she were trying to hold
back tears. Again, he decided to tuck his thoughts in
tight and keep his desire for her thoughts in check.
He didn't want to overstep; he didn't want her to see
his fear.

"Hi," he said, standing up as she sat down, his legs
slightly wobbling, enough so that he put a hand on
his thigh, trying to bolster himself.

"Hi," she said, sliding into the booth, arranging
herself, maybe even fussing a little too long in order
to calm her own nerves.

"I'm glad you could come," he said.

Mila nodded, her hair sliding blond and light
across her shoulders. "I thought about not coming. I
thought about telling you that I never wanted to talk
to you again. But I can't just let this drop. There is so
much that I want to know."

The waitress came up to their table, offering
drinks, mentioning the specials. They both asked for
water only, and though Garrick could have used a

scotch, he knew something nonalcoholic was best. He had to be clear when the subject was so murky.

"Listen," she said abruptly. "I don't think we can figure this all out at once. But, well, maybe we can get to know each other."

"I would like that," Garrick said.

She blinked, nodded. "We can learn about each other. Whatever this is—whatever we are—might just sort of fall into place. Maybe together we can come up with something. Lord knows I've tried. I even clicked on a Web site called 'Time Travel for Beginners.' "

Garrick laughed, but then the sound ended on his tongue. "Did you learn anything?"

"I learned it was possible, at least theoretically. I learned that Einstein believed in it. I read that he believed that I should be able to travel through time and space, which I have. Not too far, but definitely to different places. From one room to another, that kind of thing. He thought that time moves at different rates for things. I felt like one of those things. But it never made that much sense to me."

Garrick knew that he wanted all the answers right now, but he had to be patient. After all, he had waited twenty-eight years. He could wait a few months longer. All he had to lose was time, and he knew he could go back to find it if he wanted to.

"I think it's a good idea," he said. "Together, we should be able to come up with something."

He looked over at Mila, noticing a red swish of blush spread on her cheek and then disappear. "Maybe, finally, we will know who—I mean what—we are."

The waitress brought them their water and took their orders. Garrick wasn't hungry at all, his stomach prickly, as if filled with tiny sea urchins. He wanted nothing more than to get up and leave. He didn't really want this problem. He didn't want to talk about the past, something he'd lived in too long already. Wouldn't it be great if he'd met Mila as he had, but without any of the connections? He'd never reacted to the painting. He'd never learned she could read minds or travel through time. Maybe in another universe, this was just a normal date, the kind that would end as all his did. In bed.

Mila looked up at him, her eyes searching, maybe for a thought. She was so clean, so clear, so trusting. He knew he had to finally go about something the right way, even if it simply led to them understanding why they could do what they did.

"Who are we?" she asked, her hands on the table, her fingers slim, unringed, the nails short with faint bits of scrubbed-away color under a couple of the nails.

"I—" he started, feeling that burning tingle again, the one that warned him not to touch her.

"What?" she asked.

"I think. I think—" Garrick felt sweaty, out of control. "I think I can answer some questions."

"How—" Mila began, but then Garrick leaned over and grabbed her right hand with his left. He pulled her up to a standing position, wondering what he was doing. Taking her out of the restaurant? But something warm and wonderful began to flow through him, and he turned, his front facing the double doors opened to the kitchen, hers facing the rest of the dining room.

He had no idea what he was doing, but he decided to open his mind fully now, letting her have and see it all. Without his asking, he felt her do the same thing, her mind like a warmth he wanted to sit by, curl around.

"Close your eyes," he said, and as he did and so did she, he heard the waitress ask if they needed to know where the restrooms were. He wanted to bolt, to pull Mila out of the restaurant so that whatever was happening wouldn't happen in front of people. But he'd not thought this through. Not at all, and he couldn't let her go, not now, not with this warm lovely pulse beating between them.

Garrick was about to nod politely to the waitress and tell her all was well even though it certainly wasn't, when another feeling overtook him, the same feeling he had when he moved back through time. There was the hush of emptiness, of stillness, the whoosh of no air, the lightness of the world stopping for a moment before whipping him into the past. All he could feel was Mila's hand holding his and the slight yank in her arm as something seemed to pull them apart.

And as he was ready to land into the past, he realized that he and Mila were in the grainy time between time, the gray spot he'd been able to reach only once or twice, stalling in a gray lurch as time's line clogged. It never lasted more than a millisecond before he was dumped into the same old life, the past a dreary repeat. But this time, the spot was different, a glimmer of colored light on her side, the same glimmer on his, the glow like doors they could both walk through.

He squeezed her hand, and she looked at him, looked at herself, the gray, the glimmer. They were both standing but on what? His feet seemed to squash into the gray, his leather shoes rising and falling, almost as if he were standing in sand as the tide rolled in and out, in and out, the ground a moving, uneven place. Mila was visible, but waves of gray moved in front of her, obscuring her dark eyes, her blond hair, her serious face.

We're here, she thought.

I've been here before, he thought back. *But it's different.*

She nodded. *We are here together.*

Garrick felt himself smile. *Yeah, we are. Together.*

Together. Garrick felt the word forming in his mouth, the thought swirling in his mind. He'd never really understood the word *together* before, never felt together with anyone. Not his parents. Not his friends. Not his lovers or so-called girlfriends. Not even, really, at work with his colleagues. His work seemed somehow just off from what the professor wanted and from what everyone else was creating. Maybe sometimes he felt connected to Linda, to Jim even with all his weirdness, but everywhere else—*always!*—he had felt like he was standing just outside the crowd, invited in but unable to attend the party. People called out to him, but it was as if nothing they said could make it better.

Mila nodded. *I know what you mean. But how could you possibly know that this would happen? How did you know I could do this with you?*

He shrugged, shook his head, squeezed her hand harder. *Something has been keeping me from you all this time. Wanting to push you away. Almost as if I knew that the moment we touched, something would happen—something that we couldn't back away from. There's no going back from here.*

Mila looked as if she wanted to weep, to just lie down on the shifting, roiling ground beneath her feet and cry.

What is it? he thought. *What are you feeling?*

Why did it take twenty-eight years for this to happen? Why did we have to wait for any kind of answer?

Garrick felt the gray float around him, the space a twirl of energy. *I think it's time. I don't know what for. But it was meant to happen now, just like this. I saw your painting, I met you. I felt the connection from the beginning. I didn't want to feel it, but it seems I have no choice.*

But I needed this years ago. I needed you way back when.

But at least it has happened, he thought. *Some people wait forever, and they don't know what they are looking for. I—I knew. I know.*

Garrick felt her warm current literally in his body, felt her hand, heard her mind, joined her in jumping out of time. Not since he'd flung himself back in time and out of trouble or sadness or upset had he felt connected to something real. Someone real.

This is really happening, she thought.

Garrick nodded, shrugged, smiled slightly, looking past her to the glimmering spot next to her.

What are those spots? she thought. *Can we go through them?*

I don't know. I've never seen them when I've been here by myself. But I think we can go through them. I think that they are doors.

No, Mila thought *We can't try them. Not now. We have to go back to the restaurant. We have to stay in the time we were in. And I have to find out—I have to ask my parents about what you said. I have to find out the truth about that. And then I'm hoping you'll help me find out more.*

Through the gray, Garrick could see her need.

She was flushed, her eyes bright, and so very beautiful as she floated next to him. And he quickly banished the wicked notion that he'd touched her and only good had happened. Look at this amazing thing they could do together. And with a quick flick, he pushed away the thought of what else he could touch, what else besides her smooth, small hand.

We can't do it all at once, he thought. *I have some ideas. I could be wrong about your parents. I just dug around in my life a little. I had the time to. All the past I needed. I just had to pay for all my sliding back by living through the time again. I couldn't bear to live through my childhood again, even though I think I could do it better now.*

Garrick sighed, the past in front of him again, those years, the kind Mila thought about, the sad ones where no one knew a thing about him.

You're right. Let's go back, he thought. *Let's eat. We can figure everything out later.*

Garrick knew he had other things to say, other things to simply contemplate, but all of that could wait. He and Mila needed to get back to the time of their dinner at the restaurant, eat together, talk, and plan. Plan for finding out the truth. Plans for so much more, Garrick couldn't even think about it now.

And he let himself slip into the rush of time, both of them flinging into the world again. Then he was standing in the restaurant, the waitress holding their plates of food, waiting for them to sit down and start the rest of their lives.

Chapter Four

When Garrick came to her loft this time, Mila felt so different from the time before when he'd called her wild and upset in the early morning. He wasn't the good-looking, unattainable jerk that had totally blown her off in front of her parents, who would rather hike up hills than sit next to her in a car.

Instead, he was the one person on the planet who knew what she could do and could do it, too. How was that possible? Mila still wasn't sure any of it had happened, and Garrick's phone calls these past two nights hadn't made this newfound discovery more real, even though they had talked for hours. She finally understood the saying "I had to pinch myself to make sure it was real." If she'd followed through with that dictum, she'd be black and blue by now. And she was excited, thrilled almost, her days since the night of their dinner at Amarata filled with anticipation. Maybe even joy.

When he rang the bell this time, Mila smiled to

herself, lit one last candle quickly, and walked to the
door. She opened it, and when she saw Garrick, her
body did something it had never done before, sort of
a physical cliché: it lurched. Her heart did what only
could be described as leapt, moving as fast and hard
as it could against her ribs. She felt herself breathing
faster, felt her pulse beating. Mila could somehow
feel the current that had bound them in the no-time
place even now, slick, hot energy between them.

"Hi," she said, feeling herself blush hot, glad for
the low lights.

Garrick smiled, ran a hand through his hair, and
Mila wondered if he was nervous.

"These are for you," he said, handing her a beauti-
fully tied bunch of calla lilies, the long red ribbon
dangling in a soft curl.

"I love these," Mila said, letting him in the loft,
smelling his cologne, something sweet but hard-
edged. "These flowers always remind me of Georgia
O'Keeffe. Thank you."

He smiled, his teeth white in the glow of the room,
and put his hands in his suit jacket pockets. His suit
jacket. He dressed up for her, wearing a suit even
nicer than the one he'd worn to her parents' house,
a luscious chocolate color, his button-down shirt butter cream.

He was like a truffle, something she could put in
her mouth . . . *God!*

She looked at him, flushing, knowing that she was
broadcasting on every possible channel. Tamping her
thoughts down, she gave him a glance. And to her great
relief, he didn't give her any indication that he'd been
listening in. So at least she'd saved herself from that
embarrassment.

Mila wondered, though, how she was going to make it into the dining room without doing something stupid. She might start blathering or trip on the bare floor or blurt out that as of two nights ago, she was suddenly, majorly attracted to him. Any adverb would do.

Of course, what if this was some kind of attraction built on the fact that he was the only one on the planet who understood her?

What's wrong with that? Doesn't that make perfect sense? she thought to herself, shaking her head, realizing that Garrick was still smiling at her, both of them still at the door.

"Sorry," she said. "I'm not myself lately."

They walked into the loft space and toward the kitchen area.

"Who are you, then?" he asked. "I was hoping I was having dinner with Mila Adams."

"I don't know if I am Mila Adams," she said, the reality of their situation overtaking her ridiculous, well, crush. "I may be someone else entirely. From some strange tribe that can do magic."

Garrick leaned against the kitchen counter while Mila looked for a vase. "I don't know about magic earth tribes," he said. "I've tried to locate one, trust me. Every time I met someone 'psychic' or 'otherworldly,' I've asked a few questions. But no one said, 'Yeah, I can travel through time or space or make fire.' And I would have believed anyone who did say that."

She nodded, arranging the flowers. "I guess this is a better place to be in than thinking I'm insane. Or totally alone. But I just don't know what we should do now."

Garrick started to say something, then stopped.

He looked at her for a second, breathed in, and then moved closer to her. He raised his arm, brought his hand to her face, letting his fingers skim her jawline gently.

At his touch, she took in a breath, certain that in a second they would be floating in the gray, out of time again, staring at each other in a haze of nontime.

"Don't worry," he said. "I think one or both of us has to want to move into time. Some kind of intention. And that's not what I want to do at all."

"You aren't reading my thoughts, are you?" she asked.

"No," he said, and that's all he said. Because then he moved even closer. She could smell him—something like tea and spice and fresh-cut wood—and then his lips were on hers. "I don't need to read anything," he whispered before he kissed her. "I can see what I need right here in front of me."

This was a kiss. A real kiss, the kind she had always thought was improbable or at least unlikely, especially for someone like her, someone who could never let herself be known to anyone.

But she was learning to be known, learning to know. Garrick was teaching her. He put his arms around her, his chest and thighs against hers, his strong hand slipping across and then holding her neck. Pressed close, they opened to each other with mouths and tongues and heat. It was a kiss that was a balancing act, so much like when they brought together the present and the past and turned it into the gray, but this time, with this kiss, it was their mouths that were conduits for joy, for desire, for recognition.

Because he could see her. And she saw him back.

Garrick brought his arms more tightly around her, holding her waist, letting his hands move along her body: the light bump of ribs, the slide of waist, the gentle flare of hips. She touched him back, her hands moving on his back as if she were reading Braille, sliding down to his belt, pressing tight.

And what were they saying to each other? Mila wasn't open to his thoughts, but she knew he was saying so much with his embrace. He tasted hot, alive, needful, his tongue against hers, asking and telling.

She answered back, wanting nothing more than for the two of them to disappear into time so that this moment could last. Finally, here was something she wanted to have again and again and again. How had she lived without this?

The excitement from this embrace was almost so overwhelming she could barely stand straight, and she felt her knees start to tremble.

Garrick put his hands on the side of her face, and then gently pulled away from her, looking down at her. She breathed deeply, trying to steady herself.

"What?" she whispered.

"I want—I need to be with you, Mila. And not just like this. Not just with our bodies."

She blinked, took another breath, smiled. "But—but this is pretty amazing, isn't it?"

Garrick smiled back. "Yes, it is. It's—you are—amazing. And I want it, but I want more. I—I want it all."

He looked down at her, his eyes she seemed to recognize, their darkness almost light, something magic inside. But she didn't say a word at first, putting her hands gently on his chest, nodding.

"Me, too. And even more than all. I want the truth, too. I want the story about us. About you and me. I need it."

He nodded, and she took in the heat of him, the smell of outdoors, the smell of desire.

"I'm not sure we can ever find the story we are looking for," he said, his hands stroking her shoulders, running down her arms. She felt her skin prickle, everything alive to his touch. "But I want to try."

Mila didn't wait this time. Instead, she pulled back a little and found his hand with hers, turning and walking them toward the back of the large space.

"I know it's so art student of me, but my mattress is on the floor. No box spring. No frame. And I can't quite vouch for the comforter's origins."

Garrick laughed. "I don't care where your bed is or what it looks like, frankly. I'm okay with the floor at this point."

Mila turned to him, and he brought her near again, his hands holding her neck, his thumbs under her jaw. He bent to kiss the spot above her collarbone, and she wanted nothing more than to feel his lips right there.

"I want—I want your hands," she whispered.

My hands want you, he thought, letting his mind into hers.

Without moving his mouth from her skin, he brought his hands to the front of her blouse. Then he pulled back, watching her as he slowly undid the tiny shell buttons one at a time, from the bottom up.

"God, you are something. So firm and then so soft," he said, letting his fingers travel along the fabric lines of her bra, down to her belly. "Beautiful."

"Oh," she said, finding a small word, unable to fully look him in the eye. Her heart thrummed against the stairs of her ribs.

"Yes," he said back, pulling the sleeves off her shoulders and arms. "You are smooth everywhere."

As her clothes started to come off, she found the courage to look up. "I can't stand the idea of being undressed alone. It's not fair."

Garrick slowly took his hands away from where they encircled her bare wrists. "I am a huge proponent of shared nudity," he said. "And I want everything between us to be equal. And we are perfect equals, perfect matches, here and in time."

Stepping closer to him, the lace of her bra lightly grazing the fabric of his shirt, Mila began to undo his buttons, her hands steady.

"Let me help," he said, and he brought his hands up to finish the last few buttons, shrugging off his shirt and bringing her to him.

"Wonderful," she said, letting her hands move softly up his back, finding the flare of lats, the curve of obliques. "You feel wonderful."

"I do feel wonderful," he said. "I've never felt this good in my life."

She laughed, the sound vibrating into his chest. "Then I feel great, too."

"You do. You feel amazing," he said, and with that, he undid her pants button with one quick move, pushing them down with his hands. She laughed again, and helped him.

"I have hips," she said. "Things don't slide off so easily."

Garrick closed his eyes. "Don't talk about your

hips anymore. I might not be able to wait until all your clothes are off."

Mila thought he was kidding, but his face was alert with desire, a look she'd never seen before in a man. He wanted her, needing her body. And she was glad that in a moment she was standing in front of him in her bra and panties.

"Beautiful," he said, unbuckling his belt and unzipping his pants. "You are a beauty."

"You have to say that," she said. "I'm standing in front of you almost naked. It's basically pro forma!"

He kicked off his jeans and then took her face in his hands again. "I would never say anything I didn't mean. I would never say anything because it was expected. Not to you. Ever."

She looked up at him, taking everything in: his words, his body beating out a pulse to hers, their shared magic. This was time she wanted. This now was time she would never want to push through to get it over with. In fact, she wished that she could do what he did, letting events happen again. This was one she could live through a hundred times.

"I believe you," she said. "I believe it all. I don't need to get into your thoughts to see that."

Garrick kissed her and then picked her up in his arms, ignoring her laughing protests.

"I'm too heavy," she said, putting her face against his neck. But he felt strong enough to carry her for miles.

"No, you aren't. Not for me. Not for anyone," he said, not stopping his journey to the bed for a second.

And before she could wriggle free, he placed her

on the bed, laying his body against hers. Mila looked up at him, knowing that this—both of them together as they were now— was a miracle. Two weeks ago when her mother had planned the fix-up dinner, Mila would never have imagined this scene. Garrick had been so rude from the first second he'd walked into her parents' house, so horrible in the car on the way home, that she'd ignored her attraction to him in order to protect herself. He was too good looking, she thought then, and that made him dangerous.

But now here they were, in her loft, on her bed, kissing, connecting, finding meaning out of their separate pain.

Not separate, he thought. *Not ever again.*

He leaned over her, kissing her again, their conversation of lips continuing, their bodies now truly able to join in. Mila wondered if she were in a dream. With each move that brought her closer to him, to lovemaking, she wondered if she would wake up. But no. She stayed awake; time didn't throw her forward to the art studio or lunch with her mother or a drive along Van Ness with Mr. Henry.

No. It was Garrick and more Garrick. His clean hot smell, his body hard and smooth, and excitement were all over her. As they moved together, she could feel his erection against her belly, and like never before, she wanted this passion, wanted him.

He slid off her panties and let his fingers slowly move them down her thighs. Mila slithered out of them once they reached her ankles and then opened herself to him again, her legs locking him on top of her.

"You're mine," she said, laughing a little from nerves, but she really didn't feel like making that sound at all. She wanted to cry out, to moan with readiness, but her arms and legs weren't laughing.

I'm ready, too. His thought was full of a low, lovely laugh. *Maybe too ready.*

He kissed her just under her right ear, and then on the same spot on the left. She let her hands move through his short, soft hair. As they moved together on the bed, their skin pressed warm together, she let herself take in his thoughts, see how he felt about what was happening. She let loose her sensations, focused on the pulse of blood throughout her whole body, the need in her chest and mind for him, her want of him, his hardness, his urgency.

Me, he thought back. *Too.*

And then there were no more shared thoughts. Only their bodies. He pressed close, and she arched just enough to let him into her, and he slid slowly and gently into her.

Oh, perfect, she thought, feeling him fill her up completely.

Mila moaned against his ear, holding his back as she slowly started to move with him. She pushed up at him, wanting to move, to feel more and more. Garrick matched her for a moment and then slowed his movements.

I want this to last, he thought. *I want this to go on all night.*

We can always do it again, she reminded him, both hands on his back. *You and I have time both ways. And we have now.*

At her thought, at her encouragement, Garrick began to move more quickly, a rhythm of kissing and moving, of muscles and wetness and moans.

"Garrick," she cried out as she came, her body contracting around him. Her entire body was wild with nerves and feeling. She held on to him, feeling his body flex and harden as he pushed into her slickness.

His thought was a groan of pleasure as she came, her body contracting around him. Everything inside her relaxed, released, enjoyed.

She put her hands on his back, sliding them down to his ass, pressing him into her, wanting his enjoyment as much as she'd wanted her own.

He moaned against her ear, and he came inside her, filling her, holding her tight as he did, his thoughts, about his body, in the body, rested and complete and happy.

They lay tangled in each other and the blankets, Mila's head on his chest. She ran a hand along the smooth hair of his chest and belly, wanting to feel more but feeling a little shy, even though they'd made love twice now.

"You better keep your hand still," Garrick said. "Or you are going to have more of me to deal with."

"I think I can handle you," she said, leaning up on an elbow and looking down on his smiling face. "I'm getting some good practice."

"Well, you know what they say. Practice makes perfect. We will just have to keep this line of instruction open," he said.

She lay back down, holding him, blinking into the dark room. "You were such an ass at my parents' house! I can't believe you are the same man."

Garrick kissed her shoulder, ran his fingers up her

arm. As he did, Mila's entire body tingled from her toes to her hair. "I wasn't that bad."

She shook her head but not enough to move him away from any part of her he was touching. She loved his touch, and she didn't want to end it, even if she needed to make a point.

"Hello! You were horrible. You barely looked at me, and you wouldn't even shake my hand!"

He shrugged, her head moving as his did. "I'm sorry. I was—after I saw your painting, I felt that I had to protect myself from what you seemed to already know about me."

"Why did you come to the house at all, then?" She listened to his heart beating as she spoke. "Why didn't you just forget about it and me?"

"I kept telling myself it was for Linda. She's really the only family I have here. I couldn't disappoint her one more time. But . . ."

"But what?" She let her hands wander his ribs, his flat belly, the band of muscles by his hip.

"That wasn't it. It was you. I had to see you. I had to find out how you could have painted what I've had in my mind my whole life. And even now"—he squeezed her shoulders and kissed the top of her head—"I still don't really understand."

"About the dream?"

"About the dream. I don't have a dream as much as an image. Of time moving. Or movement. Going somewhere with a bunch of children."

Mila breathed in, feeling the movement, the metal, the sounds of children laughing. That was her dream. How could he have it, too? Was he one of the people in the dream story? And how could they have shared that?

"How can we share being able to push time around?" he asked. "There is so much we don't know about what we can do and who we are."

She nodded and then she yawned. "What about maybe just forgetting about it now? I think—I think knowing you are here makes me feel I can stop thinking about it. You answer so many questions."

Garrick laughed, rolled on his side, his hand on her face. "If I am the answer to some of those questions, we are both in trouble."

He kissed her, and she pressed close to him. "You are in so much trouble right now," she whispered in the middle of their kiss, her words between their lips.

That's what I'm hoping. This is the kind of trouble I like, he thought, and he moved on top of her, his skin the best answer of all.

Mila knew she was asleep, but it was the kind of sleep she had never fallen into before. Of course she knew she was drifting in unconsciousness, but the entire time, she felt as though she were in conversation with Garrick, who held her with both arms, his muscles keeping her exactly and totally against his skin. In her waking/sleeping state, she heard him whisper to her, tell her that he loved her.

"I love you, too," she said, not caring that she let such precious words loose into the air, not scared as she would be in the real world where there was always the possibility of rejection and betrayal and despair. Always, *always*, she had been certain that her boyfriends would discover her secret, find out that she was wrong. Or she would hear their thoughts, find out what they really felt about her.

She's too intense. Too fucking artistic.

I should have gone out with her friend instead.

I really don't like her hair.

That skirt is butt ugly. And what about those shoes?

Adair is a bitch—a total buzz kill. I might take the daughter if the mother would disappear.

What a princess. I'll break up with her after the holidays. Or before. I don't know how long I can last.

But in this dream, in Garrick's arms, with his voice somehow all around her, she let go of the old voices of men she didn't want to be with anyway, her old fears that arose from not having the man she was supposed to be with. In her sleep, she found herself moving into Garrick, touching him, feeling him, breathing in his breath. Were they making love again? She wasn't sure, the dream was so deep and long and slow. But she didn't really care. She felt his lips, his strong mouth touching, kissing, licking, pressing her skin, all of her. She felt her body respond, open wide, take him in. She heard what they said to each other.

You are beautiful.

You are beautiful.

I love you.

I love you.

I need you.

I need you, too.

They seemed to almost dance together, their legs and arms and bodies part of a routine they were just learning but didn't want to stop practicing. At certain points, she was sure she'd slipped into his skin, hearing not only his thoughts but his blood and heart. They were alive together, both wanting exactly the same thing.

The night shifted, cracked into early morning.

Mila sometimes tried to open her eyes, managing only to see the city's gray light flow into her loft before she had to close them again. The dream went on, her fatigue pulling her into a deeper, darker sleep, where she was unable to feel even Garrick's strong arms. His movements were replaced with the familiar rumble of the dark place, the children's voices, the hum of adult voices above her.

In her old, familiar dream, she turned as she always did to the boy who sat next to her, the blond boy with the dark brown eyes. The boy who talked to her so seriously. Mila knew this was her old dream, and she was about to let it slide away so she could search out the more pleasurable one when she realized that unlike all the other times she had the dream, she could see. The floor she sat on was metal, shiny, black. The little girl who had always been almost impossible to see at all was sitting next to her, her blond hair short, perfect for her pixie face. Her knees were scraped, and she kept saying, "Florsey," a word Mila didn't understand. And that's when she realized Mila didn't understand a word anyone was saying, the language a ragout of disparate sound all around her.

But this was her dream, and she knew that she next turned to the boy, and she did, seeing him clearly, sharply, as though she'd finally been able to adjust the focus of a broken camera.

When she saw him, Mila felt her body react, even as the dream played on in her head. He was so serious, his eyes so intense for a boy of, what? Four or five? He looked at her with his intense eyes—so dark and deep and thoughtful—and spoke to her quickly, his mouth familiar and known. He spoke in the same strange language that filled and echoed in the dark place, and Mila felt herself nod as she always did in the dream, and it was then that she began to understand what he was saying.

"Home," she caught from the sentence. "Go back . . . parents . . . escape . . . wait . . . twin. Magic. Always together. Find."

And as always in the dream, it was her turn to speak, and she said the words in the language she didn't know she knew.

"When will we go home?"

"Soon," the boy said, pushing his hair out of his eyes, his fine, blond hair just like hers. "Mata said soon. She told me to tell you all to wait and they will come to get us. Mata and Pata will come right away."

"But I don't want to be without them," Mila was saying. "I don't want to wait. I want them now."

The boy leaned over and pulled her close to him. "Don't cry, Mila. Don't cry. I will be with you always. You will always see me at night. And then I will find you. I promise. And things will be better. Things won't be scary anymore. I will find you. And you will have your twin. You will have the one who will make you whole. He's not far away from you ever. And neither will I be."

The dream Mila looked up at the boy, turned to the little girl, and in her sleep, Mila knew that she couldn't let Garrick be the answer. But together, she understood that they could find the boy and the girl, these children so important to her she'd dreamed about them her entire life. She and Garrick did have the power to find them and the world they came from. Somehow, even if this dream was about—well, travel to another . . . place, wherever it might be. In her waking sleep, she held her lover tight in her arms and saw the work that they had to do.

But she was tired from the dream, from so much love, and from thinking, and she let herself fall back into unconsciousness, knowing that in the morning, she would have some explaining to do.

"So, can you run this by me again?" Garrick asked. They had finally made it out of the bedroom, Garrick's lower half wrapped in a sheet, Mila standing by the coffeemaker, wearing a nightgown, and trying to remember how to make coffee. Her body seemed disconnected from her brain this morning. She turned to look back at Garrick, smiled, and then flushed. He was so handsome and he was sitting at her table, waiting for her to get her act together and make coffee because neither of them had slept too much or too long.

"Okay, in my dream there are two children sitting next to me."

"The dream about the dark place. The painting. *The Ride.*"

"You said it was something you knew," she said. "Understood."

Garrick nodded, sitting back in his chair, the muscles in his stomach flexing as he brought his arms up and folded them behind his head. "I did. I do. It feels like somewhere I went to long ago."

"Where could it be?" she asked, wanting him to look long and hard. To see what she saw in his thoughts.

"I don't know. Maybe it was in a dream I had, too.

Maybe we share more than just the ability to move time and read people's thoughts. But dreams are dreams."

"It's not just a dream. It's real. I know that now. It's the dark place," Mila said. "From my dream."

"The dream that you've had your entire life."

"Right," Mila said, finally finding the ON switch, sighing as she turned to face him. The coffeemaker gurgled into life, and she sat down at the table.

"So I had the dream again last night. Only this time, I could understand everything that the boy said to me. Being with you, or finally accepting who I am, made the dream different. More real."

"Do you know who the boy is to you?" Garrick watched her, his eyes never leaving her face.

She shrugged a little, picked up a spoon that was on the table, and examined it for a moment as if the metal shine held the answers. Then she sighed, put it down. "I think he must be my brother. And the little girl is my sister. Or they are close friends, but we must be connected in a bigger way if I've been dreaming about them for all these years."

"So you think we can find them? You think they are in the Bay Area?" Garrick leaned his elbows on the table, the morning light glinting gold against his hair, his eyes lightened to the color of caramel.

"Maybe," Mila said, biting her lip. "But maybe they aren't here. Or aren't—aren't on this planet."

Garrick crossed his arms, moved closer to the canvas. "What is the dark place? Is it an airplane? A train?"

Mila shrugged and tried to stop the words coming out of her mouth because they were crazy. She wished she could be normal, for just a second. But if she wanted the truth, she had to let it loose into the air. "I think . . . I think it's a spaceship. Or something like that. Something that moves through space. And these abilities that we have are probably normal where we come from."

Garrick laughed, an amazingly light sound. "A spaceship. Where we come from! So, are you trying to tell me that the boy and the girl are little aliens? And we are, too? That you and I aren't just humans with bizarre abilities? That we are aliens with bizarre abilities?"

Mila flushed. "You were the one who said we were adopted. We came from—we came from somewhere and we were left here. In San Francisco. And maybe the others were, too. But it was us. Four of us. The two of them, you, and me. That's all we know for now."

She sat back and crossed her arms, suddenly embarrassed about her theory, even though she was talking to a man who could go backward in time.

"Don't be embarrassed," Garrick said, stroking her right arm with his hand. As he did, her skin prickled with desire. "I'm just not as far along as you are. I haven't been having this dream. I'm not sure that we all were left here, but it makes some sense."

At the word *sense*, Mila started to smile. Only Garrick would say that to her now. *Sense.*

"But when you first talked about the dream, you said something about a twin. You said it twice. What does that mean?"

When he asked her the question, she realized that she could show him everything with her mind. Her words and explanation were not doing what she wanted them to do. But the pictures she had in her mind would tell a thousand tales.

"Let me show you my dream," she said, standing up from the table. "Let me give you what I know and then we'll be able to figure this out together."

He pushed the chair back and stood up, taking Mila in his arms and kissing her. She closed her eyes and then started to laugh. "We will never get to the dream if you keep doing that," she said. "Keep doing it—no, no, let me show you first."

She took his hand and touched his cheek, talking as she did. "I've had this dream my entire life, since I can remember. And not until tonight was I able to understand what was going on. It's as if being next to you gave me the final bit of energy I needed to see and hear in the dream. What I think is that everyone in that spaceship is running away from something bad. Something evil. The children were somehow saved, and we were going to be—to be dropped off. Our parents were supposed to come and get us, and they didn't. Who knows why? Maybe the bad people or bad thing did something to them. But all I know is that we are the ones who are left."

Garrick stared at her, looking at her with the eyes that had been watching her for her entire life. So intense, like always. Finally, he took in a deep breath, letting it out slowly. "Take me to this place. Take me on *The Ride*."

Mila had never let anyone so far into her mind, to places she'd only expressed in her artwork.

It will be okay, he thought.

Here, she thought, and she opened up her dream like a novel, a stream of information turning into a picture they were both pulled into. First, she let him feel and hear the dark place, the spaceship, the machine that carried them somewhere.

Yes, he thought. *This is it. I remember.*

She went slowly as she opened up the memory, letting him taste the air, the warmth of all the bodies crammed into too tight a space. Mila let him hear the rolling murmur of voices, the reassurances given from child to child, adult to child. She let him hear the language that she hadn't been able to understand until tonight, the words of hope and faith and love.

What is this dark thing they are—we are—running away from? Garrick asked, and she opened up the fear that shadowed everyone in the dark space. She showed him the images that the girl in her dream had, the thoughts of something hard, full of hurt and pain. In the dream, there was a memory of dark smoke, a smoky shade pulling down over intense light. Then escape. The bad things. The bad ones.

Who are the bad ones? he asked. *Are they after everyone here?*

I don't know who they are. But I think they want—they want to kill everyone. All of them. Us, Mila thought. *They've killed so many already.*

Where are the two children? Garrick asked. *Where are the ones you think are your siblings?*

She swung the image around to the wall of the dark place, focusing on the three blond children seated at the end. Slowly, as though she were a camera, she brought the children into close-up view. There were the two little girls and there was the boy, looking up for a second at someone passing in front of him. As the boy stared at the adult walking by, Mila stopped the dream image like a freeze frame.

* * *

For a moment, she felt Garrick circle the boy's image, his mind working into the crannies of the shot. He allowed his imagination and intellect and curiosity to flow around the boy and toward the two girls, his interest on the older one, Mila. And then he backed away, and it was as if he were circling a statue at a museum, gathering all the information he needed to understand the art.

I'm doing a better job here than I did at S.F. MOMA, he thought.

Mila felt herself smile, but pulled the picture closer, letting him see all that she knew about the dream.

Garrick moved closer with her, listened to their talk, and she realized that he, too, understood the language somehow. The little boy was talking about Mila's twin, reassuring her that everything would be all right.

Can't we find him in here? Garrick wondered.

I've never seen that person. Not once in the dream. I don't know if the twin is a boy.

Think, Mila, Garrick thought. *You've got to open yourself up to more than what you already know about this dream. You've had it so many times, there are likely things you've never seen before.*

What did he mean? She knew everything about her own dream. For God's sake, she'd been having it for years. For her entire life! After all those nights of being in the dark place, Garrick wanted her to see something she hadn't?

The more I know, the more help I'll be, and the sooner we can start figuring out who we are, Garrick thought.

You're right. I'll try, she thought, and she opened up the picture, allowed all the images and sensations

and feelings and hopes and reactions to whirl in her
mind. They whirled into the corners of the dream
she had not examined for years, riding on the
thought that always came to her in this dream: *there
was someone she was attached to that was not the boy or the
girl. Someone else.*

Where? Garrick thought.

I don't know.

Think, Mila. Bring us there.

Again, she allowed herself to relax into everything
in the dream, but for a few moments, nothing shifted
or opened. It was just her dream, a well-worn path in
her subconscious. Then something shimmered in
the corner, a flicker of movement. An arm, a body, a
whirl of thought.

Is that him? Garrick asked.

I don't know.

Go closer. Let us see him.

Mila relaxed even further, and the flicker of movement became a full body, a giggle, a laugh. There
were words that were too quiet for her to understand, even now that she understood the language.
This was a part of her dream that she'd ignored for
so long, probably from the first time she'd had it.
What had always interested her most had been the
children, the boy, his intent to protect her, her feelings of safety and warmth in the clutch of family.
Mila knew this was family. This place, these people.
All of it, home.

As they both looked toward the new movement,
Mila saw something else in the corner of her vision,
and she turned away from the child that so enthralled Garrick.

What is that? she wondered, her mind floating toward something dark, a twist of wind or smoke or vapor. The substance moved and writhed above the scene, an almost invisible apparition. But then it began to take form, turn into a shadow, a figure, a body.

Who is that? she thought, knowing somehow that the darkness was a being, a person, sentient and slightly evil. And then she shivered, pulling away, wanting to leave, until Garrick's excited thoughts caught her up and held her still.

That's a boy, Garrick thought, his relief clear. *Take us closer. Let me see!*

Mila turned to look back toward the swirling darkness, but it had disappeared, vanished like smoke. Shaking her head, she breathed in, started to move closer to the new boy, but as they always did, every single time she had the dream, the images began to fade, the colors of the dark space dulling to a grainy gray. She could do nothing as the dream drifted into confusing parts, the sounds, the warmth, the smells becoming nothing more than air.

No, Mila. Stay, Garrick thought. *Keep us here.*

I'm trying, she thought, concentrating on the boy's image.

Do you think it's me? Is it me? Can't you stay here?

But it was too late. The dream ended, the boy shimmering into a wash of static, and then all was darkness.

"I want to go back," Garrick said, looking up at Mila over his cooling cup of coffee.

He sat with his elbows on the table, his eyes alight with this new knowledge, this thought from when they first began. She couldn't take her eyes off him, wanting to hold the image of his thoughtful face, his intense eyes forever. Staring at him, she still couldn't believe he was the same rude man she had first met. Oh, he'd been beautiful then, too, but now she understood him. And now, after she'd shared her dream with him, her ideas, he was even more beautiful than he had been last night in her bed, her arms. "I didn't get enough of a look. I didn't get a chance to understand—to get closer to the other boy."

"I'm sorry. That's how it ends. The dream always ends," Mila said. "Always. I can't give you any more than that. We could go back, but it would end the same way. I can't let us stay there any more than my mind allows."

He shook his head, his eyes suddenly filled with sorrow. "I don't understand. I didn't get a dream. All I have is an image, something that your painting had to shake out of me. All of these years, and now I'm able to see? I feel like it's my only clue. Of seeing who I am. Of knowing where I came from. You're lucky."

She laughed. "Lucky? All my life I've been different. All my life I've had to hide my secrets." Mila stood up and walked to the counter to pour herself another cup of coffee. "I know for a fact that I'm that little girl, the one on the right of the boy. And I know that boy is my brother. I know that the other little girl is my sister. She keeps saying, 'Florsey. Florsey,' and I know she's talking about an animal. An animal we played with. And mostly, Garrick, I know it's not a dream. It's a memory. Something that happened to me. That happened to us. You recognized the spaceship when you saw my painting."

Garrick was leaning back in his chair, his eyes never leaving her face. "We have to find out more."

"How can we find out?" Mila asked. She'd been trying to not find out all this time. She'd been trying so hard to fit in, feel normal, feel in the flow of everyone else that she'd forgotten what it was like to need to know. To have to find out where she came from and who she was. "What should we do next?"

Now Garrick stood up, walked to her, took her in his arms, her face against his chest. She heard his words from deep inside his body, the rumble of sound pressed against her cheek.

"We are going to find out, Mila. I promise. I don't know how, right now, but I am going to find out. I guess that means right off the bat accepting that we were in a spaceship. We are aliens. Fine. Done."

Mila felt herself want to laugh, but it wasn't funny because it was true. She nodded against his body.

"So you looked like you were about two, maybe three," Garrick went on. "We can look into records, find your birth certificate. We can see what your parents were up to. What mine were. We can find out who gave us to our families. Why our families have lied to us. And if I have to, I'll go back in time all those years and live it again just so I can remember!"

"No, Garrick," she said. "No! You can't use time. No. We have to solve this in the present. I can't bear for you to be . . ."

"Say it, Mila," he whispered.

"To be where I am not. When I am not," she said, knowing that she meant it. If he went back in time, he'd have to live all those years and months and days without her. Maybe he could go search her out, but she wasn't ready to meet him until just now, after having let go of the life prescribed to her by her upbringing, her parents. She'd left her job, her neighborhood, her beliefs, and she hadn't finished *The Ride* until just a couple of months before. Right now was exactly the right time to meet.

"You know there is one more thing I have to do," she said.

"What?"

"I need to find my brother and my sister, too." Mila paused. "And, Garrick, if I have siblings, you might as well. You might have people now, right now, who belong to you."

His arms flexed, relaxed, flexed. For a terrible second, she reached into his mind and felt the horrible pit of loneliness he'd felt his entire childhood.

"Maybe. Maybe I do."

Garrick held her tight again, and Mila closed her eyes, and after a moment of feeling his strength, his muscles, his body, she imagined the soft, smooth rhythm of the dark space taking her away from what was dangerous, saving her as it had over and over again, her entire life.

"I just told you so. I knew that you two would hit it off. Aren't you glad you listened to me? Do you finally see how I have your best interests at heart? And you didn't want to come to dinner," Adair said into the phone, her voice a lyric of self-satisfaction. In her desperate imagination, she probably had Mila and Garrick already married, living in a five-bedroom house in Mill Valley with their three children, and taking the financial world by storm, art cast by the wayside. Little did poor Adair know that they were trying to find a way to get back home, home being somewhere not on the planet. Even though she felt very serious about discovering who she and Garrick were, she almost giggled, imagining Adair's face upon hearing, "Yeah, I'm leaving on a spaceship. Don't know when I'll be back again."

It was all so crazy. Mila shook her head and listened to her mother as she sat at her desk in her loft, looking down at the list of questions she and Garrick had come up with for each of them to ask their parents. Garrick had left a couple of hours ago, Mila spending the time since wandering through her loft looking at everything she owned as if she'd never seen it before. Who was the person who had painted these paintings? Bought this rug? Shopped for this couch?

Was it she? She wasn't that person anymore. She felt totally different, entirely brand-new.

As Adair raved on and on about Garrick's charm and looks and business acumen, Mila ran her hands on the written sentences. Mila and Garrick agreed that they couldn't dump the seemingly random questions on their parents all at once, but slowly, over some time, gleaning clues as they could. The hope was that someone would slip, hedge, release some information to the wind. And if none of them did, then that was information, too. That would mean that someone else—something else—was keeping all four parents from telling the truth. That would prove that there was some kind of bad magic out there holding tight Garrick's and Mila's secret.

But which question to ask first? They seemed so ordinary and known.

What hospital was it I was born at?

What time of day was I born? (This question, Mila thought, could be explained through the desire to have an astrological reading done, a crazy idea that Adair would expect from Mila at this point.)

When did I crawl? Walk? Run? Talk? Sing?

What was my first word? Second word?

What was my favorite story?

Mila closed her eyes and rubbed her forehead with the back of her hand. She had to start somewhere, so she coughed a little into the receiver, and Adair slowed her words for a millisecond.

"Mom. It was great. I really am glad I met Garrick." She paused, feeling a sudden, true thankfulness to her mother.

"Oh, Mila," Adair said. "I am so glad. I knew it had to happen, and he can only, well, you know. Get you back on track."

"Hmmm," Mila said, wishing she could say something pointed and clear to her mother about how she didn't need to get on track one tiny bit, small angry feelings stirring in her throat like birds. But she couldn't. Not right now. Maybe not for a long time. She needed to get her mother to tell her something, anything. "Listen, Mom. I had a question. I'm, um, well, I'm looking to have—to have my astrological chart done."

"You are doing what? A chart? Oh, Mila. How ridiculous."

"Wait. I mean, it's about making sure Garrick and I are aligned. You know. You want to check all sources. We are . . . I think, you know, so perfectly matched that I just want to have it validated. Anyway, it's nicely done. Sort of a fun present for him. And you know those people are quacks, so they'll make it a good one. A good omen." Mila rattled on, the lie getting too long every second.

"Oh, in that case. All right. Sort of as a joke present. Very cute. Well, have fun. But—"

"Mom, wait. I need to know the exact time of my birth. You know. Hour, minute, second. Place, time, all of that. I know I've heard all the stories, but I need some specifics. You know, info from that birth certificate you can't seem to find. You know I need to renew my passport. It's getting ridiculous."

For a moment, it was hard for Mila to recognize what was different. She was still sitting in her chair, the sun was shining on the table, the honks and roars and bursts of engine noise were still coming in the window from the street traffic below. The Spanish twirled up from the *panaderia* from the first floor along with the smells of yeast and sugar. Nothing was seemingly out of the ordinary. Then Mila realized what it was. Adair had stopped talking, the sound coming in Mila's ear nothing but phone static.

"Mom?" Mila asked. "Did you hear my question?"

There was a pause, and then Adair spoke, her voice almost rote, the pattern strange, unnatural for the forceful, talkative woman. "I'll have to look that up, dear."

"Mom, I know the date, of course. But time? You know, what time did you give birth. Morning, noon, or night? I think the story goes it was in the morning."

"Oh, I don't really remember right now," Adair went on in that eerie, staccato voice. "I have to go. Nidia needs me in the kitchen."

"But, Mom. This should be easy. You remember

what grades I got on my fifth grade history paper on Sutter's Mill and the gold rush. So what about the hour when I was bor—"

But then the phone clicked, the air popping into silence. Adair had hung up on her.

Mila sat back in her chair and stared at the phone in her hand. Her mother had never done *that* before. In fact, Mila had been the one to hang up in a fit of rebellious college pique, wanting her mother to understand why she needed to backpack through the Pyrenees with her Swiss college friend Josette for the entire summer between her junior and senior year or why she had to take the spring semester class on the African Diaspora instead of statistics. But Adair? Adair was a harper and talker and hang-in-there kind of phone conversationalist, a nag-till-you-drop kind of mom.

Sighing, Mila stood and pushed in her chair. She had no choice. She had to go to the house and confront her mother. She had to find out the answer to one of these questions. There was no other alternative but look her mother in the eye and ask.

By the time Mila had showered, dressed, and driven through the Mission District and onto Geary up to Pacific Heights, Adair had made her escape, clearly unwilling to talk any further about birth certificates and time. There was no sign of Mr. Henry and even Nidia was gone, the house echoing with Mila's loud "Mom? Dad?" when she answered the door.

"Damn it," Mila said, dropping her purse on the foyer table and sighing. She clacked her way on the

tile and then hardwood floors, pushing her way into
the kitchen. But no one was home, and it didn't look
like anyone would be for a while—nothing left out
on the granite counters for later preparation. Nothing defrosting, nothing rising, no pasta left to dry on
the drying rack.

Mila walked to the fridge to see what she could
scrounge up before going home to her basically
empty larder. She hadn't eaten much since Garrick
left, and the night and morning of lovemaking had
left a ravenous hole in her stomach. She opened the
large brushed stainless steel door and stared in at the
neat rows of Tupperwared food, everything easily
identifiable: grilled chicken, sliced steak, broccoli
florets, green beans. And then there was a decadent,
mostly untouched strawberry cheesecake. As she was
about to pull the cake from the shelf, she suddenly
imagined Adair's desk drawer, the desk in her parents' bedroom. The middle drawer, the one Adair
seemed to keep something important in, telling Mila
once when she was looking for drawing supplies,
"Don't rummage in here. If you need paper or pens
or whatever, look in your father's office." And now
that Mila thought about it, that comment was accom-
panied by the only physical punishment she'd ever
received from Adair: A quick grab of arm and a swift
walk out of the bedroom, the door banging closed
behind her.

She slid the cake back on the shelf, closed the
fridge, and pushed out of the kitchen, almost running for the stairs. It was unclear how long she had
until everyone came home. Her father was at work,
and Adair could have Nidia along for a shopping ex-

pedition, Mr. Henry at the wheel. They could be gone for three hours or forty-five minutes, so she needed to find some kind of clue quickly.

"Mom?" Mila asked as she opened the bedroom door, pushing on it so the only sound was the light *whoosh, whoosh* of the door against the carpet. "Are you there?"

She looked into the room, finding everything immaculate except for one scarf in a silk pile on the neatly made bed. Mila walked all the way in and sat down on the floor in front of the desk and pulled open the middle drawer. For a minute, Mila stared at the contents of the drawer, not knowing where to start or if to bother because the drawer seemed full of only bank statements and bills in tidy manila piles. Adair had everything labeled clearly: ACCOUNTS 2004, STOCKS 2004, and FUNDS 2005. Even in this day and age of computer files and spreadsheets and programs that kept track of everything, the entire contents of the drawer seemed like an accountant's dream, years of spending and saving in organized, chronological heaps.

What could Mila possibly find here that would help? Why would Adair have cared that much about the younger Mila opening the drawer at all? And how could anything in a drawer help Mila understand what the dark space was and why she and Garrick could move through time?

Mila laughed, knowing that she was crazy. Doomed, just like she had tried to tell Adair two weeks ago. Doomed to be forever confused. D-O-O-M-E-D.

Shaking her head, Mila put her hands on the envelopes, pulling them up and looking underneath.

Nothing but envelopes. She opened one, and just as she thought, the papers were neatly inserted: bank statements by the month.

She slid her hand under the bottom envelope, hoping to find a smaller envelope, something stashed just so. But there was nothing odd or irregular, just her mother's careful order.

Mila closed the drawer and then opened the one above it, surprised, really, to see rows of folded scarves. Her mother had a huge wardrobe in the walk-in closet, the small, special room that had been Mila's favorite play space as a child. In fact, Adair had kept castoffs in the bottom drawer for Mila to play dress up with— year-old party dresses, hats with feathers and jewels, glittery belts.

She looked back on the bed at the swirl of silk, and then she carefully slipped a hand into the rows, feeling for something harder, something odd. And she found it as the prick of an envelope corner hit her hand as she searched. Carefully, she pulled it out from the froth of the scarves and held up the business-size envelope. Her pulse whirred in her throat and her skin felt clammy. Something important was in here. Something that would change her life.

What is it? Garrick asked. *Are you all right?*

Mila jerked upright, frozen, and then she breathed out. *I didn't know you were there.*

I wasn't until just now. I had this feeling that something was wrong. What are you—what did you find? Are you okay?

She put the envelope flat in her palm as if to weigh it. *I don't know. Probably nothing. But I called my mother and then she just seems to have run out of the house to avoid me.*

Mila looked around the room again, making sure she had not been discovered.

Open the envelope, Garrick thought. *And then get out of there. I don't feel right about this.*

Mila examined the envelope, turning it in her hands. This wasn't going to be easy. She needed steam to melt the gummy glue, the old-fashioned spy trick she'd seen on TV. Or she needed some other kind of power like X-ray vision.

Mila!

Okay, she thought, standing up and walking to her mother's bathroom. On the way, she listened for sounds from downstairs, but she was still alone in the house.

In her mother's bathroom, she turned on the hot water and let it run until steam flumed up in front of her face. Carefully, she brought the envelope over the steam, moving it back and forth, hoping to effect the glue and not the paper. With a fingernail, she slowly edged open the flap, pulling away from the steam as the glue loosened, ready to disgorge the secrets.

What is it? What's in there?

But as the folded piece of paper slid out of the envelope and into her hands, Mila couldn't speak, breath seeming to leave her body. Slowly, she walked back into the bedroom, staring at the envelope as she did. She couldn't wait. She had to know, so she let the envelope fall to the carpet and opened the paper, reading as she did.

Mila! What is it?

What indeed. Finally, here was her birth certificate. When she was a child, her parents had taken care of the process, sending all the information and her pretty wretched passport photos to the right authorities. But when Mila wanted to renew it just the year before, Adair couldn't seem to find it, blaming a lost safety deposit box key or a mix-up in her filing system.

"Really, darling," Adair had said. "Don't you think you should take care of your problems in this country before rushing off to another one? You aren't going to find the perfect job or perfect man there if you can't find either in San Francisco. And anyway, didn't you spend enough of your time as a child in Europe? Take care of business here first."

But now, right in front of Mila were her dates, the ones she'd always known. These were the facts from the wild birth story she'd been told her entire life. The understory of the certificate was still intact. Here was the proof, right? The morning dash to the hospital, the happy mother and father, the pink and so, so wonderful baby. No, nothing was different: May 1, 1980, 8:32 AM. Dr. Ron Golden. St. Mary's Hospital. Parents . . . parents . . .

She felt her breath hitch somewhere in her throat. Where were her parents' names? Why weren't they listed on the lines they should have been? Garrick had been right, after all.

Mila, I'm getting in the car. I'll be there in fifteen minutes.

She felt Garrick's movement, his thoughts about rushing to her, his agitation, his concern. Still, Mila couldn't breathe, and this time it wasn't because anticipation of the secrets she would uncover but because of the names in the spaces. The names that should have been her parents'.

"Why do I find you here?"

Mila almost flew out of her skin, imagining herself hovering over the scene, her body a flat, empty shell on the carpet by her mother's desk. She couldn't turn, though she knew who it was. But somehow Mr. Henry's voice seemed different. And once she found her regular breathing pattern, she wondered if the difference in his language, in his body, in his manner was disappointment in her.

"I—I was looking for a scarf," she said, standing up, pressing her birth certificate tight against her thigh.

"Really?" Mr. Henry said. "There is a very fine scarf on the bed."

Mila blinked, looked at the pile of soft material on the bed and then back at Mr. Henry. He didn't have on his driver's hat, so he must have returned from his drive, set it on the foyer table as he always did. That meant her mother must be home as well. Mila needed to get out of the room now.

"I didn't find anything I liked," she said, moving toward the door. But Mr. Henry moved in front of her, keeping her trapped in the room.

"I suppose that's what can happen when one goes looking for things. Often, one is disappointed by what one finds. Never what is expected, wouldn't you say?"

Mila started to walk toward the door again, but then something in the sentence that still floated in the air struck her. Mr. Henry didn't sound like Mr. Henry. What was different? She stopped and stared at him, noticing the sweat on his brow, the slightly messy hair, as if he'd ripped off his hat upon entering the house and run up the stairs. As if he knew what she'd been doing. As if he didn't want her to find her birth certificate.

"That's the truth," she said, her heart pounding out a scary movie sound track. "Well, I think I'll go see what's in the fridge. I think there's some cheese-cake."

"I think we need to have a little talk," Mr. Henry said, placing himself this time right in front of her.

If it was possible, Mila's heart beat even faster, her other body systems seeming to want to commiserate by speeding up as well. She felt sweat start to pool under her bra line; the hair on the back of her neck prickled to standing.

I'm coming, Mila, Garrick thought. But she could tell he wasn't close enough to get her out of this situation with Mr. Henry. *I'll be there as soon as I can.*

"Everything's fine," she said, watching Mr. Henry's face start to swim, somehow, as if he were melting. "I'm just going to go downstairs."

His face morphed into a leer, and without thinking about it, without knowing what she was doing, Mila felt herself slip into the space of moving time. Her heart slowed, her mind cleared, and she pressed her birth certificate as close as possible to her body, understanding that she needed this clue no matter what time she ended up in. The next thing she knew, she was sitting at the kitchen counter with Garrick, eating a piece of pie. Mr. Henry was nowhere to be seen.

Mila dropped her fork, stood up from the chair, and patted her pockets. She looked on the counter, under her chair. Where was it? Where was her certifi-cate?

"What's the matter?" Garrick asked.

Mila turned to him, knowing that for the first time in her life, she could actually ask a person what happened in the time that she had pushed forward, someone who wouldn't think she was insane. "Did— where is Mr. Henry? Did you feel it? Did you come with me?"

Garrick looked at her, nodding. "Oh God. I get it."

"What, Garrick? What? Please, you have to tell me what happened. You have to help me find it."

He pushed back from the counter and stood up, taking Mila's shoulders in his hands. "I know what it feels like now. It's a rush. I was on my way to you, hearing what you were saying to Mr. Henry, feeling what you were thinking, and then time just pushed me. Like a wave. And then I was sitting here, completely unconcerned about what was going on in your mother's bedroom. Like the push knocked away my thoughts. I don't think anyone in your life probably ever noticed before."

Mila stared at him. How horrible. So all those times that she'd moved time forward, she must have moved those close to her or connected to her. She'd wasted their lives, too. "How do we know who we move? Is there like a radius? An emotional connection? What?"

Garrick shook his head. "I don't know. I was about a mile away."

Mila looked around the kitchen again, sighing as nothing continued to change. No certificate. No Mr. Henry. "Did you see him?"

"No. All I remember is being here. Just like this. But what did you find?"

Mila bent down to peer under the counter one

more time, stood straight, touched her pockets again, and sighed. "My birth certificate. And it's weird. You were right, Garrick. I think I would be more shocked about it if I hadn't accidentally escaped and pulled everyone along with me. I'm so sorry. I was just scared. He wasn't himself."

"Who?"

"Mr. Henry. He was acting flat-out weird. Like he wanted to keep me from learning what I did."

Garrick hugged her, rubbing her back. As he touched her, she felt her body slowly relax, and then she felt every single part of her begin to respond. Underneath her clothes, she felt her skin prickle with desire, goose bumps on her thighs, stomach, forearms. Her joints seemed to loosen, and she thought she might actually faint. Was she going to swoon like some southern belle? Swoon when something so bizarre had just happened?

Mila thought so, and grabbed on to him a little harder. In this instant, she didn't care about Mr. Henry, her bizarre birth story, Garrick's relationship to her. All she wanted was this feeling of wanting him.

There is something completely wrong with me, she thought. Her body was taking her places she had never been before. Look at her! Her breathing quickened, and she wished she could take this great man up to her childhood bedroom and make love to him.

Mila closed her eyes and pushed away from him with her fingertips, locking her knees lest she fall down. "Mr. Henry. My birth certificate," she said under her breath. "My parents' names aren't listed. Other people I didn't know were—strangers. Or maybe they weren't even real people at all."

There was a pause, and the story that belonged to

both of them filled the space between them. There was the dark place, the ride that rumbled them to safety, the voices of the children all around them, even as the bad people tried to find them. There were their four parents, their caretakers, really, the people both she and Garrick had been given to. There were their childhoods, filled with confusion and upset. Orphans. They were both orphans.

"Oh, Mila. I wish I hadn't been right." Garrick reached out and then pulled his hand back. He shook his head. "But who was listed?"

She looked up into his so beautiful black eyes and shrugged. "I have no idea who they are. They seemed like names pulled out of a hat. Mary Jones and Steve Smith."

He nodded. "But you said you had the birth certificate before you moved time. Where is it?"

"I don't know. The next thing I knew, I was here with you."

He looked at her, his eyes wide. In his mind, she heard his thought and knew that it was the way they could understand this mystery. "Okay. But I don't want to go back into the bedroom with Mr. Henry. He scared me. I know you can't really predict how far you will go, but don't send me there."

Garrick shook his head. "I think—remember how we held hands? I think that we can go together. I think we can make choices when we are joined. And I don't think we pull people with us when we are."

"You mean, go back to the same point? Be in the past together?"

"I mean, watch time. See it together but not be in it. I've been thinking about this a lot, and those luminescent spots we saw? That's what we can use. Portals. Doors. The entrance to the past and the present."

"How do you know this, Garrick?" she asked.

This time, he shrugged. "I don't know. The same way I knew when I saw you for the first time that you could hear my thoughts, read my mind. The same way I knew that you were the one I want."

He stopped, looking at her, and Mila felt her breath in her throat stop. The one he wanted!

Garrick took her hand. "It was the same way I knew that if I took your hand, you could go with me into the gray space. So trust me. Let's go. Let's find out what happened."

Chapter Five

"Are you ready?" Garrick asked, looking into Mila's eyes, knowing that what they were doing was so new, so frightening, both of them should be scared. He had never moved into the past with anyone before. Of course, he'd wanted to. Oh, how he'd wished he could prove to his parents that he wasn't lying or making up a story or trying to drive them crazy.

With Mila, he'd moved into the gray. With Mila, he could move into anything, and now he needed to be strong, to help her find out what had happened with Mr. Henry, a man she had trusted her entire life.

"Yes," she said, and then she thought, *I know it will work*.

"Okay," he said, and then he reached out his hand again and took hers, so soft, so light, so strong. "Just stay with me. Don't let go. Don't let your energy go anywhere else."

When their hands touched, Garrick felt her current pulse through him, find his pulse, his movement. They blended together, flowed in a single unit of energy and flesh, and suddenly, they were no longer in the Adamses' kitchen standing by the counter. They were in the gray, the shimmering portals at either side of them.

Now what? Mila asked. *Do we go through? Or in?*

Never having tried this before, never having had any inkling of control over his movement through time, Garrick thought about pulling her back into the present, giving up before they even started. But he couldn't. Not now.

In, he thought, knowing somehow that this was the right answer. *And through. Follow me.*

Pulling her gently, he moved them toward the shimmer of color to his right. He reached out his other hand and slipped through it as if it were soft, parting water, his hand disappearing as he did.

Oh, Mila thought. *Where—*

I don't know, he thought back. *Stay with me.*

He moved in, his body now in the shimmer, Mila coming along with him. And there they were, in the Adamses' house, standing in the foyer by the stairs. Before Garrick could conjure something to think about, an earlier Mila pushed through the kitchen doors, rushing past them and bounding up the stairs.

I'm off to go look through my parents' room, Mila thought. *And God, what a racket I made.*

Garrick smiled, hearing the next thought she tried to smother.

That can't be my ass!

He turned to her, letting her know that her ass was just fine—more than fine—wishing that he'd already moved them into a place where he could show her with touch. For a second, he was back in her loft bedroom, holding her ass, her whole body as they made love. Her skin was soft and warm, her muscles firm, everything about her body perfect.

Stop. Don't, she thought. *We have work to do.*

Garrick nodded, and together, they walked up the stairs, following behind Mila. At the top of the stairs, they turned and stood in the Adamses' bedroom doorway, watching Mila riffle through Adair's scarves. Then she found the envelope that contained the birth certificate.

So it was just there? Garrick thought. *Why do you think your mother would hide it in the drawer? Sort of in plain sight really. Your mother seems a little more organized than that.*

Mila turned to him, the shimmer of time illuminating her, making her almost glow. Her blond hair was white, light itself, her face golden. *I don't know. You're right. It seems pretty strange. She would have had it under lock and key somewhere, you would think.*

Just then—without the before Mila seeing him—Mr. Henry walked almost through Garrick and Mila standing at the door and into the room. Garrick stared at Mr. Henry, remembering the first time he saw the man at the Adamses' dinner party and then from the ride home in the limo, when he couldn't wait to get out and take a breath of the night air.

Garrick, Mila thought, pointing to Mr. Henry. *Oh my God. Am I seeing that?*

Garrick followed her outstretched hand, starting when he saw what she was pointing to. The back of Mr. Henry's head seemed to shift, move, the landscape of his hair moving like black grass in the wind.

What is that? Garrick thought, holding on to Mila tighter, even though nothing in the time past could hurt them physically now. *What in the hell is going on?*

Mila was transfixed, watching her earlier self talk with Mr. Henry and then studying Mr. Henry's hair, the rippling movement of something just under his skin and bone.

Mila!

She began to walk backward as her prior self came toward them and the door. *Watch me. Pay attention! I'm going to shift out of time any minute. Right now.*

And then, just as the earlier Mila seemed to fall into a trance and the world of the past went on fast forward—the room seemingly dissolved into a fuzzy swoosh of wallpaper, furniture, and hardwood floors—Garrick saw Mr. Henry lean forward quickly and pluck the envelope from Mila's grasp and stuff it in his pocket.

Look what he did! How did he do that? Mila thought. *He took it from me. He took my birth certificate and his hair moves! His head is alive. That's not Mr. Henry. That's not him!*

Garrick held on to her hand tightly, sure that they should leave immediately and go back to the future that they had landed in earlier. But then Mr. Henry seemed to turn to them both, though Garrick wasn't sure the man was really looking at them. It seemed as though Mr. Henry was slowly being influenced by the time shift that Mila was creating, his body almost being sucked out of the room as if he were being vacuumed away. But he must have known somehow that they would come back. He looked around the space where they stood and then beyond and said, "Why do I find you here?"

Mila gasped, and even Garrick felt a tug in his stomach as the man's face seemed to blur, his mouth a leer, a gaping rectis. But at least from the front, they couldn't see the lumps and rolls of his head.

Get us out of here, Garrick said, knowing he only wanted to move forward. Not backward. And in a flash, they were standing by the kitchen sink, talking with Nidia as she informed Mila of the exact ingredients of the cheesecake.

Mila nodded and smiled at Nidia, trying to act as normally as possible, but Garrick could feel the agitation in her thoughts. The images in her head jumped from Mr. Henry's head and mouth to her own search for information to the wicked moment that Mr. Henry had turned to them.

What are we going to do? she thought, all the while keeping up the innocuous conversation.

We have to go and find him. We have to find out how he managed to talk to us when we weren't even really there. And we have to find your birth certificate and the people on it. If, in fact, there are even people to find.

Mila nodded imperceptibly, and then she reached down and grasped his hand. Her touch was loving and kind and known, the very touch that Garrick wanted more of, always.

Nidia smiled at them both. "I am happy you have gotten to know each other better. I wasn't sure after that first evening, though."

"It is a surprise, isn't it?" Mila said, leaning into Garrick for a second, seeming to forget for just a flip of time what they had just seen. "After the way he acted."

As Mila turned to smile at him, Garrick wanted to say so many things. He wanted to tell Nidia that he loved Mila. He wanted to tell Mila that, fighting his desire to get down on one knee and say something he didn't know he ever would, words he'd never before strung together in a sentence.

He wasn't sure how all of this had happened, could happen when he'd just watched a man's scalp crawl around his head.

Nidia was staring at him, so he nodded, breathed in, said, "I was on my worst behavior that night. It won't happen again, especially if you promise to make that gazpacho for me another time."

Nidia smiled, blushed, turned to the counter. Mila looked into his eyes, and more than anything, he wished they knew who they were so they could be who they were together. He didn't want to look for anything or anyone. All he wanted was her warm arms around him.

Garrick hugged Mila, felt her nerves and excitement and fear beating just under her soft skin.

He had no choice but to look. For her and for himself.

We will figure it out, he thought.

Thank you, she thought back. *Thank you for being here with me.*

Where else could I possibly be? Where would I go that you are not?

Work maybe?

I'm serious, Mila, he thought.

She pressed into him, and Garrick ran a hand down her smooth hair. He looked up to see Nidia smiling, and for the first time in his life, he felt recognized. Almost normal. Home.

"This is his room," Mila whispered. They stood in the hallway on the third floor in front of a closed door. The Adamses' house was three floors, each floor slowly diminished in finishing touches. This hallway was without the crown molding and wainscoting of the first two, but the hardwood floors still gleamed, a function, Garrick imagined, of Adair's constant housecleaning vigilance. And, of course, Mr. Henry and Nidia had rooms on this floor, the one out of the way.

"Don't think my mother is that classist," Mila said. "There are only three bedrooms on the second floor."

"Three in use," Garrick said. "What about those four rooms under renovation? Your mother could invite a small country to move in."

"Maybe I'll suggest that," Mila said. "Tell her that you want to be dictator."

She gave him a tiny, sweet smile that disappeared as she looked at the bedroom door again. Garrick reached out and put his hand on the wood of the door, wishing he had some other kind of magic. The kind that would let him see through wood, like Superman.

"But what are we going to do now?" Mila asked. "Walk in and ask him why his head moves? This is too damn weird. I don't think I can take it. In fact, I can't. Let's get out of here. Now!"

"Shh," Garrick said. *He might actually be in there.*

Of course, he didn't really think so. In fact, he imagined that whatever Mr. Henry was or whatever was inside him had long since left the house. What worried him was that he thought they'd find the real Mr. Henry—or parts of him—in the room. Whatever the thing inside him tossed aside.

And the truth was, if the thing in Mr. Henry could hold on to time in a way that most people could not, likely he could read minds, too, and had long since discovered their plan and had left the house, the city, maybe even the state. Maybe, Garrick thought, even the planet.

But he took care of me when I was little, Mila thought, looking at Garrick with such sadness that he pulled her close.

Whatever that thing was, Garrick thought, *it wasn't the Mr. Henry you grew up with. It wasn't a human. Or if it was him, something has gone wrong. Very wrong. But from what you tell me, the man you know would never hurt you.*

Mila put her hand on his arm. Her touch, her heat, went through his shirt, through his skin, to his bones and blood. He wondered if there would come a time when her touch wouldn't do this to him, but he doubted it.

Come on, he thought, trying to ignore his own desire.

Her hand still on his arm, Mila sighed, but she didn't start when Garrick turned the doorknob slowly, opening the door to Mr. Henry's bedroom. Garrick was ready to push them back into the past at a moment's notice, and he was sure that Mila was geared to do the same with the future. If that creepy, lumpy-headed man came at them, they would be out of the room in a flash of time and motion.

He's not here, Mila thought.

Garrick looked around the small but nicely decorated bedroom. The four-poster bed was made up, the curtains drawn, sun shining off the waxed mahogany furniture. Nothing was out of place, no clothing on the bed, no personal items on top of the bureau. No body or body parts on the floor. No strange live thing that resembled the fluid movements on the man's head crawling around like an inchworm.

He's gone, Garrick thought. *And I mean, for good.*

Mila looked up at him, her brown eyes full of sadness. *He always understood me. He always knew what was bothering me.*

Garrick nodded, but he wondered what that meant. How could Mr. Henry have known what Mila was needing or wanting? There she had been, just like Garrick, alone with her secret, confused, scared. What if Mr. Henry had been sent to the Adamses' house to watch over Mila, to spy on her, to keep track of her growth and her use of her powers? Maybe it was he who had given the baby Mila to the Adamses. Or maybe he was just an innocent bystander in whatever war Mila, Garrick, and their people were waging.

So, who would have sent him?

For a second, a part of Mila's dream seeped into Garrick's mind, the part about the bad people, the bad things, the bad feeling. The wetness, the heat, the pain. The dark, curling smoke.

Who are they? Mila asked. *What do they want?*

I have no idea, he thought, clearing his throat because he needed to use his voice, tired of the floaty quality of speaking in thoughts. "All I know is that we need to find whoever or whatever Mr. Henry has become and make him give us your birth certificate. We need to find those people listed on it. Your fake or real or proxy parents. Whoever they are, they have answers to questions we don't even know how to ask."

Garrick felt his breath ache under his ribs with each inhale. He wanted to find Mr. Henry now. He

wanted to forget about his real life at Calder Wilken
Brodden. In fact, he wanted to quit everything but
this. Quit everything but Mila. It didn't matter how
much money he had or where his career was going
or who he knew. He never wanted to talk with Jim
Ryan on the phone again, joking about women or
the Dow Jones or life. All he wanted was this woman
and the understanding of who they both were, sepa-
rately and together.

"Okay," she said. "I do. I have an idea."

Mila took his hand and they walked out of the
door, into the hallway, and into the mystery of everything.

"When I was little," Mila was saying as Garrick
slowed down and parked on the corner of Masonic
and Fell, "he would always take me here. Right at the
panhandle. It's all new now, but there used to be an
old swing set and a curly slide. My mother would
want me home by a very specific time for some kind
of after-school activity. But if there was a second to
spare, he'd bring me right here to this playground.
Let me run around a little. Play on the jungle gym.
Try to climb—there, that tree."

She pointed to a cypress, its limbs high, but its
bark thick and solid enough for little feet to be able
to use it as stairs.

"Sometimes," she went on. "'Sometimes he was the
only friend I had. I never told him about what I
could do with time, but it was as if he understood me,
everything, all of it."

"Maybe he did," Garrick said. He shrugged,
opened his door, and stepped out, careful to avoid

the speeding traffic. Walking around his brand-new BMW 5, he realized that he suddenly didn't care as much about the car as he had even the day before. It was black and shiny, had overhead cams and a six-speed manual transmission, and so what? Everything until now meant nothing to him. The car had been a way to spend the money he earned because there was nothing else to do with his time, the time in the past or the present.

Now there was. Now there was Mila.

Garrick opened Mila's door, watched her slip out of the seat, and then stand next to him, her heat a gentle wave lapping at him. He didn't want to tell her that maybe all along, Mr. Henry was planted here or that maybe something else was planted to watch Mr. Henry and wait until the time was right.

"But I never knew anything about him, really," Mila said. "Nothing about his family or his friends. What he did on his time off. I've never really thought of this before, but it's like he existed only to care for me. For my family. Like—"

"Like maybe he wasn't really a person?"

"That can't be true!" Mila said loudly. "How can that be true?"

A woman walking a pug rolled her eyes and clacked by, as if irritated by the idea of truth and trying to find it.

"Come with me," Garrick said. He took Mila's arm, and they walked across Fell and stepped onto the sidewalk. Garrick took a deep breath and kissed her, wanting to give her the happiness he felt even in the midst of this strangeness. Kiss her without worrying about how much feeling he was showing or how weird it would look to anyone but them. No longer caring about the past or how things used to be.

Next to the park where an alien-infested driver might be hiding out, next to the park where Mila had spent countless childhood hours escaping from the curse of her gift, Garrick kissed her. And kissed her again.

Her lips opened to him, her tongue soft and warm and wet and wanting. He moved his arms gently around her, holding her tight, and she responded by pressing her body against his. Garrick knew that she must be able to feel him so hard against her belly, the sure sign of all his want, desire, need for her. He wanted to feel her skin, her heat, her breath on him.

"Oh," she whispered against his mouth. *Oh*, she thought.

Yes, he thought back, feeling the wings of her shoulders under his hands.

Garrick had never kissed a woman like this, wanting not just her mouth but all of her. Her heart and soul and mind and thoughts. Her companionship. Her voice. Her laughter. This is what he wanted his lips to tell hers. Yes, he wanted her body, too. That lovely body, her curves and planes and smooth long limbs under and around him. But this was the truth he knew: he'd never known how important a kiss was before kissing Mila for the first time. Probably he hadn't known a thing about just anything until this moment, on this busy San Francisco intersection, cars whizzing by well over the speed limit. Speeding just like his heart.

Do you think we will ever be a normal couple? she thought, pulling her lips slowly away from his. "Do normal things like go out to dinner and not slip into some kind of time thing?"

"That's what we're trying to do here," he said. He took her face between his palms, staring into her dark eyes. "I want us to have our life together, whether it's normal or not. And we need answers before that can happen."

She tried to pull away when the tears started, but Garrick wouldn't let her, watching as they slipped wet and quick from the corners of her eyes.

I really don't know how to believe all of this. No one has ever been, well, you, she thought.

How reassuring, he thought. *Given what we know about powers and bad forces and all, I'm glad no one has been me before.*

She laughed, and Garrick kissed the sides of her face, her salt on his tongue.

"I have such a vested interest," he said. "I mean, you know. I figure this out, and look what I get."

She smiled. "What, exactly, is it that you will get?"

"You," Garrick said. "You."

"A bargain," Mila said, wiping her eyes. "What a steal."

"A deal at any price," Garrick said, moving his hands away from her face and running his thumbs gently under her eyes, whisking away the last of her sadness. "The deal of a lifetime. My lifetime."

Garrick breathed in and took her arm again, and they started walking slowly down the sidewalk, turning left and walking across Fell, into the panhandle, passing by huge eucalyptus trees and wide green lawns. Bicyclists, parents with strollers, and runners passed them by—in the middle of the lawn, a group of teenagers wearing tie-dyed shirts and ripped jeans laughed and passed a bottle among them.

"They'll grow up to be accountants," Garrick said.

"Maybe they'll be lawyers or dentists," Mila said, shaking her head. "Or work in finance."

"Touché," he said. He knew that his assistant, Brody, was likely wondering where he was right at this very moment, concerned that Garrick wasn't picking up e-mails or voice mail from his BlackBerry. His colleagues were likely fending off harassing calls from his clients, the ones who watched the Dow like an ongoing soap opera. Money all over the world kept pouring from one bucket into another, splashing and filling or flooding or evaporating, and for today Garrick wasn't there to keep track of it. Work had always been the place he could bury himself in, pulling up the blanket of busyness over his head as he tried to forget what he had never understood.

"Haven't you ever thought about doing something else?" she asked. "I mean, not that there's anything wrong—"

"Let me guess. Some of your best friends are in finance, huh?" He butted her lightly with his elbow and turned to look at her. Her cheeks flushed red, but she met his eyes and shrugged.

"I just couldn't do it anymore," she said. "It seemed so fake. So pointless. Money seems so ridiculous, as if at times it's not even there. It isn't really. It's all a social contract, and I got tired of that contract. And once I realized that, I knew I had to get out."

"It wasn't about money or a contract. You had no choice. You had to paint your way to this. To us," Garrick said. "You are the one who remembered. You are the one who is going to bring us back together."

Mila stopped. "Who do you think they—we—are?"

Ever since Mila showed him her dream, her memory, Garrick had asked himself the same question. As he'd floated through her images of the dark, moving place, he'd noticed that there were so many more children than adults. And the adults didn't seem to be attached to particular children but to all of them, hovering over and around them all, each group as important as the next. Maybe that in and of itself wasn't so odd, but it was the look that all the adults and the children in the dark place wore that caught his attention the most. They were not only afraid, they were filled with loss, a loss that weighed on them like ropes of stones.

And then suddenly in his thoughts, the adults were gone. The dark place a place of children.

"I'm not sure, but I think that you—we—were being taken someplace. Being taken to safety."

"But where did the adults go? Why are we all alone now?"

"I think they were trying to protect us. Put us in a place where we wouldn't be hurt. And maybe," he continued. "Maybe they didn't make it. Maybe whatever was following the . . . the spaceship found them. Maybe they sacrificed themselves for us."

Mila gasped, her hand on her mouth. Her eyes glistened. "They put themselves out as bait. They put us first. They saved us."

A wind picked up, pushed Mila's hair in front of her eyes. Garrick gently pushed away the strands from her face. "You must have been worth it."

"We were worth it," she said. "All of us. All the children in the ship. You were in the ship, too."

"And we will find the rest of them. You aren't the only child any longer. You will never be the only child ever again."

"Do you really think so? Do you think we can find them? Do you think we can stop being so alone?"

Garrick nodded. "We already have," he said, and they kept walking, heading toward the play structure and a low squat building that housed the restrooms. Garrick scanned the area, looking for Mr. Henry. He didn't really feel there was any hope of finding the man here, but it was Mila's only idea, and he certainly didn't know where else to go. His one notion was to go to the hospital to see if her records were available, but first she needed to calm down and accept the fact that the man she'd counted on all these years had changed. Garrick knew he'd be more than a little distressed if he'd just seen his childhood pal's head move as if there was a snake under his hair. Hell, he was distressed anyway.

They neared the bathrooms, and Mila stopped and turned to him. "I really don't want to go in there, but I sure could use it. Do you think it's okay?"

Just as Mila asked the question, a woman pushing a full shopping cart rolled around the side of the building and stopped in front of the women's bathroom door, her cart clanging and clacking to a halt. It was impossible to discern what was in her basket, even though objects seemed to flop right out of it in dirty tendrils. Everything had been so mixed up— rags and cans and paper—that rather than individual items, it seemed the woman was toting a glob of garbage. She herself was strangely attired, her coat not a coat but a dress. Her shoes not shoes but boots, everything the same brown color of a crowded city street in the summer, dust and heat surrounding her.

"Does that answer your question?" Garrick said, and he was just about to lead Mila away, when the woman spoke to them.

"I wouldn't go that way," she said. "Lord, it takes them time to get here, and once they does, my, you are in luck. Yes, indeedy. Lucky, lucky day."

Okay, I'm with you, Mila thought. *Time to go look at the playground. I can use another bathroom.*

"Oh, they aren't in any old bathroom. No, sir. Not them. Them's got the sneaky heads and fast ways. I've seen what they does, slippy-ing and slidey-ing around here, sort of creeping like them little white spiders in the corners of rooms. For years and years. Oh, gee, Bob, I told them shelter folks about thems, but they only want to put me on those ass-nasty pills. Big old lozenges that make me sick. They's got the damn nerve to tells me I have a problem, when those bobble-headed, invisible freaks is everywhere."

She heard you, Garrick thought. *Heard your thoughts. And she has seen something pretty damn weird.*

"Damn weird? Sheet. More than that, honey. And I haves to say I ain't deaf. Never has been, never you mind what those nasty health boys want to do with me. Sticking theys little pieces of plastic in me. In me! Using that light and all. Feeding me all of that gobbledegoo. No, I tells them, but they try. I tells them I can hear just fine indeed. And I can sees just fine, too."

She stared long and hard at them for a moment before smiling. Then the woman snorted, slapped her heavy thighs with her mitt-covered hands, looked up into the sky that was turning gray with fog, a chill licking them all.

Garrick tried to move inside the woman's mind as it seemed she was open to thoughts, but all he found was a swirl of language and color, an inaccessible kaleidoscope of images.

"What's your name, ma'am?" Mila asked.

"Gertie. Name's Gertie. That much I know for sure."

"Gertie, tell me about the slippy-slidey people that you have seen. Where are they now?"

Gertie smiled at Garrick, eyes wide and smug. "Oh, they's not here right now. I wouldn't be all here by this bathroom if they was. I know what I'm doing, that's for sure. Ugly things, they is. Looks like they have some kind of earthquake going on under their skins, all rumbly and shit. I runs when I see them. Hightail it out of here and sits by the Starbucks on Masonic and collect some for a piece. Folks never very good to me there. Not like at The Sacred Grounds or anything, but it's too damn far to push my cart!"

Mila grabbed Garrick's arm, her thoughts fast and quick. He could almost feel her body thinking, wanting the answers Gertie could give.

"When do they come here? Why do they come? Who are they? Do you ever see a man with short black hair?"

Gertie started to rummage in her cart as if she hadn't heard Mila's questions. Cans and silverware clacked and clattered, paper flew up and whisked away in the breeze. Garrick tried not to notice, but he had to almost stop breathing to avoid the fetid, wet blanket smell that wafted around the woman as she flung her arms about.

"Do you think they will be here later?" Garrick asked.

"I told you I ain't deaf. Here." Gertie looked up from her cart and pressed something hard into Garrick's hand. "Now, if that don't help you, then you've been talking to the wrong person all this time. And I think you have. I'm just going to roll out of here and leave you to those skanky-looking thangs. People, they thinks they is. Jee-sus. My God. All slippy-slidey and shit . . ."

Gertie pushed into her cart and it lurched into movement, her conversation continuing as she walked away.

"What did she give you?" Mila asked. "Let me see."

Garrick looked into his palm and struggled to keep himself in time, wanting to push back into the past to escape what he was looking at. Cradled in his palm was a beautiful-looking coin, flat and thin and silver. For the slimmest of seconds, he'd wanted to admire it, pick it up between his fingers and examine the craftsmanship, the delicate, raised artwork on the front, a small cityscape on the front. Impossibly, Garrick remembered the city, as if from another dream, a memory, a childhood fairy tale. He wanted to go there, slip into the early morning streets, wander in the parks. Oh, it was beautiful there! Oh, the orange sky, the warm air around him, the pink clouds overhead.

But then some other feeling took over, a revulsion that went beyond anything he'd known, certainly nothing he'd felt when looking at coins.

"What is it?" Mila asked again, pulling on his wrist, trying to see the coin in his hand.

He felt his throat contract, and he had to swallow once, twice in order not to retch, in order not to run away from the memory that had just intrigued him. But why? It was just a tiny piece of metal with an image on it, but there was something else guiding his feelings. Something red and dark and painful. A pounding hate that made him want to hide.

"Garrick," Mila said, her voice soft, and then she put her hand over his, covering the coin, and Garrick found his breath and opened his eyes. There she was. Mila. His Mila. The world wasn't full of pain, a swath of red and hurt. It was only the color of her dark eyes, her hair, her hand on his. She was the world of their time together, their bodies pressed close, their hearts beating strong. He breathed in deeply and relaxed.

"Let me see it," she said, and slowly, he opened his hand, the fading light glinting dully off the coin.

She picked it up, held it to the light, looked at the ordinary disc. "A coin. It looks so old. Ancient, maybe. Like something from a museum."

Leaning against the building wall, Garrick shook his head, pushed his hair back from his forehead, feeling his cold sweat on his fingers as he did. "I don't know. Maybe she found it in the bathroom."

Mila laughed, put the coin in her palm. "Yeah, an ancient coin-operated bathroom in the panhandle restrooms. Probably sponsored by the De Young Museum. It will be installed here until November. There was corporate funding."

He started to laugh at her joke, but then he looked

in the door at the woman's bathroom. According to Gertie, that's where she spent so much of her time. And she had been trying to tell them something with her wild stories of the rumbly people. Garrick shook his head. He was slow to get things sometimes. But like Gertie said about herself, he wasn't deaf.

"In here," he said, moving into the doorway of the restroom.

"Garrick, you can't go in there."

"Mila, this is a homeless hangout. Not only that, it's San Francisco. I think gender isn't going to be a problem if the cops show up."

She shrugged, smiled, and put her hand in his. Garrick pulled her into the bathroom, and they looked around the tiled room. The stalls were metal, only one with a door, the white toilets clean but old, seatless, and burbling.

"No coins needed," Mila said. "Looks like you can go for free. Finally, there's your bargain."

It can't be that easy, he thought, turning to leave. None of their questions could be answered that easily.

But then Mila gasped. "It's pulling me," she said.

"What is?" he asked, but then she answered his question with her body. Her hand was held out, hovering, her palm open, the coin vibrating on top of it. It pulsed, beat out a silver shimmer, shone into the bathroom gloom.

For a beat, Garrick felt nauseated, afraid of the slick, sick feeling slipping over him again. But like before, there was Mila, her hand, her voice.

"Don't let me go," she said, squeezing his hand tightly, and he responded by grabbing the fine bones of her wrist. "Don't ever let go."

I won't, he thought, knowing that even if it wasn't the way he wanted it, they were finally headed toward an answer. Then the bathroom started to vibrate in the same manner as the coin, a jumpy flame of movement.

"Run," he said, his voice disappearing before Mila could even hear.

Run, he thought.

Garrick tried to pull them both out of the door, back into the foggy air, but he was stuck. No, he and Mila were being slowly spun to the movement of the room.

What's happening? she thought. *I'm slipping. Something is pulling me. Something is swallowing us.*

And they were being swallowed, the room folding up, triangulating them into nothing.

Hold me, Mila. And conjure time. Like we did before.

Garrick thought hard, felt the gray space of time, the connection between them. There it was, the glimmering sheen of space and time, the place they found together. And even as the strange, sad bathroom around them folded into nothing, taking them with it, they were protected by the power they shared. They were nowhere and in no time, but together.

Before all was darkness, Garrick smiled, hearing Mila's thought, a thought trying to cover her fear.

Off to see the slippy-slidey people.

And then the world folded shut.

Chapter Six

All Mila could feel was Garrick's hand. Actually, all she could do was feel his hand warm and strong and tight around hers. In this terrible, still place, he was the only thing that reminded her that she was alive. Nothing else touched her, nothing else came in, not through her ears or nose or skin. No air pushing against her face. No sounds reverberating around them. Nothing to see but the heavy darkness. It was like they were in a sense vacuum, the world reduced to this one tight grip.

In the midst of all this, she felt part of herself pull away, look down, and wonder how in the hell this could be happening.

Don't let go. Hold on to me, Mila.

I won't let go, Mila thought. *If I do, I'll never find you in here, wherever here is.*

If you do, I won't know who I am, he thought, and she felt his smile. Garrick squeezed her hand, and then he seemed to tug at her, pull her forward. Slowly, the dark opened up slowly to the gray of in-between time.

Here we are, Garrick thought. *Here*—

And then in a sickening ache of seconds, he was gone.

Mila turned around, floating in the no-space, wanting to cry out, but she had no air, no breath.

Garrick, she thought.

"Garrick!" she cried out. "Where are you?"

She waited, her lungs still, her eyes wide open and waiting. The no-seconds went by, the gray swirled around her, and for a long time of no-time, she hung on the hope that Garrick would come back, appear as he had that day at her loft. There Garrick had been standing in front of her, holding out his hand, bringing her close to him and somehow, closer to herself. Then later, there he had been in her bed, kissing her, touching her, showing her with his thoughts and his words how much he wanted her, needed her. Since then, he had been in her thoughts and heart and mind, nothing and no one as important. But now he was gone. How could she go back to the time when he wasn't with her? She was alone in a place that was no place. She was alone in a place that might lead her to the horrible people Gertie had described. To the people who did something terrible to Mr. Henry. To Mr. Henry who might actually be a slippy-slidey person.

At that thought, she began to cry. And the tears came so fast and hard, she knew they weren't only about this bizarre situation. No, this was for losing Garrick, for living and feeling alone, and for the mystery of the children in her dream. Finally, she let out the sorrow, let her tears come. There was nothing to make her stop. No Adair to tell her to "Get that look off your face or go to your room until you can smile.

What would anyone think when looking at you?" No classmates, colleagues, cohorts to ask questions about her feelings.

Instead, there was just the quiet of nothing and Mila's sobs, and she let them flow.

You shouldn't cry, really, came the voice. *It's not as if this very scene wasn't expected for your entire life. It was only a matter of time before we found you all, the precious ones, the ones they tried so hard to hide. You we have managed to find. You we managed to keep under control. It was only a matter of time before you found your twin. You all are like magnets.*

Twin? That's a disturbing word. Mila shivered.

Twins. Doubles. Magnets. Twins.

What do you mean?

Ahh . . . The voice trailed off, the sad, sick sound of a laugh echoing in the space.

Mila looked up, her eyes full of the grainy gray, nothing to see but light and dark and flow and flutter. She wiped her cheeks, scanned the space around her. *Who are you? Where are you?*

Oh, I'm in time. You thought you could pull a little trick on us, hiding in the in-between, trying to watch. But since we know you and your people so very well, we anticipated this. So here you are, my dear. Happily ensconced in our little laboratory.

Where is Garrick? What did you do with him?

Her thought quivered in her mind, fear making the idea almost crack in two. She didn't know if she could bear to talk with this voice, the sound so slickly evil, grating. From her dream, Mila pulled the dark, red, wet badness forth, and knew that that feeling, that image was this voice exactly. How could she bear this? How could she survive being close to the very people who had killed her real parents?

Maybe she would have to push through the years and get to where it was over. She could do that. She could find her death right now, search it out, make all of this stop.

But you would never see your darling again, would you? the voice thought. *You would never find out about the dark place and who you both really are. Wouldn't that be a shame? Wouldn't that just about ruin everything?*

You need to tell me who you are, Mila thought, her words pounding in her head. *If you've been looking for us, well, then, you've found us! Do what you need to do. Get it over with.*

The space crackled with electricity, a hum of thought rippling through the waves of no-time.

We are doing what we need to do, my little one, the voice thought. *But we've decided to bring you out of this horrible space you've put yourself in and take you with us.*

But what about Garrick?

The voice said nothing.

What have you done to him? Mila thought.

But there was only silence and then as she listened and waited for any response, the space around her started to flicker and dim.

Don't leave him here, Mila thought. And as she started to feel faint, slightly dizzy, her neck barely able to hold up her head, she knew it was over. After twenty-eight years of waiting, after finally finding her true match, she would never see Garrick again.

In her dream, Mila sees a city, as if she is standing on a hill looking toward the urban silhouette against an orange sky. Tall buildings glint in the light, nothing green any-where, everything orange, yellow, full of heat and bright-ness. At first, she imagines this glow is from fire, but as the image seeps into her eyes and mind, she knows that this is simply the way this world looks, warm and golden and inviting.

But then she notices that there is a darkness slinking across the ground headed toward the city, something that moves like smoke, like fog, like hate. Slow and deliberate and unrelenting.

She wants to cry out, and she turns to the people next to her. She doesn't know who they are, but she points and they seem to understand her, nodding and pointing at some-thing else. Mila turns back to the city and sees small black things flying up and out and away, puncturing the orange sky and disappearing.

What are they? Who are they? Where are they going? *she thinks, but the people don't tell her because this is her dream and they really can't see her at all. But Mila knows they are sad, feels their melancholy build in her head.*

We have to leave, *they think.*

We have to save the children.

We will stay until it's over to give the rest time to escape. They must make it. They have to make it.

Mila knows what is worse is that they clearly under-stand. As they stand here on this hill and look out to the bright, lighted, wonderful city, they all know they are going to die. Everyone who stays will. It is only those on those tiny specks of black flinging into the air who will live through the fog, the hate that is coming.

But I'm not ready, *she thinks, and then she is no longer on the hill but inside something—inside the dark space. Somehow, she knows that the dark space is one of the black things she saw leave the city. Somehow she knows that the people on the hill are already dead.*

And now she is hurtling somewhere, moving fast, voices and thoughts loud. This is not her other dream, she knows this even as she dreams on. This is another part, a sadder part, the part she has never seen before.

And she is a child again, a toddler, held in someone's arms. Who is it? Who is holding her?

Mila peers into the dream to see a woman, a tall blond woman holding her against her shoulder, bending slightly as she weeps. But even with the tears, there is comfort and love and warmth.

Oh! This is her mother. This is the flesh-and-blood mother Mila imagined in the long nights she lay awake hating Adair's rules and judgments—and even in the time of Adair's love and hope and kindness. That love led her to want this other, greater love, the love she has missed since she can remember. But finally! There it is, the feeling she's craved her entire life, and Mila bends into it, knows that there is nothing like it in the world, love passed down from mother to child, mother to child forever, no matter what planet one comes from. No matter how wonderful the surrogate mother. No matter what other kind of love one can find.

For a second, she is tugged to another memory of another kind of love, something different but as warm, as loving.

No, she thinks, shaking off the intrusion.

No.

She slides back into the dream, and Mila wants to hold on to her mother's warm flesh, to breathe in a smell that is so familiar—a flower, a perfume, a lotion. Lilies. Lavender. Vanilla. She doesn't want to let go, but then she is sitting, leaning against the wall with the children she has dreamed about her entire life, the blond children, her siblings. As she

*sits there in her toddler self, she knows that the next best
thing to her mother are these children, the ones who know
her best. These children and . . . she doesn't know who else,
but she moves into the bodies of the children, knows they will
keep her loved and safe and warm.*

We will come back for you, *comes the thought.* Take
care of each other if you can. Find each other, *and
then Mila knows that the people she loves best in the world
are gone.*

Tell me who we are, *she thinks now, in her dream. But
the dream children say and do what they have always done,
and the story, as it always does, plays out until it ends.*

Mila startled awake, blinking into darkness, hoping that somehow, she would turn over in her bed
back in San Francisco, reach out her arms, and find
Garrick next to her, their story somehow an ordinary
one. But the stiffness in her shoulders and back told
her she had not spent a night on her own mattress.
Slowly, a light began to glow at the end of the room,
the radiance yellow, round, the shape of a lightning
bug, moving slowly toward her.

"Just tell me what you want from me," she said. "I
can't take this cloak-and-dagger crap anymore. Take
what you want from me and leave me alone."

Mila wished she was as brave as her words. Inside
her clothing, she felt herself shaking, her skin a field
of goose bumps, her breathing quick and shallow.

The light kept coming forward, and for an instant—yes, there!—she felt relieved. The form holding out the light was familiar, known, Mr. Henry as
he had looked coming down the hallway and into
her room the nights her parents were out late and

she had a bad dream. Mr. Henry as he walked toward
her as she sat on the school play yard crying because
she felt so alone, so afraid, accidentally moving time
and unable to tell a soul. His quick, authoritative
steps always made her feel that she was just on the
cusp of being saved.

But now? She remembered his head, the way the
thing or things moved under his scalp. She shivered
again, held herself tight, but forced herself to keep
her eyes open.

"Why are you here?" she asked. "I don't understand why you are involved in this, Mr. Henry."

Mr. Henry stood in front of her, silent, watching
her with his dark eyes. The light in his hand swung
back and forth, a bobbing yellow ball in the gloomy
dark.

Mila was scared to look at him too closely, not
wanting to see any lumpy movements. Not wanting
to see who or what he really was. But then she had no
choice but to look. Mr. Henry put down the lantern
on a table that was suddenly visible and took her face
in his hand, cupping her chin in his smooth hand.

"I'm not Mr. Henry," he said, smiling. "But I
thought I'd take this brief but pleasing shape for you.
I know how much you think of this human. He was
mildly useful to us."

"Was? Where is he?" She stared into the face that
was so familiar. "What have you done to him? And
what have you done to Garrick?"

"You ask too many damn questions," the not–Mr.
Henry said. "And almost always the same ones."

He took his hand away from her chin, leaving behind a warmth that flickered and flared and then
dimmed.

"What would you do?" Mila said. "What would you ask?"

"What about 'Where am I from?' " Mr. Henry said. "That would be a good start."

Mila sat back, breathed out. She needed to just escape. She would conjure time and travel to some other place on the continuum and leave this situation to memory. Or maybe she'd just keep going until it was over, tumbling into darkness and never having to deal with any of this.

"I wouldn't do that, if I were you," Mr. Henry said. "Sadly for you, your powers are anticipated and you aren't going to slide out of here so easily."

The air in the cramped space hung on her like lead. For the first time since first grade, time was immobile.

Fine, she thought. *Good. Tell me where I am from.*

"You've always known where you are from. You just chose to forget. You had the opportunity just recently to see it all. But both of you were like little children, wandering around unable to see what was exactly in front of you."

Mila shook her head. "But I could only go forward. And together—"

And then she was silent, thinking about Garrick, his warm touch, the way they slid through time together without having to pay and pay for doing so.

"Exactly," said Mr. Henry. "Garrick. Your twin. Your other half. All that joined power."

Of course, Mila thought. It was what the little boy in her dream said. Garrick was that other one, the one who would help her. They'd been together from the start.

"Earth has done something to you. Sort of sucked

your smarts up. Ate away at what made you so useful
in the first place. The air. It's too heavy, makes you
slovenly." Mr. Henry stopped laughing, stood in
front of her with his hands on his hips. "Sometimes I
wonder why we make all the fuss over you all. In an
instant, you could all be gone. We should have finished what we started long ago."

"So you haven't answered any of my questions,"
Mila said, pushing tears away off her cheeks with her
hand. "You haven't told me where I am from. Or
what you are going to do with me. Or Garrick. Why
all this mystery? Why not just do what you need to do
and get it over with? Why not—"

"Silence!" Mr. Henry said, and with a wave of his
hand, she felt her throat go numb, her vocal cords
seize, her body tingle with goose bumps.

Mila wanted to think something at him, throw her
words into his mind, but she pulled back, let her
mind clear, her body soften under his tight grasp.
She had to play nice so that he would tell her what
she needed to know. He was frightening, but not as
horrible as the images she had of the bad people—
the red wet hurt. She had to stay calm to save Garrick
and all the other children that had been with her on
the ship, those who might still be alive. She wouldn't
let happen to them what had happened to her
mother. And no matter how crazy and weird and insane it sounded, they had all come from the light,
bright, orange planet years ago. Then they were scattered to the winds, and what Mila had to do now was
play the game so she could find them all. Every single one of them, especially the two next to her, the
girl and the boy.

She swallowed, kept her eyes closed, listened to

the sound of Mr. Henry's calm, light breathing. She needed to be calm, keep quiet. She needed to marshal all the silence she had developed as a child, use the strength she had found inside herself as she'd grown up alone, without anyone else like her on this planet. Or so she'd thought.

In the cold room, Mila Adams made a decision to do what she was told. For now.

Blinking, Mila looked up at Mr. Henry. "What do you want me to do?"

Mr. Henry crossed his arms, raised his eyebrows.

"Everything I ask," he said. "And you know what the consequences will be if you don't." He flashed an image of Garrick, still in a dark room as she was but he was bound, immobilized, gagged.

"Of course," she said, and she stared at Mr. Henry without moving, unflinching. She wasn't going to react. Not now, when she was so close. Garrick had worked too hard to get them to this place and she wasn't going to mess it up. She wasn't going to make it easy for these terrible people to hurt him.

"Good," Mr. Henry said. Turning away from her, he moved his arms and said something in a language Mila had never heard, a language that as it faded from the room she found herself recognizing. Before she had the chance to ask him what he had said, the room was filled with light, heat, zinging flashes, and she was moving through energy, away from the room, away once more from Garrick.

When she came to this time, Mila thought she was sitting in a chair, but there was no visual evidence, only the hardness of wood or plastic under her rear and back, her legs dangling. She hung in the middle of nothing, an invisible chair under her, the space filled with images of the city she had seen in her dream. But this time, there was no scary dark fog creeping over the landscape.

Mila brought her hand to her neck, tried to keep herself from lunging into the scene, needing to be here, be back, be—be home. It was so amazing, so wonderful. Her throat seemed to clamp down, tears tingling in her eyes. She could almost feel the glow of the suns on her skin, and she wanted to throw her arms up and close her eyes, taking in the heat she could still imagine.

How different this view was from her dream. Now instead of a war zone, it was just a beautiful orange day, the sun glinting off the metal and glass buildings, iridescent clouds swirling past in pink and blue and green, hiding and then revealing what seemed to be three suns—one large, the other two tiny amber orbs—and the ghost of a large white moon that hung at the edge of the horizon. The image reduced, zoomed in, and she could see swaths of green, lush, rolling hills dotted with thick trees and shrubs amongst the buildings. What looked like tiny spaceships—space cars?—zipped along in orderly lines between the buildings, around the city, out of the city into the distance where, Mila could see, was another city and another.

"Do you remember?" the voice asked, and the scene zoomed out again, Mila high above all the action. She looked into the clouds, wondering if she was in some kind of auditorium on display or in a cage like some kind of lab rat. And who was speaking to her? The voice was like Mr. Henry's, but deeper, fuller, combined with something she couldn't recognize. But she understood the language, she heard every word.

Mila looked around for Mr. Henry or someone or anyone, but she seemed to be alone in the space, the clouds rolling out under her feet, the buildings tiny below her.

"Not until today," she said.

"Do you know where you are? Do you know what this place is?"

Mila looked around the setting, breathed in the air that felt as though it should taste like apricots or honey. "I guess home. But isn't that the question I'm supposed to ask? Isn't that what Mr. Henry told me?"

"True," the voice said. "And you are right. This is your home."

"Where is it?" Mila asked. "What solar system has three suns? I barely made it through college astronomy." She tried to keep her voice light and unconcerned and slightly jaded, but her hands were shaking. She clasped them together, breathed in deeply, trying to hold her thoughts in place.

"Cygiria," said the voice. "One hundred and forty-nine light-years away. Or, at least, away from Earth."

Mila took this in, and then stopped moving, her breath, her blood, her thoughts frozen. *From Earth?*

"Where are we right now?" she asked. "Have you taken me somewhere? Am I close to Cygiria?"

Without making a sound, the voice seemed to chuckle, a horrible knowing in the sound. And then there was a pause, a beat, a shift in sound.

"No, we aren't close to Cygiria. These images are but memories."

"Whose memories?" Mila asked.

"Your memories," the voice said.

Mila felt her mouth open, her thoughts still. Her memories. How old had she been in the ship? How could she have noticed the city like this if she'd only been a toddler? She was going to ask the voice this question and so many others, but before she could, it interrupted her.

"You haven't been contacted by anyone else?" it asked.

"What do you mean?"

"Please try not to be so slow. Your life on Earth has shut down almost all your powers, but you are a big girl now. Try to keep the pace. Try to remember who you are. What you can do."

"Screw you," Mila said, her words coming out before she had a chance to shut down, swallow them back. "I don't have to keep pace with you. You are interrogating me, remember? You've taken me here. You've pulled me away from Garrick."

The voice was silent again, and Mila knew she'd crossed the line she'd wanted to stay clear of. She was supposed to be protecting Garrick. This was about getting him back. Keeping him safe.

"Okay. Okay," she said quickly. "The answer is no. No one has tried to contact me. I don't know who else could. The only weird things that have happened to me have been meeting Garrick, seeing Mr. Henry's head turn into earthquakes, and falling into a public restroom vortex and ending up here. I think I'm fast enough to remember all that."

The voice laughed, an eerie, smooth sound like snakes sliding against silk. "Maybe this air is helping you after all. Who knows what you will be able to do given time?"

Mila clasped her hands again, tried not to shiver, clamping her thighs together to keep from falling off her chair. Time. She'd had too much of it at so many different times that she'd squandered it, rushing past moments that could have changed this one. If she'd just stayed focused. If she'd just hung in there with the teasing or hurt or boredom or pain, maybe this situation wouldn't be unfolding right now in front of her like a weird nightmare. Maybe if she'd behaved better, Garrick would be sitting across from her at her parents' house and she could have done everything differently. No touching hands. No learning that they were the same, related, twins. No sex. No love. No falling into vortices. Instead, she'd be at her studio right now, twisting blue felt over a layer of cerulean acrylic, waiting for her professor James MacNaught to tell her, "It is a slight contrast, but . . ."

She should have been smarter, just like the voice said.

"Oh, how sweet your thoughts are," said the voice. "And slightly sad. Life does not unfold in a neat line. How do you think it is that we are here together now? But I suppose you can't quite comprehend what I am saying. You've become so linear."

"What do you want with me, then," Mila asked, "if I am so linear and boring and worthless? Like Mr. Henry said, why do you bother? What did you want with this entire planet? How could you who are so, well, perfect need them, need us, for anything?"

She moved her hand to indicate the world just under her feet. "Why did you want to ruin this, ruin us, if we are so linear and slow and useless?"

The voice laughed its slick laugh again, and then laughed even louder, the room or auditorium or cage filling with the sound. "We have the two of you now. There are only a few more that we truly need. And we will have what this entire world couldn't give us. Refused to give us. Not even as we did this."

As the voice spoke, the scene below Mila's feet changed, the orange turning amber, umber, brown, black, the buildings no longer reflecting light, the green suddenly shadow. And then came the explosions, the silent plumes of buffeted curling black smoke that tore down everything, leaving, finally, nothing. And that's what Mila saw as the smoke curled away. Nothing. Only the flat landscape of the destroyed.

"And even when we had them," the voice said. "Even when we took them one by one and extracted what they wouldn't share, they refused to tell us about you. To show us where you were. So we waited for our searchers to find you. Or at least that's what you would understand. We simply were there until you appeared, without us even really asking. Now all we have to do is wait until the rest follow suit."

Mila listened, waited to understand, feeling some kind of knowing circling her thoughts. Somehow, she saw a pie, a time pie, something large and flat and full, everything happening all at once. Time wasn't a line. Time didn't happen forward or backward or in the moment. In this pie, the past, present, and future were happening all at the same time. Here, the future could affect the past, the present could change the past. The past could be changed to make a different future.

"Ahh," said the voice. "Yes."

Her breath caught in her throat, Mila saw that they could be waiting for them back in the time before she and her siblings ever got on board the spaceship. The voice and the people or creatures or *things* it represented could finally get them before there was an escape. She wouldn't be an orphan on Earth—she'd be a slave to a force that wanted to use her.

Mila's thoughts popped, raced, and she wanted to jump up and run through the clouds to save her early self, save her early family. Save the mother who held her in soft arms. It wasn't too late. If time was a pie, there was, in fact, time.

"Ahh," the voice said again.

"So why don't you do it? Why aren't you already there?"

The voice was silent, and Mila knew. They really needed her and her kind to do anything.

"Time for sleep," the voice said, and even though Mila tried to keep her eyes open, loath to let go of the memory of the orange scene, she felt her body relax, her eyes shut, her brain slowly relax its worry, its fear, and she was asleep.

It wasn't the movement that woke her up, but a smell, something familiar and known, like straw or morning air or saltine crackers. A smell that was light and known and comforting. Mila tried to move, but she was trapped, her arms pressed against her body by something—rope or cord or tie—her legs immobile.

And then, there was not just the light, bright smell, but a sound, a flicker of movement at the corner of the room like wings or the thinnest of paper being thrown or the slight crush of eggshells. Everything about the disturbance was light and calm, and she knew that it wasn't made by the voice from earlier or from the Mr. Henry facsimile.

Who is it? she thought. "Who are you?"

Shhhh, someone thought, and Mila realized that along with the thought, she was picking up personality—someone who was nervous, scared, really, but smart, quick, and clever. He knew the size of the room, Mila's exact location, the magic that was holding her down.

Stop guessing, he thought. *I'm going to get you out of here, but you have to keep still. Don't think. Just wait.*

Okay, Mila thought, stilling her thoughts, letting the stillness and torpor of sleep fill her. She wanted to get out of here, she wanted to save Garrick, so she let her mind fill with gray, let her body pull in and back until she felt nothing, heard nothing.

And then she is dreaming again, back at the orange world. Her world. There she is watching the glinting golden buildings stream by as she—as she travels through the air. Who is she with? She turns to the person next to her, and it's the little boy from the dark place.

"Who are you?" she asks him, but she knows now that she's almost too little to speak. The boy pats her head, lets his small fingers touch her kneecap. He laughs, and Mila smiles, looks toward the front of the car at the adults. They are laughing, too, talking about something Mila understands but doesn't really need to know about, the patter of adult sound she's accustomed to. All she wants to know is who the boy is and why they are so happy. And it is only at the end of the dream that she is able to turn the other way and see the little girl, the one who has always been there, too. Oh, she is so small! Smaller than Mila, and she's asleep,

160   *Jessica Inclán*

her head bent at an angle that would pain an adult, crooked like a discarded Raggedy Ann doll. But she is breathing lightly, the crown of her head resting against Mila's shoulder.

"Now," the voice said, and Mila felt her entire body lift out of the invisible bonds that had held her down.

"Hold on," he said, and she knew he didn't mean hold on to him, not that she could see him in the darkness. These words were not said in the same way Garrick had used them during those last minutes before he vanished. No, this man meant hold on to herself, and in a second, she knew why. It was as if she was being flung by a giant catapult through heavy air, her body pushing and flying at the same time. And somehow, there seemed to be something supporting her, holding her from either side of her body. Even though she certainly had never had this flinging experience before and Lord knows, she'd never been away from Earth, learned about the destruction of her home planet, or lost someone she loved to aliens ever before, she had a slight, consistent feeling that everything might be better now because of this support, this man's voice, this man's actions.

You could be wrong, thought another voice, a woman's. *He could be the psychopath he seemed to be becoming before all this started.*

Shhh, thought the man. *We aren't out of here yet.*

And if history serves, it will be a close call this time, too.

Kate, the man thought.

Yes, my love? Kate thought. *Yes, Michael my sweet? Could we please just escape? We have a guest with us.*

Mila wanted to laugh as she listened to their banter, but something in the feel and dialogue between them made her sad. Even though she felt their anxiety and fear, there was an undercurrent of satisfaction and happiness just from being together, even as they rescued her. Just from being side by side. And Mila knew that they were connected by and through the same kind of energy as Garrick and she were. But these two were together. And she had absolutely no idea where Garrick was. Or where she could find him. Or if he was even still alive. He might have pissed off the voice. He might have fought back. These two had not found him.

Michael is right. Don't worry, thought Kate. *Or go ahead and worry, but not yet. We are going to help. And we are going to find him. We are going to find all of them. And then all of us will change everything.*

Chapter Seven

Garrick wasn't sure if he was awake or asleep. He could feel his body, the long plane of his back as he lay on something hard, the tingle of his skin from the cold, crisp air, the rolling emptiness of his stomach. But he could not open his eyes. He tried, but they felt glued, trapped together, his only view a grainy black. He tried to turn over, but it was as if he were being held down by ropes. The only thing he could do, really, was listen, and that was proving as temporarily useless as everything else. From what he could discern he was awake, but trapped in the middle of somewhere cool and empty.

A lot of damn good that did him.

And the thing Garrick knew the most clearly was that Mila was gone. He'd lost her. One second she was holding his hand, and the next, he was being flung to this place, where he'd been held for what seemed like days. As he lay pinned down like a bug on a board, he conjured her: her soft light hair in his hands, her face next to his, her voice at his ear, telling him what she did at least initially. "Yes."

Oh, when she said yes. Oh, when she put her arms around his neck and pushed her soft body against his. After all the years he had spent alone, hiding his ability, afraid that someone would spot him for the freak that he was and strap him down just like this and put electrodes on his head and fry his mind one more time, he was not going to let her acceptance, love, beauty, and fire go without a fight. He needed to find her so that they could finish what they had started. He needed to get back to the place where she would hold him again, be with him, live her life with him.

"Goddammit!" Garrick cried out against the grainy blackness. "Let me go!"

That might be arranged, thought a voice. *But first you need to be of some great service to us. If you are, well, then maybe we can discuss your release.*

"What do you want from me? And who the hell are you? Are you people like Gertie? The woman from the park? Or are you those slippy-slidey people? Whatever in the hell those are."

"I see that you would rather speak," the voice said aloud, the room echoing with his sound. "No, we are not like Gertie. But she does guard our portal, whether she knows it or not."

"So if you can create a portal why do you need me?" Garrick pulled against his bonds, tried to open his eyes, thought of Mila. Her smell washed over him, a waft of vanilla, something citrus, a drop of lemon oil, a squeeze of grapefruit.

"There are just some things you will never be able to figure out. None of you have. Those that are left."

Garrick yanked upward, an invisible rope against his chest. "None? None who? Mila? Where is she? What have you done with her?"

There was silence, and in the no-sound, Garrick heard something he wasn't supposed to, a slice of anger, wistfulness, irritation, frustration. He saw the image of air, of movement, of escape. Something in his body relaxed, his heart opened, closed, held still, even as he knew there was no way this was over.

"She is none of your concern right now," the voice said. "What should concern you is how you will help us. And then how you can get what you want."

What I want, Garrick thought to himself and to the voice. *What I want is to be free. What I want is to know who I am. What I want is to know where I came from and what I should be doing with the talent that I have. What I want is to be with Mila, now and forever. That's what I want. Can you give that to me? Can you promise me that I can have all that? If you can, then I will do everything you ask.*

There was a pause in the dialogue, in the thoughts, and the voice sighed, laughed a low, soft, ugly laugh. *If we could promise you all of that, wouldn't we give that to ourselves?*

Garrick breathed in quickly. "What do *you* want?"

For a moment, there was nothing but the darkness behind his closed lids, and then Garrick thought to blink, and would have several times if he were really seeing the images flickering before him. Everything was bright, light, golden, orange, crimson. He wanted to step back, to cover his eyes. His heart was pounding under the cage of his ribs, sweat trickling down his sides, his breath in quick hard pants.

"Where is this place?" he asked. *Where have you taken me?*

There was no verbal response, only the flash of silver, a landscape of cities, a swirl of vehicles floating—not driving—around the tall metal shapes. Three amazing orbs of heat and light shone in the sky, everything drenched in yellow.

"A world? A place?"

Without answer, the voice went farther into the image, floating above the scene and then diving into one of the buildings. There Garrick landed in the vision of a large room, in the midst of a meeting. All those attending seemed to be focused on a panel of speakers who sat at what looked like a golden dais. Those who were speaking and those who listened were all dressed in the shades of the landscape: orange, red, pink, green, gold, brown. Just looking at them made Garrick want to squint, just as if he were taking in the first bright image.

For an instant, Garrick wanted to ask the voice questions, but instead, he walked through the scene, looking at the people. And they were people. Just like anyone he'd met his whole life, the life he'd lived on Earth. None of the people here seemed to be aliens with secret hands or feet growing in strange places. No one with lumpy heads like that freak Mr. Henry. But people.

And yet—there was something he recognized in the room. It wasn't anything he could see, but instead, something he could feel. A current of energy that was the same beat and pulse as his own blood, a strand of electricity that connected everything, everyone. These weren't strangers. These were his people. These were people like Mila.

This is not a case of live and let live, one of the men at the dais was thinking. As he did, Garrick noticed words in a language he knew but did not know pop up on tiny gray screens that sat on the tables or were held in people's hands.

This, he continued, *is about self-preservation.*

A woman stood up, her hands out, her mouth still. *But they want more than they say. They want what we have. They want our powers. They want our bodies. They want our air and our trees and our longevity. They want everything. What is worse, they want our children. The ones with the powers they need the most.*

In the back row, a man stood up slowly, turning to look at the audience. *If we don't let them in, we lose. If we do let them in, we lose. We can leave, and then we still lose.*

We must, at least, save the children, thought another woman. *We don't have to subject our children to our mistakes. Our mistakes for beginning a dialogue in the first place. We owe it to them. We have to give them a chance to live free. We have to get them out of here.*

There were nods, murmurs, a group leaving the room, communicating in thoughts as they left: *children, now, go, home.*

Garrick found himself hopeful, excited, tears licking the edges of his eyes.

But just as the group left the room, the image began to vibrate, shift, shake, slakey gray tiles falling from the bigger picture, leaving large gaps in the view. The people in the room began to turn from side to side, looking up in the corners of the room, pointing fingers, mouths open. Some yelled; others screamed, the sound a wicked echo in the large room. Garrick recoiled as chairs and tables flipped upward, hurled against the walls, the air humming with electricity, fire bursting and then puffing wild before extinguishing in sad, gray poofs of smoke. He could feel the power in the room, knew that all the people there were trying to use their powers, but it was as if the weight of the atmosphere were being pushed down upon their shoulders. Everything stopped, the air empty and dry and dead. And then there was nothing.

Do you want to find out about them? the voice thought.

Garrick's eyes still closed, his body pinned against the flat, hard imaginary surface, he nodded. He didn't care about anything else except finding Mila and the world of orange and flame. And if he found the people or at least knew who they were, he would know himself. Know who he was. And then he could know Mila. Completely. Totally. One hundred percent.

Yes, he thought. *I want to know everything.*

At first, he thought he was in a dream. The situation was similar to one he'd had as a child. In that dream, he'd been sitting at a long table in front of a huge book, the pages under his fingertips. His hands working the large pages, he flipped through the book, scanning each carefully before he actually realized what he was looking at. And as he began to see, he knew he was looking at his life, the past a story in pictures. There it all was again, the horror of his loneliness, the terrified looks on his parents' faces, his sojourns into the past. As the pages took him back, back, back, his vision became clearer, keener, and then he woke up, just before he got to the point that didn't make sense. Everything stopped when he arrived at the place he'd never had the nerve to go back to: his infancy, his birth, the time before he was born.

He never believed he could see what he wanted to and come back alive.

He never thought he could handle living through his life all over again.

He had always been too afraid.

Now, though, this wasn't a dream and it wasn't his ability to jump into the past that was in front of him. He was being given all of this; the voice was guiding him through a series of slowly sharpening images.

First, the world again, orange and lovely and hot.

Next, there were the cities again, spread out on this world with three suns and a huge white moon, all the buildings gleaming, everything clean and shiny.

Then he was in a roomful of people, all of them dressed as they had been in the prior vision. But this was no meeting. There was no imminent war or danger. In fact, this was like a party, everyone paired up, dancing, talking, eating.

As Garrick watched, he noticed that the pairs—and the pairs were men and women, men and men, women and women—had something connecting them, something bringing them together, an energy that Garrick could see, a waver of light, a flicker of heat, like a mirage on a hot asphalt highway. It was as if an arc of wave and particle arced up from one body to the other, holding them in proximity, knowledge, and effort. But no one was doing anything. There weren't flames or fire or smoke or sudden changes in anything. It wasn't like when he and Mila held hands

and moved through time. And then, for a second, he
felt her absence in a way that was like feeling her
near him. The space between them was huge, palpa-
ble, empty. Not like what these couples were feeling,
this way of being the second half of another. This obvious but hidden pairing.

There was a burst of laughter, two people suddenly disappearing from the room. Then poof! they
were back, bringing with them a child that others
walked over to see and "ooh" at.

Then the image shifted to a work scene, a man
and a woman at a table over what looked like an ex-
periment of some kind. There weren't any trays or
dishes or tiny burners on the table. In fact, the marble in front of them was empty save for their folded
hands. But it was clear they were working on something, and as Garrick watched them, he noticed that
something was growing on the table. But not really
growing. That was the wrong word. Emerging.
Sparkling gold from out of nowhere into a pile in
front of the woman. And as the image strung out, the
pile grew and grew.

And then, just as it had appeared, it disappeared,
and somehow, Garrick knew it was the man who had
made it so.

We aren't whole, Garrick thought.

No.

We need each other to do the opposite part.

Halves.

And can we do anything?

*When you are properly paired. Like you and the woman,
your twin.*

Twin? Garrick thought.

Your other half, the voice thought. *In power. Twins in*

thought and action. But opposites. You know that. Otherwise, you wouldn't be here with us now.

The images of the people at the marble table flickered and passed, and another took its place and another, each with couples doing things in opposition. Apparating and disapparating. Causing fire and putting it out. Changing the weather to storm and then making it clear. Like a strange deck of cards, the images flipped past so quickly and so fast, Garrick felt sick. Here was where he came from. Here were the people who were like him and Mila. Here was the place where his whole life would have made sense.

How could they have just abandoned him and Mila on Earth? How could they have not left someone there to tell them about being twins, about their powers? Didn't they know how hard it would have been to survive? To not go crazy? To not wish every day to be dead? To find a way somehow to keep going?

Garrick thought about the last few years of his "normal" life, the way he pulled back, kept himself in a tight center in his body. The way he'd managed to stay far enough away from everyone so as to avoid getting hurt. If he'd revealed anything about himself, the closeness would have ended. Or worse, he'd end up strapped down on a table one more time with eager doctors standing over him trying to fix him.

How could his people, these people, have allowed that?

Garrick turned to where he imagined the voice came from. What had scared them so much that these talented, happy people would have allowed any of this to happen? It must have been the people or things that chased them. There was no other expla-

nation. And the voice knew. The voice was the cause.
The voice had to be evil.

Who are you? Garrick thought, but as he did, he
wanted to pull the question back, make it disappear
because the voice began to show him. But the showing didn't start in pictures but in a feeling. His muscles began to clench, as if everything at once went
into spasm. His nerves prickled, rows of gooseflesh
ran up and down his arms and legs. The hair on the
back of his neck rose in stiff spikes. His heart
thumped out a fast, beating message: *Run!*

Again, he tried to free himself, and again, the images started to flow. First he saw an almost luxuriant,
crawling black smoke creeping over the orange city,
moving into the streets, filling the air, covering up
the brilliant orange. What looked like spaceships or
some kind of flying vehicles spit into the air and
twirled away, escaping the smoke. But not everyone
made it out. There wasn't time. As the smoke filled
the landscape, Garrick knew he was hearing the cries
of thousands. Maybe millions. He felt pain, the hard
press of something implacable against bone, the
dizzying darkness of death. He saw blood, the heat of
life pooling on floors. He felt fear scurrying like a rat
into the darkness.

And then he felt nothing.

His heart pounded against his ribs, his breath
short and tight in his throat.

Why show me this? he cried. *Why let me know what you
did? Why should I help you? Why do you need my help
when you can kill us all? What could I possibly do that you
can't?*

The last image was of stillness. The buildings were
still there, the suns glowed hot and bright in the sky.

But nothing else moved. No vehicles. No people. And then the images disappeared, the sounds of the dying fading into the echo of the hollow room.

We can do this all over again. We can kill all the people on your new home planet just to make sure you are all gone. All you orphans. But we want you.

You need us, Garrick thought. *There's something about us—we have something you don't.*

Without another word, lights went on, though there was nothing electrical about the light. It was a stark, radiant white, that shone almost blue on Garrick. He blinked, realizing he could open his eyes again. And then he wished he couldn't.

In front of him were what could have been people or should have been people. Maybe they had been at one point. He could see in their flickering forms a semblance of bone and blood and tissue. But they were see-through, wraiths, wisps of form. They moved like ghosts, like clouds, like the tiny glassfish in his fifth grade class aquarium, their spines visible from brain to fin.

Garrick almost laughed, his mind casting about for answers. He remembered a *Star Trek* episode where a group of aliens had evolved to such a level that all that was left of them were their pulsing brains. Those terrible aliens had wanted the crew's bodies. They'd forgotten how it was to be in the flesh. They missed gravity, the pressure of the atmosphere against their skin. They wanted to press up against each other and be real.

We need your magic, the voice said.

And now Garrick saw that the voice came from one of the forms. A heart pounded in the middle of his chest, two black eyes darkened a pale, almost-face.

We always have, the now-body said. *You have never wanted to help us.*

So you killed everyone? To make us pay?

We didn't kill everyone. And all we wanted to do was make you listen.

Garrick wished he was free, and then he was, his body falling to the ground, his limbs loose. He pushed his body to a sitting position and stared at the forms before him, wishing he was able to use his power. How much easier to go back into the hell of his whole life than live through this time. He'd take every second again, every strange doctor visit and every terrible procedure. The knowledge of all this death, this massacre was worse. Everyone was dead. Her real parents. His. The true parents they would never know. Family and friends, the world they would never live on. And then there were the siblings she had and maybe he did as well. Scattered to the winds.

I can't make you flesh, Garrick thought. *I can't give you what you need.*

No, thought the form. *But you and your twin can give us time. And there are others who have what we need.*

Garrick blinked. Of course. Time. He'd been cavalier with time, knowing he could rewind when he needed to. But it was what everyone else craved. There was either not enough or too much. People lived so fast through it that they forgot to pay attention. They moved so quickly that they ruined things before they realized.

And these flickering forms in front of him had done something to themselves so heinous that their only hope was to take over the people who could help them.

But it didn't make sense.

If all you need is time, why not just find Mila and me? Why destroy everyone? Why hurt the rest of the world?

There is more to fix than you know. We need much more than time.

But if you can stop my magic, why can't you make it yourself?

The form shook his pale, ghostly head. *You don't know anything.*

Garrick wanted to fight back, to disagree. But the form was right. A week ago—no, a month ago, he hadn't known anything about these disgusting beings and their murderous anger. No. Garrick thought he'd be living out his life in his twenty-first-floor office, looking out over San Francisco and trading other people's money. He thought he'd be going out with Jim and his aunt Linda and meeting women he could sleep with when he wanted to. He imagined himself living out his life in his apartment alone, unable to talk with another person about his life.

And then he met Mila.

And then everything changed.

You can find her again, said the voice. *And bring her back.*

Where is she? Garrick thought. *What have you done with her?*

But the form didn't answer. Instead, it and three others moved closer to him, holding something black and twisty and disgusting. Something slippy-slidey. Something that undulated in the form's hand.

You are going to find her and bring her back. You won't come back here until you have her.

Before he blacked out, Garrick was surprised to see that the forms really did have hearts, round wet organs that beat in their chests just like his. As they held him down and hovered over him—the black, twisting thing writhing in the form's scrawny claws— he watched the red pulse move blood in highways through their bodies, watched the *beat, beat* of their pulses as they touched him with their horrible hands.

The last thing he remembered was the form's voice incanting in his ear.

You will find her and bring her back. You will find your twin and give us what we want.

Chapter Eight

Mila hung in the energy bubble Kate and Michael held her in, half dozing, half dreaming. For as long as she could—riding on the bumps and turns and spins of traveling through the utter, rolling black carpet of space—she fought back her old dream, knowing that seeing the dark space only confused her now. What she did know was that they were all orphans, the remnants of an entire world, nothing but a bunch of children, toddlers, and babies, the only ones to survive the attack. The only ones saved.

It hurt too much to think about her mother, the woman who held her so tightly in sad arms. Mila didn't want to feel the lull of the gentle ship as it took them to Earth and the rest of their confusing lives. She didn't want to think about how many ways her life had been forever changed by the slow crawl of black smoke across an orange landscape.

And to think of home—Adair, Paul, Nidia, Mr. Henry—made her start to breathe too quickly, knowing that Adair had likely called the SFPD, the

San Francisco Chronicle, the FBI, the CIA, Mila's school to report her sudden and strange disappearance. Even now as she was hurtled to some unknown place, Mila almost laughed, wondering if the James MacNaught she knew had the balls to stand up to Adair Adams in full primal motherhood.

"What have you done with my child?" Adair would say. "I know about you artists and your dreadful ways with models. I know what you've been thinking about each time you look at my daughter, you sick man. So help me find her. Now."

Adair would have no idea James was gay and the last one who would have wanted more than Mila's artwork.

Paul was likely tucked away in his office, worrying and making quiet calls to friends in high places. And who could possibly guess what had happened to Mr. Henry? Or who knew what Mr. Henry was?

So instead of fretting, Mila dreamed about Garrick. Not in a way that would have been helpful, of course. Not in the Garrick as a friend, a fellow "alien" or whatever they were, a companion in this craziness. Not in a way that would have helped her find him, helped her rescue him just as she was being rescued. No, her dreamy thoughts were about the smooth slip of her hand on his chest, the way he felt so perfect inside her, the crackle of connection she'd felt when he'd touched her, entered her. She'd never thought about how a man hung there, really. Not before. Oh, sure, she and her girlfriends would laugh about body parts and size, and say, "It's not the size that matters. Ha! Right. It's not the size of the ship but the motion in the ocean. Sure!"

But Garrick had moved into her in a way that was right. He fit. They fit together.

She could still hear him say quietly in her ear, "Do you want me? Tell me that you want me."

"Yes," she'd said. "Oh yes, I want you."

And he'd kissed her neck, her collarbone, her chin, her lips, and pressed inside her, sliding into her as if no one else ever had. She was his. And here was the sad and silly part. All those things that were supposed to be completely corny had been true. His kiss was right, his body was right, he was right.

And for a second, she was back in her loft, pulling Garrick close, kissing his neck, feeling his lips on her body in the same way, both of them in and out of time, nothing as important as their lovemaking.

Okay, thought Michael. *Enough of the soap opera.*

Mila startled awake, blushed, glad for the darkness around her. *Are we there? And if we are, where is there?*

Home for now, thought Kate.

And then there was a flash, the energy sling Mila was riding in cracking, opening, letting her step onto solid ground. She looked around, confused, not knowing if she was back on Earth or out wherever she had been before. Or maybe she hadn't been anywhere but Earth, all of this just some kind of alternative universe.

Oh, you left Earth, Michael thought, and then both he and Kate stepped down next to her, all three of them outside a short, squat, beige building. A slight breeze moved gently over her skin, and she looked around, noting similar buildings placed here and there. In the distance, she saw what could have been the silhouette of a town. But there were no roads or cars or much noise, nothing but safe voices and the quiet trill of some creature in the distance. Mila knew that even if this wasn't Earth, she was safe here. Protected. She felt it.

Turning toward Michael and Kate, Mila blinked against the light and them and took in a quick breath. They were beautiful: tall and blond and lean. Kate was just two inches shorter than Michael, her eyes not quite as dark brown, flecks of green in stars around her irises. Michael's eyes were darker, and in a way, harder to see into, his thoughts hidden, her own feelings reflected back in flat, solid umber.

And that's when her stomach grumbled. The last thing she remembered eating or not eating was a piece of cheesecake at her mother's house just before the terrifying Mr. Henry experience.

"Well, let's get you something to eat. You might not recognize it as food. But it will keep your body from cannibalizing itself." Kate smiled, putting a hand on Mila's shoulder. "You've been through a lot."

"What, exactly," Mila asked, "have I been through? I'm not quite clear on the concept. I was dreaming so much, I could have made up the whole thing. Especially that damn voice. Not to mention how I got here in the first place. And where are we?"

They started walking toward the entrance to the building, Michael chuckling. "It's always a shock. I remember wondering if I had just finally gone psychotic. After the years of creating energy fields for fun, I thought my mind had finally snapped. Or maybe my family put me in isolation to keep me out of the way."

"So you were caught—or you were with the voice,

too? At that place? You saw everything they showed about the planet? The destruction?" Mila asked, looking back and forth between Kate and Michael.

"I wasn't," said Kate. "Michael and I found each other on Earth. But we have pulled others out. Like you."

Michael nodded. "We've seen the story."

Mila felt her chest empty, her heart flit against her ribs. "How many of us are there? There are people looking for us? And—and?" She stopped talking, thinking about the dark space and all the children next to her. If she could only find the blond-haired boy and girl. Now that she knew who Garrick was, she just needed them for everything to make sense.

Michael and Kate looked at her, and Michael brushed his hand through his long blond hair. The light fell onto Kate's glossy locks, blowing strands forward over her shoulders. They were both blond. Maybe everyone was. This was an impossible situation. How could she ever find the boy from her dream?

"Mila," Kate said, her eyes so kind, Mila felt herself want to break apart weeping. "You're hungry. You need to eat first. And then we can tell you everything."

Michael pushed open the door of the building, letting Mila and Kate walk in first. From the outside, this building looked like something a government would hastily build to house a Social Security or welfare office. But inside, the air smelled of toast, everything light soft browns and tans and beiges: the walls, the fabric on the sofas, the pillows on the couches.

"Is one of us Martha Stewart?" Mila asked, her words cracking through the pain around her heart.

Kate laughed. "Well, maybe collectively."

Mila turned to her. "What do you mean?"

Kate seemed about to answer, when Michael took her arm and Mila's, leading them farther into a building, stopping in a room with a large round table in the center. A woman worked at a counter at the back of the room—a kitchen or something, though Mila couldn't see a stove or refrigerator or even pantry shelves.

But it didn't matter. The room was awash with lovely smells, the savory waft of cumin and peppers and onions and roasted chicken. Mila breathed in, her stomach reacting to the smells with a long rumble.

"There is no way we can tell you everything at once," Michael said. "It will be weirder than how it was living on Earth. So let's eat and then we can talk."

Together, they walked to the table and sat down. Mila felt uncomfortable, as if she were at home waiting for Nidia to serve her. How could she have come this far and still ended up acting the same, waiting for others to take care of her?

But Michael and Kate—neither of whom seemed to have grown up in any way close to Mila's Pacific Heights existence—seemed unconcerned, and when the woman at the back of the room came with a tray of food (that didn't remotely resemble a chicken or any animal but rather an unrecognizable and lumpy mound of stuff) and drink and set it down in front of them, they both smiled.

"Thank you, Naomi," Kate said, and it was then that Mila realized the woman wasn't really a woman, but something else. It wasn't that she was a woman, but that she wasn't real, flickering a little, her body visible but somehow transparent, thin to the eye, not really there at all. The woman stood, her gaze not at but through the three seated at the table. What was she? She was a—a. . . .

She's a computer program, Michael thought. *Sort of beats Windows, huh? Blows out Google-dot-com, too.*

A computer program? With arms? And feet? Mila thought back, almost gasping. *Arms and legs that can actually move, carry things?*

Kate's next thought was interrupted when the computer program woman's body flickered and then seemed to depixilate and disappear in a crackle of sound and electricity.

For about a second, Mila wanted to know everything about this amazing program, but then as suddenly, she didn't care. The lumpy nonfood smelled wonderful, and she picked up her fork and began to eat, closing her eyes as she did, tasting all the flavors she had smelled and even feeling the texture of juicy meat, sautéed vegetables, and creamy sauce. She took in forkful after forkful, not realizing that she was almost vibrating, humming as she ate, lost in her gastronomic reverie until Kate and Michael laughed.

"I remember how that feels," Michael said. "The Neballats—"

"Who?" Mila asked, looking up from her food.

"The voice. The ones that had you," Kate said.

"I call them the see-throughs," Michael said. "But that doesn't go over too well. Nebs when I can. But Neballat is the politically correct term."

"See-through?" Mila said.

"Yeah. They are. I mean, like, literally. And that's

why they don't remember too much about hunger. They don't have much to sustain. I was there for at least two days before they thought to give me food."

Mila listened, took another bite, chewed, and swallowed. She picked up a glass of what looked like beer and sipped it, swallowing down a wheaty but nonalcoholic drink.

"So, where do I start?" She put down her glass and her fork, not quite full but ready for answers. "I know what they showed me and I know what I can do. What Garrick can do. But the rest is dreams and guesses and imagination."

"Tell me about the dream," Kate said. Mila nodded, and told of the dream she had kept a secret for so long, never mentioning it to a soul until she recounted it to Garrick. For a second, she was in the warm darkness with her people, the people she understood now better than she ever had. All the connections, all the sadness, all the fear. And then she felt Kate's hand on her arm.

"That's it. We all were given that dream. Or a form of it. Or an image," Kate said. "Some had it more vividly than others. Some unfortunately didn't get it fully, just a vague recollection or a feeling like déjà vu. And it wasn't really a dream but what happened to us on the ship as we escaped."

"We were sent away to live, right?" Mila asked. "They tried to save us."

"And they did," said Michael. "It's just that there wasn't enough time. Some of us went to Earth, and there are other planets and other children. But we don't know where yet. They were running, always running from the Neballats and there was no plan."

. Mila looked down at what remained of her food, her stomach suddenly scratchy and upset. "How could they just leave us?"

There was a silence in the room, nothing but Kate's and Michael's light breathing and the throb of Mila's angry heart.

"They had no choice. You know that." Michael stared at her. "Think about it, Mila. What would you have done? What would you have known that they didn't?"

Mila touched a crumb with her index finger and brought it to her tongue. This was something that she knew. Taste, sensation, feeling. She understood her need to create, to put images on canvases, to use color and form and shape. She knew how to move time. She knew her body. She knew Garrick's body, the sounds of his breathing, the feel of his skin. She knew the way his energy moved through her, letting them move through time as if it were just a doorway. But she did not want to understand how her mother and father and family could have left her marooned on a planet she did not belong on. She refused to wrap her head around the idea of all the adults leaving all the children to fend for themselves.

Mila looked into Kate's and Michael's eyes, wishing they would join her in her outrage. Her moral indignation. But they just watched her, and in their soft gaze, she realized that there was nothing else her parents and all the parents on their world could have done.

"What happened to them?" Mila asked quietly. "Are they all dead?"

Michael sat back in his chair. "We don't really

An odd melodic voice filled the room, and as it did, the hair on the back of Mila's neck flicked to attention, her body responding to the sound. Her eyes filled with tears and she turned to Michael and Kate. "That's our language."

"Yeah," Michael said. "It's beautiful. But listen to it, Mila."

And she did, the wave and flow of it forming in her brain, backing up in a confusion of utterances. But then, like a dam breaking, the words began to stream, make sense, telling her the story she'd always wanted to know, telling her a story that was very hard to believe. And then the screen did something very surprising. Or not really surprising, Mila realized, as there wasn't one thing in the past day that two days before she wouldn't have categorized as either a miracle or totally wacko.

There the screen was in front of her, seeming to hover and then morph in shape and size, sliding down into the chair next to her and very slowly filling with color and texture until it resembled a man. And then it was a man, his arm resting on the table. He smiled at her, and Mila's heart ached, knowing somehow that this man was related to her. He felt like an uncle. A father. A local wise man. A person of her kind, through and through.

"Mila," the man said. "What do you want to know?"

Mila looked back at Michael and Kate, but their faces were obscured in darkness, the bright screen-man taking over the room with his luminescent glow.

"I," she began. "I want to know if we are human. People. I want to know where we came from."

The man smiled, sat up straight. "Cygirians are human. Just like the people who raised you on Earth.

We came from the same inspiration, but we seem to have been on Cygiria so much longer than those who are on Earth. But like the people on Earth, Cygirians have a multitude of ways of explaining our creation, needing stories to explain or rationalize something we can never truly understand. We have gods and we have belief systems, many of which are contradictory, many of which are the same. But hundreds of years ago, when we first began to explore space, we found Earth. Once we did, we realized that we had the same bodily requirements in terms of atmosphere and climate. We all needed to eat to stay alive. We died in the same ways. The only difference was the way we developed powers. For some reason, those on Earth don't have our powers, the matched powers, the twin energies In fact, it surprised us how little the inhabitants on Earth could do. But it was no matter. We visited, tried not to interfere, took what information we needed, and left."

Mila nodded, all of this making sense, especially now, when nothing could surprise her. "So, what about the Neballats? Why did they destroy life on Cygiria?"

The man nodded, his form wavering slightly and then coming back together, the pixels forming a body puzzle. He looked around the room, as if he were taking in information from ghosts, and then breathed in.

"They were an older race than we. They've lived thousands of horrible years in the condition they are in, destroyed by their own inattention to their environment, their bodies twisted by their need for intellect and power. They forgot to care for what was sustaining them in the first place. As they grew their war machines, their businesses, they forgot about the water, the air, the earth."

Behind the man, another screen slipped gently down the air of the room and began to flicker. At first, Mila didn't know what she was seeing, some pencilly figures on the screen moving around. What were they? Cartoons? But then as she watched, the image grew tighter, neater, finer, and she realized that the thin, one-stroke figures were people. Or had been people. Slippy-slidey people. As the image opened up, showing the figures moving through landscapes and situations, she saw how their bodies clung to their bones, their skin invisible, their organs like parchment. And everything all around them was darkness, a swirl of black. There was no sun in their sky, no warmth, no heat. No wonder they wanted Cygiria, the warm, butter-orange world of light.

"Horrible," Mila muttered, and the images faded, the screen blank.

The man continued. "But like we discovered with the humans on Earth, the Neballats determined that we were compatible with them. Our atmosphere could keep them alive. Our life spans were approximate to theirs. But we had two things that they did not. Bodies that were whole and healthy. And powers that could give them back what they had destroyed through millennia of misuse. They had destroyed their environment, their bodies, their powers, their gifts. And then they came to us, wanting to take and not ask for help. They wanted us to repair their world and their flesh. And then when we refused to be enslaved, they struck out, killing us, the only ones who could help them."

Behind the man, another screen appeared, full of more of the images that Mila had seen while with the voice. There was the insidious black smoke curling through the buildings, obscuring the sun, killing everything.

She put her hands to her eyes, her mouth, trying to ignore the beating of her heart. So much loss. Her entire family. Generations of relations, a trail of connections that could have explained who she was. After all the years of not knowing how she fit into anything, the answers were here. But not completely, the full story wiped out by a race of invisible specters with too much power and too much need.

And she could see for the first time how the failings of Adair and Paul weren't failings at all. They'd been given a child and a story and thought it was all true. Somehow they had ingested a story and believed it enough to forge the truth. Adair's perfectly crafted world was as real as the computer image talking to Mila now. Clear, apparent, as thin as air.

All Mila's suffering on Earth had been nothing compared to this.

And there was no end to her loss in sight. She was without Garrick, her twin, her power source. The one who made her complete.

Behind the man, the screen flared into use again, showing the evacuation of Cygirians, the dash to space, the fighting, the rush to save the children. And then there were no more images, just a slow fading to gray.

The man looked at Mila, waiting. She knew there was so much more she didn't know, she'd never be able to take it in now. A whole civilization had just come and gone in front of her. Millions of people (and they were people) were gone, just like that. Until about a few hours ago, she'd thought that humans were the only race of sentient creatures in the universe, and here were two others. Here she was, an alien.

More importantly, she'd learned that there was a reason for her existence, for her being alive, for the amazing connection she had with Garrick.

Mila shook her head. Taking in her decision, the computer-man disappeared, too, and the room opened into light.

"So, what do we do?" Mila asked Michael and Kate. "How do we save Garrick? And how do we find the rest of them?"

"One at a time," Kate said. "Just like with you."

"One at a time? Aren't there thousands of us?"

"Yes," said Michael. "And if we are lucky enough to find two at once, then bingo. But for now, this is what we have."

Mila stood up. "First Garrick."

"Of course," said Michael. "But before we start, you need to meet the others."

Mila nodded, breathed in, and followed them out of the room, down the hall, toward all the people who would change her life.

Chapter Nine

He was moving. He was in a ship. He was going forward. All of this was like an old dream, something he remembered in images and symbols. Dark. Metal. The rush of stars.

Or was this even his dream? He couldn't tell. He felt in pieces, parts, bits, the only constants the whirling whoosh in his head and his certain knowledge that he was moving through the deep silence of space, but he didn't know who he was. When this trip first started, a name, a word, a thought kept coming to him. Something that sounded warm on his mouth, made him want to make a sound, to moan lightly into the empty shell he was sitting in. But now he couldn't even remember that name, that sound, that feeling. All he knew was that he was moving. Going forward. His head ached. His body hurt, and he'd had this feeling before, so long ago, back when somebody else put something on his head to hurt him. How many times had he awakened to ache and muscles cramped and sore, his jaw like wood? But as he thought about the pain, something softened, slid softly around his thoughts, and he was comforted, lulled, put fast asleep.

When he woke up, he sat straight in the chair, blinking. He waited for information to wash over and through him. *Yes*, he thought, *of course.*

He stood up, moved toward what looked to be a door, and waited. Something was going to let him out of this place. And then he was to go—he was to go to her. Bring her back. Her. She. The one.

He blinked, knowing that her name might be caught in his mind, but it wasn't. In fact, he felt something slam shut, close, lock.

Find her, the voice said, and it was the voice. His voice. The voice that promised him everything. He wasn't exactly sure what the promise was, but he knew that if he did this one thing perfectly right, something very good would happen. He would be rewarded. He would have what he needed.

But what did he need?

He wanted to shake his head free of the voice, the control, but then that urge was gone, evaporated like smoke.

Something flashed wide and open in front of him, and he gasped, reeling back against the bright light of this beautiful place. Everything was orange, amazing, warm.

Home? he thought.

No, thought the voice. *Not home. This is home.*

And as quickly as seconds earlier, the scene flashed into gray, black, the acrid cling of smoke in his nose.

Do you want this? the voice asked.

No. No. He knew this in his bones and blood. He

wanted orange. Warmth. The same feeling he got from . . . from . . . her. Yes. The one.

Then go into this, the voice thought, and the scene changed again.

He knew this place. This place he knew. He could name it. He recognized the sights, the smells, the taste of the air. This was home, too, a place he understood. This was a city, San Francisco. He looked up, seeing in front of him the red metal tower that he saw every morning from his office. Sutro Tower. He breathed in cypress, the quick cold gush of ocean air, a whiff of car exhaust as traffic hurtled toward the avenues, streets, freeways.

And as he watched people walking along sidewalks, some pushing strollers, others walking dogs or holding hands, his mind began to clear. He was Garrick McClellan. He was twenty-eight years old. He worked for Calder Wilken Brodden, and what he needed to do now, more than anything else, was to find the woman he loved, Mila Adams, and bring her back to this very spot. He would give her to the voice. And once he did, he could have her forever. That was the promise. As Garrick stepped out of the ship that suddenly was not there at all, he knew that nothing would stop him.

"Where on God's green earth have you been?" his aunt Linda asked. "I have . . . This is . . . Well, Garrick. After I learned that Mila Adams was missing, too. Both of you—like that. My God. Where in the world are you?"

A thread of annoyance circled Garrick's mind as he held his phone against his ear. Something made him want to throw the phone against the wall, but something else told him that this would not be productive. This act would not lead him where he wanted to go.

"I'm home. Mila and I—we went away for a couple of days. A surprise. Spontaneous, you know?"

"Surprise? Spontaneous!" his aunt cried. "You've got the whole SFPD looking for you. Paul Adams pulled some strings and even got the FBI on the case. He's a judge, you know. For goodness' sake. What were you thinking? Why didn't either of you answer your cell phones? Your mother and father are beside themselves. It was all I could do to keep them from flying in."

"Don't worry," Garrick said calmly, his words like a tape he'd heard somewhere else, somewhere before. Mother and Father weren't important. This woman was important. She could lead him where he needed to go. "Everything is fine."

"Well. My. All right. As long as you are safe. But where's Mila?" Linda asked. "Why hasn't she called her parents? Adair will have the Coast Guard involved by now."

"I dropped Mila off at her loft," Garrick lied. "She hasn't called home yet?"

"Not that I know of. I'll call Adair. I'll tell her you, at least, have called."

"Are you going to go by the house?" Garrick asked. "I think you should go there and calm Adair down first. Let's meet there. Mila can tell you the whole story of what we did during our time away."

"Some of that story is probably not ready for public consumption," Linda said, her voice lighter now, less concerned. "But you can tell me if you want to!"

The slow, smooth roundness of his thoughts whirled. Find her at home. Bring her back. Find her and bring her back and then—and then he could have what he wanted.

"Sounds great, Aunt Linda. I'll be there in a flash."

"Don't forget to call your parents," she said. "I can't wait to see Adair's face when she sees you are home. That woman is amazing when she's upset. Let's just put it this way. She's not ready to be on the cover of *San Francisco Magazine* just yet."

Garrick agreed, and clicked off the phone. All he needed to do was get to the house. Then he could keep time sliding backward until Mila showed up. And he knew she would. He wasn't sure how, but he could see her returning. Over and over again, he saw an image of her walking through the front doors, her smile wide, her arms open. In fact, since he'd returned, that was all he saw, and he wanted to see it for real. He wanted to see it now.

"Garrick McClellan, you had us completely unnerved," Adair Adams said. In the short time since he'd last seen her, Adair seemed to have aged ten years. He thought of the few things Mila had told him about her mother—her control issues, her adherence to appearance and social norms, her relentless need for Mila to succeed in school, business, and love—but all he saw now as she stood before him without makeup or her normal composure was her need for her child's safety. For her daughter to be safe.

Something inside him wanted to reach forward, hold her, comfort this woman, but then a force inside him, something stronger and more forceful, kept him back, held him still. Made him only smile gently, made his words wise and calm.

"I am so sorry that we made you anxious," he said, finding a smile on his face he didn't feel. "I promise you we had no intention of doing so."

"You know that Garrick would never have done this on purpose, Adair darling. It was just one of those impetuous, impulsive things of youth. Of love," Linda said, holding on to Garrick's upper arm as she spoke. "Mila must be just crazy about him."

"Well, really," Adair said. "The least you could have done is call us. After all those messages? Verizon and Cingular were about ready to call in the marines after Paul had words with them." Adair stared at him, her eyes fixed on his. "Where is Mila? I still haven't heard from her. Even after Linda showed up and told me she was home."

"She said she was on her way over," Garrick said, and that was when he rolled time back. Just for a minute.

"Garrick McClellan, you had us completely un-nerved," Adair Adams said, and Garrick heard himself responding to her, but as he did this time, he looked around the living room, needing to find clues. He could find no evidence of Mila's having been here before him. Or after him. Or in the future time, for that matter. But he was stuck here in this foyer, in this room, with these two women.

"Well, really," Adair said. "The least you could have done is call us . . ."

And then he slid back again, crossing the thresh-old of the Adamses' house one more time, paying attention to everything. He had to find Mila. He had to bring her back. He had to do what the voice said or—or what? His head started to throb, and he pressed the heel of his palm against his temple. All he knew was that he had to find her. Now.

"You know that Garrick would never have done this on purpose . . ." Linda talked, squeezing Garrick again and again. He wanted to push her away and run up the stairs, storm each room until he found Mila. Then he could grab her hand and they could move out of time together, without having to live through it interminably as he was now doing with these women who wanted answers to everything. He didn't need them! They were in his way. The others were the way to—he didn't know what. They would just help him have Mila from now on.

He slid back through time again, hearing Adair talk about being unnerved, and he knew that he couldn't keep living through this. It was pointless. What was he expecting to happen? Mila just come to him from wherever she'd gone to? She obviously didn't know what the voice promised him. That they could be together forever if they just went back. There would be no worries about who they were or what they could do. They would be safe and protected. For the first time ever, they would be able to be who they truly were. But only with the voice. Only.

Garrick's head throbbed, and he brought his hands to his temples and tried to rub out the incessant pain, the whirl of ache under his fingertips.

"Well, really," Adair said. "The least you could have done is call us. After all those—"

He swallowed, hoping to be able to get to the end

of this conversation. Again. There was his aunt defending him one more time. There he was trying to placate Adair, knowing he hadn't a clue about where Mila was. That was the problem.

His head went past throbbing and moved into stabbing pain. He had a hard time finding his body, moving his fingers so he could feel that his arms were still attached to his shoulders. He moved his feet, unsure if he was standing on the floorboards. His thoughts seemed to flitter and form into static, Adair's voice an electric whine in his ears.

He found himself shutting down, knowing that something would keep him upright. That something was controlling him, helping him.

Then the conversation changed. The fast clack of high-heeled shoes stirred him, and he breathed in against the pounding of his head.

"I'm going to call her one more time, and then . . ." Adair looked over at Garrick, a slight bit of fear marring her determination. "You don't look well. Something about your head. I—I think something has happened and you aren't telling me. Where is my daughter?"

"Adair, I told you. She's at her loft. She's fine."

Adair grabbed the phone, held it out to him. "I thought you said she was on her way over. Get her on the line. Now. Then I will stop worrying."

Garrick gritted his teeth, anger taking over his body. Rage jagged through him, and he could almost feel the woman's neck in his hands. So easy. It would be so easy to squeeze her silent, shut her down, shut her up.

"Are you going to call or not?" Adair asked.

"Oh, Garrick," Linda said. "Just give Mila a call. Then we can put this all behind us. Move on, as I say."

He turned to his aunt and saw that for once, the upbeat, often forced gaiety in her expression was gone. She was scared, her face falling into fear despite her many surgical procedures. He was scaring them both. This situation couldn't go on. He couldn't keep shifting back into the past. He had to do something.

And then it was as if Garrick were wearing a choke chain, a vicious owner yanking him toward Adair and the phone.

Don't let this happen, the voice whispered. *Silence them. You need time before Mila comes back to the house. You need to be waiting. You need to get rid of them.*

"She is probably in some ditch somewhere, and you—" Adair stopped, her face a sudden mask of horror. "You. You are—you would have brought her here if you really knew where she was. You would have been able to tell me more."

Garrick moved even closer to her, feeling his blood pulse under his jaw.

"Don't get any closer to me. Linda! I'm going to call the police! Where is Henry?" Adair began to walk backward, the phone behind her back. "Nidia! Nidia! Call the police. Linda, run outside. Find—"

He heard Linda gasp, protest, and then turn, the door flinging open as she ran outside. And then Garrick had Adair's wrist, the bones so fragile, so easy to snap.

"Let me go!" Adair said, her face betraying her now, her lips quivering, her eyes bright, wide, wet. "Take your hands off me this instant!"

He wasn't sure what he was going to say, two different sentences on his tongue, but then the owner yanked the chain again.

"Put down the phone, Adair. Put it down now."

"Mila," she said. "My daughter."

"Mila is fine," he said, his hand moving up to her forearm, squeezing more tightly. "Mila is just fine. You don't need to worry about her anymore."

Outside, Garrick heard the whoop of a siren and then Linda's muffled but frantic explanation. He had to do something before Adair ruined everything. He had to go back into the past, or he had to make Adair shut up. Or both.

He moved his hand up her arm, close to her shoulder, his head beating out a plan.

Don't let her say a word. Keep her from talking.

Yes, Garrick thought. *Yes. I know what to do.*

He felt his hand slide to her neck. He wanted to tighten his grip, clamp down, shut her up once and for all. But no, he didn't. He couldn't! There was something in her eyes, the way she looked up at him that made him remember Mila. Mila! This was her mother. Or the woman who raised her. But someone who loved her nonetheless.

Do it.

Garrick's head pulsed with blood and pain, and he knew what it would be like to press so hard on her skinny neck that Adair's breath would stop. It didn't matter that she reminded him of Mila or anything else.

Now, he thought. *Now.*

But then there was a crackle of electricity, a whoosh of hot air, and Garrick felt something take his hand, wresting him out of the scene. The last thing he saw before disappearing into darkness was Adair's face—surprised, relieved, afraid—and then everything was energy and time and the hard, heavy beat of his head.

Something was twisting in his forehead like a bad dream. Or it was a bad dream, the images dark and slimy and round, the smell wet and acrid? He wanted to cry out with each tug and turn and press, but someone whispered into his ear or mind, *It's almost over. It will be okay.*

Garrick wanted to believe the voice. But he'd believed voices before, and he'd ended up with Adair Adams' throat in his hands. In his delirium of pain, he wondered how he could have done what he had. How was it that he could have gotten over to the Adamses' house and almost strangled Adair? He'd wanted to kill her. What had possessed him?

This god-awful thing is to blame, thought someone. *It's not the first of its kind we've seen.*

He couldn't place the thought, the voice, but he knew that it wasn't from the same people who'd sent him to find Mila. No, everything was different here, calm and warm and safe.

Oh, Garrick, thought a voice. And then he knew. It was Mila. He tried to open his eyes, but he couldn't, the white-hot shots of light in his head too intense.

Stop, thought another voice. *Relax. Sleep. Sleep.*

And he did.

* * *

When he woke up, he tried to blink, but his eyelids felt heavy, as if it would take all his strength to see anything.

He breathed in, sighed, and then he felt her hand on his shoulder.

"We are twins," he whispered. "Together—"

"Together we are magic," she said, and he felt her heat on his face, her breath against his lips, and she kissed him gently.

We are more than what we imagined, he thought, words too hard to push into the air.

You're my twin, my partner. My love, Mila thought. *And together we are going to do amazing things.*

Where are we? Garrick thought, feeling her kisses on his neck. He wished he could turn to her and take her in his arms, but he was so tired, thinking was almost impossible.

A safe place. With people like us. There are more of us. We aren't alone, Garrick. All that terrible aloneness. It's over.

Garrick sank back into the soft mattress he was lying on and relaxed. When the voices had shown him the destruction, he knew that some had escaped, the ones the voices wanted. But he never really thought he'd ever find them. All he'd wanted was Mila. But to know there were more of them?

Of us. More of us. And we are going to help, too, Mila thought. *We are going to find the rest of us. And then we are going to stop this. We are going to take back what is ours.*

All that's mine is you, Garrick thought. *All I want is you.*

She pressed her lips against his again, and he

knew he was dreaming, knew this was a miracle, and then he was asleep again.

As he lay with his eyes closed, he heard them talking, and he smiled, feeling something that he never had before. It was some kind of comfort, peace, joy. He didn't have to wake up knowing that he had something to hide. He didn't have to carefully orchestrate his day because he might or might not wish to move away from the present moment into something stale from the past just to avoid whatever it was: a fight with his parents, a confrontation with a fellow student, coworker, boss, friend, or a date where the woman looked at him expectantly, wanting answers to questions he could never answer for anyone.

What do you want most out of life?

How was your childhood?

What is your biggest fear?

Garrick never knew what to say, knowing that the truth would only hasten what would happen with the woman anyway—he'd run her off through inattention and unconcern. And he'd have to start all over, dreading the day that the questions would start all over again.

But now he was—he was home.

He turned, opening his eyes into sunlight. Or suns' light. He didn't know where the safe house was, really, and from what had happened to him, he knew he could be anywhere. Some faraway planet, an asteroid, a spaceship made up to look like a room with sunlight slipping through.

And for all he knew, Mila's voice could belong to someone else entirely. Or something else. Blinking, he let his eyes focus, and slowly she came into his vision, her eyes on his, her smile just her smile. It was true. There Mila was in front of him, kneeling at the bed and looking at him. The door of the room closed, and he knew that they were alone.

"Hi, there," Mila said, and he drank in her voice, the sound he'd only been able to carry around in his head, the sound that saved him through everything. Struggling a little, Garrick found the strength to sit up, pull her close, feeling her soft and warm against him. He paused for just a moment to see how his head felt, and the long, dragging ache was gone.

He stroked her arm, feeling the fine, soft hairs under his fingertips. He put his mouth on the soft curve of her shoulder and kissed it. She smelled like citrus, sugar, heat.

"That's not going to happen again," he said.

"What's not going to happen again?" she asked, her voice muffled against his neck. She kissed him back with soft kisses, letting her lips travel his jawline.

"You being away from me for more than about an hour."

"You are going to have some explaining to do with your boss," she said. "He might not understand why I am at the board meetings."

"I don't think we are going home to that old life, Mila. You know that, right?"

She looked down, shook her head. "This is so weird. All of this. I barely got over finding you. And now to find out about us being twins, paired, like—"

"Like it was meant to be," Garrick said, feeling the old truth on his tongue, not one syllable feeling like cliché. "You aren't going to be anywhere I am not. Not again."

Mila laughed, lifted her head, and kissed him on the lips. Garrick was tired, his head feeling empty and full of a light buzzing energy, but he wanted her. He had no idea what had made him do what he did or feel so terrible, but there was time for that story later. What he needed now was her skin, her body, her laughter, her pleasure. Right now, in the middle of . . . in the middle of—

"Space. We are in space," Mila said. "Our known universe has opened up since we were in high school and studied the constellations. Can you believe it, but there are things that Mr. Hedwig didn't tell me in high school."

"That's all well and good," he said, pulling her close. "But for now, *shhh.*"

Very slowly, he pulled off the simple cotton T-shirt she was wearing, closing his eyes and almost gasping when he saw her breasts. Maybe there weren't bras in space, he thought, and that was a good thing because he could touch her now. And he did, cupping her breasts and leaning down to kiss each, taking first one nipple and then the other into his mouth.

Mila moaned, and he slid his hands down to the waist of her pants. She was wearing loose-fitting pants similarly light and cotton, and he was able to push away the fabric just as easily, skimming them off her body, taking her sandals with them as he moved down her body. He had to shut his eyes against the lovely curves of her ass, the beautiful V of her. He wanted to savor her, take time with all of her, but first he needed to get her undressed. Then he needed her to be ready.

"You should be resting," she whispered.

"*Shhh*," he said again.

"You've just been through something very traumatic," she said.

"*Shhh*," he repeated, letting his finger touch her upper lip.

"We haven't even told you what it was," she said.

"*Shhh*," he said one last time, kissing the corner of her mouth.

"I didn't expect—I didn't think you . . ."

He stroked the smooth skin over her breasts with his fingertips. "You should always expect me to love you. To want to make love to you. Even under the influence of whoever they are, I did what I did for you. And I always will be able to love you. I have no choice."

Taking her by her shoulders, he pushed her gently to the bed, kissing her as he did, taking in the sweet taste of her mouth, her skin, her love. He let his entire body feel hers, feeling her flat stomach, the roundness of her hips, the smooth skin of her thighs. He took in the slight, sweet fragrance of her skin between her breasts, moving his mouth up and over the lovely swell, taking each nipple into his mouth, first one, then the other, loving how she moved under him as he did.

He kissed her again, wanting to breathe her in, all of her. Breathe in her breath, her smells, her voice, her moans, her skin itself.

And she opened to him, just like she had that first night at her loft. Just like that night, it felt as right as anything ever had. The one thing Garrick had done his entire life that felt true.

As he entered her—she was so wet, so tight, so

warm—he felt their combined heat and then he felt the tingling of time ready to shift, the push and rise of the past and the future.

Where are we going? he thought.

You mean when, my love.

But it wasn't a when, it was a where, the same in-between-time place they'd found together at the Adamses' house. When was that? A week ago? How could he have only known Mila for such a short time? It felt like centuries. But here they were again, together in the time that wasn't time, holding each other, supporting each other through their combined energy. Floating gently in the gray static, they stroked each other, moved to a rhythm that was as known as if they'd done this hundreds of times before. And that's what Garrick wanted more than anything: the luxury of having Mila over and over again, all his life, all their lives.

I love you, Garrick thought, feeling her body tighten around him.

Yes, she thought. *Oh yes.*

Garrick knew that the time they were given was a luxury, so he asked her questions he wouldn't have had they been back in San Francisco, lying in a sweet postcoital tangle in her bed or his. But he knew there wasn't time for this now, and the minutes they had pressed up next to each other were precious.

"So, what did they do to me?" he asked. "What made me follow all their orders?"

Mila sighed, ran her hand across his chest, talking into his side, her voice muffled. "It was the same kind of thing that the Neballats—"

"Neballats? That's what they are called? The ones—who've done everything?"

She nodded. "Yeah. They put in you what they put in Mr. Henry." She sat up, brushed his hair back with her hand. "They have this thing. Kate and Michael call it a simulator. I guess it simulates what a person would be like and then controls at the same time. It's alive. A live thing."

"Yuck. Sounds like a prop out of a B movie."

Mila shrugged. "If I could have made it up, I think I would have made mind control a bit more high-tech. Implants and such. But Kate and Michael—"

"Kate and Michael," Garrick said, smiling. "I'm going to meet my first aliens, and they are named Kate and Michael? Shouldn't they be called Burag and Gluck?"

"We all are aliens," Mila said, smiling back at him. "I mean, I think I knew that the first time I met you! The way you acted."

He squeezed her, nuzzling her neck. "I was trying to tell you something."

"Yeah, it was get the hell away from me. I got the message."

"I'm glad you didn't take the message to heart," he said, meaning it, holding her tight, grateful to the two aliens, Kate and Michael, who saved them both.

Mila was skimming his thoughts and picked up the thread. "They are great. And they are just like us. We come from the same planet, and they grew up on Earth, too."

"Figures," Garrick said. "No exotic, tail-wearing aliens for me."

He started to laugh, and then he remembered the Neballats. He swallowed, seeing in his mind the black dots of the escape craft leaving the planet. That terror, that fear was more exotic, more alien than he wanted.

"So," he went on quietly. "What did they do to me?"

"Mind control. Literally, in the mind. The simulator is a living thing, a creature they plant inside you. They must have one in Gertie, too. That poor woman. Anyway, they can code it with behaviors. It transmits their ideas to you, tracks your behavior, and reacts to it. You followed along with what the Neballats wanted you to find."

"You," Garrick said. "They wanted you."

"They want us tog—"

"Together," he said. "Because of our powers."

"Power. What we can do together." She nodded. "We are all like that. All of us."

He sat up, his arm around her. "I saw it. They showed it to me. The voice—the Neballats. I saw how we connect with each other. And I saw that there were so many of us. All living together on that world."

Mila rubbed a finger on the top of his hand, her body so warm, her skin the color of sunlight, of summer, of a California beach. "We belonged there. That's where we were born, Garrick. That's what our parents died fighting for."

For a moment, they were silent, and Garrick wondered at how easily he was sliding into this crazy story. He was an educated man, a man who had met the world in terms of books and art and culture and countries. He'd known the inside of crazy while being treated as a teenager, and this? Being from another planet? Having another group of people out to either kidnap or kill him? This made 100 percent total sense.

"Because it's true," Mila said. "Nothing before really was."

"So, what are we going to do?" he asked. "How do we fix it?"

Mila kissed his shoulder and then pushed herself up, her hair falling over her shoulders.

You look like a goddess, he thought.

I don't have many followers for a goddess. I think I need to improve my religion. Give it a little spice. Make it more entertaining.

You only need one follower, Garrick thought, sitting up next to her. *And I guess we have to wait for the entertainment until we do what we need to. Until we, well?*

"We need to find the rest of our people," Mila said. "We need to find the other planet where we were left."

"And then—"

"And then we figure out how to find the rest of us. And then how to fight back. Stop this now. For our generation."

Garrick ran his palm on her smooth waist, loving the feel of her smooth, silky skin, knowing that he wanted to spend all his time right here, with her, danger from genocidal aliens be dammed. "Maybe there will be other generations now. Maybe that now we finally know who we are we can go about living."

Her hair falling down around his face, Mila smiled, bent lower, kissed him, her breath sweet and soft.

"I hope there are many more generations to come. And that we could actually live together, in one place, on one planet. Have children. But, Garrick." She sat up, wiped her eyes quickly, her tears instant and strong. "They killed everyone. Everyone but us. We are all that's left of our people, and we don't even know where the rest of us are. We don't know if we have siblings left. We don't know anything."

He pulled her close. "Two weeks ago, we didn't know that we had each other. Two weeks ago, we were living our lives in San Francisco, our biggest worry how to get out of the blind date we'd been set up on by invading relatives. But in that time, we found each other, found out what happened to our planet. We know so much more. We can't give up. Not even if someone puts something absolutely disgusting in our heads."

Mila laughed a little, sniffed, bent into his shoulder.

"It must have looked just, well, violent," he said into her neck, nuzzling her, feeling himself grow aroused.

"You don't even want to know," she said. "Michael knew what to do."

"I think I know what to do, too," Garrick said, pushing her back down on the bed.

"We don't have ti—" Mila began and then stopped, her mouth covered with his, her arms moving around his neck, pulling him closer.

Meeting Michael and Kate and the rest of the small group of Cygirians wasn't as strange as Garrick thought it would be. As they walked down the hall toward the meeting room, he tried to hide from Mila the fact that his legs were shaking and his arms felt like the slippery slick rubber of rubber cement.

I would think you were crazy if you weren't nervous, she thought. *You should have seen me when they first showed up!*

And he could almost feel her thoughts run up his body. Since he'd arrived at the safe house, they'd been more connected than they ever had been. All of their thoughts and emotions and ideas were swirling between them like a moveable chalkboard. She would remember something—a day at school, a moment with her mother, a lick of color in afternoon sunlight—and Garrick would catch it, hold it in his mind, lob it back to her like an idea softball.

He would startle with a memory of what the voices said to him, feel the cold, hard pallet he lay on as they showed him the terrible visuals, and she would nod, explain what she understood about his thought. But she explained it all to him with her mind, her ideas. All of her enveloped him like a wonderful garment, so soft and loose and free.

And instead of making him want to run away from her, to hide like any *normal* man (if withholding, retreating, or running away was truly in the realm of normal) would from such omnipresent "knowing," he wanted to stay. To sink in, to float in the knowingness between them.

I don't know why I'm so unclear about this, he thought. *Why am I nervous?*

Because you are finally meeting who you are. You are going to see yourself in them. You won't be able to help it.

Garrick breathed in, took her hand, and as they made it down the hall and turned left into the large meeting room where everyone sat, he had a flood of feeling. But it wasn't fear or anxiety or nerves or terror. Instead, it was if he'd walked into a party of known people, a group of family, his best friends from college, lifelong companions. He felt he would be able to sit down and talk with every person in the room about their childhoods, their families, their hopes and dreams. They were known to him. They were his. Almost as much as Mila was.

A tall blond man walked up to him, clasped Garrick's shoulder, smiled. "It was a long haul to get you standing. But you seem to be doing quite well."

"Those simulator things are disgusting," said a woman who was almost as tall as the man. "I'm still trying to wrap my head around them."

"I think you have it backward, Kate," the man said. "It's the disgusting things that wrap around your mind."

"Very funny, Michael," she said, punching him lightly on the shoulder and then holding her hand out to Garrick. "I'm Kate. This guy is Michael. He and I are—"

"Twins," Garrick said, clasping first Kate's and then Michael's hands. "That I can tell."

"When they saved you," Mila began, "they created a sort of like . . . um . . ."

"We make an electrical field that's moveable. Sort of an electrodynamic bubble propelled by electromagnetic energy," Michael said.

"How in the hell did you figure that out?" Garrick asked. "That's not something I would have imagined."

"Like moving through time is?" Kate asked, laughing. "Alone I would push myself around like a top, but I couldn't go anywhere. I always assumed that I had some kind of warped telekinesis. You know, a power with a hang-up. Mostly, I tried to not think about it."

Garrick nodded, understanding that impulse.

"But then one evening we met at Carmen's in Boston over a beer, and the next thing we knew we were in flight. Whoosh!"

"The next thing you knew," Garrick said softly. And that was exactly right. It all happened like magic.

"Well, we had to practice, but space travel, well, it was just the next step," Michael said.

Garrick listened, feeling Mila's soft presence behind him. He couldn't believe he was hearing this, but then, what could really surprise him now? He looked around the room at the people staring up at him, and knew that the dozen or so people in front of him had powers that would at first astound and then make sense, too.

We aren't in Kansas anymore, Mila thought. *What they can do! Disintegrate matter, reintegrate matter. Absorb light, throw light back. Perceive the future, perceive the motives of others in the past. The list goes on and on.*

Garrick shook his head, putting a hand on Mila's arm. It was overwhelming, but now he was here, thanks to Michael and Kate. "I can't tell you how much I appreciate you getting me out of the Adamses' house. And for taking out that simulator. Mila told me about it."

"Trust me, always a pleasure to get rid of one of those things. Forcing it down the garbage disposal is always a chore, though," Michael said, laughing, taking Garrick by the arm and introducing him one by one to everyone. And as Garrick shook hands, said hello, he felt an excitement he'd never known, a quickening of nerves and adrenaline and heat. Something good was going to happen. Even though his race of people was on the brink of extinction, hunted down by the very people who had tried to off them all in the first place, things were going to be all right.

"So good to meet you," he said, knowing that it was good. He wasn't sure how he could actually feel optimistic, but he did. Oh yes, there was going to be hardship, but he felt the hope in himself and the hope in the room. Somehow, with his people, with Mila, he was going to be able to finally do what he was born for.

Chapter Ten

Although Mila knew she should be focused on other things—important matters, such as basic life-and-death issues, the search and rescue of the rest of her tribe, the learning about the skills of her groups—all she wanted to do was take Garrick back to the tiny room the group had allotted them and make love to him. For days and days. Weeks, maybe. Even a year.

While she was strategizing with Michael and Kate and the rest of the team, she had to tamp her mind down because without her even meaning to, she would sail back to Garrick's recovery bed and the love they made there. Oh, his skin! Oh, his mouth.

A couple of times, Kate glanced over at Mila and smiled, and Mila pressed her thoughts tight, imagining them surrounded by tinfoil. She knew how important it was to stop the Neballats. Not only had they virtually obliterated the Cygirians, but what was stopping them from taking over Earth and the other planet the remaining orphans had been left on? The

Neballats could find the rest of them and then swoop down on unsuspecting Earth and repopulate it. Use the planet as a base camp while they fixed their wasted, sad bodies and lives. What would the Republicans think about that? Wars in the Middle East and global warming wouldn't even be arguments anymore. No one would talk about term limits, taxes, or teachers' salaries ever again. Even the Democrats would have to stop politicking.

Maybe that's what they need. Make all those politicians work together for a change, thought Garrick, slipping into her reverie. *Maybe a little alien invasion is worth its weight in gold. It worked in that one movie, the one where a scientist and a soldier save the day.*

There's only one invasion I am interested in, she thought back. *And it has something to do with you invading me.*

But before they could think more or sneak away to their broom closet, they were pulled into a conversation. Just, really, as it should be.

Of course, they had time to slip against each other's skin during rest periods enforced by the artificial day and night in the safe house, but by then, both of them were exhausted, having spent most of the day planning and the rest learning about their world, the world that had been. But how wonderful to be with him. How lovely it was, even so. Just to breathe in deeply as she lay on his chest barely awake was enough.

Not hardly, Garrick thought as he fell asleep, his arm tight around her.

The fourth morning they had both been at the safe house together, Mila, Garrick, Kate, Michael, and four others, two additional set of twins—Porter and Stephanie and Whitney and Kenneth—sat in front of a computer screen that had morphed into a 3-D computer image of a solar system. The little planets circled in their orbit through the room, periodically disappearing when passing through someone's head or torso and then reappearing and continuing on. The focal point was a smaller planet, Upsilia.

"I don't even know what the order of our planets are!" Whitney said. "What's that thing—you know, the way we learned?"

"You wouldn't mean 'My Very Excited Mother Just Served Us Nine Pizzas'?" Porter said, his voice a stick ready to snap.

"That's it!" Whitney said.

Whitney and Kenneth had found each other by the simple fact that they'd never moved from the childhood homes they'd been raised in. The few remaining Cygirians whose role it had been to place the children had obviously run out of time and luck, placing them in homes close to each other. By some lucky coincidence, neither family moved, and they knew they were connected when they sat next to each other in third grade. Both of them were pleasant to look at, round in face and body, happy, but the biggest irony was that their power was so intense, neither had ever tried it out fully, discovering their skills when touching plants and bugs and animals: Whitney could bring someone back from a near fatal injury, and Kenneth could injure someone with only a touch.

Of course, the power had hurt Kenneth more than Whitney, so he had used it only by accident all these years. But even so, he was as solid and down-to-earth as Whitney.

"You are like the alien *Leave It to Beaver* story," Mila said to Whitney. "Sort of the happy-orphan, world-destroyed saga we all know and love."

Like many Cygirians, Stephanie was tall but she was striking to Mila at first because she was not blond. Now seeing more Cygirians, Mila knew that blond was just one sort of model, Cygirians coming in the same varieties as humans.

Stephanie's black hair was short and spiked, her big eyes dark and bright and slightly wicked. Porter was similarly dark, but he looked irritated by just about everything anyone had to say. His saving graces were his sense of humor, his long, languid body, and his amazing lips.

"I thought I was the only man you could see. That I blinded you with my great, good looks," Garrick said, picking up her thoughts one day.

"You don't have anything to worry about," Mila said. "About an hour with him and I'd want to kill him dead."

Grumbly with each other and not in tune as all the other twins seemed to be, Porter and Stephanie were able to create and then destroy electricity, bringing forth or tamping down energy, everything from a watt to gigawatts.

"Lights on, lights off," Garrick had said to Mila after meeting them. "And the way they snipe at each other, wow. I wish it were lights off!"

As they sat listening to Michael, the planets swirled around them, Porter rolling his eyes. Stephanie sat with her hands clamped tight between her clenched knees, as if to keep them from slapping him down. Mila tried to ignore the planets and the people, remembering the solar system from grammar school, the Styrofoam balls whirling around the painted sun ball in the middle. But this system had one sun and twelve planets, though the sun was slightly bigger and hotter than the one Earth circled.

"Don't be so sure they are planets," Whitney said. "Remember what happened to poor Pluto! I guess Mom is going to have to serve up something different now besides pizza."

"What ignominy," said Porter. "Reduced to a rock."

"*Ignominy,*" Stephanie whispered.

"No, not a rock. A *trans-Neptunian object*. A dwarf planet," Mila said.

"Where do you pick up this stuff? Isn't that word *dwarf* politically incorrect?" Garrick asked. "Shouldn't it be a 'little' planet?"

"The diminutive is just as degrading," Stephanie said. "Who are we to know what constitutes a planet or not?"

"People," said Michael. "Please. Who cares about Pluto? It's hard, it's in orbit, we can fly past it if we want to later. So can we now get back to planning how we are going to do this?"

For once, Michael didn't seem to be joking, and Mila breathed in, found Garrick's hand, and squeezed. She was scared, and she knew that the rest of the group was, too. How could any of them not be? They were going to go down to find their people, risking exposure to the Neballats. Not only that, who knew what the "people" were like on the planet they were going to invade?

I know, thought Kate. *I feel like I'm a part of* War of the Worlds. *But it's me who is invading.*

At least you don't have a death ray, Mila thought back. *Or do you?*

Garrick turned to Mila and smirked, his lip twitching enough to make Mila want to kiss him. He turned back to face Michael.

"So," Garrick said. "We think—we know—this is the planet. Upsilia."

"You've seen all the archival footage that was left behind," Michael said. "The charts."

"Of course, that's what they left for us before they were annihilated," said Stephanie, rubbing her forehead. "We haven't had any contact with the planet, have we?"

"None that we know," Porter said. "If it weren't for the first twins finding their power and managing to use their powers to get themselves here, we wouldn't know anything."

Mila nodded, looking out the window again at the first twins, Jai and Risa. They had found each other on Earth, and slowly developed their ability to move through matter. They'd shared the dream that most of them had, and with their ability, managed to find this place, the safe house.

Alone and confused upon their arrival, they followed the oddly compelling voice that called to them and were abducted by the Neballats, put through the same interrogation and seductive intimidation that both Mila and Garrick had gone through—as so many others had, too. Fortunately, they'd also been assisted by a rebel Neballat, the same individual who was feeding the Cygirians information still.

Jai and Risa had done everything that Mila and Garrick had but without any outside help. They had been manipulated, starved, tortured, teased, wooed. But they'd made it out, gotten free, broken loose.

And though they were barely older than she, just looking at them made Mila tired. They'd been through so much, waiting and waiting until this small group grew, two people at a time. What Mila had heard whispered was that Jai and Risa believed that there was one among them, one who would lead the battle against the Neballats.

"All we need is a messiah complex around here," Porter said. "Why must there always be 'the one'? Such a tiresome cliché. So biblical. So *Matrix.*"

"I don't know about you," Kate had said. "But I sure wish someone would take over. Make me feel a lot better. There is something to be said for 'the one.' He or she always takes charge."

But for now—no messiah in sight—the group had given Jai and Risa a less arduous mission—collecting the remaining twins on Earth. How less dangerous the mission was, Mila wasn't sure. The only dangers there were the Neballats and the unfortunate humans trapped by simulators into helping them.

"And your point is what exactly?" Stephanie asked Porter, her eyes dark slashes.

"My point is—" Porter began, interrupted as Michael took over the conversation again.

"There is a beacon. We've seen that on the charts." Michael pointed to a spot on the chart. Mila nodded, but felt she was back again in college, trying to find Mercury or Mars in a field of white dots. She'd dropped that class, irritated from the cramp in her neck from looking upward for two hours at a time, all the stars and planets just that. Random, blinking lights.

Once, though, when she'd been at a film where the main character was shot through a wormhole, she'd laughed at the silly computer graphics at first, but then as the astronaut went through nebulae and galaxies, clusters of stars all around her, Mila gasped.

She looked at her viewing companions—friends from work—and they munched on their popcorn and sipped their sodas, eyes wide on the screen. But no one else seemed to want to stand up and shout, "I've been there. That's right. Home."

That's what it felt like—the path home. But, of course, she wasn't in space at all. She was in San Francisco, with her colleagues, at a nine o'clock showing of a science fiction film Hollywood had spewed out for her viewing pleasure. There had been a raffle for discount movie tickets before the previews. Chitchat about business before the main feature began. An overheard conversation about a terrible love.com date gone horribly wrong. A night out. Nothing more, nothing less. Or so Mila had thought.

Michael switched the computer screen to a map of the world Upsilia. "We arrive approximately a hundred kilometers from this main contact point using the emergency ships and land right about here, the point we've determined was the elders' selection point." He pointed to a spot on one of the continents, a yellow patch in the midst of a green and blue piece of land. "Yes, yes, Mila. It is a desert, but with the cloaking device and the isolation, we should go undetected. And Kate and I can get us out of there before we even think to be thirsty."

"When did you learn to fly with a ship?" Garrick asked. "Did you take a refresher course in the last eight hours? Gee, I sure know since freshman year that I've forgotten how."

The screen flashed from the map to the schematics of a ship, and this view gave Mila a shock. She turned to Garrick, his dark eyes full of understanding. It was the ship from her dream. The dark place. But now it was labeled with information that didn't make much sense to Mila: propulsion system, oxidizer tank, electric servo full-flying horizontal stabilizers.

"Flying these things doesn't seem to require much training other than pressing buttons. Or just thinking things, really. You know, 'accelerate' and 'orbit,' " Kate said.

"Right," Garrick said, but before Kate could even argue with him, he nodded. "I bet."

Kate went on. "The good news is that we came from a technologically advanced culture. More and better toys. Easier directions."

Mila looked outside where a group of Cygirians sat under a tree, close to Jai and Risa. All of them had been through more than Mila could imagine. And none of it, not even flying a spaceship with a "brain," had been easy.

Kate waved a hand. "Okay. It's not going to be a cakewalk. But Michael and I have tapped into the training programs and we are going to do the best we can. We'll get us there. And the other group will be responsible for Earth. By the time we all return, it will be just as we planned. A larger group of us. A better sense of where to go from there."

"What if they've already mobilized in some way? Like, maybe they've already figured this out, too. You know, abduction, rescue, panic. They could be on some kind of whacked-out safe planet or something, trying to find us."

Kate nodded. "You're right. But this is all we can do from our end. And if we meet in the middle, the two plans coalescing, then they do. Like I said, we just 'go from there.' "

"That's the plan?" asked Porter. "We will 'go from there'?"

"That's what we've been doing all along, Porter," Stephanie said, shaking her head. "We weren't left with many instructions, you know? We are just doing our best."

Porter didn't argue, looking instead out the window. Mila leaned against Garrick, knowing that they had no choice. They would put all of this information into a clear and concise package, prepare the ship, and go, but how it would unfold was as unclear as anything had been. As strange as every single thing had been from the minute Garrick walked into her parents' house. As dangerous. As unpredictable. As wonderful.

That night, Mila dreamed her dream again, but this time, it was as if she had been fitted with special glasses. Nothing was unclear anymore, unfocused, confusing. The dark place was clearly a ship, the same kind that she had spent time in this afternoon with the group, learning how to maneuver it through space. There were the controls. The seats. The hatches ready to let them all out onto their different worlds.

And this time, when she turned to the little blond boy next to her, she could see that he was only about three, the wise face she'd always imagined simply the face of a vulnerable, scared child. As she listened to him, she heard him say, "I see you again, Mi'a." No L. Just Mia.

Her heart pounded against her ribs, even as she dreamed on. Mila was her real name. Her name, something that her real parents had given her. How had that happened? How could that be? She looked to the boy, seeing what a tiny thing he was. Mila wanted to scoop him up and hold him to her adult body, comforting him as he was trying to comfort her younger, dream self. But he was strong. And now, finally, she could also see how this boy was never Garrick. How this boy was himself. He moved differently, his fingers and arms and body all his own. What would he look like now, she wondered, this little boy all grown up? This man of now about twenty-nine or thirty. A man whose life was just about to change. Or maybe already had.

Turning to her left, she saw the little girl again and this time, was reminded of herself. Looking down at her dream legs, Mila saw that she and the little girl were almost exactly the same size. The little girl blinked, smiled, feeling the same way Mila did, reflecting everything right back.

Garrick shifted next to her in his sleep, adjusted the blanket, put his arm tightly around her waist. And the little girl and the little boy smiled, faded, leaving only shades of blond and beige and white.

"I love you," Garrick said, half in the waking world, half in dream, his voice at her ear.

"I love you, too," she said, moving as closely as she

could to him, needing his breath, his smell, his sound not just next to her but in her. If the world could be reduced to this and only this—this close swim of skin and love and heat—it would be enough.

The remnants of her dream broke into darkness and she pressed back against the warm chest and stomach and thighs of her lover and breathed herself back into sleep, down and back into the morning where she would go to try to save her people.

Sometime, somewhere, Mila felt she had seen a movie about this, too. How else would she have known about setting off for a trip in space? This wasn't a lesson she'd learned in school, no computer screens that morphed into solar systems there. But this was different from any movie she'd seen. There were no puffy orange space suits with bubble helmets. There was no steeplelike launch pad pointing up to the sky. No crowds oohing and aahing. There was no psychotic computer ready to take over the craft. There was no sound track, either, though a little music might have lightened the mood.

You've got that right, Garrick thought, nodding toward Porter and Stephanie, who were arguing, Stephanie's arms gesticulating, Porter's crossed, his eyes half closed.

Whitney and Kenneth were busy organizing and packing supplies with Kate and Michael. Most important was the gear they would need on Upsilia when they were away from the ship, trying to fit in as they set off the beacon, searched for their people.

"We could possibly be living there for a while," Michael said the night before. "We have to fit in."

"I still don't get it," Garrick had said. "I mean, all

of us are the same. Even the Neballats. Was it some kind of seeding program? Or if you believe in God, he just did repeat performances on various planets?"

Michael shook his head. "Dude, I don't know. I just work here."

Kate put an arm on Garrick's shoulder. "It doesn't seem to matter what planet you come from. No one remembers the beginning, and everyone has a story. Most of them are astoundingly the same. All we know is that our people knew to plant us in places we could live. So that's where we are going."

Mila knew that there were never answers to questions everyone asked. *Who am I? Why are we here? Where do I fit in? What is my purpose? What should I do with my life?*

It was all about figuring out an answer that worked. What she did know was that a huge question had been answered when she met Garrick. And that's all she needed for now.

"Come on," Garrick said, grabbing her bag and his and taking her arm. "I think we should say good-bye to the lookie-lous and get this show on the road."

For a second, she thought about her father, Paul. One of his favorite expressions was "Let's get this show on the road." Adair would roll her eyes, but move Mila along toward Mr. Henry's open limo door. And in the moment of the memory, Mila felt a pang in her chest, sorrow for all that she had taken for granted. Her former, maybe troubled life. Her art. Her parents. The people who had done their best, all along, even if what had seemed best hadn't been.

"You can tell them later," Garrick said. "I promise."

Mila and Garrick walked toward the ship, smiling

and nodding and saying hello to the group as they did. For a moment, she stopped and looked around. If she were at one of Adair's volunteer committee projects, Mila would be worried that her mother would flip out about the lack of help, the paucity of volunteers.

"It's incredible! An outrage. A mission to space, and no one to pass out the bags of food," Adair would say. "We only have enough people to fill them. I am going to have a word or two with the organizer."

That's what it looked like here. A scant thirty people packing up supplies, adjusting machinery, making last-minute plans. How could they expect to do anything? They just weren't enough, Mila thought. Not enough.

"Listen," Garrick said, stopping her, staring at her with his dark eyes. "You have to believe in this. When you believe, anything can happen. We ended up here, didn't we? We ended up here, together, knowing that we can be together for the rest of our lives. In fact, we know we kind of are stuck with each other. Think of how far we have come, Mila."

She breathed in, nodded. Yes, she'd seen the destruction of an entire world, her people cast to the winds, thrown like pepper into a burning sky. Yes, she'd felt alone her whole life until Garrick. Yes, a trusted and loved man had been turned into a puppet of the very people who wanted to kidnap and use her, the same thing happening to Garrick. But Garrick was right. Here they were, together.

She closed her eyes, brought her hand to his face, feeling the slight stubble, the softness of his cheek, the planes of bones just under her hand. Here was ground, terra firma, home. Here was where she belonged. It didn't matter who they were with or how many there were. Together, they might be able to do anything.

"Okay," she whispered, and he took her arm and they walked up and into the ship that might help them change everything.

She'd dreamed about this flight for so many years that the rumble and hum of the machine under her was as known as riding the Muni in San Francisco, not that Adair had ever wanted Mila to take the bus anywhere. But hurtling through space was as simple as that. Except, of course, she never imagined this coffee klatch sitting with her. Here she was, with four other Cygirians, sitting at a metal table, drinking some dark hot liquid certainly not Peet's coffee and eating light fluffy muffins as they passed by galaxies. No bone-jarring shaking when they took off, no booms of noise, no g-forces pulling her skin from her bones. Just this, this easy flight, this strange picnic in space.

"I'm glad you feel that way," Garrick said, sitting back against the metal chair, his arm around Mila's shoulder. "I could use some Dramamine about now."

"Breathe," said Whitney. "It will pass."

Kenneth laughed. "How do you know, sweetie? You've never flown like this before. It's been the Kate and Michael method for you."

Whitney blushed. "My mom used to say that when I would get carsick. And she was right. It will pass."

"Or not," Porter added. Stephanie rolled her eyes at him again, making Mila imagine the woman's eyes stuck in a permanent whirl because of Porter's comments. How would they deal with a lifetime together? It certainly wouldn't be like the relationship she had with Garrick. And Mila knew for a fact that Stephanie and Porter did not share a bed or room at the safe house, seeing Porter tossing and turning on the common room couch one night.

Not everyone is as lucky as we are, Garrick thought as he sipped his coffee, one hand still on her shoulder. *In fact, I don't think anyone is.*

You have got to stop listening in on me.

Can't help it. You're like a radio I can't turn off. Don't want to. Won't.

Mila smiled, nestled closer to him. Outside the window, stars and the wide void of space streamed by in flumes of white and black.

"So," Whitney began. "We've looked at everything in the database. All that the elders could leave for us before, well, you know. And I was paying attention when Michael went over the entire history of the universe."

"Like Michael could know that," Porter said. "He was a volleyball coach back in wherever the hell it was."

Stephanie closed her eyes. "Anyway!"

Whitney continued, ignoring both Porter and Stephanie. "But I still don't get it. How could this world we are going to be enough like Earth so that we can just waltz in? I guess I don't know how we really managed to live on Earth so well."

"Some of us didn't," Garrick said, and Mila brought her hand to his knee, wishing for a time when he wouldn't refer to his adolescence, to the time when no one believed him.

"What do you mean, Whitney?" Mila asked. "What's your question?"

"It's the ants," Porter said.

"Ants?" Mila asked, nudging Garrick.

"Well, of course." Porter raised an eyebrow, a very irritating habit, Mila thought. No wonder he slept on the couch.

He paused, waited for everyone to look at him. "You put four ants on a pile of sand with a food and water source, and the ants will do the same thing. You know, dig holes, search for food and water, reproduce. They go about their little ant lives, still ants even though they are on different piles of sand."

Stephanie shook her head, clearly familiar with this argument. "But what if one pile of sand is just a tiny bit bigger? Or the texture of the sand is just that much finer? Those ants are going to develop different ways of adapting to their different sand piles. Maybe over time, their bodies will evolve differently. Generations of people on Cygiria learned to do things with their minds and bodies that people on Earth didn't. I mean, look at us. We can do things my mother at home certainly can't."

Porter pushed back his hair. "Yes, yes. All of that is true. Adaptation and all. But the point is, the two ant colonies will have had the same origins, the same beginnings. Enough so that you could put an ant from one pile onto another and everything would be just fine."

"Probably rip the dude's head off," Garrick said. "Ants are a bit more territorial than people."

"Really?" Mila said. "Have you looked at the history of Earth? Have you ever considered Rome? Ger-

many in the twentieth century? How could ants be
any less territorial than say the United States—"

"No politics," Kate said as she walked into the main
cabin carrying blankets. "We have enough problems
of our own."

There was a rumble of laughter and then Kate
began passing out the blankets. "We have about eigh-
teen hours before we arrive, and there's not much
else to do until then but play cards or sleep. I'm all
for the sleeping because who knows what will happen once we land? There are cubicles with pads aft."

"Aft," Porter said. "When did you pick up that
word? Seems like you are taking this spaceship stuff
way too seriously."

"You are a complete idiot," Stephanie said. "She
grew up in Florida. On a boat."

Again, there were rumblings—Kate flipped Porter
the finger, flicked her hair behind her shoulder, and
walked off—and then people stood up, grabbed
blankets, headed, as Kate said, aft. Porter stayed at
the table, his cup in his hand. There was no couch
on the ship.

She wanted to turn and laugh with Garrick about
poor lonely Porter, but then something horrible
slipped into her chest and curled around her heart.
She tried to breathe it away, but she was suddenly
scared, her mind filled with ants not happy with each
other, a violent fight on piles of sand too much like
their landing on a desert. The Neballats could have
anticipated this, now that she and Garrick had escaped. They might have found the safe house. Or
worse. What if the people on this other world detected their arrival? Had aircraft ready to shoot them
down? What if none of them ever made it off the

ship, all their plans cut short on a hot stretch of arid land?

Mila started to breathe more quickly, her heart racing like a rat on a wheel. What if—what if something happened to Garrick? She could never live through that again. She barely made it in the few days she'd had to survive without him before. All that worry! If it hadn't been for Kate and Michael, she would never have gotten through it.

And what about all the years before meeting him? Everything until then had been a half-life, partially colored, mostly monochrome, sick with longing and loneliness, busy with very little that made her feel whole. While her art had been her passion, it had only been a dim interlude, really, a place she could try to let her feelings out, look at them, understand her hurt, finally see it in color and texture and form.

Mila felt herself grow resentful, harden against this mission, even as her own people were stranded just as alone as she had been on Earth. Everyone just needed to go home and learn to hide better from the Neballats. Everyone had to because there was just no way they could all be found and saved. There was no way the very few Cygirians that had survived could take on the beast that wanted them dead. And besides, she wouldn't live alone again. She refused. Mila stopped walking, knowing she had to make this whole mission stop. They could live at the safe house. They could just stay put.

Everything in her body felt cold. She wanted to shake herself out of the sensation, but she couldn't. When had she become this afraid? This needy? This desperate to keep what she had? She closed her eyes, knowing that she was almost angry at Garrick for showing her what she could lose. At how much could be taken away, just like that, in a puff of evil, black smoke.

It will be okay, Garrick thought, now by her side, his warmth, his heat against her. *You will never be without me again. No matter what happens.*

Oh, she thought, leaning against his chest. *How can you be sure? I couldn't bear it. Not again.*

You won't have to, he thought.

How do you know?

Garrick pulled back and looked at her, his gaze steady and full with understanding and love. *Let me go show you what I can. Let me prove to you the best way that I have that you will always be with me. Right now.*

Mila took a breath, and despite the flurry of anxiety of fear in her chest, she smiled.

Oh, really? How will you ever do that?

Just let me show you.

And then he took her hand, led her back to a bunk, pulling back the thick, utilitarian curtain, and then gently helping her in and getting next to her after she lay down. Inside, her body was still humming but no longer with anxiety. Just his hand on her waist as they were walking to the bunk had given her shivers from her earlobes to her ankles.

Now his hand slid up under her shirt, skimming her stomach, her ribs, his fingers warm and soft. His mouth was on her neck, her jaw, behind her ear.

Do you feel better yet?

"Hmmm," she said, the end of her sound almost a moan. "Almost. Not quite yet."

"Let me see if this works," he whispered, his hands gently shuffling off her T-shirt, his lips on her breasts. "This better?"

He slid the straps of her bra away, down, his lips finding first one nipple, sucking gently, and then the other. "What about now?"

"Oh," she said. "Almost."

"I guess I have to give you the total treatment," he said, sliding his hands along her waist, slipping off her pants. All the while he touched her, Mila felt her body tingle, as if he'd flipped a switch, every single nerve and fiber reacting to his fingers, palms, mouth, tongue, breath, voice. In fact, it was as if he'd turned her on and left her on, her body always receptive to him, his body, his voice. All day long, even in the midst of action, she would look up and see him and slicken, as if her feelings were rain that needed to fall.

He moved his mouth along her neck, down her sternum, across the plain of her stomach and pelvis, finding her, just, just, just . . .

There, he thought, his lips holding her, moving against her, urging her toward pleasure.

Take it, my beauty, he thought. *Take what you want.*

What about you? she managed to think before thinking was impossible, before she lapsed into that floaty place she loved to go with him.

Oh, he thought, his voice a laugh she could almost hear. *Don't worry. I'll get what I want. I already have.*

And his tongue moved against her, and she began to float and spin in pleasure, his hair beneath her hands, her sounds only thoughts, only *Yes, yes.*

"Time to get up," Kate said, but when Mila opened her eyes, Kate was clearly not in their cubicle, her voice coming to them through either an intercom or their thoughts. Either way, Mila knew, it was time to start the mission. To leave the safety of this bunk. For a second, she looked around and wondered how she and Garrick had managed to make love—some pretty amazing love—in this cramped four-by-six-foot space.

"Love knows no bounds and has no space requirements," Garrick said, kissing her on the ear, the cheek, the lips and then pulling his clothes on. "I have a feeling I could make love to you anywhere."

"Really?" Mila said, slipping on her shirt.

"Just bring it on. We can make it a reality TV show."

"It's called *porn*," Mila said. "And I'm sure someone has thought of it already."

"Never on top of current trends," Garrick said, getting to his knees and buttoning his pants. "Come on, girl, it's time to do this thing."

Mila nodded, and though she tried to keep smiling, a slim line of worry threaded her thoughts. She tucked them away and blocked them from Garrick because there was nothing he could do now—the time for lovemaking had passed. And Mila understood that no amount of passion could change the basic fact that they were going into a strange, unknown, potentially dangerous situation. One where everything was at stake.

Garrick looked at her, his hand on the curtain. She nodded, but then before he could open it and step out of the cubicle, she pulled him down to her, kissing him, thinking, *Be careful. Please be careful.*

"Mila, I will. I have too much to lose. And you know, when you are so busy worrying, worry about yourself, too. It's not just you who has something huge to lose, okay?" He held her gaze, his eyes dark and sparkly in the dim light. "You are what I have. You are what I want, and I won't live without you or it or anything ever again. Understand?"

She smiled, and he kissed her one last time.

"Come on," he said. "Let's go."

Garrick pulled open the curtain, and they stepped out, hearing noise from the galley. He laughed.

"What?" she asked as they walked toward their group.

"I just had the feeling I could say, 'Let's go save the world.' "

"Well, maybe we will," Mila said.

"Or at least our own," Garrick said. "And then we can have our life."

He kissed her forehead, and they moved forward, melded into the group, took part in the conversation. For a second, Mila relaxed, knowing that no matter what her life had been like before and what it would be like later, she and Garrick had made this moment, this second, and had already saved each other.

Chapter Eleven

As a child, Garrick had seen the movies about aliens and space. Maybe, he thought now as he gripped the edge of his seat with one hand, he'd always known that he was meant for space travel—that he'd actually already flown, his first ride to his new home on Earth. But when he watched *Star Wars* or *Star Trek*, he didn't remember that, the dream of the ship, of Mila's dark place eluding him.

So while watching the big screen, he'd landed a dozen times on a dozen different planets—desolate, lush, humid, arid, freezing—enduring all the bumps and grinds and crashes and implausibly perfect landings that the casts did. And sure, Kate and Michael had brought him to the safe house and yes, the Neballats had taken him back to Earth in their craft. But in one case he'd been cradled in energy and in the second, he'd been a zombie with a head stuffed full of a simulator.

But none of his own flights nor the films had prepared him for a totally conscious real landing on a real planet. How could it? He was a stockbroker, damn it, not an astronaut. His classes on decision modeling, marketing management, and strategy had not taught him to do anything in space, obviously, and never before had he had something so dear to lose. Mila. When he'd heard her fears, he'd tried to make her feel better about the mission, but truth be told, he was as nervous as she. So much could go wrong. So much in the history of the Cygirians already had.

But for now—if he could remember to stay in the now—he was simply sitting next to Mila, their backs against the padded wall, his body vibrating slightly. That was fine. He was with his love, holding her hand, feeling her warm, comfortable self next to him, but then suddenly the ship began to move more slowly and—at the same time—descend into what must be the atmosphere of the planet.

"What's happening?" Mila asked. "It's like a carnival ride."

"Probably what's supposed to happen when you hurtle tons of metal toward a planet," Garrick said. "You know, rattle and shake and—"

"It's called descent," Porter said. "Not much more than going down. I mean, even from just growing up on Earth, you've seen the space shuttle landings."

"Please don't evoke the space shuttle," Mila said. "That's not a very reassuring image, especially in recent years."

"For God's sake," Porter said. "In this group alone we have enough power to keep this thing from crashing. Just sit back and relax."

Garrick wanted to fight back, to come up with something witty to shut Porter up, but the man was right. At the very least, Michael and Kate could harness their power and settle everything to ground. And he and Mila could push time back far enough to where things were safe.

Maybe, Mila thought, her voice a smile in his mind. *Or we could rattle and shake ourselves to bits.*

I thought I tried to do that to you earlier, Garrick thought.

Oh yes. I remember that ride. What a descent. Mila smiled at him, and Garrick wished he could pull her close and make the trip stop. But he couldn't even hold her as they were strapped down.

"Here goes," said Whitney, and the ship began to hum and then almost moan, the metal reacting to gravity and friction.

Just as Garrick was feeling that the ship might snap into parts, all of them flung into the sky unprotected, the movement stopped completely and then there was a space, a holding of energy, and then a settling onto something solid. Or something that felt solid.

The shields retracted from the windows, and the ship flooded with light.

"Thank God for this sun. God, it is bright," Stephanie said as she unstrapped her belt and stood up. "At least we won't freeze."

"What kind of sunblock does one need for something like this? Ninety?" Mila asked, laughing. "We might get a really good tan."

Porter looked at her and shook his head, his lip curled just enough that Garrick wanted to throttle him and then knock that sneer right off his face.

"If the sun were that extreme, there would be no life here. And clearly, there is."

But Mila was not upset, pushing on Porter's shoulder. "God, you are so literal. No one would ever suspect you could actually create electricity. You are such a wet blanket."

And to Garrick's surprise, Porter shifted, relaxed, blushed, smiling at Mila.

You get to everyone, Garrick thought.

The only person I want to get to is you, she thought, leaning over and kissing him. *And the good news is that I think I've managed it.*

Oh, you have. No question there, Garrick thought, wanting to kiss her back and then some. But Kate and Michael came into the galley carrying their gear. Garrick felt himself ready, as if expecting a blow. He had to be ready. He had to make sure nothing happened to Mila.

"So," Michael said. "Kate and I are going to take us all through the desert. If we need it, Mila and Garrick can shift time, or whatever it is you do. Depending, of course, on what we encounter. I can't think how Kenneth's and Whitney's power might be useful, but you never know. However, there are probably a number of machines with currents that Stephanie and Porter could turn on and off. So just be ready."

"How long before we reach the city?" Whitney asked.

"Not long at all," Kate said. "Less than an hour. But we thought we'd stop before entering to check our bearings. Make sure things look okay. There's a mountain ridge not far from it with a clearing and a straight-shot view to the city. We can land there and make sure we haven't been detected."

"Or be detected because we've stopped," said

Porter, no trace of irony or sarcasm in his voice. "Maybe it's better to just go in."

"Maybe," Michael said, agreeing. "But at least we'll know who has spotted us. And then we will know how to fight back."

For a moment, the group was silent, all of them looking out to the flat brown desert of Upsilia. Without the mission and the imminent danger, the hot expanse could be any desert on Earth, Garrick mused. The Mojave, the Sahara, the Gobi. All those hours of watching the Discovery Channel while being parked in mental ward common rooms as a teenager had taught him the terrains of the world. Now he was off to explore one he'd only seen on a floating computer screen. And this time, what he discovered could change everything.

Michael pushed a button and the door to the craft opened, more light pouring in, making them all stare wide-eyed and then blink against the glare.

"Okay," Mila said. "Maybe I don't need ninety sunblock. But some shades would do. Just about now."

Porter actually smiled at Mila instead of sneering his asshole sneer. Garrick took Mila's hand, squeezing her soft fingers with his own. Just about now, Garrick thought, he needed to be somewhere with Mila. Somewhere where things were safe. Somewhere where he didn't have to fight for his very existence.

Like you said, Mila thought. *It will be fine.*

Garrick closed his eyes and didn't think a thing back, letting her words enter into him, settle into taste. Yes, she was right. Everything was fine right now. Her hand was in his, her body next to his. They were going together into something bigger than they were but as crucial to them as breath.

He opened his eyes, watching Kate and Michael join hands, creating a bubble of energy Garrick could just see, a waver of caught light, whirling energy, a focused storm.

"Hold on to your hats," Michael said, and the two of them flung up the energy as if they were handling a parachute and pulled it down and around the group. Like before, Garrick was lurched into air and space and pulled forward, with his Mila holding his hand.

Let's go save the universe, she thought. *Vanquish evil. Find all our loved ones. Right wrongs.*

Let's, he thought back, and he looked around at the group hurtling through the wide-open desert sky, and hoped they could.

At first, he thought that Kate and Michael had done something wrong. Very wrong. The six of them in the bubble were being knocked together like wooden soldiers, the energy punching at them and then suddenly collapsing, tossing them up and down, all of them trying not to injure each other as they slapped together. Mila was down at the bottom of the bubble, pressed against the wall with Whitney, and Garrick tried to figure out how to help them all. He glanced around, noting that Kate and Michael—outside the bubble—weren't holding on too much more easily, seeming to slip and slide as they tried to grasp their created energy.

And then there was a sound, a blast, a shattering sound like knives against a tile wall, a huge rent in the fabric that was carrying them. And then there was nothing but black and the feeling of falling. Finally, there was a hit, hard to his solar plexus, and there were stars, hundreds of them.

Garrick hoped his eyes weren't open, because all he could see was a grainy darkness. But he could feel his eyes moving, his lids blinking.

Anyone there? he thought, his frequency open to all.

He held himself still, waiting for a thought, a sound, a flick of feeling. And then there was a cough, an arch cough, as if the cougher were slightly put out.

"Yes," said Porter. "I am here, though where here is is up for conjecture."

"Grabs," Garrick said. "Grabs. Up for grabs."

"What-ever," Porter said.

There was shuffling—almost an irritated step and pause—and Garrick moved toward the sound, feeling Porter's body heat and then touching the other man's shoulder.

"We clearly didn't make it to the clearing," Porter said. "And I don't hear anyone's thoughts. No thoughts. You wouldn't perhaps have one?"

As Porter spoke, Garrick imagined but didn't hear Porter say, *No Stephanie.* And like Porter, Garrick felt the loss of his other half. No Mila. Not here. Not right now.

"What about light? Did you see if you could flick a switch somewhere?"

"Gee," Porter said. "I didn't think of that. Hmm— I've been turning crap on accidentally all my life, and I just couldn't think to do that here."

"Oh," said Garrick. "No dice, huh?"

"Not a light in the house. Or not one that works with my current," Porter said.

"That sucks," Garrick said, trying to think about what to do next.

"So the plan would be?" Porter asked.

Garrick felt the pull of his power, the time before this moment providing clues they'd been unaware of—images, senses, feelings they hadn't thought to pay attention to. "Let's go back. See what we missed."

"Only you will know that we've moved back in time, though, right?" Porter asked. "I'll just be reliving it without being able to pay attention."

Garrick nodded. "If Mila were here, we could all go. But I can't do it on my own."

Porter shrugged. "The story of my life. Okay, let's do it."

Grasping the other man's upper arm, Garrick let the feeling of stillness come over him and then within an instant, they were both back in the bubble. Instead of focusing on his body this time or the noises, Garrick watched. There were Whitney, Kenneth, Mila, Porter, all of them trying to right themselves. Outside, there were Kate and Michael, trying to recharge their energy, their faces panicked, afraid.

But behind them, within the darkness, was—was light, a flicker of iridescent color, yellow, slightly pink. Then there was the sound and the darkness and Porter's irritation.

"Yes," said Porter. "I am here, though where here is is up for conjecture."

"Believe it or not, we've already had this conversation."

Porter was silent for a moment. "Things must not be good if you already went back. Did you see something new?"

"Yes," said Garrick. "I saw some kind of light."

"Praise God," Porter said. "We're saved at last."

Garrick sighed. "No, I mean outside of the energy bubble. I couldn't tell what it was, so I think I need to do it one more time. At least."

"Have you ever," Porter asked in the darkness, "found a way for other people to remember when you are going back? I feel like some kind of freak show."

"Only with Mila," Garrick said. "I can only do it with her."

"The story of my life. Okay, let's do it."

Laughing, Garrick put his hand on Porter again, suddenly liking the man, despite his sarcasm. "Believe it or not, you've already said that."

"See what I mean? Freak show."

Relaxing again, letting time wash over him, Garrick was back in the bubble, seeing his friends, watching their fear, finding the light. Each time, he had to push away the sight of Mila, knowing that he could barely stand watching her so afraid, knowing that when this part was over, he'd not know where she was and be even more unable to help her. He wanted to tell her what to do, but he didn't know what that was, either. What he had to do was focus. He had to pay attention, so he centered his sights on the light, waited in the brief, scattered, flickering seconds that passed, and there. There! Within the light was a form. Forms. People. Someone moving, pulling open Kate and Michael's energy. There seemed to be a struggle, the energy shifting, pulling, as if two groups were arguing over a tablecloth.

But who? Was it the Neballats? Or was it Upsilians? Or both?

Before he could see any more or figure out anything else, Garrick heard the cracking noise, found himself in the darkness with an ironic Porter.

". . . I am here, though where here is is up for conjecture."

"There was someone outside the energy bubble."

"What?" Porter said. "From whence does this conversation spring?"

"We've been back twice, and there was a light, an opening into the energy, and people."

"Alas," Porter said. "I would have figured that someone was responsible for us not getting to the clearing. So who? Are they working for good or for evil, pray tell?"

Garrick was about to reply, when the darkness burst into a filtered light, all of it streaming from one large, deeply set window. Blinking, he imagined that they were in a cave or a spot within a mountain or—

"Not a bad guess," a female voice said, and both Porter and Garrick turned to look behind them.

"Who are you?" Garrick asked, knowing that he didn't really want to know. Lately, every time he asked that question, he got an answer he didn't really want.

He waited, turning to Porter, who shrugged, both of them keeping their thoughts firmly clamped shut.

Another window opened, and Garrick turned again, this time noticing a very slim, plain woman with long brown hair and almost golden skin standing behind him. She held up her hand, nodding as she did.

"It's all right. You are safe here."

"Really?" Porter said. "And our evidence for this is where?"

Garrick stared at the woman and was surprised when she smiled. "Good point. You don't have any evidence except that we managed to pull you two down and get you to safety."

"What about the others? The people we were with?" Garrick asked, everything in his head screaming *Mila. Mila.*

The woman walked closer, the hem of her dress *shiff shiffing* in the dirt. And as she came closer to him, Garrick realized that while she was like him, like Porter, a "human," she was somehow different, lighter, more air, more thought. In some strange way, it was as if her body was not quite as important to her as Garrick's was to him. None of these thoughts made sense, but when he shook his head and briefly looked at Porter, Garrick could see the other man was picking up something as well.

She stopped moving, clasping her hands in front of her. "We've known that the Neballats have been on the planet before. We've had evidence of this for years, starting with the abandoned ones."

Garrick glanced at Porter and then turned back to the woman. "The abandoned ones?"

She nodded, walking closer still. "The ones who were left. The ones who appeared."

"Appeared from where?" Garrick asked, the image of his wrecked, ruined planet in front of him, the vivid orange sky washed black, the escape ships flinging spaceward.

know. But if they'd been caught, the Neballats wouldn't be after us now. At least, that's what we are thinking."

"So they left us on Earth."

"Some of us."

"Some?" Mila asked.

"Like I said, as far as we can tell, there is at least one other planet used as an emergency drop-off point. Not that we've been able to find them." Michael indicated the room they sat in. "So we are collecting ourselves here. It's small enough to avoid the Neballats' notice but big enough to hold anyone who needs to land here for a while."

Mila shook her head. "I—I don't understand."

"There was enough time before the annihilation," Kate said, "to create a resting point between Cygiria and Earth. On an asteroid. Of course, it was easier to get here with ships, but others must have had the talent Michael and I have together."

Ships, safe place, asteroid. Mila wanted to laugh out loud, clutching her stomach and falling to the floor. Or cry. It certainly would be easier, she realized, to be back at home battling Adair or dealing with bad dates or even sitting in the wide parking lots of commuter traffic on the freeways. But to use a cliché, there was no going home again. At least not easily.

But she was here on this safe place, with her people, the ones she'd been dreaming about forever. And she needed to find Garrick.

He's your twin, Michael thought.

I know. But how does it work? How do we all find each other? How do people know?

"We just know," Michael said. "It's just the way it is. All the people we've met, helped rescue—those who helped us, the seekers who found us—said the same thing. They met the person that finally made sense of their power. They met their other half. The Neballats call us Twins, and I think that they got the word from our people. So that's what we are in an energy way. Nothing will keep you apart from him."

"Tell me everything," Mila said, leaning forward, pushing plates and cutlery out of the way. "Tell me everything and then let's go find him."

"How did you know they'd found me?" Mila asked. All three of them were still at the table they'd eaten at, but now a large, pellucid screen hung in front of them. Or didn't really hang. Had appeared, as if this was where a screen should hang for those being debriefed on their entire lives.

"We have an informer. Someone who is on our side," Kate said. "But we don't really know who that informer is. We get messages. Cryptic but clear."

"How can there be sides?" Mila asked. "I mean, aren't we almost dead as a race, whatever race that is?"

"Cygirians," said Michael, and that was when the screen flickered, images emerging. First it was a similar image to the one the voice showed her, the warm planet bathed in smooth orange light.

"Are we—well, are we like humans? Are we people? Or do we have extra parts or something?"

The image on the screen flashed to Cygirians, a man and woman standing placidly and naked before them. Mila flashed to fifth grade sex education and the diagrams of bodies and body parts, and these people were people. Nothing odd about them.

The woman stared at them for a second, seeming to decide what to tell them. Then she tilted her head. "They were left with families. Someone had tried to put a thought bind on them, making them believe that these children were theirs. To ask no questions. To take them in without a thought and build a life without a moment's pause. But it didn't work. Whoever they were, their culture was not as advanced as ours. Or simply advanced in other ways."

"What happened to them?" Garrick asked.

"Most stayed with the families to whom they were given. But some—some were unhappy. They never quite fit in. They felt displaced. Rejected. They felt as though they'd been given away—"

"Just like us," Porter said quietly, quickly, no trace of anything but sadness in his voice.

The woman stopped speaking, looking at them each carefully. "You are abandoned ones. This is good. We thought that maybe you were sent to rescue them. To warn them about the Neballats."

"We are abandoned. But we weren't left here," Garrick said. "On another world."

"Do you have the power?" the woman asked, a flume of energy infusing her face. "Are you two doubles?"

"Not us," Porter said. "Our doubles, our twins were with us. But we don't know what happened to them or what happened to us, really."

Garrick breathed in, looked up at the woman. "So, where are the abandoned ones? The ones on this planet?"

"Most are in the Source."

Garrick looked at Porter, and then put his hands on his hips. "The Source?"

"The Source Yes. Of course. They've gone into stasis. It was too hard for them here, and we didn't know how to make them feel any better. Sometimes, they come back. Sometimes, they learn to live here. Like us. Even if their doubles are with them. Sometimes, life is just too hard and they—"

"That's a better word," Porter said. "I think I like the whole notion of doubles better than twins. Twins is frankly too incestuous. Vaguely revolting. Very disturbing."

The woman ignored him and stared at Garrick. "You don't know of the Source?"

"Listen," Garrick began, his body wanting to move when he knew that he had to listen. He didn't know where he was or what to do. He didn't want to hear about the Source or Porter's ideas about word choice. What he wanted was Mila. Here and now. Next to him. Safe. "I don't have a fucking clue about what you are talking about. I don't know what you are saying to me at all, even though I understand every word."

She smiled. "I'm not speaking this, well, English. But you understand me. That's what's important. It's what we all can do."

Garrick started to question her but there was no time. He didn't want to fight with her or make her angry. Even though his heart was pounding so hard he wondered if she could see the bounce on his shirt, he knew not to react. All the years of thinking of his power as a disability had taught him to shut up and deal with what was in front of him. "Listen, do you know where the rest of our group went? Who took them? Do you know where we can find them?"

The woman moved closer, not put off by his anger. "We had to take you in groups. The power that created that energy was very strong. And we had to make sure that none of you were with your doubles."

Porter slapped his sides. "So tell us, then. What is going on here? What do you need to know?"

The woman smiled, and Garrick wanted to kill her for being so complacent. There was something wrong in her placid replies, her smooth and simple movements, her even and clear tone.

"Let me first find out what you want with us here. You speak of the abandoned ones. We need to know what you want here with us. With them."

Garrick swallowed, breathed, tried to pull up his patience from his core. "We came here to find the people you call the abandoned ones. We"—he indicated himself and Porter—"we were abandoned on our planet, and very slowly, we've managed to find each other. Group together. Figure out what happened to us, understand why we have our powers. Accept that we don't have to feel alone."

Garrick wanted to simply be angry, force the woman to help them find the rest of their group and then these abandoned ones. But as the sentences slipped out of his mouth, he was overwhelmed by sadness and longing. For such a short time, he'd managed to feel whole. He'd held on to Mila with a grip he didn't know he'd possessed. He knew now as he stood in this smooth, cool cave that he'd allowed himself what he'd told himself he never would: love and peace and contentment. Even in the midst of all this struggle.

"Look, we're under attack," Porter said, irritable.

"We are going to be killed by the Neballats if we can't find a way to fight back. We need numbers. We need all our powers. All the 'doubles.' "

Garrick took in a deep breath and found his strength. "We knew they were here. We wanted to ask them to come with us. To try to find a way for our people to live again."

He walked closer to her, wanting her to see in his eyes that he wasn't lying. That he wasn't joking at all.

The woman continued to smile. "As I said, the Neballats have been here and we have protected the abandoned ones. If you are indeed who you say you are, we will help you. But first we need to determine that."

"Plug us in," Porter said, and in the tightness of his voice, Garrick could see that he was worrying about Stephanie the same way Garrick was about Mila. "Do the DNA test or whatever scan you want. But help us find the rest of our group and then the rest of our people before those transparent grotesques make the decisions for us all."

The woman stared at them with her wide, clear look and then nodded. "Follow me," she said, and she turned, walking toward the darkness that suddenly opened up into another room, the flume of light pouring into where they stood. "Come."

Porter turned to Garrick as they started to follow her. *This could be a big mistake,* he thought.

Garrick shrugged. *I know. But we won't make any progress standing still here.*

Porter rolled his eyes, and Garrick almost laughed. Somehow, nothing Porter did bothered him anymore.

So literal, Porter thought.

Garrick almost laughed, but he couldn't find the sound inside himself. Not yet. Not until he found Mila.

"What is it?" Porter asked. "Like a CT scan?"

The three of them stood in front of a light, slim machine that had a platform sized—it would seem—for someone to lie down on. Garrick touched it, the metal not metal but something lighter, something that seemed that it should almost sail through the air. He turned to look behind him and noticed the shadows of other people, as if there was a curtained audience watching them and the procedure the woman was prepared to proceed with.

"CT scan. I don't know what you are referring to," the woman said as she pressed a button that made the front of the machine slide back a little, allowing more room on the cot part. "But this will tell us about your—your energy."

"You know, you are asking quite a lot here," Porter said. "You rip us out of our energy bubble, separate us from our friends, throw us in a dark room, and then ask us to lie down on some machine that could do anything to us. Turn us into—"

"I think we just need a little more information," Garrick interrupted, sure that Porter was about to say "turn us into *you*." Which, Garrick admitted, would be very frightening, becoming a Stepford Wife type of person, floating around the universe. But he didn't want to piss her off—her or the people surrounding the edges of the room.

The woman, however, was unflustered and undeterred, indicating for Garrick to arrange himself on the bed of the machine. "This will simply give us a look at your patterns. That way, we can match you with what we know of the abandoned ones. And what we know of the Neballats."

As he sat and then moved to lie down, Garrick realized that this seemed fair. What would he have done if some strangers decided to float around his planet in an energy bubble? Again, he wanted to laugh because until about two weeks ago, he hadn't had a clue about life beyond NASDAQ and San Francisco social engagements and the relentless phone calls from his aunt Linda and Jim Ryan. If he'd seen anything strange, he'd probably have called CNN or 911, reporting the weirdness and then sitting down in front of the television to have it explained by the experts. Or more likely, he would have shut up, turned from the window, certain that once again, he'd managed to move into a place that marked him as different. Strange. Odd. Mentally warped.

But he knew that he was not warped. And he also knew there were no experts. No one who could know about Cygiria, Neballats, this planet, twins/doubles, or Mila. No one who could explain it all.

Garrick arranged himself flat, trying not to remember being strapped down, the depressor on top of his tongue, the nurses hovering over him waiting for the surge of electricity to go through his body. Each time how he wished he'd come to and not be who he was. How he wished he'd have forgotten about time, moving backward through it like a terrible river.

Strangely, though, even with these thoughts, he felt calm. The light metal of the machine was warm, and he blinked, looking up into the soothing opalescence of the room above him. The woman moved about at his side, pressing buttons on the side of the machine, humming slightly as she did. And just when he asked her when she was going to begin, she touched his shoulder.

"All right. You are done."

Garrick sat up. "Done? Did you find what you wanted to find? Or didn't find what you didn't want to find?"

She smiled. "I would like to scan your friend now."

Garrick got off the table, and turned to Porter. "It's your turn."

"Turn at what?" Porter said as he sat down. "I thought maybe she was going to give you a facial, and then it was over."

But despite his complaining, Porter lay down and the woman went through the same motions she had done when Garrick was on the table. In a few seconds, it was over, and Porter and Garrick stood by the machine. The woman smiled her incessant smile, staring at them for a moment, and then saying, "Follow me."

She must have gotten instructions from the mother ship, Porter thought. Bring the prisoners to us! *Should be loads of fun.*

Garrick sighed, rubbed his forehead. *Let's just be good for now. Seems like we've passed the test.*

The woman walked into the room, lights flicking on as she passed and then first one door and then another opening as they continued to move. Finally, one very large door opened, and Porter and Garrick were led into a large wide room, the air warmer than in previous chambers.

What are those? Porter thought.

Garrick turned his head to see a number of what he could only call pods—long, white, person-length tubes. They lined both lengths of the room, and Garrick could see that there was a small window in each. Had this woman and her people put Mila and the rest of the group in these things? He breathed in sharply, wanting to run to peer into each window and not wanting to at the same time.

Invasion of the Body Snatchers, he thought back. Alien—*you know, when she goes into hyperspace and the monster infects her as she sleeps. Everything bad in sci-fi you've ever thought of.*

Great, Porter thought, putting a hand on Garrick's shoulder. *We need to find the group and get out of Dodge. Now, before we turn into the automaton our lovely tour guide is.*

"She's not an automaton," said a voice at the end of the room. Both Garrick and Porter turned to see a small man walking toward them, his robes flicking at his feet. Garrick held back a laugh because the man wasn't wearing elegant sandals to go with his flowing robes, but footwear that looked like running shoes. If Garrick imagined being greeted by an alien on an alien world—a scene he'd watched in so many films—this man would not be from his imagination.

It's the geek squad, Porter thought. *Or they've sent in the clowns.*

Garrick huffed a small laugh, thinking that the man with his short round body swathed in fabric perhaps was the entertainment.

The man drew closer.

"Well, then, if she's not an automaton, what is she?" Porter asked, looking at the woman who continued to smile. "I hate talking about people in the third person. I don't really hate it, but I can't help it with her."

The man walked to the woman and put his hand on her shoulder. She didn't change her smile, but just turned and walked back the way that they'd come, the doors opening, the flashes of light, and then she was gone.

The man nodded. "She is a little rote. An early version. But dependable."

"She's a . . ." Garrick began. "A robot? An android?"

"A roomba?" Porter added.

"She's an anthro," the man said. "You might call her humanoid. I guess android. I'm not sure I can give you a word you would understand."

"You seem to be speaking it well enough," Garrick said, but then he held up his hand. "I know we are understanding it. Part of our ability."

"Exactly! My name is Andras Borshow." Andras held out his hand, and Garrick took it carefully, shaking it, noting the man's slim hands, fine bones. Andras smiled, his eyes bright as Porter grudgingly shook hands as well.

"I have been studying Earth for years. I have a small group of cohorts, but the study isn't very popular. Extraterrestrial study has focused mainly on Cygiria since the abandoned ones came, and before that, we only had the most minimal of contact. Of course, there are the Neballat colonies."

"Colonies?" Garrick asked.

"Unfortunately, they have a web around the galaxy. But our study of them has been defensive study. But enough of that! I have so many questions to ask you. So much to find out. We must get started immediately."

"Whoa," Garrick said. "Wait a minute. We aren't here to be your field study. First of all, we came here with a group of people. Same as us. And then, what or who are these people in the pods?"

Andras folded his hands, his wispy hair wild over his head. "Those are the abandoned ones who went to the Source."

"If they went to the 'Source,' then why are their bodies here? Or is this the Source?" Porter looked around. "How sad if it is. I want the Source to have a little more joy. More light. And certainly more color."

Andras walked over to the nearest pod, Garrick and Porter following him. All three of them peered down into the window at a woman who seemed to be in the cradle of deep sleep.

"No," said Andras. "This is where we keep their bodies in stasis. A very few Upsilians go to the Source, but we isolate the abandoned ones here. Keep them together. Just in case—in case whoever left them here came back. And you seem to be back."

"We didn't leave them," Garrick said. "But our parents left them and left us. Our world was destroyed by the Neballats. But you must know that if this is your study."

"Yes," Andras said. "And we fostered the ones that came. But it is hard here. Being different. It must not be the same on Earth."

Garrick looked away from the pod window at Andras with his running shoes, short stature, and wispy hair. How easy was it to be different on any world? Where was it truly possible to let individuality steel around you like a divine costume? No, it could never be easy, humans or humanoids like pack animals, mammals still, hierarchical and full of insider/outsider behavior. It was so much easier to hide, to steep oneself in history or the stock market or art or sarcasm to avoid feeling it.

"So these—these abandoned ones—couldn't handle life in some way? And they go to the Source. Where is that?" Garrick asked.

Andras stared at him, his mouth open slightly, his eyes blinking one, two, one, two. "You don't know about the Source on your world?"

Porter began to shift on his feet, a guttural moan of irritation in the back of his throat, his rumbles only loud enough—at this point—for Garrick to hear.

"Listen—" Garrick began.

"Come. Let me introduce you to others like me who want to help," Andras said.

"Do they have the rest of our group?" Garrick asked. "Are you going to let us see our—"

"Doubles?" Andras answered. "In time. Come. Come on now. There is time for everything to be explained."

Garrick sighed, wanting to make time go forward, to push past all this inane talk about a Source. He wanted to move into a month from now when everything was finally over. When he and Mila were back in San Francisco in his apartment—no, her loft. No, no. In a place they both lived in. A house. When they could lie in bed and touch each other and think about only the present moment. The now. No past, no future, just her skin under his hands.

But as he followed Andras into yet another room, Garrick knew he couldn't go forward without living through this now. He couldn't move forward without Mila. Without her power or without her being. So he would follow the geek squad and do what the man wanted to make sure that the result of all of this was Mila.

Let's hope you are right, Porter thought, and together they followed the man in the robes and running shoes down a corridor, the door to the room the abandoned ones were in shutting behind them.

Chapter Twelve

"So," Mila said. "Let me get this straight. The Source is like—okay. The Source is like a soul repository. Where every individual soul in the universe comes from. Every soul, no matter what tribe or species or whatever. It's the place where we all return to when we die—and the place we can choose to go to if we want."

The woman named Teca nodded, and Mila glanced quickly at Whitney, who sat next to her at a small metallic table.

"Is it like heaven?" Whitney asked. "I mean, isn't that where our souls are supposed to go?"

"I think that would mean we were dead," Mila said, remembering that Whitney had been raised in a very small town in Iowa—Hampton, or something like that—and while she was now on an alien planet talking to an alien about souls leaving the body, she'd never been east of the Mississippi River. She hadn't gotten around much, so figuring out heaven might be too much to ask.

"When you are incarnated on a physical plane, you don't bring your entire soul with you. A little bit stays in the Source. The converse is that when you choose to go to the Source before death, you leave a little bit behind."

"I don't get it," Whitney said. "If your soul goes back to the Source, how can the body stay alive even with just part of a soul?"

Teca kept her gaze level, answering them as if speaking to children, which, Mila realized, was what they were acting like, asking question after question. "The bit of spark, of energy, is enough to keep your body going. Your body works on its own, so all the biological needs are met. We take care of the ones who go."

"Do all the abandoned ones go to the Source?" Mila asked. "Why don't they stay? I mean, if they have found their doubles, then things should be okay for them."

"Most do choose to go," Teca said. "This is not the most hospitable of social climates. While we did recognize the abandoned ones and give them shelter, they were never integrated fully into our society. And when we discovered their doubled powers—people were a little nervous."

"What do you mean?" Mila said. "Nervous how?"

Teca blinked. "Of their powers. We found that together, they could do so many things. We have our own small abilities. Some telekinesis. Energy sourcing. Telepathy. But nothing like what the abandoned ones can do. Create climatic changes. Evaporate water sources. Turn night into day. Things that we'd only imagined from stories our ancient ones told."

Mila felt the ache that had been building inside her all day pulse. The space of the pain was where Garrick wasn't. Since she'd discovered him, since he found her, this place had opened up inside her body, her heart, her mind. When they were together, it was wonderful, a full and overflowing place of love and joy. And when he wasn't? Like right this very second? She was barely able to take in breath. Now, looking at Teca, she knew what this culture had done to the abandoned ones was worse than death.

"You kept them apart," Mila whispered. "You wouldn't let them see each other."

Teca nodded. "At first, when they came of age and realized their connections to each other, we let it happen. But they had no elders teaching them what to do with their powers. They had no guidance. At first, we tried to help them learn, but some ran off. Some took over different, well, areas. Businesses. Natural resources. It took some time before we were able to gather them together and then pull them apart."

Whitney gasped, brought a hand to her heart. Mila knew she was feeling the same rent that she was, the space where Kenneth was not.

"We had no choice. We didn't know what they would do."

"So you made them go," Whitney said. "You forced them—it's like you forced them to almost die."

Teca nodded again, her face pale, her hands folded in front of her. "But there were some like me who wanted to help, even if we couldn't give them what they wanted. I am part of a group who studies them. Who work on their behalf."

"And when we talk about 'them,' " Mila said, "we are talking about us. We are the same as they. We are abandoned ones, too."

It was all Mila could do to keep herself together sitting down. She needed to grab up Whitney and get out of this room. She needed to find Garrick and the rest of their group and get off Upsilia. There was no time to save this planet's abandoned ones. Not now. Not when this woman and her world just wanted to knock them all out. The Source! As if! The whole stupid story was just a way to make a long-term drug-induced coma seem palatable.

"In the Source," Teca began, her voice becoming soft and light. "In the Source they can be together. With everyone. With all the souls from all the planets. In the Source, there is no way to fight. To control. To take over. To hurt or kill each other. When we enter into it, we go back to the beginning, where we are all part of the one. You need not worry about the abandoned ones. They are happier there."

Mila gasped, letting her arms fall to her sides. "What a lie. What a terrible rationalization. You put them out like animals and call it for the best."

Standing up, Mila took Whitney's hand and pulled the other woman to her feet. "You need to bring us to our group. You need to let us go home. You can let us take the abandoned ones with us or not, but we are not going to stay on this planet for one more instant than we have to."

Teca stood as well, her face placid and calm as it had been the entire time. Through the testing, through the stories, this woman was impossible to ruffle. None of Mila's nor Whitney's complaints or protests or confusion seemed to matter a bit to this woman. Something inside Mila wanted to jump at Teca and strangle her, make her see that all of this was horrible. It was torture. It was wrong.

"We can't let you leave," Teca said, the same way she might have offered Mila a tuna sandwich. "Your departure will attract the Neballats. We need to send you all to the Source."

"I don't want to go to the Source," Whitney said, her voice breaking. "I want Kenneth. I want this to stop."

"In the Source, you will find him," Teca said. "You can be together in a way you could never be together on any plane. On any planet."

"I don't want him in the Source. I want him where I can touch him."

Mila gasped, thinking about a place where she couldn't brush her fingers along Garrick's shoulder, feel his skin against her lips. Maybe they would join in some New Age spiritual soul way, but it wouldn't be the way she needed, wanted, had to have. His hair, his smells, his breath, his voice.

Teca nodded, again as if Mila had refused the tuna sandwich but preferred the egg salad. "We will send you back to the Source. There you will find the peace you never found in life."

"I did find peace," Mila said. "I finally found it. I don't need you to send me anywhere but home. It's not your responsibility to fix us or help us or trap us."

From a place of strength she didn't know she had, Mila pulled herself forward and walked toward Teca. If she were alone, she could move through time and get away from this moment. But she couldn't leave Whitney. And Whitney was probably trying to figure out how to touch the abandoned ones and bring

them back so that they could band together and get
out. But who knew where they were kept? Mila and
Whitney were only halves. Together, but only halves.
They would have to get away from this woman with
only their ordinary attributes.

Teca kept smiling her calm, placid smile, her eyes
steady and still. How could she not see how angry
Mila was? How could she just stand there? Mila felt
herself flag a little when Whitney stormed forward
and pushed Teca out of the way, grabbing Mila's
hand.

Breathe, Whitney thought, and somehow, without
Kenneth or Garrick, they were spinning in some
kind of energy, a jumpy, lurchy movement that
seemed to lift them up and over Teca.

Go, Whitney thought, and with time and thought
and focus, they were out of the room and in a hallway.

How in the hell did we do that? Mila thought.

Anger, Whitney thought. *Desire. Magic. Who knows?*

Mila breathed out. *Well. Okay. Let's keep that one in
mind.*

What now? Whitney thought, looking around.

Run, Mila thought, and they ran down the dark
corridor, their hands in front of them. At any moment, Mila expected to be caught by something
metal or wire, hurled into a room alone. But nothing
happened, and they ran until they stopped at the
end of the corridor and a door opened as they approached, light streaming on them.

Shit, Mila thought, looking around, sure that more
calm smiling women would surround them. Whitney
grabbed Mila's hand, both of them breathing hard,

winded by their escape. The door closed hard behind them with a loud whoosh.

Mila looked around the room, ready to pull Whitney even farther on their flight. But there was no one
in the room. In fact, the room was empty save for
strange-looking white cylinders lining each side of
the room.

"What in the hell are those?" Mila asked, not waiting for Whitney to answer but taking her hand and
moving her forward quickly so they could both look.
Maybe, Mila thought, these were escape pods, like
the ones she saw in the vision the Neballats had given
to her, little black specks leaving a planet, so hopeful
for survival.

But as they raced toward one, breathing hard,
Mila noticed that a small yellow light emanated from
each, and on top of each cylinder was a small window.

"I don't think you mean what. I think you mean
who," Whitney said, and they both peered in, looking
behind them as they did, certain that Teca would be
close behind them.

"I don't know what I mean," Mila said, staring
down at a man's face, his eyes closed, his face peaceful in what appeared to be a deep, dreamless sleep.

But then she knew. Who else could they be? How
else? Where else? The cylinders contained the bodies
of the abandoned ones who were currently in the
Source. For a quick second, Mila wished she could be
in the same state—nothing bothering her, no longing nor worry for Garrick, no problems except a
dream of the beginning.

We have to get them out of these things. These tombs.

These cages, Whitney thought. *We have to bring them home with us.*

Mila looked down again through the window at the peacefully sleeping man, his blond hair long and flowing down to his shoulders. For what amount of time had he been at the Source? she wondered. If this whole thing was even true, how long could the body survive without the whole soul? She stared at the man, thinking of him as a dim votive candle about to flicker into smoke, like the candle left in the jack-o'-lantern at the tail end of Halloween.

We have to take them home, Whitney thought, and Mila shook her head a little, clearing her mind of the floating, easy Source, souls lit and unlit. *We need to get them to the ship.*

How? How do we get them out of here? Mila thought, and then, without asking, Whitney walked over to the nearest wall and pressed a large, flat pad randomly, pressing all over the spot.

Whitney! Mila thought, worrying about all the abandoned ones in the cylinders, here and otherwise. And there had to be more somewhere, all the troubled people, all the irritants that had bothered the Upsilian culture. So they couldn't just bring them all back! What if they turned them off accidentally? What if their bodies came back to life before the souls returned? Would they be like zombies? Half alive, half dead?

Zombies were a possibility. Zombies were everywhere in film at home, so why not? An idea made real. More than ever, Mila knew that anything was possible. Nothing was unbelievable. Not anymore.

Her heart and head spun as she thought, and she grabbed Whitney's hand, feeling the woman's rat-a-tat pulse in her own palm. In that second, the lights went on in the room, and a hum commenced, something clicking on in the cylinders with a slight whir.

We have to. I know it's scary, but there's no other hope, Whitney thought. *If we don't wake them up now, they end up having to stay. To live here. To be stuck in that Source without their twins. That's death. That's the worst punishment of all.*

Mila looked into the window of the cylinder, waiting to see if the man moved or opened his eyes. As she watched him, she remembered something, but she wasn't sure what exactly. Was it the way his hair fell in front of his forehead? Was it the constant up and down of his chest as he breathed? Who was he?

Mila! Whitney thought, her mind full of prickly nervous energy.

Looking up, Mila saw the door opening. With the lights on, there was nowhere to go, nowhere to run but out of the room, leaving the abandoned ones for good.

The cylinders whirred even louder. Then there was a vacuum sound, like a hundred coffee cans being opened at once—the make-believe sound from movies she'd seen all her life, the sound she associated with air locks opening into the deepest, darkest space. But this was real because the cylinders *were* opening, all of them at once, and just as they did, Michael and Stephanie ran into the room and the door closed behind them, as it had for Mila and Whitney.

They both looked around, watching the cylinders open, the doors sticking up straight like fins. Mila and Whitney came to them, Mila noticing that both looked just as she felt—bereft without their twin.

"Don't tell me," Stephanie said. "The abandoned ones. Coming back from the Source."

Mila nodded. "We have to get them out of here. And us. All of us."

"Have you seen the rest of our group?" Whitney asked. "Have you seen Kenneth?"

Michael shook his head. "No. We were interviewed and tested by a pretty strange man, given all sorts of information we didn't know we needed until right now, managed, surprisingly, to escape, and ran right into this room with you. And, of course, none of us are paired up here with our twin. Fancy that."

The ache that was Garrick's absence flumed and sputtered in Mila's chest cavity, and she sighed, knowing that what Michael was saying was dead-on right. If these people didn't want them to escape, they wouldn't have. If they didn't want them to find the abandoned ones, they wouldn't have, either. More than likely, Whitney's pounding on the pad had very little to do with the cylinders opening.

"So, is it going to be like *Night of the Living Dead* around here?" Stephanie asked. "Or will they pop out just fine?"

Mila shrugged, looking over at the cylinders. Nothing had happened. No body had peeked out, spouting Source lore. No one—not even the long-haired man—had stirred.

"Let's go see," she said. "Let's go find out what we are supposed to do."

The four of them looked at each other and then walked back toward the cylinders. Mila walked a bit more quickly, wanting to see the man, knowing that somehow, she had something to say to him. And as she reached the cylinder, she almost stopped moving, fearing the worst. Fearing that the doors opening would make something horrible happen. Something might have happened to their bodies. Their air supply might have stopped. They might all be dead, saved by incompetence from an endless life in the Source. But was there death if there was the Source? Mila was so confused, and she wished she could simply think about these things rather than look down and see what they had done.

"Mila," said a voice, and Mila jumped, put her hand on her chest, feeling her heart pound against her ribs.

"Yes?" she answered, turned to look down at the man, who sat up in front of her. He smiled, pushed his hair behind his shoulders with a slight laugh. He smiled a smile that she'd never imagined a person could have, wide, broad, full of a joy that seemed to pour from him, radiate off him like heat.

"Who are you?" she asked, moving closer, noticing his long blond hair falling over his shoulders, his intense dark eyes.

"Don't you know me?" he asked, and as he did, Mila felt something old stir inside her, unlodging, falling away to reveal the truth.

He laughed quietly, his eyes full of the same heat as the rest of him, obsidian and shiny. "It's me. Edan."

Stephanie, Michael, and Whitney stepped forward, all of them looking at this man, Edan. Mila breathed in, and then she knew for certain. How could she not? All of it—all the time alone—all the dreams, the hope, the need, the desire came back, and she fell to her knees, her hair hanging forward in front of her face.

"What is it?" Whitney said at Mila's ear, but Mila

couldn't speak, couldn't say a word. Finally. She was almost full, complete, whole. She had Garrick or had at least found him for a time, and she had the blond man—the blond boy with the short hair and dark brown, almost black eyes. The boy who tried to make her feel better, who told her it would be okay, all right, just fine. Finally after all of these long years, he was right.

"How did you know it was me?" Mila whispered. "How could you tell?"

There was silence, a long enough pause that Mila felt compelled to look up, stand, take in a deep breath. "How could you know me, Edan?"

He still sat in the cylinder, his smile still there but not as full of delight, everything suddenly more serious. All around them, the other abandoned ones were coming to, waking up, getting up out of their cylinders.

Edan looked around the room and then put his hand on Mila's arm. His touch was warm and calming, his skin making her feel something like peace. "In the Source, everything is there. But there won't be much time."

"We don't have the time to go into metaphysics right now. But do you want to come with us?" Michael asked. "Do all of you want to leave this world?"

Edan nodded, stepping carefully, slowly out of the cylinder. "They want us gone. They always have. If it weren't for the group that maintained our lives, we'd have been—well, it's hard to say. They think that the Neballats want us because we are like them. That we will take over with our powers."

Mila put out her arm and helped Edan get out of the cylinder. In that instant of contact, she was the little girl in the dark space, leaning against the small, strong body of the blond boy. And he was there to help her, to protect her—to protect her and the other one, the girl. Their sister.

All at once, the loss of so many years ago connected with the longing she'd had since then and she wanted to weep. For all three of them—Mila, Edan, and their sister—for all these abandoned children in front of her, for Garrick and everyone else who never fit in, who paid the price of the Neballats' desire for power.

And now there was a sister, too. The blond boy was Edan. And the girl—the girl . . .

"Sophia," Edan said. "Her name is Sophia, and I think I know how to find her."

Sophia. That's who they were. The three of them. Edan, Mila, and Sophia. They were who was left. They were a family.

"I hate to break up this happy reunion," Michael said as he helped Mila with Edan, holding his arm as they walked away from the cylinder. "But we need to get the hell out of here—I think something is happening outside this room."

As Whitney and Stephanie helped the other abandoned ones who were waking up, Mila listened to some noise outside the room, large bangs, the muffled sound of an engine, voices yelling, calling out. Michael was right. They all needed to get the hell out of here, but how? And where were their twins? Where was Garrick?

Mila looked around the room as if Garrick would suddenly appear out of nowhere. But that was possible. Anything was, and she knew she couldn't just leave without knowing what happened to him.

"They kept you apart on purpose," Edan said as they walked slowly forward. As she noticed he was just fine on his feet, she increased the pace, the noises frightening her at every step.

"Because of what we might do with our powers?" she asked.

"Yes. But they aren't here anymore. The noise isn't coming from the Upsilians."

"It's the Neballats," Michael said.

"And look what they will finally have," Mila said, sweeping her arm, looking at all of them together, all of them with their powers. "Just what they always wanted. All of us together. All of us with all of our powers."

And as Mila gazed at the abandoned ones struggling to come to, standing, looking around and trying to find their twins, their doubles, she could feel their energy, their power, their heat. This warm, orange feeling inside her whole body was like the world she saw destroyed, the terrible image the Neballats gave her. The image here of these people *was* her planet—her life. This warm, connected, wonderful feeling was like what she felt when she was with Garrick.

Garrick, she thought as loudly and with as much force as she could. *Where are you?*

In the pause that hung in her mind, she thought she heard his soft, deep voice. She thought she could almost feel his skin brushing against hers. But then the pause dragged on, the noise of the room filling it with what was real. She couldn't reach him.

Even though they should have been lurching around like zombies after being out of their bodies for so long, the abandoned ones seemed to know what to do. They moved through the room, out the door, taking Mila and her group with them.

"Where are we going?" Mila asked Edan.

"There are ships," he said. "We've always known about them. It was either going to the Source or leaving. And we didn't know where to go."

The door of the cylinder room closed, the hall dark all around them. Mila held Edan's arm. "You've got to tell me. What is the Source? Did you know who I was because of it? Did you recognize me? Did you know who I was right away?"

For a second, Edan turned to her, his black eyes like glass in the dim light. Some light, almost invisible color seemed to radiate from him, her eyes taking in his brightness as they stood together. He blinked, slowly, his face suddenly so wise, too wise, lines where no twenty-nine-year-old should have them.

"The Source is everything. It's what people are always looking for and can't seem to find," he said. "If I got anything from all of this life, it's—"

Before he could finish, there was a loud, dull throb, the sound of an explosion, the force of heat and energy pulsing through the room.

"These ships you mentioned?" Michael said. "I think we need to go."

"But Kenneth!" Whitney cried. "I can't leave him here. I can't go on without him."

Mila looked at the group collected next to her and saw that Whitney's cry was all of their cries. No one in this room—not one of the Upsilian abandoned ones—had their twin, their double. All their magic, all their love, all their feeling of connection was broken. All of their power was useless.

"No, it's not," Edan said. "We can still use what we have."

"What?" Michael said. "And it better be fast."

Mila looked around the group of thirty or forty people, and realized that only her group seemed distraught.

My twin, she thought. *My love. Garrick.*

Yes, thought Edan. *Don't worry. We learned more than we had ever imagined in the Source.*

Edan nodded, and the abandoned ones began to form a circle, their bodies encompassing Mila, Whitney, Stephanie, and Michael in a swirl of speckled energy.

It's like nothing you could do with a twin, Edan thought. *Nothing like it at all.*

Mila wanted to ask him more, to grab him and let him hold her through whatever it was that was happening. But as she raised her arm, she realized that she was not solid flesh anymore. If she had a face, her mouth would have been opened in a question, a frightened murmur, but she saw as she looked around that all the people who had once been standing with her had turned into flickering light, their forms only vibrating outlines of the energy they all were.

And Edan must have been guiding them out of the rooms and structure they had been in, because suddenly there was light. And then just as suddenly, there were the heavy shadows of the Neballats' ships, the hulking metal bodies of spaceships hanging in the cerulean sky, the same oppressive ships Mila saw in the image they had forced on her. And when she looked carefully with her eyes that were no longer eyes but atoms of seeing energy, she saw their wraithlike forms creeping like horrid spiders into where they thought they would find all the abandoned ones.

Except they were away! They were flying, soaring, moving in a mass of movement all together, a river of being that moved up and over the mountain ridge and back into the desert and then past it, sailing, sailing, sailing until Mila knew she could no longer be breathing. She didn't know where she was or who she was. She didn't know where her own body ended and everyone else, everything else started. Everything was wide and wonderful and full. It was too much, too intense, and Mila knew that she could only rest into it all and be the energy, be the wave that was taking them all to safety. Taking them all home.

In the dream, she doesn't know where she is because it is dark and closed in and crowded. She is sitting, her back against something hard. This dark is a place she only sees in the dream. But it is not scary. It is a place where she is surrounded by the children and by adults, who talk in soft whispers. Everything is so fuzzy, just like it has been all her life, her perception so small, so limited, so scared. But slowly, the images begin to pull together, take shape. Mila turns, looks to her right, and there he is, the blond boy. He is helping her, making her feel safe, touching her arm softly. The image shifts, focuses, and changes, the room brightening, opening, and she wakes.

"Mila," Edan said.

She blinked. He was no longer a boy, but a man. A tired man with a sad but happy face. And she was on a ship, but it was not the ship of her dream. It wasn't even the ship that had carried her to this planet in the first place. The interior was white and sleek and smooth, and she and Edan were sitting on a long bench with a few other abandoned ones who slept sitting up, leaning on each other.

At the end of the room, she saw Stephanie, Whitney, and Michael at a table talking. Whitney was being comforted by Stephanie, who looked pale and unusually afraid, needing Porter openly, showing the connection with him she must have always felt.

"Mila," Edan said. "It's not a dream."

"I know this isn't a dream, but what about everything else?" Mila asked, blinking. "How can any of this have happened?"

Edan shook his head. "We have to go back to the time on the first ship. The one from your dream. The dream all of us always shared. That's when it all started."

"No," Mila said, turning to face Edan full-on. "I just don't understand how any of this can be true. I grew up—I grew up in a place where there was no acknowledgement of aliens. Well, no real acknowledgement. We went to movies and weirdos looked up into the night sky for strange lights. There were writers who wrote about being abducted and having all sorts of crazy experiments done on them. But no one really believed this. I grew up knowing I was basically one of those weirdos and tried to make the best of it."

Her brother touched her face, and Mila wanted to weep, knowing that gesture from memory, by heart. She took in a deep breath. "And now? I'm running for my life from the Neballats who want the powers no one ever knew about. And now I find you and lose Garrick all in one morning."

As she spoke the last words, her body seemed to contract, shrink, but the pain inside her chest cavity expanded, taking her completely. She leaned against Edan's shoulder and he brought his arm around to hold her tight. While she still missed Garrick, needing him like a vital organ, her brother's touch calmed her.

Edan stroked her hair. "I grew up with a family who did what the government on Upsilia told them to do. Keep them involved in daily life, don't let them use their powers, and when we started to figure out that we had counterparts, that our powers matched, they took us into their deepest mystery in order to protect themselves."

"The Source?" Mila asked, lifting her head. "How did they know about it? Why aren't all of them there if it's so great? Shouldn't they be more evolved people if they've had the Source all this time?"

"You would think," he agreed. "Leave it to people to discover the answers to their most cherished mysteries and to keep on looking for answers anyway. But it's only a small group of people who know. Or who practice travel to the Source. They are ridiculed by the society, in the same way we were. But even though they traveled to the Source, they were afraid of us, too. So they offered it to us as an option. It was that or leave, and we didn't know where to go."

"People on Upsilia seemed to know about the Neballats. I guess aliens aren't really a concept there but a real thing," Mila said, thinking about UFO fanatics on Earth and how right they had turned out to be.

"Yes," he said. "They'd always known that there were more abandoned ones. They've always known about the Neballats and about Earth. I don't really know how or why, but they'd anticipated your visit and prepared for our escape. They needed to make sure you were like us, matched our genotypes. But that's not what I wanted to tell you, little sister."

Sister, she thought. *I'm someone's sister.*

At that thought, he turned to her and gave her one of his otherworldly smiles, the kind that seemed to almost come from, well, the Source.

"I hadn't found my twin," Edan said. "But I knew that somewhere, there had to be someone to match my power. Someone who could do what I could do, only backward. My gift was too horrible to be left by itself."

"What is it?" she asked. "What can you do?"

"I've only done it twice, once by mistake, once on purpose to see if I had really done it in the first place," he said. "It wasn't like there was any way to really check. Perhaps I could have gone to a physician to have a scan. But even without it, I felt something. Something in my bones. And I don't have any control of it."

Mila felt a ping of fear patter down her spine. What could be that frightening? Was it the ability to control life and death? But how could Edan have *done* death once?

"What can you do?"

"Aging. I can make myself older. I think I've lost about ten years. Maybe more."

Mila gasped. "How could you tell? Was it time that passed?"

"No. It was more like my skin. The way I felt. The

feeling inside me. My blood, my bones. The first time it happened, I ran to my almost-mother to see if she looked different, to see if she noticed anything about me. But she was just as she had been before I'd gone to my room to get my schoolbooks. The second time, I didn't even bother to check. It was all in me, not the world."

"So your twin could go the other way. Together, you could get back all those years. Back and forth. You could even stay about twenty for your whole lives, not that being twenty was anything I'd want again," she said, thinking about the sadness of almost every year until this one, all the unrecognized longing she'd had for Garrick.

She pressed her hand against her sternum, trying to push away the ache. Edan took her free hand, squeezed her gently.

"I suppose we could be twenty forever," he said. "From what I've seen of powers, maybe we could give that 'gift' to everyone. But I never found out what we could do for each other or anyone else. And without my opposite energy, I'm useless. A person with a power no one needs or wants."

"You know," she said, "I can tell we are related."

Edan finally smiled, his face like a sunbeam, his teeth white, his eyes bright. He seemed to be radiating whatever he'd picked up in the Source. Joy. He suddenly radiated joy. "How? Because we have blond hair?"

"Not so easy. I think it's because we move time, either in the world or in us."

He thought, nodded. "I never found my twin in the Source. It was like I could see her shadow, her form, but she wasn't really there. It was comforting to know she was around, so I relaxed into it. I found you and Sophia. I learned to not worry so much, but I always felt my body back on the planet wanting to live. Wanting to touch her. Find her. Finally learn who we were together."

"How long were you there?"

Edan let go of her hand, sighed. "The authorities rounded us up and took us to the holding place in the mountains. They explained to us what the Source was and put us in the cylinders. That must have been about five years ago."

Five years? Mila let out a quick breath. Five years.

"Out here, that number seems longer. There— well, even though I wasn't living my life, I was in this most amazing place, Mila. I wasn't scared there. I wasn't worried that at any moment someone was going to come and take me away from my home. I didn't feel different. I was one with every bit of energy in the universe. I was—I was home."

Flashes of Earth, San Francisco, Adair, and Paul passed through Mila's mind. The panoramic view of Cygiria came back, the warm planet before it was blackened and destroyed. Garrick. Garrick's arms, skin, chest. Garrick's face. His laugh. Home.

"It's all in the Source. And you were there, Mila. I knew who you were the second I moved into it. Sophia. We have to find her. We have to all be together."

"Do you know where she is? Is she on Earth?"

"I have an idea, but I need to think about it," Edan said, looking down at his hands. "I just know she wants to be found. None of us are complete without family. And without our twin."

"Did you ever find out anything about our parents? Who they were? What happened to them?"

Edan looked down at his hands, rubbing his thumb unconsciously. "No. I never saw them or heard anything. Sometimes, I would think that I'd hear something, see a shadow. Remember a word, a touch, a voice. But no. I never saw them. I don't hold the image of their faces in my mind."

"I saw our mother once. In a dream. Or an image the Neballats gave me. She smelled like lavender and cookies. It's all I have," Mila said. "It's all I can remember."

At her words, Edan sighed, and Mila turned to look once again through the cabin. Here they were. The abandoned ones. The only children scattered to the winds in order to be saved. Their parents had done so much work, and yet look what still had to be done. And now she was only half again.

"We will find him," Edan said. "All the rest. Don't worry, little sister. I can tell—I can feel that we will all be together soon."

For a second, Mila wanted to snort, the same way she used to do when her friends at home used to talk about being in the "now" or staying in the present or relaxing into the moment. She hated it when people told her that "Everything happens for a reason." She wanted to hurl when anyone dared to say, "It all works out as it should." She scoffed at making better agreements with the universe or trying to believe she was simply part of the larger whole.

But look at what had happened today. Her atoms had opened up and merged with everything. She'd moved into the greater whole and now she was flying through space. So maybe Edan was right. She had to relax into this and wait.

She nestled closer to her brother, breathed in the feeling of comfort that she had always known from her dream. She took his hand, looked at it for a moment, and then giggled. "I think I need to recommend a special cream. One for antiaging."

He turned to her with that incandescent smile, the one that told her that everything would truly be fine. "You better watch out, or I will turn my evil power on you. And then you might need a bit more than cream!"

She laughed again, and put her cheek on his shoulder, and stared into the ship, waiting for what Edan said to come true.

Chapter Thirteen

One minute Andras was leading Porter and him into a room, and the next moment Andras was gone, the slam of another door closing the clue that whatever was going on wasn't over. Not even close.

"This gets better and better," Porter said. "I am just having a marvel—"

Garrick was about to roll his eyes, picking up Stephanie's habit without wanting to. He stopped himself and sighed. "Come up with another plan, then, Porter. What should we do? What great idea do you have for us?"

Porter walked around, moving close to a cylinder, and put his hand on it. "I think we need to—"

But before he could finish another word, there was a hiss, a whir of machines or gears or something metal, and one by one, the cylinders began to open, a whoosh of vapor escaping as they did.

"Shit," Porter said, standing back. "I didn't mean to do that. What's going to happen now?"

"You didn't do that," Garrick said. "I think that

someone wanted all of them to wake up. Right now. In front of us."

And the people in the cylinders were awakening. Garrick and Porter walked toward the cylinder that opened first, slowly peering into the now open window. Garrick wasn't sure what they would see, and he almost bolted when a woman sat up, her eyes wide open.

She didn't look the way Garrick imagined she would after being in the Source that Andras had told them about: dazed, confused, disoriented about where and when she was. Since being sent there was kind of an exile, Garrick hadn't imagined that anyone would thrive. But, in fact, she looked calm, peaceful, smiling slightly at them, almost as if she knew who they were and why they were there. She didn't say a word at first, watching them carefully, and then, as if they had been speaking to her, she broke into a broad smile, her eyes filling with tears.

"Cygiria," she said. "Oh, finally. At last."

Garrick looked at Porter and then back at the woman. "How do you know that?"

Still smiling, the woman blinked, started to move slowly out of the cylinder. "I knew you would come. I found out in the Source."

Garrick wasn't sure if he could believe what she was saying, but he didn't really know how to believe anything anymore. And frankly, there probably wasn't time to figure any of this out. He put a hand on the woman's shoulder and asked, "Do you know where the rest of our group is? Do you know where our—"

"Twins," she said. "That's what you call them. And they are . . . they are . . ." Her sentence trailed off as she saw the rest of her group starting to emerge from their cylinders. She clambered out, Garrick and Porter helping her as she did. "They are—"

And then there was a horrible noise, something like an explosion, the sound resounding metal, steel, and pain. At that same moment, another door opened and then closed, the room flooding with light and then cast back into semigloom.

"Garrick?" someone called, and then Kate pushed into his view. Kate and Kenneth. And about forty additional people, probably more of these abandoned ones. "Porter?"

Garrick rushed forward with Porter behind him, not knowing what shape their friends would be in, but they looked fine, the same way Garrick felt. None of them had been harmed on Upsilia.

"What happened to you?" Garrick asked Kate.

"No time for that. The Neballats are in the structure. I saw a group of them just before the door to this room miraculously opened. We need to get out of here now."

"But then what?" Porter asked. "You can't do your parlor trick without Michael."

Kate was about to answer, but the group of people she led into the room began to shout out to the ones coming out of their cylinders, people rushing toward one another, helping the ones not quite aroused to awaken and get out of their cylinders. Then there was kissing, touching, hugging.

"Do we have time for this touching reunion?" Porter asked. "I'm about ready to call *People* magazine."

"Oh, shut up, Porter," Kate said. "Look, there has

to be some twins or doubles or whatever amongst this group. Someone will be able to find a way out of here."

The woman Garrick and Porter had helped was suddenly at Garrick's side. "We don't need our double powers. And we can leave here very easily."

"That's fabulous news," Porter said, his sneer just under his words. His sneer and anxiety. "Do you think we might want to go now?"

Despite his attitude, the woman remained unflustered, and she nodded, moving toward the end of the room opposite from the door that Kate and Kenneth had come through.

"I guess this plan is as good as any I could come up with," Kate said.

"What? 'Follow me'?" Porter asked.

But Garrick noticed that Porter was following the woman and so was everyone else, heading toward the end of the long room where a door opened and they all filed out. As they went, they could hear more explosions, more clanking metal noises. Garrick thought something should happen now, immediately, at once before those disgusting Neballats slinked into the rooms, enveloping them all with their horrible need. He couldn't bear to have to look through the clear body of another one again, see their transparent flesh, see the absence of any soul, any conscience.

They moved into a wide, dark corridor, and Garrick felt his skin crawl, the same way it had back when the voice had been interrogating him. The Neballats were here. A light flickered at the end of the corridor, angry metal sounds pushing in. And then there were the voices, or the thoughts, their slinking, slimy thoughts. Again, something, someone, had escaped.

We will have you, was the thought that hurled itself down the hall. *We won't let all of you disappear again.*

Garrick wanted to grab Porter and anyone else he could and bust out of the structure. He wanted to force some kind of power from alternate energies, making something happen, wounding the Neballats, stopping them. Or more.

He swallowed, knowing that he wanted them all dead. There it was. He wouldn't tolerate being tied down ever again. And that's what would happen. They were going to come and strap him down and make him do what they wanted. They wanted the time that he and Mila could give him, millennia of chances to avoid their fate, their invisible bodies, their destroyed world.

They can't have our powers, the abandoned ones thought together, their idea a chorus in Garrick's head. *Our parents wouldn't give them what they wanted, and neither will we.*

The abandoned ones turned, watched the light at the end of the tunnel broaden, watched the Neballats come down the hall, and then they lifted their arms, an umbrella of radiant energy filling the corridor with red light. For just a second, Garrick saw the Neballats as they approached, their bodies illuminated, their organs and bones reflecting the light of the abandoned ones' energy.

And they kept coming, their horrible, long limbs slinking forward, a wave of power seeming to emanate from them, ready to burst forth and plunge forward over Garrick and the group.

Without thinking, Garrick felt himself slip into stillness, everything around him hushing, and then they were in the past, only a few seconds before.

Without having to tell them, the abandoned ones seemed to know what had happened with time. They threw another wave at the Neballats and this time, startled, they began to fall, one by one, as if the energy were a tidal wave they couldn't run from.

Now, came the thought, and the combined group of abandoned ones turned, facing their rescuers. This time, they didn't conjure up some wonderful feat of transformation or movement or fire or wave. Instead, they began to encircle Kate, Kenneth, Porter, and Garrick, moving closer and closer until they were all pressed together like sardines.

"This is kind of weird," Kenneth said, his voice slightly muffled. "But preferable to those things."

"What isn't weird?" Garrick said, thinking in a flash about every single weird thing he'd experienced lately, especially the bodies of the Neballats. And he didn't care how they got out of there. He didn't care if they evaporated into the air itself and steamed their way home to the safe house. All he wanted was to get away from them and find Mila. Too many times they'd been separated, and he didn't know if their luck would hold out. He didn't know if he would ever see her again.

Just before they began to dissolve (and that's how he would later describe it), he heard the woman's voice in his mind.

It will be all right. We will get away from them, she thought. *Just float with us, and I know that things will work out.*

Garrick felt a slip of anger pulse inside him. Just relax. Things will work out. Right. Surrounded by Neballats. Isolated from their entire culture.

Mila vanished.

How often had he heard some obnoxious person say those words to him and to others? How did things just work out? You had to work for what you wanted or hide it. That's what he'd always believed before Mila. As he thought of her, he realized that Mila had just worked out. He'd relaxed into the stupid blind date, and there she was. It worked out.

So maybe the woman was right. Hard to believe, but there it was. He tried to turn his head to find her, but he couldn't see anyone anymore, just the pulsing flicker of energy, of all their energies merging and melding into one plane.

He wanted to ask the woman a hundred questions. What did they do to the Neballats? He wanted to know not only what in the hell the Source really was, but what else she had learned while she was in the Source. What was there that made her so confident? Why did she believe what she learned there? Did she know where Mila was right now? Did she know if they would ever bring Cygiria back, at least all its people?

But there was no time to ask anything, and together, all of them seemed to soar and move and sail away, far from the structure, far from the Neballats that wanted to own and use them. They'd escaped. Somehow, surprisingly, things had just worked out.

On the ship, sitting with his back against the wall, Garrick closed his eyes and tried not to feel Porter's upset. He had his own to contend with, and even though for once Porter wasn't saying a word, his thoughts were a flickering ticker tape of worry.

Stephanie. Cygiria. Neballats. Home. Stephanie. Fight. Cygiria. Stephanie.

Kenneth wasn't doing much better, nor was Kate, but both of them sat surrounded by a group of the abandoned ones, listening to stories about their lives on Upsilia. Garrick thought to sit with them and learn what he could from these people who seemed to know so much more than he, but the only story he wanted to hear through was his own and Mila's. The story that brought them back together for good. The story that had no terrifying sequel but only a happy denouement as the man and woman went off into the orangey sunset.

Garrick sighed, turned his mind inward, knowing that he likely had a tape similar to Porter's broadcasting for all to hear. And there was something else, something that felt different. When he thought of Mila, she felt richer, deeper, not as though she were missing. In fact, it was as if she were happier. Better off somehow.

Garrick crossed his arms and sighed again. How could she be better off? They were separated. She might still be back on Upsilia, running from the Neballats. They weren't able to meld their powers together. They weren't able to be together in any way. So where was this feeling coming from?

He called out to her in his mind. *Mila? Mila! Where are you?*

For a second, he held his breath, waiting for her voice to come sailing into his mind—her soft, strong presence—but there was no answer. Slowly, even though he clung to the idea of her reply, the sounds from the ship filtered into his thoughts, along with the repetitive cant of Porter's whining.

Nothing. No Mila.

He opened his eyes and shook his head, but then

something pulled at his memory, tugged at his thoughts, reminded him to have hope. What had the Neballats thought just as the abandoned ones flung the energy wave at them? What were their words?

We won't let all of you disappear again.

Garrick sat up straight and then stood.

"What is it?" Porter asked, standing as well.

"Did you hear their thought?" Garrick asked.

"Which one?" Porter asked. "The one about taking all of our power or destroying us? A fine group of people."

"No," Garrick said. "The thought about not letting all of us disappear. Maybe that meant that some had."

"For such evil, powerful people, they seem to let us slip through their invisible fingers quite a bit," Porter said. "You'd think they enjoyed the chase."

"You aren't listening to me," Garrick said. "It could have meant that Mila and Stephanie and the rest disappeared. That they made it out. That they were the ones who slipped through the invisible fingers."

Dropping his sarcasm, Porter looked at Garrick, barely breathing. "How do we find out?"

Garrick didn't answer, but walked to the group of abandoned ones sitting by Kate and Kenneth. The woman that he and Porter had awakened sat calmly listening to Kate talk about Earth, but when she saw Garrick approach, she beamed her wide, open smile. Before he said anything to her, Garrick wondered how these people could actually be related to them. They didn't seem to struggle against what was happening or worry about it. After being treated like social outcasts and thrown into the deep freeze, he'd expected some bitterness or resentment. But none of them seemed to have any. He imagined that if any of them were subsequently strapped down to tables and given electroconvulsant therapy, they'd smile about it afterward.

"Are there other ships?" he blurted out. "Were there others like you in cylinders?"

The woman smiled again, and Garrick wished she'd stop. "Of course. There are hundreds of us."

"Where we were? In that place?"

"Some," the woman said.

Kate looked at Garrick and then back to the woman. "Ava, why didn't you say anything? We might have been able to get more of you off the planet."

"When it's time for them to leave, they will. Upsilia will have their hands full with the Neballats. There will have been sightings that will have to be covered up, and then the secret discussions and negotiations will begin. But Upsilia will keep their promise to us. They won't give us up without—"

"What are you talking about?" Garrick said. "The Neballats just came down to your planet and bombed their way into almost taking you and us away. Wouldn't a bunch of sleeping Cygirians be a lot easier to take?"

Garrick felt his anger and worry turn his voice rough and hard and impatient, the same voice he'd heard himself use at work before when talking with other traders. But that voice and that life should be miles away. However, Ava didn't seem disturbed by his tone, as usual.

"It's all going to be fine," she said.

Porter snorted. "Yes, it's all one large cosmic design, the universe unfolding exactly as it is supposed to. Yadda, yadda, yadda. But come on! Do you think the rest of our group got off Upsilia? What do you know?"

While Ava's smile slipped gently off her face, her eyes stayed steady on Porter. "I don't know why I can tell you this. But I can. It's all going to be fine. There is a plan. A design, as you say. And we wouldn't be here if there wasn't."

Porter seemed to move forward, and Garrick caught his arm, thinking, *No.*

At that thought, Porter relaxed, stood back on his heels. "Fine."

"We just need to know about our twins," Garrick said. "You must know what it feels like to be separated from yours. If you know anything. If you know what the Neballats meant about some already disappearing, you need to tell me. Look at us."

Garrick indicated Porter, Kate, and Kenneth. "We just can't do it. We just can't go on."

By now, all the abandoned ones were looking at him, and instead of feeling stupid, Garrick felt stronger. "We need to get back to the safe house and find our other halves. Nothing will work without them."

Ava stood up, walked up to Garrick, placing her hand on his arm. "Not everything that comes from the Source is specific. But I can tell you what I've told you. Everything will be just fine. If that means our doubles are returned to us, then we are lucky. Then we are blessed."

"Don't you miss him?" Garrick asked, his voice losing its anger. "Don't you need to know where he is?"

"I never found him," Ava said, her voice changing tone, lowering, softening. "I was put in the Source

over five years ago. I've had images. Feelings about
him. In the Source, I imagined that I caught
glimpses of him. Like a spring shadow. Like a flicker
of flame. But I never saw his face. I don't know who I
am looking for."

For the first time since meeting her, Garrick saw
her sad, slightly confused, not beaming her opti-
mism and hope at one hundred watts. And he saw
that, of course, she knew how he felt, even if she'd
never laid eyes on her twin once.

He found her own words almost slip out of his
mouth: *everything will be just fine.*

Garrick didn't say it, but Ava heard him all the
same, and she smiled, her face taking on her hope
again, her joy.

Kate stood up and walked to Garrick and Porter.
"We will be at the safe house soon. We'll know if they
made it. They will have tracked the other ship."

As she spoke, Garrick could see that she both
wanted and didn't want the information. Yes, it
would be available, but it might not come in the
form that any of them wanted. He knew he wasn't
alone in any of this feeling; he knew he would never
really be alone again.

"Well, for God's sake, let's sleep our way through
this ride," Porter said. "Better yet, send me to the
Source so I don't have to endure it."

Garrick shook his head. "I'd put you in the Source
just to get you to stop talking."

The group laughed, and Garrick felt a small hope
rise in his chest like a tiny balloon, something he
needed to nurture and watch and hope for.

Porter punched him lightly in the arm, and they
walked back toward the sleeping cubicles, knowing

that when they woke up, they'd know what happened. They'd know the truth.

Unlike a 747, this ship landed without a bump, and Garrick only awakened from his sleep because of the excited voices filing past him. Thoughts flickered along with the walkers, the abandoned ones hoping that the other ship had arrived and in it possibly were people they knew or even their doubles.

He stuck his head out of his cubicle to see if Porter were still asleep, but the other man was gone. Garrick hitched himself up to leave the ship, but it was as if an invisible hand was pulling him back. So instead, he lay back down on the pillow, blinking up at the cubicle ceiling.

He wouldn't be able to bear it if she weren't out there, waiting for him. He had never thought of himself as a soft man, a weak man, but his actual bones and muscles wouldn't work right now. The thought of never seeing Mila again was too much for his body to bear. Even his jaw seemed broken, hard and tight against his upper teeth.

And if it were all true, he'd go back. He'd move time back through the needle of action and make it all the way to the ship they had traveled to Upsilia on. He'd play that time over and over again because at least there, he'd be able to see her, touch her, feel her against his body. She'd make him laugh, she'd love him, and even though he'd spend all of that time knowing it wasn't going to last, Mila would be his.

If you won't come find me, came the thought, *I'll just have to find you.*

Garrick jerked up, hitting his head on the ceiling. He blinked stars away in order to take her into his vision, into his arms. Mila.

"Are you really there?" he asked, reaching out to pull her down onto him, kiss her hair, her forehead, her cheek, her lips.

"Hmm-hmm," she mumbled, kissing him back. "I am never going anywhere again."

Garrick laughed, holding her even closer, knowing that he didn't want to go anywhere else again, either. He knew that was ridiculous because they would eventually have to leave this cubicle and get off the ship. They would have to meet with the abandoned ones and the rest of their group in order to decide what to do next. They would have to fight the battle for their people and for their lives.

But for now, there was Mila.

And she was all over him, sloughing off his clothing with her hands, kissing his neck, her tongue leaving a delicate, wet line along his skin. He couldn't stand another second of not having all of her. He pulled closed the cubicle curtain and pushed her down on the bed, looking into her dark, wonderful eyes. He ran his hand along her smooth shoulder and then placed his lips right at the apex of her throat and chest, breathing her in as he moved his hands under her shirt.

There was so much about Mila that was right. Of course, there was their combined power, but even now the ability to move through time somehow seemed normal, like breathing or blinking, a thing automatic and necessary. What was truly amazing was her voice, her smell, her laugh. There was the way she moved, pushing her hair off her forehead; the way she crossed her legs; the way she clapped her hands when she was happy. Her face when she woke up in the morning and turned to him, smiling, her hair splayed out across the pillow, everything about her he simply loved.

And there was this moving together with her, this love, this sex, that was different from anything Garrick had ever known. He had never once believed the fairy tales anyone had told him, the stories read to him by his mother and father. Later, he laughed at love stories and soap operas and his friends' tales of overwhelming attraction to first girls and then women—the long e-mails written after three beers, the late-night phone calls, the stuttering first dates.

But now it was different. Now he had what everyone had tried to tell him all along.

"You are so soft," he said, knowing that "soft" didn't do her justice. There were words not invented for how she felt, but his hands knew how to read her, understand her sighs, her slight moans.

He took off the rest of her clothes, running his hands along her body, and then shrugged off his own, needing her skin, her flesh, her feel. Every second that was between his body and hers was a second too long.

"Yes," she murmured as he pressed against her.

"Where have you been?" he asked, moving his mouth down to the lovely mound of her breast.

"Saving the world," she said, laughing. "Waiting for *youuu.*"

Her last word moved into sound as he found her nipple, sucking it gently as he moved his hands under the sweetness of her ass, pushing her thighs apart gently with his body.

And then he was inside her, the slick warmth of her holding him tight and wet.

"You feel amazing," he said, or at least he thought he said it, his voice caught into stillness as he just felt everything about this touching. Finally, he had permission to feel. To be who he was. She allowed him to be the man he always wanted to be.

It's you, she thought. *You are amazing.*

Together, they rocked and moved, her sighs turning into moans, his heart beating against his ribs, spilling, it seemed to him, out of his body, into hers, where they were caught together, forever, in love.

"Do you remember my dream?" she said, running a hand along his jaw. "You know, the one about the dark space?"

Garrick pulled his mouth away from her neck, nodding. "Of course."

"You remember the blond boy?"

"Of course," he said. "The one you think is your brother."

"He is," she said. "I met him. I found my brother."

Garrick stopped kissing her, leaned up on his elbow, stared down into her face. "You did? How? Was he here?"

"No," she said. "I woke him up."

"He's one of the abandoned ones," he said. "He was asleep in a cylinder."

Mila smiled, her face opening in a way he'd never really seen, and despite his attempt to push the feeling away, a slit of jealousy opened up in his chest. He knew he shouldn't be jealous. She had been waiting her whole life to understand her dream, to find the boy sitting next to her. And thank God he wasn't that boy! But Garrick knew that her brother would always have a place in her heart he couldn't have. Sure, that was normal, but he was greedy. He wanted all of her, even if that want was unreasonable.

"I couldn't believe it," she said, pushing herself up on her elbow so that their eyes were level. "He was the first one I saw. What are the odds of that? And when he woke up, he recognized me. From the Source. Something he learned there helped him know who I was. I can't wait for you to meet him. For you both to know each other. And maybe he can explain about the Source."

At the mention of the Source, Garrick shook his head. "I don't really understand that idea. That place. It seems to make them, well, a little wacky."

"I know. Edan—that's my brother—seems so calm. Sort of, well, really evolved. Like he's lived a few years or decades at a Zen monastery."

"Edan, huh?"

"It means fiery. Or zealous. Or something hot," she said. "But he seems anything but."

She shrugged, her hair falling around her shoulders. Garrick pushed a strand back, feeling her soft hair against the back of his hand. She'd found her brother, and she was happy. She was lucky. He could only wish to find a family, to have a connection to the life he knew he must have had—the life he'd hoped he'd understand surviving all the years of unhappiness.

"I'm glad," he said finally, realizing he meant it. Maybe he'd never be the only man in her life and he shouldn't really want to be. Together, he and Edan would help her, give her strength just as she would do for them. "I want to meet him."

Mila stroked his face, and he wanted to push her

back down and start all over. He looked at her with a smile.

"You know, we could move time back a little. We could have all of this over again," he said.

Mila laughed. "Yeah, and we could go forward and see how everything turns out. We could see who wins the fight and figure out how we find my sister and your family and everyone. But—"

"But you don't want to," he said, finishing her thought.

"No," she said. "The more I live with people who acknowledge my gift, the more I fight against people who want to steal it, the more precious I think time is. This time. This now-moment. I know it sounds ridiculous, but I only want time when I have it."

Nodding, Garrick took in a long breath. He wanted to argue, to say that together, they didn't affect time the way they did when they churned through it alone. Together, time was like a hallway with doors they could walk into, choose to enter, choose to move through, choose to leave to come back to this now-moment. But he understood her, and he wanted the same thing, too. This life as it unfolded.

"Well, then can we stay here for a while? No one might notice." Garrick kissed a spot on her fine line of collarbone, letting his lips take in her heat.

"We can't," she said. And she was right. They had to leave the ship. They had to go out and start this new life, the one with their people. With Mila's family. With their fight against the Neballats. "But I want you," she said. "Now and always."

"Now?" Garrick said, kissing her chin.

"Not *now* now. But you know what I mean."

"I do," he said. "I do know what you mean."

Together, they moved quietly dressing, and in those simple moments, Garrick knew that despite everything, all of it, he knew this. Her. And now.

Once outside the ship, Garrick almost stopped still, looking out the small outdoor space of the safe house, all of it completely filled with Cygirians. After seeing the images that the Neballats had shown him, after knowing about the quick, frightening getaway off the planet all those years ago, it was amazing to see so many Cygirians safe, together, whole.

"My God," he said. "Did we—did you bring them all home?"

"Not all. But we did. You did. And the other group from Earth did. And there's so many more still on both planets. People in hiding. People who actually haven't discovered their abilities," Mila said.

Garrick turned to her, amazed. Could there actually be someone who hadn't found his or her talent the hard way? Had someone managed to keep everything underground and lived, well, normally? "I can't imagine it, either. But we have to go back to Earth and to Upsilia to find us all. And then we can finally deal with the Neballats. We can finally live our lives."

"But there's some bad news. We think that the Neballats managed to capture some of us. There are people that Kate and Michael haven't been able to rescue. We have to find them, too."

He nodded. "No one should suffer any more of that abuse."

Something came over Mila's face, a look he'd seen the first draft of—when she was determined to find Mr. Henry or when she stood firm in her resolve to not sleep with him because he might be her brother. Then he'd known it was her strength showing—the firm line of jaw, the steady gaze. But now there was a light glowing inside her, lit by the knowledge that Edan was alive and well and that somewhere, her sister was alive, too.

"We can't live in fear of them. Not anymore. Not ever. Look at all of us."

Garrick turned back to look at all the people below him, wanting to believe that what Mila said was possible. But he'd seen the insides of the Neballats, literally and figuratively. They wanted what they'd lost along the way and would do everything to get it back. They wanted what they didn't deserve.

And why wouldn't they? On Earth, those were the people who ran everything. Who owned everything. He knew that from living the life he had lived. Power and privilege corrupted, and if the Cygirians wanted to fight back, they would have to play rough, play hard for what they, he, wanted.

Mila squeezed his hand, and Garrick relaxed, looking around again at the throng. Then he laughed. "Is this place going to sink or implode or deflate?" he asked, wondering where all of them would fit. The safe house wasn't big enough to support them all for very long. "I guess we actually do need our own planet."

"Or figure out how to live on one of them," she said. "Somehow make everyone accept us. I don't think anyone should have to go to the Source if they don't want to. There has to be a way. There won't be another big bang just so we can find a place to live.

And I don't think we can build up a whole civilization in time to retire!"

Garrick smiled, thinking about her hopes. She pulled on his hand, and they walked into the crowd, heading toward Porter, who seemed to be standing on something—a chair, a box, a bench—telling a story, moving his hands. Garrick was about to shake his head, knowing Porter well enough already to almost hear the sarcastic, amused story he was telling. Garrick wanted to join in, add a true commentary to whatever load of crap Porter was presenting, but then something stopped him, made him glance to the left. Later, he wouldn't know if it had been a feeling or a sound or a motion, but right then, Garrick realized he saw Edan before Mila could point him out. He stood quietly in a group, listening to someone, and then he turned slightly, seeing Mila and smiling.

Of course, Garrick could blame the recognition on the fact that Edan looked just like Mila—the same long blond hair, strong, lithe body, and dark, intelligent eyes—but Garrick knew he would have noticed Edan even if Mila wasn't related to him. There was something amazing about him—amazing and spooky.

"I know," said Mila. "It's like he shines. I mean, like it comes out of him. It's like heat. Or light."

"But from what? From being in the Source for years? From living on that crazy planet with androids?"

She shrugged. "Some of them seem a little spacey, but mostly, Edan is just different."

"What is his power?" he asked, imagining that it was something like turning dirt into gold.

"That's the sad part," she said.

"What?"

Mila sighed. "He can age himself. Time doesn't go by like it does with us. But his body ages. He thinks he's lost about ten years. And he's only used his powers twice."

"Unbelievable," Garrick said. "Or not, really. But what about his twin? His double?"

"He never found her," Mila said, reaching out and touching Garrick's arm. "They never made contact."

"That's—" Garrick began, knowing that no matter how amazing Edan might seem, not having his twin invalidated that shine. But as Garrick looked at Mila's brother, he wanted to ask more questions. He wanted to know what Edan and his twin could do. Together, could they keep each other from aging at all? Did their power move to other people? Was there an antiaging wave they could create? Were they like some kind of human fountain of youth?

And he wanted to know more about the Source, this place that had given him so many answers. He wanted to know if he could go, if he could try to find out who he was in its murky pool of soulness.

But before Mila could sense any of these questions and tell him to knock it off, Edan had noticed them, excusing himself from his group that included Kate, Michael, Stephanie, and Porter, who seemed to be bereft when he left them. As he walked toward Garrick and Mila, his hair behind his shoulders, his eyes alive with happiness, Garrick knew that if this man ever found his twin, his center, he would be a force unimaginable, like wind, like water, like magic.

"I am so glad to meet you," Edan said, putting his hand on Garrick's shoulder. "Mila wasn't sure what had happened to you on our planet. But I had a feeling you would be all right."

"I'm glad you thought so," Garrick said. "In the short time I have known your sister, I've had more than a few moments of doubt."

"There's no time for doubt," Edan said. "Look around! Look at all of us. We are back with each other. We are ready to take back what is ours."

Without really thinking about it, Garrick blocked his thoughts, not wanting his doubts or his cynicism to show again. Standing by this confident man made him feel like Porter.

"That would be, well, amazing," Garrick said, finding Mila's hand with his own. "And I guess you are right. With all of us, so much more is possible."

"Yes," Edan said, smiling. "Yes."

He smiled and squeezed Garrick's shoulder again and then hugged Mila. "I'm going to go speak with Jai and Risa about what to do with all of us from Upsilia. And then I think we are all going to meet. Together. All of us abandoned ones."

"Found ones," Mila said. "We are found, Edan. You, me, Garrick. All of us. We aren't abandoned anymore."

In the first second of hearing her words, Garrick could see Edan accept them and then reject them, based on one thing—Edan hadn't found his twin. For that tiny moment, his shine faded. Dimmed, really, before rekindling, blaring, blasting so high, Garrick wanted to blink.

"You are right, Mila. We are found. Not lost anymore." He smiled again, and then strode back into the crowd, his hair flowing behind him.

Garrick turned to Mila, shaking his head. "He is one intense dude!"

Mila nodded. "What did you expect? He haunted my dreams my whole life. Even as a little boy in the dream, he was like this. Serious, comforting. Intense."

"I don't know if I want to be around when he finds his twin. That will be some kind of fireworks."

"Like with us," she said, kissing his cheek. "Just like with us."

In the midst of all his people, Garrick turned Mila slightly and hugged her, pressing her as close as he could without hurting her. Under his hands, he felt her skin, her ribs, her breath.

"Yes," he said, nothing cynical in him now. Nothing Porter-like. Nothing worried. "Just like with us. Just like it will always be with us."

They stood there together in the crowd, her mouth against his neck, her arms tight around him, their hearts beating, beating into the next second and the next.

Chapter Fourteen

"So, we have to figure this out just right," Mila said. She and Garrick were sitting under a fake tree in the fake outdoors of the safe house, one of the few quiet spots available now that people were meeting and organizing all day long, planning everything about the resistance movement, the rescue of the remaining Cygirians on Earth and Upsilia, the eventual move to one of those planets. The air ached with plans of the future, but for this short time, Mila felt she and Garrick had to figure out their return to Earth. More specifically, their return to San Francisco and their families.

"Right. Everything is in the timing."

"Is that a pun?" Mila asked. "Are you a punster?"

"What we have together is time. Time is of our essence. No time like our time. Time for—"

"Okay," she said, reaching her hand out and touching his hair, the fake sun beating heat down on the gold strands. "I get it."

"I don't know if you really do," Garrick said. "How could you know how much I love you?"

"I can float around in your head, silly one," she said. "I've seen some of those thoughts and they aren't G-rated."

"Don't get me started," he said. "Or I will have to finish here, in the fake outside with people just around the corner. We need to figure this thing out."

"All right," Mila said, stretching out, feeling her skin, her bones, her flesh, the parts that Garrick touched so well. "Tell me your plan."

"All right, then," he said, running a finger along her arm. "We want to make sure Mr. Henry has been divested of the simulator and that my parents and Aunt Linda aren't too freaked out about our sudden disappearance. It seems wise to work it so that your mother hasn't called in the world's air and armed forces to find you and kill me. Or the CIA, FBI, or KGB. The next thing we know, James Bond will be sitting on her sofa with a martini."

Mila smiled, suddenly yearning for home. Yes, home. Adair and Paul and Nidia. And Mr. Henry. All the rules and social norms and horrifying charity events. But more than anything, she wanted to see her mother's face, her raised eyebrow, her smile. And the good news was now that she and Garrick were united, she wouldn't have to field Adair's demonic blind date setups.

"Yes, yes. I know. There will be men with semiautomatics at the door. But more importantly, Mr. Smart-Ass, we don't want any Neballats lurking around, putting another simulator in someone just as we show up," Mila said, knowing that the Neballats were likely figuring out a strategy as the Cygirians were.

Garrick leaned forward and kissed her. "You're right, as always. So when should we go? When will you be ready to leave Edan behind?"

Mila was about to say she could go right now, when a pang as old as her dream banged hard in her chest. Leave him. She had to. Just as she'd had to leave Garrick behind on Upsilia. This new life seemed to be as much about leaving behind as her old one had been about trying to live through. To take each day as it came even though nothing had ever made sense. Now everything made sense, but she kept having to let it go.

"Sweetheart, we have to leave now. We have to go back to our lives so we can leave them again. We have to make happy those people who love us. Who have taken care of us."

"I know," Mila said, closing her eyes and letting herself just breathe Garrick in.

"And we'll come back and do what needs to be done. And think of it this way, we won't have to miss any time at home. They will blink their eyes, and we will be there. They will blink them again, and we will be gone. We can show up for every holiday, every birthday, every party, and still do what we need to here. For Cygiria. We won't miss our old lives. We will actually have two."

Garrick pulled her close, and Mila nodded against his shoulder. For so long, she'd railed against the old life, wishing it would disappear—*poof!*—in a puff of smoke. No more harassing calls from Adair, no more job she didn't like, no more dating issues, no more artistic boyfriends who ran off with models. But from millions of miles away, that life seemed like a small, tender jewel she wanted to watch and polish.

"And then put back on the shelf," Garrick said.

"The only part I can't put on the shelf is you," Mila said, kissing his neck.

"I told you not to get me started," he said. "But it's too late. I'm started."

"I like what happens when you get started. So listen, they do call this a safe house." Mila disentangled herself from Garrick, stood up, and held out her hand. "Let's go check out how safe it is. Maybe we can find a few minutes to ourselves."

He took her hand and stood up, grabbing her and pressing her close, thinking, *I don't want minutes, I want a lifetime.*

It all starts now, she thought. *And now and now and now.*

Together, they walked toward the building, ignoring the noises around them. Mila felt Garrick—his hand, his leg brushing against hers as they moved, his side—and knew that though together they could replay this moment over and over again if they so chose, it was now, in this fresh new minute, that everything was exactly as it should be.

"So you are going home just as the story heats up," Porter said, shaking his head as Mila packed up her few possessions. "How you could want to go back home now is beyond me."

"Will you keep quiet?" Stephanie said, handing Mila a folded shirt. "Will you *ever* keep quiet?"

Porter turned to Stephanie, and from the looks on their faces, it was clear they were having an argument Mila was glad not to be a part of.

"Fine," Porter said finally with a sarcastic sigh, a

trick Mila had never heard anyone accomplish. "I hope you have a marvelous trip. I hope you are able to solve your family troubles, financial issues, work situations, artistic crises, and social obligations before finally heading back to us."

Mila looked up from her packing, about to tell Porter to go do something unspeakable to himself, but then she saw how he really felt, his face full of the sad words he couldn't say.

"Porter, we will be back soon. We just have some loose ends. I know they don't seem very important to you, but I won't be able to focus on all that we have to do for Cygiria if I don't go home first. And you know you could come with us. Garrick and I will take you home, bend a little time for you if you want. Just say the word."

Porter shook his head, put up a hand, and walked away. Stephanie put her hand on Mila's forearm and pressed gently. "Ignore him. He's just nervous. All these people here now and no way for him to subdue them all with his rapier wit. And he doesn't need to go home. There's no one there for him."

"Then this is home," Mila said. "Where you are. Wherever you are."

Stephanie smiled, blushed, shrugged as she took her hand away from Mila. "He and I have a long way to go. But we are growing. We aren't like you and Garrick, but we are figuring it out."

"Just keep your electricity under control, and I think you'll be fine."

Stephanie nodded. "I don't know. Sometimes, I think all I want to do is put Porter out. Stop the madness."

But she laughed. Then she leaned over and kissed

Mila on the cheek, and walked away, leaving Mila to her packing, which was done. Now all she had to do was wait for Garrick to finish talking to Jai and Risa and find Michael and Kate. Michael had been sure they wanted to "go home the way they got here," even though there were ships available now.

"If you insist," Mila said, knowing that the bumpy energy rides—though fast—weren't half as wonderful as sitting in a comfortable ship, Garrick at her side.

"Kate and I might even hang around. Go to Pier 39 and do some touristy things," Michael said. "I've been itching for a 49ers cap. Or maybe the Giants."

"I don't think so," Kate said. "But we will be ready to come get you when you finish your work there. You know how to contact us. Just make sure the us from the past has come and gone."

The work they had there. Mila sighed. She and Garrick had figured out the exact time from the past that they would return, shortly after Kate and Michael had taken out the simulator from Mr. Henry and before Garrick had shown up with his own. In that small slip of time, they could appease their families, prove Mila's wholeness and happiness, and then prepare to leave again.

"You won't be able to be on rewind forever," Edan said.

Mila started and then turned to see her brother standing in front of her, his hands clasped.

"At some point, real time and your real life will have to merge."

"That's easy to say when you come from a planet where people have a clue about other world cultures, spaceships, angry, invisible aliens, and time travel. Try coming from a place that doesn't even think global warming is caused by man-made sources."

Edan smiled. "I'm not sure what you mean about this global warming, but I know it's not as easy for you on your world. But at some point, you will have to tell them. Both of you will. All the Cygirians from Earth will have to make themselves known."

Mila picked up her bag, and both of them walked down the hall and then outside. Garrick was there, talking with Kenneth and Whitney, shaking hands and then hugging them both. He saw Mila and Edan, said a few more words, and then came over to them both, smiling a slight, wistful smile, his head full of regrets.

Family, home, miss them, a place, Aunt Linda. Aunt Linda!

This isn't easy. You know we have to go, Mila thought. *And then we will come back. Think of it this way, if you play your cards right, Aunt Linda will never have to matchmake again.*

What do you mean play my cards right? I thought I'd already laid down a royal flush!

Laid down, huh? Mila thought. *Is that what this has been all about? You sure had me fooled with that poker face of yours.*

"It's possible you might actually end up staying," Edan said. "This argument could go on for quite a while."

"I hope it goes on forever," Garrick said, taking Mila's arm. "I hope this particular argument never stops."

And then Garrick kissed her quickly, leading her

down the path to where Michael and Kate were waiting, talking with Edan as if he'd known him a lifetime.

For a small second, everything seemed in align-
ment, and Mila forced herself to keep breathing. She
heard herself answer questions, felt Garrick next to
her, watched her brother talk with the technicians who
would help them lift off and leave the safe house.

Except for her missing sister, this might be her
dream. Her true dream. All the connection she always knew she wanted was right here in front of her,
right now. Neballats or no Neballats, Adair's poten-
tial wrath or her slanted eye aimed at Mila's love life,
Mila Adams was 100 percent happy.

Moving together in Kate's and Michael's energy,
buoyed by space and movement, Garrick held Mila
in his arms. As they embraced, they shared the time-
line in their thoughts, flicking over what they knew
would happen and when, showing each other snip-
pets of the past.

*There, you see that space, just before I came to the door.
My aunt and your mom are together in the living room talking. My aunt is trying to persuade your mother that all is
okay.*

Mila smiled, seeing that even in her obvious dis-
tress, Adair had put on her St. Johns suit, nylons, and
heels.

Woops, Mila thought, just as Adair turned to look
at the front door. *Here you come. We have to get there before then. Or your simulator-raged brain might have some
issues. Or you might send us all back into the past.*

And where is Mr. Henry?

Not around by a long shot, Mila thought. Kate and Michael had already gotten to him.

Too bad we didn't bring Porter. He would disarm your mother in a second with his evil tongue, and she might ignore us altogether.

Mila shook her head, smiling. *There is no way we are getting out of this easily, Porter or no Porter. I might be waving good-bye to my Christmas shopping spree at Neiman's.*

Garrick chuckled low and soft, holding her tighter. *You hate Neiman's. You don't even really seem to like clothes.*

Not when you're around, Mila thought.

Okay, you two, Michael thought. *We are almost there. Don't start moving time until we leave, though. I don't want to end up back home eating Frosted Flakes and listening to my mother watch Judge Judy.*

Don't worry, Garrick thought. *We won't send you home. Just leave us at the place we agreed on and make sure you leave at the same moment. We don't want to have to try to explain one more thing!*

Garrick held on to Mila, and together they watched as Kate's and Michael's energy brought them closer to Earth, breaking into the atmosphere with a whoosh, moving slowly, slowly down onto the planet. The earth spun on its axis, the great groan of the Northern Hemisphere turning into sight.

Home, thought Mila as she saw the Pacific pop into view.

Yes, Garrick thought, and then Kate and Michael seemed to accelerate, bringing them into daylight, blinding light, the air softer, warmer, and then they were both standing on the sidewalk in front of the Adamses' house, Kate and Michael only a crackle of energy in their ear and then there was silence.

Or, really, the sound of Adair Adams talking loudly in the foyer of her home.

"Some things," Mila said, "never change."

"Thank goodness," he said. "But we better move time back to *when* we want to be, oh, about now."

Both of them turned to see the front door opening. Quickly, they took hands, and Mila closed her eyes, feeling for stillness, finding the gray whoosh of the time of no-time, seeing the portals that she and Garrick could enter.

Find us there, Garrick thought, and Mila imagined it. The time, the place, and the world shimmered, and they walked through the portal to the left, into the very same spot where they had started the process.

"How much time do we have before you show up? About ten minutes?" Mila asked.

"We have as many of those ten minutes as we like. We just need to keep your mother and my aunt busy until Kate and Michael can come and get me and rescue me from myself. There has to be enough time to get Mr. Henry out of there, too."

"Later," Mila said. "Later we have to go back and find him. I have to know that he's okay, especially now that we know what they did to him."

"We will," Garrick promised. "And he's fine. Look how well I did after having a simulator-ectomy!"

Mila nodded, and he went on. "So we manage to get them out of the house. I will arrive, and I won't be able to find Adair at home. Mysteriously, she and my aunt will be out on a lovely stroll or something."

Mila nodded and pulled Garrick up the stairs. When they reached the door, she just about rang the bell but then stopped, turning to face him. "Even if we can't make it right with them, any or all, I am going to be with you, Garrick. No matter what. You know that, right?"

Leaning forward, Garrick kissed her, his lips soft on hers, his tongue warm and wet and barely there. Mila wanted to open to him, take in his feeling, his passion, his body, but there was so much to do, and, to use a cliché, time was of the essence.

Okay, he thought. *But you know what I want to do after this is over!*

They pulled apart and Mila rang the bell, knowing that with the urgent *clack, clack, clack* on the marble foyer inside, Adair Adams was just seconds away. And then the door opened wide, and there was Adair, staring at Mila. And then Garrick. And then Mila. Her face, for once, was still, her mouth hanging open, no words coming at them. But then it was as if she was being chipped out of ice, her face slowly showing her amazement, her grief, her joy, her irritation.

"My God, Mila. My girl," Adair said, swiftly walking to Mila and taking her shoulders in her hands. "Where have you been? Why didn't you call? Why didn't you let us know where you were? We have had everyone we know on this. The mayor has been calling me every hour. We . . . we—"

"Mom," Mila said, letting her mother's whirling questions creep into her body. "It's okay. I'm all right. I'm home now. And I'm sorry—"

"We have all the authorities on the case. Your father was about to call Washington."

"We can call everyone off now. The worry is over," Garrick said, and at his voice, there was a shriek from inside the house, another set of *clack, clack, clacks*, and then his aunt Linda was in the doorway. Her face full of amazement, she launched herself at Garrick, grabbed him hard around the neck, and hugged him in a death grip.

"Aunt Linda," he said, his voice muffled. "Aunt Linda!"

He took a hand and gently moved his aunt's arm from his mouth. "Like Mila says, it's all okay."

Linda grudgingly pulled away, looking closely at Garrick. Then she turned to Mila, her face widening into a huge, wrinkle-free, blindingly white-toothed smile. "I knew it. I knew it before I ever set you up. You two are in love. This was a getaway, an escape from everything. All just has to be forgiven!"

Adair stood straighter, clenched her jaw, narrowed her eyes. "Love is all well and good, but it's no excuse for rudeness. It's fine and well for you to tell us, young man, that we don't have to worry. But have either of you ever heard of a cell phone? My God, you don't know what we've been through because of you two." Adair tapped her shoe, crossed her arms, made small clucking noises at the back of her mouth.

Mila wanted to comfort Adair, to tell her the truth really. But, of course, that would take days and vials of Valium, and as they stood there in the doorway, Mila felt time click by in huge seconds. She could almost sense the metal mechanism of a spaceship somewhere, perched and ready to take captives back for interrogation. "Mom, let's—let's go on a walk and talk about this. You and Linda and Garrick and I. Let us tell you the story."

"A walk?" Adair looked at Mila. "A walk? At a time like this? I most certainly have to get on the phone with everyone to stop this madness."

Mila breathed in, trying to remain calm. "But it's lovely out, and we want you to hear the whole story. Not be interrupted by telephones or reporters or whoever else that's interested in this. In us."

Linda held on to Garrick's arm, nodding, agreeing with every syllable of Mila's words. "Adair, let's. Let's hear the story of how they ran away together and fell madly in love. That's a story that I want to hear, especially because they seem so happy!"

"And especially because you arranged it," Garrick added, looking at Mila over his aunt's head.

We have to get out of here, he thought.

I know, Mila thought. *I know.*

Adair's mouth opened again as she looked back and forth between them. "A walk."

Behind them, traffic moved slowly up and down Broadway. Mila could envision Garrick with the thing in his head driving toward them, trying to find Mila and take her back to the Neballats. After the mission to Upsilia, the discovery of the abandoned ones and Edan, the fighting with the Neballats, it would be ridiculous to be captured on Broadway in San Francisco.

"Yes, a walk." Mila held out her hand, and her mother took in a deep, slow, heavy breath and then sighed.

"Oh, all right. How odd," Adair said. "How very strange." But she went back into the foyer, grabbed a sweater, and closed the door behind her.

"And there's something even more strange," she said. "I just don't know what has happened to Mr. Henry. Totally vanished. Quite a mystery."

Mila knew she couldn't tell Adair how strange it in fact was, but she agreed with her mother. Everything was a mystery. Here she was, back in the past with her mother, the woman who had raised her from a baby, somehow receiving the infant Mila and never questioning the implanted story. Somewhere else, Mila's sister, Sophia, lived her life, not knowing why she had powers or who she was. Back on the safe planet, her long-lost brother was organizing to take back their lives from the Neballats.

In space, she had friends and families. Anywhere, no matter where she was and if she was with Garrick, she could move time, traveling in it like a river.

And more mysterious, the most mysterious thing of all—stranger than space or magic or murderous aliens—was that here, next to her, on her arm, was the man of her dreams. Not just the man in her dreams, but the man of them. Her twin. Her equal. Her love.

For a few silent minutes, they all walked together, the soft spring air full of salt and sea. The wind pushed through a giant cedar overhead, a helicopter buzzed in the sky miles away.

Just as they turned the corner of Broderick and Broadway, Garrick's car pulled up in front of the Adamses'. Mila quickened her pace and kept her eyes forward, not wanting to encourage any talk until she knew they were safe.

I think we are in the clear. We made a clean escape, Garrick thought. *I hate to think about what I would have done if I had not found you.*

We don't have to think about it, Mila thought. *Let's just think about this.*

They walked a little farther down Broderick, and then Adair stopped still in her tracks.

"Not another step until you tell me everything."

"Oh yes," Linda agreed. "Everything. Every little detail."

"Everything but the parts you won't believe," Mila said.

"Everything that's G-rated," Garrick said.

"Young man. My goodness," Adair said sternly, giving Garrick her famous evil eye. For a second, Mila felt her heart beat a sharp *one, two, one, two* against her chest, the exact response her mother had always inspired in her.

But then Adair laughed, took Mila's other arm, and they walked into the warm San Francisco afternoon.

This time, Mila's dream is different. As always, she is in the rumbling dark space, the sounds muffled and hazy, but now she is with Garrick at her side. On their sides, really, facing each other. No one else is in the space, not Edan, not her sister.

Garrick ran his hand from her neck, over her shoulder, and down the smooth sides of her waist. She breathed in, his very touch sending a wide net of shivers over her whole body. She felt herself slicken with heat and desire, her body wanting nothing more than his, his alone.

The dark space rumbled, the air full of the same, still heat. Mila looked into his eyes, saw his love, saw herself reflected in their darkness. She brought a hand to his face, feeling the soft, shaved skin under her fingers.

Twins, she thought.

But thankfully not related, he thought, letting his hand rise up her hip, pulling her closer so that her breasts were against his chest.

That would have changed the end of this story, she thought, wanting to think more, tell him how she loved that he was here, in her dream, just as she had always hoped.

But there was no time for thinking, only for feeling all of Garrick as he turned her over, moved on top of her, pushed gently, so gently inside her. She pulled him down on top of her, needing his weight, even in the dream.

And then, unlike all the times she'd had the dream before, it did not end, dissolving into gray. Instead, she slowly awoke to Garrick moving over her, thrusting himself so deeply into her she took a sharp, pleasurable intake of air. Outside the window, the sky seemed to burst into orange, a beautiful Cygirian sunrise.

"Yes?" he whispered in her ear. "Feels good?"

"Always," she said, opening herself to take all of him into her. "Always yes."

Don't miss the rest of Jessica's innovative series!

INTIMATE BEINGS

When you least expect it, love finds you . . .

Lately, Claire Edwards feels like she's floundering. A ho-hum teaching job, a string of terrible dates, nights spent with only Netflix and bizarre dreams of spaceships for company . . . life isn't working out the way she hoped. But Claire has an extraordinary secret ability—she can go anywhere at all, just by wishing it. And if the intensely attractive man who suddenly materializes in her car one day is any indication, Claire's not the only one . . .

Ever since Darl James learned of his true origins, he has been searching for his partner and life mate, the one whose gift will complement and complete his own. Now that he's found Claire, he vows to never lose her again, or their soul-searing, sensual connection. But keeping her safe won't be easy when they've been marked for destruction by an evil, power-hungry race. A fierce battle is brewing, one that will test Claire and Darl's new bond to the limit, and decide the future of all their kind . . .

O kay, she thought. *Okay. Just a few more miles and all this will disappear.*

As she rounded the park, heading toward Stanyan, she wished for the nth time that her mother were alive. Like so many things, she wouldn't be able to tell her mother about the voice, but she could at least sit by her and maybe watch a TV show. Or work out in the garden, digging up weeds or planting the latest in heirloom vegetables. Anything to take her mind away from the craziness.

But, of course, her mother wasn't here anymore, and there wasn't a person she could confide in. Claire was pretty sure that Yvonne would listen politely and then call 911. Ruth would likely do the same. Maybe it was time to go to a therapist and just spill it all and wait to see what a trained professional would suggest. Maybe she would do it. Maybe she would just finally take care of this problem.

"You don't have a problem, you nut," the voice said.

"Stop it!" Claire shrieked, braking hard at the corner of Stanyan and Hayes, a Muni bus squealing to avoid hitting her.

"Shit, shit, shit," she said, turning right onto Hayes and stalling right behind a FedEx van.

"You need to stop this car right now," the voice said.

Breathing in small, shallow breaths, Claire pulled over, parking in a rare open spot, ignoring the stares from passersby and the FedEx driver. The voice might be a product of her own imagination, but it was right. She was a danger to herself and others.

"Who are you?" she whispered, convinced now that she was talking to nothing but her own sad thoughts. "Where are you?"

"Due to the powers of others, I have managed to render myself invisible this once," the voice said. "But I don't hear that well."

"Who are you?" she asked again, her voice louder, clearer, even though she felt her heart pounding in her throat.

She looked down at her hands in her lap, shaking her head, almost wanting to laugh out loud. Was she this lonely and sad that she was conjuring up a voice? A male voice. A man. A man who was focused on her. She had finally cracked. All these years she really had been crazy. Those times she thought she'd gone to another country or town or place had been psychotic breaks. A psychotic break. She had been delusional, was so right now. When she thought she could hear other people's thoughts, she was merely deep in some horrid fantasy of her own creation.

She was paranoid, schizophrenic, maybe bipolar with an affective disorder. Top it off with panic and anxiety, and she was a psychiatrist's dream. A master's thesis. A doctoral dissertation.

So it was clear. She had no choice. No more debate here. Nothing else to argue about. Claire knew she needed to drive herself right now to Langley Porter Psychiatric Institute at UCSF and check in. Forever. Get some kind of commitment. What did they call that? A 5150. At least she'd never have to deal with Annie and Sam again.

"Oh, what a drama queen!" the voice said, and as she heard the words, a body began to take shape and form in a wave of pixilated air.

"You are a jerk," faded from her tongue, and she blinked, tried to focus on what she could hardly believe was happening next to her in the passenger's seat.

For the moments it took for him to appear, Claire knew that even though she had felt odd her entire life—even though she'd made herself appear with a *poof!* all over the place—she'd never really believed that magic existed. She never really thought about the concept of superpowers or abilities. Everything truly odd was contained in her and her alone—she was the holder of the world's weirdness. Actually, she thought she was some kind of genetic anomaly, a creation of some weird fluke in a DNA strand. No one else was like her. No one on the planet.

"I would have to say that no one is like you. But you aren't alone in this power business," said the man now sitting next to her. "Believe it or not, soon you are not going to be all alone anymore, ever again."

Claire couldn't focus on what he was saying. Instead, she slowly moved her gaze from his thigh (a very nice thigh in what seemed to be cotton pants) to his body (strong), shoulders (stronger), neck, and then face. His face. Claire wanted to stop breathing because if she did, she would die, and she wouldn't have to sit there completely embarrassed, her body roiling in heat, her mind just about everywhere.

"You are just some kind of delusion," she said, relieved in a strange way that at least she knew what she was dealing with. "Some kind of sad last gasp of hope in me."

"Really?" the man said. "Strange how I feel so *here*. You know, like in my body."

"Sorry. You're not," Claire said. "It's all about me. Finally, the cliché comes true. Hold on to your hat. We're going to Langley Porter. It's close by, so that's good. Put on your seat belt."

"I don't think that's where I want to go. From the sound of it, there are madwomen screaming in the attic there," he said, and for a brief second, she allowed herself to look at him. He was so—so perfect. His eyes were dark, looking at her with an intense humor. Like he liked her and wanted to laugh not at but with her. His dark brown hair hung in soft curls to his shoulders, gleaming in the sunlight coming through the car window. He smiled, his teeth white, his lips full. As if hearing her, he licked his lips, his eyes sparkling, his hand almost reaching out to touch her.

"Whoa, buddy." Claire started giggling, laughing, resting her forehead on the steering wheel and then sitting up and looking back at him. "Keep your fake hands to yourself. If I'm going to be crazy, I'm not going to add to it by letting the figment of my imagination touch me. Haven't you ever seen that movie *Fight Club?*"

When the man didn't answer, she answered for him. "Of course you did, because I did and you're me, so you did. I've split my psyche. If there were a movie of this car scene, I'd be talking to air. It's Brad Pitt and Ed Norton all over again. The next thing you know, I'll be hitting myself thinking I'm beating you up."

"This is not going the way I wanted it to," he said slowly. "It would be easier if you would just be quiet for a minute."

"So you have practice in this?" Claire wondered how many other unfortunate women were out there, all certain a handsome man had just appeared one day, especially for them.

The man sighed, shook his head, and put his hands on his knees. Turning to face the street, he sighed.

"Look, I know this is weird. And I tend to be a pain in the ass. So can we start over here?"

Claire stared at him, breathing in quick breaths, nervous and scared and amazed. And then she smelled it. Him. He smelled like soap and something citrus, the tang of whatever he used to shave filling the car.

Do hallucinations have smells? she thought. *Is this a multisensory projection of all my sorrows? Can I hear, smell, see him? God knows if I could taste him, and I didn't let him touch me. But smell?*

"You know," he said slowly, "I haven't had much practice with this. You are the first person I've rescued. And, of course, I have a vested interest. But I really would like to start over. If I get out of the car, would you promise not to drive away?"

As he spoke, the man seemed to become more real. His movements had weight. He filled the car space with what Claire could only call maleness: smells, words, muscles actually rippling under his clothes. Rippling. She'd thought it was only a cliché, the men she'd dated skinny or maybe filling out their Dockers a little too fully around the middle, their expensive leather belts pulled tight.

He smiled again, his eyes so bright, dark but seeming to be full of pinpoints of light. "Do you promise?"

Claire nodded, took her hands away from the wheel and folded them in her lap. What would it hurt to listen to him? Maybe once he left the car, he would simply disappear. Hallucination over. A wonderful hallucination all gone.

"I promise," she said.

THE BEAUTIFUL BEING

Together, anything is possible . . .

As leader, Edan Mirav must protect his people from the enemies who wish to destroy them. Despite his extraordinary abilities, Edan has not been able to locate his double—the one person who could make him whole and help him control his remarkable power to age himself with a simple thought. With her, he can grow even stronger. Without her, he is doomed to an uncertain fate. Just when he's about to abandon all hope, she stands before him in the blazing hot sun of the desert like a shimmering mirage . . .

Recently rescued and freed, Ava Arganos has been working in the desert—and waiting for the day that her double finds her. When Ava first lays eyes on Edan, she doesn't recognize him immediately even though she feels the charged, sizzling connection between them. Now united, Edan and Ava surrender to a fiery, explosive passion that only renews their bond as they combine forces to battle their most treacherous foe yet . . .

There was a movement behind him, and Edan turned his head, looking behind him at a group of five people moving along the dried pathways with a cart of food and water that seemed to float with them. As he watched, he breathed in a sweet aroma of fruit and butter, of other things savory and tasty and rich with flavor. The air tasted so good, his mouth began to water.

"Damn, it's about time," Siker said. "I've been dying for some of that chick's food. It's, like, so good. Awesome. I mean the best stuff you've ever had. Makes working in this heat almost worthwhile."

Turning slightly to follow Siker's gaze, Edan found his eyes holding the figure of a woman. He blinked, wondering why he couldn't get her in focus. For some reason, he couldn't really see "woman" at first, only her blur, only her essence, like the way he could taste the food that was coming without even eating it.

He blinked again, trying to find a focus, feeling as if he were underwater or in a dream he couldn't

wake up from. Slowly . . . slowly. There. There! He
could bring her into view. But he didn't see her form.
What he saw instead was color—white and gold and
red. This twirl of color, this amazing vision of her hit his
eyes, and he felt the impact of the sight in his head,
throat, chest. For a moment, he imagined that he was
paralyzed, his feet like lead, his body stiff. He wanted
to move forward, but could not, nothing in him seeming to work at all.

"What's up, man?" Siker said. "Are you okay? Is it
sunstroke or something? You need some water? Man?
Are you going to make it? Should I like call someone?"

Edan took a breath to steady himself and tried to
nod, but he was stuck in stillness.

"Dude?"

Again, Edan tried to nod, his chin moving a little.

"Okay, then. But you look like you've seen something totally freaky," Siker said, his voice trailing off
as the woman, the cart, and the four other people came
toward them. As they did, they handed out food, the
smell growing more delicious as they approached.

"Hey," Siker said to the woman. "You have any of
that, like, tart thing?"

Edan couldn't move, couldn't speak, watching as
the woman came toward him. He wanted to call out
her name, but he didn't know what her name was,
though he thought the sound of it would feel good
on his tongue. Her name would be as tasty as the
food she was handing out, something soft and lovely
and delicious. There would be heat and softness to it.
And beyond her name, everything else would be
wonderful, too. The citrus taste of her, the smell of
the delicate skin behind her ear, the warm feel of her

skin under his palms. She would whisper to him, her voice a lazy cat in his ear. He wasn't sure how he knew any of this, but he could almost feel the silky smoothness of her upper arm, the shimmering slope of her neck, the dip of her lower back. How could his hand know that? How could he know anything about her at all? How could he have sense memory of someone he had never touched?

"Man," Siker was saying from what felt like a million miles away. "Are you, like, hungry? You should get some of this."

The woman came closer, her blond hair a wave flowing behind her, her dark brown eyes taking him in. Edan knew her eyes, had seen her gaze before, as if she'd looked at him before, so serious, so calm. Her face was smooth, unlined, flawless, so clear and clean he wanted to reach out a hand and touch her. But at the same time, he almost wanted to hold up his hands to avoid her direct gaze, her eyes seeming to dig into him and beyond, into the desert behind him. She was seeing too much, taking him in as he was taking her in, and he managed to tamp down his thoughts, not wanting her to hear and know any more than she already must.

"Would you like something to eat?" she asked, her voice just as he imagined, smooth and low and assured. But there was something faraway about her, too, as if she'd thrown on some kind of protective covering, thoughts, feelings, and even air seeming to push past and around her.

Edan struggled to find words, wondering if his tongue would move to form the fricatives, plosives, and bilabials that would make words that she might understand. If he didn't focus, he realized he might find himself grunting like an animal, a primordial, prehistoric beast.

"Please," he said, pushing the word out too fast. "Yes."

Her eyes still on him, she handed him a package, the food warm in its wrapper.

"I hope you'll like it," she said.

"Do I—do I know you?" Edan asked, gripping the food a little too hard in his hands, the soft contents underneath his fingers slightly squishing.

The woman stared at him with her same still look, and then shook her head. "I don't think so."

"Where are you from?" He was almost barking out his words, and she stepped back once, twice, staring at him as she did.

"Here," she said. "Just outside Dhareilly."

"Were you in the Source?"

She shook her head, her eyes narrowing. She put a hand on her hip, shrugged slightly, her mouth in a slim, irritated line. "Why are you asking me this?"

Edan wanted to put his hands on her shoulders and shake her. Where had she been? Why hadn't she shown up before this? Why now in the desert? How could she be here, now, finally? Where had she been all this time? How could their meeting be as silly as this? Now she shows up carting food around, unable to truly see him. Her twin, standing right in front of her.

But maybe he was wrong. Maybe he was just lonely and tired and desperate to discover her. Maybe he was suffering from heatstroke, dizzy from dehydration, needing nothing more than a cool shower to calm his nerves. Despite his limited vocabulary, Siker was right. Edan needed rest, food, and water. That's all.

"I—" Edan began, about to introduce himself, but then a group of workers rounded the corner from the other side of the building and approached the cart, laughing and eager to eat the delicious food, the smells wafting everywhere.

Distracted, she turned toward the approaching people, and Edan stepped back, trying to find his breath.

"Man?" Siker said. "Looks like you've got a major thing going on. Some kind of animal instinct. Some kind of tribal reaction. Like you are about to—"

"Eat," Edan said. He turned away slowly, wondering where he could go to run away from this feeling, this impulse, this need. He wasn't sure if he could, but he put one foot in front of the other and moved, heading back toward the temporary shelter Jai and Risa had allotted him earlier.

The hot desert air against his face, the sun at his back, Edan found it hard to breathe, hard to concentrate. He needed to go back to the city. Working here in the intense sun had been the wrong idea. He was dreaming up his twin out of the sand and shrubs and wavy lines of heat. He was trying to find what he hadn't in all his years in the Source. How could he possibly guide his people to anything if he couldn't even recognize his twin? If he was imagining that a woman handing out pie was the woman he'd been waiting for his entire life, how could he ever be a responsible leader?

"Man?" Siker called out from behind him. "Where

are you, like, going? There's more to lunch than this."

Edan held up a hand, unable to turn around, unable to answer Siker. He didn't know where he was going except away, except out of here.

Books by Bestselling Author
Fern Michaels

___The Jury	0-8217-7878-1	$6.99US/$9.99CAN
___Sweet Revenge	0-8217-7879-X	$6.99US/$9.99CAN
___Lethal Justice	0-8217-7880-3	$6.99US/$9.99CAN
___Free Fall	0-8217-7881-1	$6.99US/$9.99CAN
___Fool Me Once	0-8217-8071-9	$7.99US/$10.99CAN
___Vegas Rich	0-8217-8112-X	$7.99US/$10.99CAN
___Hide and Seek	1-4201-0184-6	$6.99US/$9.99CAN
___Hokus Pokus	1-4201-0185-4	$6.99US/$9.99CAN
___Fast Track	1-4201-0186-2	$6.99US/$9.99CAN
___Collateral Damage	1-4201-0187-0	$6.99US/$9.99CAN
___Final Justice	1-4201-0188-9	$6.99US/$9.99CAN
___Up Close and Personal	0-8217-7956-7	$7.99US/$9.99CAN
___Under the Radar	1-4201-0683-X	$6.99US/$9.99CAN
___Razor Sharp	1-4201-0684-8	$7.99US/$10.99CAN
___Yesterday	1-4201-1494-8	$5.99US/$6.99CAN
___Vanishing Act	1-4201-0685-6	$7.99US/$10.99CAN
___Sara's Song	1-4201-1493-X	$5.99US/$6.99CAN
___Deadly Deals	1-4201-0686-4	$7.99US/$10.99CAN
___Game Over	1-4201-0687-2	$7.99US/$10.99CAN
___Sins of Omission	1-4201-1153-1	$7.99US/$10.99CAN
___Sins of the Flesh	1-4201-1154-X	$7.99US/$10.99CAN
___Cross Roads	1-4201-1192-2	$7.99US/$10.99CAN

Available Wherever Books Are Sold!
Check out our website at **www.kensingtonbooks.com**

More by Bestselling Author

Janet Dailey

Romantic Suspense from
Lisa Jackson

See How She Dies	0-8217-7605-3	$6.99US/$9.99CAN
Final Scream	0-8217-7712-2	$7.99US/$10.99CAN
Wishes	0-8217-6309-1	$5.99US/$7.99CAN
Whispers	0-8217-7603-7	$6.99US/$9.99CAN
Twice Kissed	0-8217-6038-6	$5.99US/$7.99CAN
Unspoken	0-8217-6402-0	$6.50US/$8.50CAN
If She Only Knew	0-8217-6708-9	$6.50US/$8.50CAN
Hot Blooded	0-8217-6841-7	$6.99US/$9.99CAN
Cold Blooded	0-8217-6934-0	$6.99US/$9.99CAN
The Night Before	0-8217-6936-7	$6.99US/$9.99CAN
The Morning After	0-8217-7295-3	$6.99US/$9.99CAN
Deep Freeze	0-8217-7296-1	$7.99US/$10.99CAN
Fatal Burn	0-8217-7577-4	$7.99US/$10.99CAN
Shiver	0-8217-7578-2	$7.99US/$10.99CAN
Most Likely to Die	0-8217-7576-6	$7.99US/$10.99CAN
Absolute Fear	0-8217-7936-2	$7.99US/$9.49CAN
Almost Dead	0-8217-7579-0	$7.99US/$10.99CAN
Lost Souls	0-8217-7938-9	$7.99US/$10.99CAN
Left to Die	1-4201-0276-1	$7.99US/$10.99CAN
Wicked Game	1-4201-0338-5	$7.99US/$9.99CAN
Malice	0-8217-7940-0	$7.99US/$9.49CAN